BLACK TIDE

by john g rees

BLACK WATER BOOKS, 2011

Black Tide
Copyright © 2011 by john g rees
First Edition: NOVEMBER 2011
All rights reserved.

Published by Black Water Books, Hawaii

This novel is a work of fiction. The characters, names incidents dialogue and plot are the products of the author's imagination or are used fictitiously. Any resemblance to actual persons or events is purely coincidental.

Cover created by Mohamed Sadath
Interior Design by Danil Mullagaliev

Printed in the United States
ISBN: 978-0-9831920-6-0

THANKS TO:
Teddi Stransky for putting up with all the vulgarity and providing the much needed grammar control. Mohamed Sadath, cover creation Danil Mullagaliev, formatting expertise and my wife Mara for her perseverance. I still don't know what she does with the evidence.

*For Jonah, whose work ethic,
friendship and love helped lay
the foundation for the words.*

BLACK TIDE

PART ONE

***

Yeah, we were young once, like you. A dream, a future to play it out in and only so much time to do it. We lived it like there was no tomorrow because that was the way it was. You could be whacked by a semi-truck, flattening your furrowed future. Slip on a rock in the garden and have a support stake poke you in the eye. Get sandwiched in a parking lot on your ten-speed and that heart monitor you wear starts to come in real handy, for once. And, of course, the guys and gals who'd take it into their own hands. Those kids have balls, the likes of which make our shriveled raisins cringe. Unfortunately you only hear about the successes, which are far more exciting than the failures. And there are far more failures than successes.

I mean, really. What are the odds of taking a weapon you are probably not all that familiar with, trying to aim it at a target you can't really see, and expecting to get a bullseye? Of course, mass murderers seem to get it right; all that practice, I suppose. But they, too, were in the moment. Time was of the essence.

It really didn't matter and some were actually lucky, tripping the light fantastic while doing what they liked to do. Then there were others, like me, who just enjoyed the work.

It was late summer when the workboat pulled up to the dock in Corpus Christi. A hundred of us got off with a month to kill; smoke and drink away before being sent out again. When I say smoke, I mean it. There was no smoking allowed anywhere near the gulf, anymore. What began as the world's largest 'known' oil spill triggered a series of unfortunate events. Fueled more by greed than the spin-off of polluting everything, the Gulf region became a dead zone. The fishing industry became extinct a while after. The loss of sea life created songs and funds, activists ran rampant in the streets. But little was done for the fish beyond good intentions. Less even for the fishermen. Wiped out along with the fish, they sank without a second glance. What use the knowledge of shrimping when there are no shrimp and won't be ever again? Wildlife and coastal habitat retention had become a sad joke, aiding in creating the world's largest unrestricted industrial complex. Being bordered on three sides by land, a huge floating barrier cordoning off the Atlantic kept the worst of it contained. The mentality that created it got the rest of us to believe that if we were all allowed to completely destroy just twenty - no, too much? Okay then, destroy just ten percent of the planet, then we can save the rest of it. And we bought it, or we were bought out. Either way we paid for it.

Wives and sweethearts picked up some of us. Ex's, with a trail of screaming kids, nabbed a few more to get child support before it disappeared from the workers' pockets, leaving the rest of us to the slim pickings along the Gulf Coast. After a week of guy-like debauchery, some began nursing a hangover that would last until they went back to work, the lucky few to families... Me? I like kids about as much as a jackhammer in the head and prefer a book to listening to a drunk tell for the nth time about that night and how he found god, making me wonder: if god was so good why were you hammered all the time?

Jonah was a maintenance tech aboard the rig. He fled the family thing, too, but straddled the line between drug addict /alcoholic/sane person like a tightrope walker in a high wind. That is to say, he was nuts only half the time. The difference, at least in the practical sense, was that he had a truck. And like any trucker Jonah had friends with them, too.

I was waiting for a bus with a bag of clean laundry over one shoulder and a copy of Mark Twain's 'Roughing It', when his big diesel rolled into the stop, belching its smoke all over the clean duds.

"You know, Jake," he said, "a truck like this will get you laid."

"No shit?"

"Yes shit," Jonah replied with the sharp laugh and clear eyes of one who didn't owe anyone anything. "It also gets you where you're going."

"I don't fuck truckers."

Jonah laughed loud and hearty, wiping a slug of white snot from his nose and flinging it into traffic. "I ain't interested in your ass, Jake. If I was, I'd of had it already. Now hop in before some cop gives me a ticket."

Tossing my laundry bag into the bed of the truck, I climbed the short ladder into the cab.

"Get nosebleeds at this elevation?" I asked looking down out the window of the lifted rig.

"No, but this shit will give you one," Jonah said, catching my look of concern.

"It's just coke, Jake, and just for the weekend." He threw me the vial, dropped the clutch and lurched into traffic. After availing myself gluttonously of Jonah's hospitality, I rolled a cigarette and watched the decrepit urban surroundings become rundown suburbia.

"Where we going, Jonah? My pension is the other way."

"We busted some serious ass these last few months, brah. Rented the park. They cleared the homeless for us, so we could have some privacy. Everybody who put out was invited."

"What am I doing here?"

"Yeah, about that. We really don't ask divers too often. Guess the pressure hasn't pushed your head up your ass yet. But," his face went tight weaving the big truck through some particularly creative traffic maneuvers, "when your gas mix went screwy, you finished buttoning that flange and didn't start screaming as soon as you got out. Covered a few of my boys by keeping your mouth shut."

"No use busting somebody's balls just 'cause you want to blame them for being lame ass mother fuckers." Jake replied. "Besides I've seen it happen before. I think they invented the term 'shit happens' just for the diving industry!"

"Fucking ay right there, brah, you fuckers are nuts," Jonah yelled above the engine noise.

"So, kidnapping me is a way of saying thanks," I asked.

"Sort of, I wanted to get to know you a little better before... uh," Jonah began.

"Before what?"

"Before you get sent to another rig." Jonah's answer was not an honest one. When an honest man lies, he generally does so for a reason and you can always tell. I figured he had his reasons, rolled another cigarette, enjoying the smoke away from the volatile coast.

"You're just different, man. Than the other divers, I mean. When you get out of the chamber, you pitch in and help us out. It makes a big difference."

"Something to do. You guys do all the work. I'm just picking up the slack." I pushed away pats on the back like the plague. Especially on the rig and being a diver. Competition is ruthless.

"Not the way I hear it. Waylon, one of the riggers, saw you chaining Shorty's crane down just as he was lifting a load of pipes. We would have lost the load, the crane, and Shorty if you hadn't picked up the slack."

"He seemed a little out of sorts at breakfast, so I kept an eye on him," I replied.

"Yeah, he drinks too much. Hell of an operator though."

"We all got stuff." I didn't know what else to say. Shorty was a full blown alcoholic and should have been let go when his condition became chronic. Booze and heavy equipment is a bad combination. It was only a matter of time before he killed himself or worse. I kept my mouth shut as far as my feelings about this were concerned. Jonah knew. It was his crew, his business.

Soon we were heading west and north with a truck full of rig workers we had picked up randomly on the way out of town. Two other trucks had joined in the caravan, loaded with supplies and more people. The signs for Big Bend National Park were riddled with bullet holes, smashed up, or stolen, leaving the single vertical post as a reminder of something. You just didn't know what. The National Park System was opened up to the droves of homeless in the early 2000's. Well, not all of it. The most popular remained as they were, but privatized with only their names altered to pump the corporation that sponsored it. The remainder of the parks went the way of the rest of the country, tanked by poverty and apathy. Some, like Big Bend, could be rented, with or without its current population. Others like the area around 'Old Faithful,' once it started to not be so faithful anymore, became permanent cities. Heat in the winter and electricity was generated geothermally. 'Old Faithful' was lucky. In Glacier National Park, now that the glacier was gone, full time residents hobbled about strangling the life out of the area's limited resources to stave off starvation. Most were toeless from frostbite. In general, the parks were miserable places to live, yet still they were better than the cities where the rats and critters had finally won.

One thread connected all of man – whether you lived in a park, your car, a gated community, at the office, in the middle of everything or at the periphery – the internet. Early users warned of the dark side of the information platform. After a generation or two they died off, end of discussion. It was so insinuated into everyday living you couldn't imagine life without it. Well, most people anyway. I read instead. Scored books when I could, just for the smell sometimes. The rest was digital and ever so convenient. You gotta laugh though when someone complains about having to actually turn pages. Barbaric.

When conversation wore thin and Jonah began managing the party while still driving, I stared out the window. The landscape was ruined years before. The mad rush for quick money left a trail of strip malls, junk towns, junk food and a junked people that still scratched out a life from the rotting skeletons of short term capitalization.

"No vision," Jonah yelled waving at a ghost town of a mall. "Couldn't see but a few years down the road. You probably seen lots of them traveling from rig to rig."

"The shit all looks the same no matter where you go."

"Don't get all bummed out on me, Jake. Have another blast. We took Big Bend because we wanted to see nature the way it used to be. Should be cool. No net, no streaming sports, just nature."

"Do the rest of our campers know about this?" I asked this as two walkie-talkies lit up on the dash.

"Nope. You, me, a couple of the guys. This will be them now, probably just lost the signal." Jonah laughed, taking a snort before picking up the radios. "'Sup, mon?" he asked, as he released the talk button, snorfling righteously before continuing with the wireless. He looked over to see me working my jaw back and forth, a little buzzed and worried.

"Don't worry, brah. The men and their wives that have come along aren't your average net junkies. It's another reason I asked you; never seen you pick up your own phone. You got one?"

"Only the company issue callout," I said, a little embarrassed.

"Shit, man, you are in the dark ages. Speaking of, we're here."

A little guard shack sat just off the road next to the rusting pipe gate that crossed the broken asphalt. The wooden structure looked just big enough for a man and a wood stove, if the man wasn't too big. Jonah honked once, briefly. The mountain afternoon became infinitely quiet as Jonah shut the motor down to wait. On cue, the door to the shack swung outward followed by a balding head connected to a neck and shoulders that had to duck low to exit the hovel. Standing to his full height made his undersized ranger outfit comical. Short in every way it needed to be long and long in the places it needed to be short, he wore it proudly and any reference to comedy was sucked up at the sight of a menacing-looking double-barreled shotgun held in his gnarled hands or the scarred face that looked like it had taken a blast from the sawed-off blunderbuss.

Stepping from the shade of the shack, I saw he held a piece of paper under the thumb of his left hand as it clutched the twin barrels. He stopped in front of Jonah's rig, both barrels casually but seriously pointed at the windshield as he checked the license plate. Judging by the length of the barrel, the blast from the weapon would expand a foot in diameter for every foot traveled. By the time the shot met the glass... God I hoped the numbers matched up.

After a few moments the guard followed the gun to the driver's door and came to rest just beneath Jonah's chin. The barrels never left their target. A muffled conversation ensued that consisted mostly of grunts. I couldn't make out a word they were saying, but then the hollow steel delivery tubes consumed my attention.

The gun moved forward into the cab followed by the head and shoulders and stench of the guard as he pushed passed Jonah to stuff the gun in my chest. His foul breath washed over me, "Hope you enjoy your stay in Big Bend and that everything is to your liking. If not, don't hesitate to go fuck yourself!" As he said the last words he dug the gun painfully into my xiphoid. I guess it was for kicks but when he pulled the trigger I about shit my pants. There was no explosion that blew a hole clean through my torso. Just a click. He waited for a moment sniffing the air, then pulled himself out of the rig. His smile was tight, lacking any mirth in the practical joke. Nodding curtly to Jonah, the guard indicated we could continue on and returned to the shack to raise the gate. The gun remained pointed at the truck with the remaining barrel decidedly aiming at me. Our caravan rolled into the park.

"What the fuck was that all about?" I said rubbing my chest.

Jonah looked me up and down, his visage hardened as he tried to see into me. "They say Olaf can tell when a man is not a man."

"I may not be much of one..." I began.

"It's not that, Jake. Back during one of the drug wars, don't matter which one, his family was taken by one of the cartel's mercs."

"What does that have to do with me? I was just a kid when that shit went down."

"It don't. The mercs were renegades from that Megacorp experiment. Got away from the big Corp and went free agent. Anyway, they did things to that poor family. Olaf was a kid then, too. He was forced to watch as the mercs went barbaric on his sisters, parents and brothers."

"I heard it got nasty, the wars, I mean."

"Mighty nice word for what went down. From then on Olaf could always tell when one of the freaks was in our midst. Like a dog."

"Hey man, nothing's been done to me!"

"I know, cause I been watching you on the rig. My guess is he can tell when you're going to be one, too. Commercial diver, top of your game, a good rep, too. Yep, you're a prime candidate."

"What do you mean?"

"Megacorp only wants the good ones. That's why me and my crew fuck up on a regular basis. Not so much as to get our asses canned or hurt someone, but enough to keep us out of the promotions arena."

"So I'm fucking myself by having a good work ethic and run the risk of being upgraded to experimental status."

"They are called reuseables. And yup, keep up the good work and that is where you're headed."

"Fuck me," I said, wanting more information.

"That they will, you can count on it. We're here. Keep that shit under your hat this weekend, we're trying to forget."

"Roger that."

Clouds of brown dust fought for the airspace with the diesel smoke as the three trucks rumbled into the parking area. Men and women were hopping from the beds before the rigs had stopped and were unloading before the smut had settled. The campsites were just a short way to the base of a tall bluff that stood beside a cool stream. There were tents, coolers, bottled water and beer. The next two hours were spent getting all the stuff set up; most important was beer on ice, with small talk and laughter erecting tents, creating a kitchen, and digging an outhouse, for which there were no volunteers. Finding a shovel amidst the clutter I asked Jonah where they wanted it.

"You and your positive I'll get'er done attitude. This is the kind of shit I was just talking about with you. See Shorty..."

Shorty was already at the river swimming with a beer in one hand and his girlfriend Molly in the other.

"That's what you should be doing. But... since you're here..." he handed me a small sack, "Pitch the tent over it when you're done. Behind those trees should be good," he pointed.

The earth was soft, the blade sinking easily into it. Halfway through, I rolled a cigarette, sitting down to watch the activity by the riverside. Laughter and mock arguments drifted across the swale. Someone was playing a guitar as the rising colorful tents helped to fabricate a festive atmosphere. Already I was a bit jealous at the ease of the camaraderie amongst these friends as they created a dream, while I dug a shit hole. Fool enough yet to laugh at myself, I stubbed the butt, deciding to create the nicest outhouse ever. Even taking a shit is part of the dream. A couple hours later I took Jonah's advice.

The heat of the day was waning as the sun crested the butte to the west. The ice-cold beer went down easily and way too fast. With the last of the sun I stripped and dove into the cool water. The current was lazy, the water, clear. I scrubbed the sweat and dirt away but felt there was filth that remained. There was something in what Jonah said about the Reuseable Program and Olaf's nose, what there was left of it anyway. Giving up my quest of cleanliness, strong practiced strokes propelled me against the current to where my clothes lay in a bundle. They were gone. In its place was a towel that was busy keeping a couple of beers cold. Setting the coldies in the river, I dried off making a skirt from the towel.

"Hey digger," came a voice from a riverside copse of trees. Scanning the shrubs, I spied my clothes hung on a line as they waved in the breeze but saw no body to connect the voice to.

"Thanks for the towel. Want one of these?" I picked the bottles from the water, popping the tops with a rock. When I looked up, she was standing right next to me. Plucking a beer from my hands she leaned in close, inhaling deeply.

"I think Olaf has his head up his ass. You smell okay to me. I'm Julie, Shorty's daughter." She tipped her beer in salute then drew from it deeply. Jonah said to keep it quiet so I struggled with what she said while trying to think of something clever to say. She was cute and the last light of sunset did her no harm.

"A pleasure," I said reaching out and shaking her hand. They were strong and calloused, no stranger to hard work but with a woman's tenderness. "Thanks for washing my clothes," I chinned at the trees, "that bad, huh?"

"Just used the outhouse. Saying thanks, I guess. You gay? I mean you made it soooo nice. Besides I wanted to smell the real you."

"I didn't know Shorty had a family," I said, veering the subject away from me.

"Mom and Dad were divorced years ago. They get along great now. But tag'em with married and it's hell on earth. Trust me I know."

"I've seen his temper on the job and glad it was never directed at me. Hell of an operator, your dad."

"Yeah, that's the problem. He's too good at what he does. If it wasn't for Jonah, they would have taken him a long time ago." Julie must have seen my bewildered expression in the twilight. "You know, Megacorp, the Reuseables."

I didn't like the direction of the conversation, always returning to the subject of the Reuseable Program. "Listen Julie, this is all kind of new to me." I knew more than I was willing to let on about, so I played it dumb. It was something I was good at and would serve me throughout my life. Not that I knew this of course. "Jonah ask me not to mention it this weekend so could we talk about something else?"

"Sure, you want to have sex?"

"Me and my big mouth," I moaned.

"I was counting on that."

"I need something to eat." Seems I was always changing the subject.

"I was counting on that, too," She laughed, taking my hand and leading me away from the fire down the beach.

"No really, I'm hungry," I said fighting a losing battle.

"Me too!"

Dawn came with a profound silence. I listened to the wind blowing through the trees and rippling water, silent except where it bumped into the shore. Not wanting to move, I feared rustling the sleeping bag would shatter the moment. The state of grace slipped away naturally, chirping birds heralding a new day in the pre-light of dawn, and I knew I was alone. Sitting up in the lean-to, I was busy taking in the river when footsteps came up to the blind side of the tent. I thought it was Julie when a cup of hot coffee was placed where I could reach it. When I went to get it, a pair of steel-toed boots stomped down hard on my hand, pinning it to the ground.

"Fuck my daughter, will ya?" His words hid the sound of his other boot coming through the thin wall of the tent connecting with my solar-plexus, knocking the wind from my lungs and tumbling me head-long into the cold waters. Coming instantly aware an instant too late, I met with a flying leap from Shorty, who was dressed for the occasion in underwear and boots. Leading with his head, the little man nailed me in the chest, plowing me under the water. I was ready this time and took it without losing my air, letting him force me to the bottom where he proceeded to stand on me and do some sort of little dance.

Struggling when you're under water is usually a waste of time and air. It's best to relax and think rationally about things. With the breath I took before going under I figured I had an easy four minutes and a ball-busting five. That is unless Shorty started jumping up and down. His jig died down and the clarity of the water allowed me to see enough to tell what he was doing. Every diver has had it done to them, whether they knew it or not. Shorty was taking a leak. With the current running, the act was more symbolic than, say, a golden shower on dry land.

Now I'm trying not to burst out laughing and lose, prematurely, the precious moments I had left. Shorty finished up and checked his watch. He carefully got off my chest and checked his watch again. The current lifted my body from riverbed slowly pushing it downstream. From my position I could no longer see Shorty, but it was about then that he figured something must be wrong. Before I could say, 'put me down,' he had me out of the water, pumping my chest. I stopped him just before he started the rescue breaths.

"I'm okay, Shorty! Listen I'm the one who was taken advantage of." I wasn't going to apologize or beg.

"You son of a bitch!" He started to yell but as the sun came over the horizon so did a smile begin on one side of his face, reaching across to the other. "That's my Julie. You hurt her I'll kill ya. Now that the father business is over with, let me buy you drink."

"It's a little early, ya think?"

"Never too early to chain an old operator's crane down, ya think?" He laughed reaching an arm up around my shoulder. "Nice outhouse, Jake. Going to have to bring you along more often."

"Thanks, I guess. You going to fuck me, too?"

He would have missed, so instead of avoiding it I let him clip me in the jaw and caught him as he lost his balance in the sand, letting him land on top.

"You're all right, Jake," Shorty said pushing himself off and standing.

The day passed in about as nice a way as I can remember. Seemed someone was always playing a guitar along with the laughter of children and the sunlight dancing over the water. I found it was like Jonah had said, it helps you forget. As the day drifted downstream those of us that could hiked upstream, to a waterfall and swimming pool. Julie and I hung together a bit. The night before was fun and we left it at that. She was a social butterfly and this was her karass. I admired the way she worked the group but had no intention of tagging along like a dog.

The sun was directly overhead warming the tops of boulders scattered around the perimeter. We spread out blankets in a shaded spot, then everybody hit the water. Off to the side of a cliff face Jonah and a bud began spidering up a crack.

"Hey Jonah! Where you going?" I yelled from the water. All I received in reply was an arm beckoning me to follow.

Climbing out of the water and putting on my sneakers, I jogged over to where they started the climb. I looked up at the gnarled sandstone crevice, 'This isn't the first time you've done something stupid for the male bonding thing,' I said to myself. The rock was crumbly and slippery when wet, which I was. You had to push with your feet on one side of the crack and push your back against the other side to keep from falling. A trail of sand cascaded down with every step. Twenty feet up the crack widened making further progress impossible. 'Fuck me.'

"Hey Jake! Look to your left." Jonah was pointing to a ledge.

I gave him the okay signal and began descending. Had to get down a few feet to access the shelf. My back started slipping and I couldn't stop it. My feet began scrambling to keep up with my body but only ground away at the loose surface. Then suddenly - air! Swinging to the left and stretching my arms out, I hit the ledge. There wasn't anything to grab on to, so I planted my palms on the sandstone, pressing as hard as I could. If the surface wasn't disturbed, it had plenty of friction to hold you - at the price of your skin.

Feet searched for anything to gain a purchase. Nothing. Carefully, I began to kick my right foot into the vertical wall. The gouging was slow and I was tiring fast. Finally a dimple I could catch my toes on. Push up, replant my hands and do it again with the other foot. After three such steps I was able to sit down on the ledge and catch my breath. The group of swimmers, who had been watching silently from below, broke out in applause and laughter. I suppose I should have felt embarrassed, but the adrenalin had me pumped. I stood and raised my arms in a mighty way, turned and looked for the rest of the way up. There, cut into the stone, was a stairway to the top. You had to laugh.

"We made the steps last year. Started them high to keep the kids safe. How's the back? We were watching, too."

"I don't know. You tell me." I turned so he could get a look.

"Eww. Ahh, you'll be aw'ight."

Jonah made a thumbs up to Frankie who started a sprint towards the cliff. I turned to watch him blast by and take a wild leap. Frankie was pedaling all the way down to keep upright. Just before he hit the water, he balled up finishing with a cannon ball. 'And the crowd went wild!'

"Okay Jake," Jonah began, "A little heads up. The pool is deep enough but there are some big fucking rocks under there. The best is to do like Frankie and take a flying leap. If you want to do a fancy dive take a good look first. You can see them clear from up here." Jonah pointed to some light blue boulders just below the surface.

"I'll stick with the bat outta hell thing," I said, taking a sobering look.

"Okay, see you down there." Jonah ran away from the cliff, spun around and bolted for the edge screaming like a wild man.

I gave him a minute and followed in a like manner. It was worth the climb.

Julie daubed some gunk on the torn skin I received during the climb and lit a joint while we sat on one of the hot rocks to chase the chill of the mountain water away.

"If Dad had come along you would have seen some diving. He used to do it as kid down in Mexico, hustling pesos from tourists till one of the resorts saw him and hired him on."

"No shit. I'd have never figured Shorty for smiling for tourists."

"He was smiling for the money, but it gave him a hell of an understanding of people." Julie was obviously proud of her father.

"That being we are all assholes, right?"

"You got it."

"You don't see him smile too often any more. When you do it makes your day somehow."

"There's no money in it, Jake. You're a little slow, aren't you?" she asked fondly.

"Maybe just a little."

When the sun drifted away from the pool, so did we. In the afternoon, shaded areas were like refrigerators. Shorty was doing shots and chasing them with bong hits by the time we got back.

"Hey, why didn't you wake me? I wanted to do some diving," Shorty demanded.

We looked around at each other till Jonah stepped up. "Nobody that brave here, my little friend." Jonah burst out laughing, taking the bong from Shorty and refilling the bowl.

When he was through with a body racking coughing fit, I asked him, "How do you pass your piss tests?"

"We don't!" This time he was down on his hands and knees laughing.

"What's so funny?"

"We don't," he laughed out again. "You divers got one hell of a lawyer. A no piss test contract. Who ever heard of such a thing?" By this time, he had worked himself into such a dither, he had to let it finish on its own.

I didn't get it, so I poured some coffee and rolled a cigarette. Halfway through both, a hand was put on my shoulder.

"Come on, Jake, let's go have a little talk." It was Jonah and the laughter was gone, probably not far, but out of sight for now.

We climbed to the top of a huge rock, nearly a hill in itself, to catch the last warm spot before sunset.

"Got another?" he motioned for a smoke. I rolled two. We smoked in silence but before we were through he said, "You know why we don't pass our tests?" I shook my head. "Because we want to be fuck ups in the company's eye. You get good, they take you. You think you were invited here just to spend the weekend with a bunch of guys you work with all the time?"

"I was wondering."

"It's because we like you. You're all right and Julie says you're on the level, so we're asking you if you want in. Guys like you get shanghaied in their prime. They don't wait till you die. And if they do, there is a good chance they'll expedite the issue."

"Yeah, Julie mentioned that, too." He could see my eyes clouding over with confusion.

"Fuck me," I said to no one in particular.

"They will if you don't listen up." Jonah paused to see if I was getting it before continuing. I guess I was. "Take Shorty for example. Top operator, in his 60's and at the head of Megacorp's 'want' list. That is until we convinced him to join up."

"Since then he's been a drunk and they leave him alone?" I asked.

"Sort of. Their scientists can beat the alcohol thing but they can't fix a fuck up. It was planned to have Shorty tip his crane. We placed a Scuba bottle in the cab so when he went over he would have enough air to hold him till a diver was put in the water. You chained the crane at the last second, foiling that plan, but it worked out just the same."

"What do you mean?"

"We got it on vid. On the one hand Shorty still looks like a fuck up, but... on the other it made you look good. Megacorp monitors all operations looking to weed out guys like Shorty and cultivate guys like you."

"Jesus, Jonah, you make this sound maybe a bit conspiratorial."

"A bit, Motherfucker? You need to read up a little more on current events. Mark Twain didn't have to deal with the likes of Megacorp."

"I guess not. So what, what do I do?"

"That's up to you, Jake. Kismet has a way of taking care of these things. In the mean time, hang with us. I'll keep you informed."

"Who's Kismet?" I asked, innocently.

"That's the ticket," he laughed. "Kismet is Arabic for fate. Come on, dinner is ready."

For some reason, camp food always tastes better than it actually is; must be something to do with being outdoors, away from industrialization and pollution. Of course now it was just the illusion of seclusion, but it was good illusion. Live music, perhaps one of life's rarest treats these days, filled the air as the stars did the sky. Some sang, others danced, we all forgot.

Well after midnight, Julie and I left the last guitarist in his quiet melodic musings for a spot farther away from the camp next to the river. The vigorous passion of the previous night was balanced with a holding and caring that was all too absent in my life: the warmth of another's body next to mine, a quiet passion of communication. What two hands can say to each other is more than words can describe. From the blackest night to deep hues of early dawn we held each other. It would not be enough for what the future had in store. It was just enough for now.

The morning was chill, with a fog blowing down the river. We watched the ghost drift over the camp lightly caressing those who slept outside and leaving what appeared to be a trail of tears in its path. As it passed over us, the dampness clung to Julie's face, creating tears that rolled down her cheeks. It was not just the fog.

"What is it?" I asked in the hush of dawn.

"I don't know. I feel something separating us," she replied, wiping the drips away.

"Today is the last day. I feel the same way, too."

"It's more than that, Jake. I had a dream we were being pulled apart. I was screaming, you were mute."

"What was doing the pulling?"

"I don't know; it had no face."

"Come on, let's get some coffee. We can go for a walk and talk about it."

Julie was shy slipping into her clothes, I likewise. Something was dividing us. And it was growing stronger.

The lone guitarist was still at it and had made a pot of the dark master just prior to our arrival.

"Thanks, Frankie," I whispered. "Anybody else up yet?"

"Just Shorty. He headed up to the falls to catch some rays and get in a few dives."

I rolled a cigarette and drank my first cup in silence while Julie went to the loo and did her morning routine.

"Let's head up to where Dad is," she said to me. "Is he drinking, Frankie?"

Frankie rolled his eyes with a 'duh' expression.

"Back in a bit, man." Julie and I reloaded our cups and headed upstream. We didn't talk as I thought we would, but that's not to say communication wasn't happening. We followed the trail on the canyon floor next to the river. Gossamer bands of fog cut off what little sunlight entered the cleft at this time of day creating a darkened surreal atmosphere so in contrast to yesterday's picnic.

We found Shorty frying himself like a chicken in a pan on one of the rocks that stood above the billowing cloud. Slowly the fog cover began to burn off. Shorty rolled over to sear the other side. Julie stripped, going for a swim while the fog still clung to the water. She disappeared in moments with only the sounds of repetitive strokes splashing the silence. A large shelf had an undercut created eons before. It was out of the wind, dry and afforded a picturesque view of the waterfall and pool. Perfect for a coffee and smoke.

It was too beautiful and the forgetfulness of the previous evening still lingered. Indeed it was a fine moment. But like all they pass, for in that moment I felt a change. Something was in the air as the fog dissipated and reality clarified.

Shorty stood and stretched. His broiled little body glistened of oil and sweat. "Where's Julie?" he yelled over.

I made swimming motions with my arms.

"Call her in. I want some pictures when I dive." There was a slur in his voice and wobble in his steps. Frankie hadn't lied in his silent answer. Personally, I thought Shorty would quit the drinking for the weekend. I reminded myself it was none of my business when I heard Julie returning.

"Hey - just in time. Shorty is going to dive and wants you to shoot him." Julie got out of the water and dried. I drank deliriously of her unabashed toweling and dressing. Her utter lack of self-consciousness was as beautiful as was she. I wanted to hold her right then, right now and forever.

"You ready down there?" Shorty yelled from the top. How he got up there is beyond me. Some of the holds are far apart. There wasn't much time to ponder this as Julie hollered up that she was ready.

It was funny to see Shorty psych himself for the dive. He was usually busy being the clown. Seeing the other side was, well, scary. He walked forward, wavering just a bit from the booze and took a good look from the jumping off place. He paced backwards, counting his steps, gave his body a good wriggle then became still for a moment. With a hop, he pumped five powerful steps coming to the edge, as both knees bent springing him up and away from the rocks. On the way up he assumed the jackknife position and began to flip. Once, twice, before snapping open into the straightest little arrow you ever saw and penetrating the water with barely a splash. It was perfect.

"You get it?" I yelled to Julie with a huge smile. She nodded with a grin and love for her Dad.

"Man, that was killer. Two and a half, knifing into water. Sweet!"

"That's my Dad."

Just as she said this, we both looked back at the water. Bubbles still rose from the entry point, but Shorty had not surfaced. The edge of the pool was irregular with boulders and rock outcroppings, limiting one's view of the whole.

"Hey Shorty! Great dive man, where are you?"

"DAD!"

"Quit fucking around man!" I was running around the pool hoping to see him hiding on the backsides of the rocks. No such luck. Back to where I began and I started stripping off my clothes. Julie's face had gone ashen. Going to hug her, she started to collapse so I eased her to the ground, turned and dove into the icy water. He was nowhere near the entry point. The current deep in the pool, however, was moving me around pretty good. I figured it must be doing the same thing with Shorty. I surfaced, took another breath and went back under, looking everywhere at once while the current moved me around.

A shaft of penetrating sunlight illumined a gray blue hand sticking out from beneath an undercut in the stone. 'Oh shit, Shorty!' I cried silently, swimming in close to get a hold of him. A dark cloud of blood floated around his head. His body was stuck and I wasted precious seconds trying to dislodge him without doing any more damage.

Julie was at the water's edge when I surfaced. Her face went from pale to panic to what do I do? Struggling on the treacherously slippery rocks made getting his body out of the water near impossible. After a certain point, we could get no farther. I got a solid purchase for my right foot and was able to jam my knee under his ass to keep him from sliding down. It was awkward but it worked. I started CPR. Adrenalin coursed through me like never before. Chest compressions followed by rescue breaths, over and over and over and over and over. The initial chest compressions pumped the yellowish water from his lungs and beer from his belly. Blood from a nasty head wound, that we hadn't had a chance to look at yet, flowed into the foam and water. After a few minutes we were covered with Shorty. Julie through her tears remained stoic and did her part. It must have been killing her to do it. But something in the killing brought life.

As I took a break from crushing Shorty's chest, Julie continued with the rescue breaths when suddenly we noticed he was breathing on his own. I checked his pulse. He had one, barely. We both took a much needed breath, only one, before putting our backs into getting Shorty off the rocks.

Hands appeared where none had been before. Hard hands. Hands of men. Fresh men who could lift the man we could not. While Shorty was being carried into the shade, I found my t-shirt, folded it and was back at Shorty's side as he was laid down. I placed the cloth over the head wound, but not before getting one of those all too clear images of the destruction. Shorty was missing a large portion of the back of his skull; the convolutions of his brain were moist and soft. I held him there with his head on my knees. Tears rolled down my face but I was not crying. I had done all I could do, or so I had thought. Julie sat by her father's side, holding his pale but alive hand.

"Where did you guys come from?" I was out of it and a little confused.

"Julie called on her phone when you jumped in the water. Is he going to be okay?"

I shrugged my shoulders.

"I called the medi-vac chopper, too. They should be here..." she began.

The whack-whack-whack of a helicopter broke the morning's silence and shattered our forgetfulness. Frankie pulled a pair of binoculars from his shirt and focused in on the sound.

"Aren't the Med choppers orange?" His question had an ominous boding for the group. The communal silence went deep.

"Yeah. What color is it?" Jonah asked.

"Black, no markings." Replied a somber Frankie who was busy putting the glasses away. "Everybody who is not involved in first aid, let's go!"

En masse, they gathered what they brought and double-timed it out of the falls and back to camp, presumably to begin breaking down. Only Jonah, Julie and I were left at the pool.

"What's this mean, Jonah?" I asked, changing out the blood soaked tee on Shorty's head for a fresh one, like one would a diaper, all the while trying not to let Julie see it. Jonah did. Whatever his reaction was he kept it to himself.

"It means Megacorp picked up on it. They are on their way to take Shorty." Jonah was pissed.

"What? Take him where?"

"They can fix that, Jake," Jonah pointed at Shorty's head, "And you'll see him working a crane in a few years. But he won't see you."

"They're going to re-use him, Jake," cried Julie. "It's my fault. I gave the medi-vac Dad's insurance numbers. Bastards had to make sure they would be paid first." She cried in shame, squeezing her father's hand.

"All requests go through a Megacorp filter. It's not your fault, Julie. It was mine for making your dad drink too much. You see, Jake, it was Shorty's reason for joining us." Jonah listened for the helicopter. It was close now.

"Dad did not want to be reused. No matter what. 'Kill me if you have to' was the way he put it."

"We have about a minute before that chopper comes in over the canyon and hovers on the pond. We have to move, NOW!"

"I'm staying," said Julie, resisting.

While the two had been explaining, half of me was listening. The other half was coming to terms with the very near future. When I spoke, it came firmly as in the way of a command. For it certainly was no request.

"Jonah, take Julie and get her out of here. I will deal with Megacorp."

Jonah took Julie by her limp shoulders, raising her to her feet.

"I won't let them take your father, Julie. I will miss him." I didn't know what else to say. 'Gee, I'm sorry I'm gonna kill your dad,' just didn't seem to cut it.

"Thanks, Jake."

"NOW Julie, they're coming over the ridge." She had gone catatonic. Jonah bent low and picked her up in the fireman's carry and ran for all he was worth to the slot where he could climb out unseen. How he was going to do that concerned me very little at this point.

The helicopter came over the falls with a deafening roar. It dropped, where we had jumped and Shorty dove this morning, hovering instead of plunging into the water as I wished it to do. The helicopter moved sideways across the water creating a mini-thunderstorm that drenched me and washed Shorty's blood from my body. Black clad soldiers hopped out onto the shore, guns leveled in my direction. They were followed by two men and an emergency stretcher. They all came to stand next to Shorty and me. The Med techs set the stretcher down. One pulled out a waterproof clipboard.

"We are here for..." they started, but I shut them down.

"His name is Shorty. At least his friends called him that. And someone else called him Dad." Tears rolled down until blasted by the helicopters rotor wash. "He was a good man and lived a good life. He deserves a good death." The techs were unaware that Shorty's brain pulsed beneath a few layers of tie-dyed cotton.

"We have our orders..." They started again.

"And I have mine." My voice was low and mean.

"If you resist, these guards will subdue you. We have our orders. Now please step away." At least they were able to finish this time.

I glanced up to see that Jonah and Julie had made it to the top of the falls unnoticed. All eyes were on me. I gathered they never received much resistance. Besides I didn't plan on giving them any resistance.

Looking back into Shorty's face, I saw the resolve I had been looking for. "We all gotta do what we gotta do. You can't have him."

With that said, I balled up my right fist as subtly and powerfully as I could. My arm recoiled back then shot forward and down into Shorty's skullcap, splattering and destroying the cohesive mass that was once Shorty's brain. I hit again and again to be sure. A scream echoed from the hilltop. A rifle butt came into view a moment before the lights went out.

***

To be honest, it was probably reading that damned my immortal soul. Reading set me apart from my peers. We were oil riggers and salvage divers; hard–core roughnecks who were known more for rowdy activities than sitting quietly. Now, don't get me wrong, I spent more than my share of time in bar fights and behind bars on account of them. But we were young. At thirty-five years of age I was considered a geezer amongst the diving teams. It was always a young man's job. To get to my age in the industry, you moved up in management, wised up and got out while you were ahead, or were just dumb lucky. The only other way out was feet first. I was one of the dumb lucky ones.

Having had my share of all-nighters at crack-houses and opium dens, which was where the crews were now, blowing it off after a month working a salvage operation, I preferred to kick back, stay at home, and catch up on some reading while resting my weary bones. Home was the Salvor, an aging salvage vessel moored in Pearl Harbor, Oahu. After a month of non-stop noise, the sound of silence was a thing to be wallowed in. Reading an original translation of the Bhagavad-Gita, I was lost in the Song Divine when the call came.

"All available divers to the dive station, PRONTO!" came the bark of Chief Engineer Caldwell. He was old school, therefore a prick most of the time. Not being Navy myself, it was a good idea to be at the station before the regulars.

I closed the book, placing it in a plastic bag for safe keeping, swung my legs over the bunk and dropped to the floor. 'What could be the deal? It's two o'clock in the morning,' I thought, slipping on my boots. Stopping by the galley on my way to the dive station, I grabbed a couple cups of coffee, drinking my sleep away.

"Evening Chief," I said entering. Caldwell was looking at some blue prints. Since he didn't return my greeting, "'Sup?"

"Good morning and real fucking funny, Jake. You're a regular comedian at this time of day."

"And you're a tough crowd. The rest of the boys are on leave, what you got?"

"A freighter just came in from Columbia. Coast Guard and Customs want it inspected."

"What, smugglers?"

"They think so. She just tied up to the wharf at the other end of the harbor, so you got forty-five minutes until they shut her down. I want you there when they do. I'll have one of the black gang go with you as a tender. Be at Times Square in a half hour with your gear."

"Pictures and everything?" I asked.

"Yep."

If they waited till dawn visibility would be better, but by then it might be too late. I was waiting at Times Square when the Coast Guard walked up looking official and everything. Time Square is the main entrance to the heart of the ship. A huge watertight door there opens for taking on supplies and getting rid of garbage. This is the Coast Guard's gig and they take it seriously. Tony was setting up the dive gear, I was suited and having a smoke.

When the Coast Guard commander was done looking us over he said, "You the diver?"

Sticking my cigarette in my mouth, I was tying my hair back thinking, 'Got to wake up pretty early in the morning to fool you'.

"Yeah, this the boat?" I wasn't military and never had been, so I treated brass like anybody else. As a rule they're not too fond of me either. I was the anti-christ of the military and could out dive any of their boys, so they put up with it.

"The Santa Maria just came in and we suspect they have drugs on board or on the hull. We need a full inspection, everything on video. You find anything out of the norm, let us know immediately and get out of the water. My boys will take over from there."

"Sure thing, boss. Am I cleared to dive?"

"As soon as the tag-out procedure is finished you'll be notified. Finish suiting up and be on standby."

I nodded, flipping my butt over the side. After helping Tony tie off the ladder, I zipped up and Tony set my diving helmet on, snapping it to the yoke. We did a comm check and waited.

An hour had passed before an officer gave me the go ahead. Shit, I could have been done already. I knew it would be a long wait; it always is with the military. I also knew better than to fuck with them.

Less than a minute after we got the go ahead, I was in the water. Headlamps and camera activated automatically. I had two flashlights - one big, one small, a spud wrench, pipe wrench, pry bar, hacksaw, chisel, and hammer. It was a bit much for an inspection; then again I wasn't above taking a piece of the action for myself either. If there was something down there and it could be pried or cut off, I would stash it under the pier somewhere and get it later. I had to find it first. I swam the waterline on the first pass of the inboard side, then dropping down the limit of visibility, which was about a fuzzy ten feet, then another pass. On the third pass was the bilge keel; it was clean with nothing welded to the underside. For the first forty minutes the dive was uneventful, if not boring. Both sides of the vessel, the bulbous bow, bow thrusters and the bottoms flats were just as they should be. If there was anything on her, it had to be at the stern.

I suddenly got the feeling I wasn't alone. It was four thirty in the morning, my brain said, my sixth sense said otherwise. Killing my lights and listening proved a waste of time. Besides, they were getting a real time feed on the topside monitor.

"How you doing?" Tony asked, his New York accent coming through intact. "Your voice is getting a little monotonous, pick it up a bit – bossman, like that chipper voice - over."

"Yeah, thanks Tony, just not enough coffee yet. One thing, is there anybody else diving around here?"

"No, just us. Why, something up?"

"Nah, like I said, not enough coffee. Out."

Swimming aft, the next thing I would encounter was the stern thruster. It is a tube about eight feet in diameter that runs clean through the ship, with an adjustable pitch propeller in the center of it. It aids the rudder in turning the 1200–foot ship. Aiming my light into the tube revealed the reality of the Coast Guard's suspicions. Several boxes were cleated to the floor of the tube. It looked like four containers, two on either side of the prop. My adrenalin spiked.

The thruster has a row of protection bars running horizontally across the opening on both sides of the ship. They keep out the larger flotsam and jetsam, protecting the propeller. These bars are bolted in place so that divers can access the thruster to effect repairs. Most often, it's to remove rope that has spooled around the propeller hub. After smearing the camera lens with gunk, I pulled my spud wrench and went to work to remove a bar so that I could crawl inside. It wasn't long before I was taking off my tank, shoving it through the gap and following it in. Once in, I knew I hit the jackpot. The boxes were bolted to welded cleats. I didn't have much time before topside would start asking questions. Four bolts and she was free and heavy. I dragged it to the opening and pushed it out. It sank like a rock. I was right behind it, but instead of dropping to the bottom I started to reinstall the bar. Just as the bar was in place and the bolt dropped through its hole, I heard a clunk. It sure wasn't me. I killed my light.

On the other side of the thruster tube, two divers came into view. They were dim silhouettes, backlit from the illumination of the dock lights, and were diving closed–circuit scuba, no bubbles. These two men going at it had one of the protection bars removed. Because they could not remove their gear, it was necessary for them to unbolt several of the bars to get in. Whoever it was, they knew what they were doing.

Once they both went into the tube, I swam under the ship to their side. As quickly and quietly as I could, I swung one of the bars back in place, getting a bolt in before they saw me. The red glow from night vision equipment explained how they got around without their lights being seen from above.

One of them moved suddenly, and the next thing I felt was a spear hitting me in the thigh. The razor sharp prongs cut deeply, holding fast. I bit my lips, tasting blood, trying not to scream. Closing my eyes, I flipped on one of the video H.I.D., high intensity discharge lamps.

They recoiled, blinded painfully as their night vision gear absorbed and magnified 10,000 watts of instant sun.

Opening my eyes slowly so I would not go blind and keeping the lights facing them, I swung the second bar into place, getting a bolt in place, cranking it tight before one of the divers was tearing at me through the bars. Like a mad monkey, he ripped away anything he could grab. Flipping my spud wrench around and jabbing the pointed end through my attackers facemask thwarted his efforts to take my life, leaving him struggling to save his own. As he fell away, another spear hit me in the shoulder. I continued on with bolting them inside, and turned on my comms.

"Tony! Turn on the stern thruster, NOW!" Tony was in the black gang and knew going through the chain of command would be futile, so he ran for the engine room and the control board. He tore off the tag out and hit the stern thruster. I grabbed onto the bars for dear life as the force of the prop wash tried to blow me away from the ship. The two divers were flattened against the bars; their terrified faces inches from mine.

"The other WAY!" I screamed, hoping Tony had his headset on.

The rush of water slowed as the motor wound down. I could see the relief on the diver's faces. Just as the prop came to a stop, I smiled at the two sorry smugglers and gave them the finger as the thruster started to turn the other way. I sank down as the giant food processor came to life, sucking the divers through the blades. I swam back to the ladder, pulled off my fins, making the climb in no small amount of pain. I now know how a fish feels after it gets hit by a blue water hunter. It hurts like a motherfucker.

Dumping my gear on the dock and drying my hands, I had just enough time to light a cigarette before the Coast Guard came up with Tony in handcuffs.

"Let him fucking go. He was following my orders and saved my life, too. Your drugs are in the stern thruster along with whatever remains of two divers. You think maybe I could get some medical attention?"

I limped up to Tony, clipping the zipcuffs with a pair of side cutters. The M.P.'s started to stop me but were called down by their commander.

"Anything else we can do for you gentlemen today?" I asked smartly.

The commander stared at me, before turning his back and barking orders at his men.

"No? Well, good day then and you're welcome," 'Fucking douche bag', I thought at his back.

I started laughing, slapped Tony on the shoulder and said, "Let's get the fuck out of here."

Back aboard the Salvor, Tony took care of the gear while the ship's doctor took care of me. Forty-two stitches later, I returned to my bunk with a head full of Percocet. The drug worked wonders on several levels; taking away the pain and letting me go one step deeper into The Song Divine.

By noon the drugs had worn off and I had a report to write and dive to log. Popping some more Percs and pouring a thermos of coffee on the way to the dive station, I settled into a big chair at a small desk and began the bane of all divers - The Report. It's not all that bad as long as you have an education and know what you are talking about. There's the rub ... most divers are big on brawn. A dive like the one I just completed required an essay, a short story of what was found and what happened. The report would fit all the requirements of the Coast Guard, full of checkable details and nautical terminology. Some of the facts would be there, but it would otherwise be a work of fiction, keeping my dive record clean and the Chief from having to cover my ass and his.

The Chief came in while I was writing. "Jesus, Jake, you have to start watching yourself down there, man."

"I thought I was," I said, looking up to the barrel-chested Chief. He was the Chief. Caldwell didn't small talk. If he said something it was because it was important and you'd better listen up.

"No, I'm serious, Jake. We've lost a few men these past months, men like you, with skills. They go out on a routine assignment and wind up dead."

"Shit happens, man. One day you're here, the next, poof!" I'm not big on the drama thing and neither is he.

"You're not listening to me, Jake. There is something going on. They are dead, right? A few months later you hear about them working a job in bumfuck somewhere like everything is all right."

"Chief Caldwell to the bridge," came the P.A. announcement.

"This report will be on your desk tomorrow morning. Hey Chief?

"What?"

"Thanks."

The Chief was gone. Duty called, he responded. I ground out the report, fulfilling my duty. My mind kept wandering back to what he had said. It was the first time I had heard even a vague reference to the Reuseable Program since the events years ago at Big Bend. Was it paranoid thinking, or was it just coincidence that the two divers showed when I was in the water? If they wanted me dead they certainly could have done a better job. Their spears were shot from high tech pneumatic guns, the kind you carry specifically for killing someone, like packing a handgun. They were not sporting weapons.

Then there was the C.G. Commander, who let us walk, after killing two people. No questions asked, as if it was no big deal. I had expected a grilling that would last days, or at the very least rip me a new asshole for breaches of protocol. At any rate, it should have been total hassle. That's what had me bugged. As Tony and I were driving out, we passed the Coast Guard dive station as their divers were just about to get in the water. There was only one gurney and one body bag visible in the morning light; that bugged me, too.

Finishing the report, I sent a copy to the Chief's office, downing some cold coffee before I limped to the galley. The chicken fried steak looked as lonely as I felt, sitting in the dining room, gravy disguising whatever the patty-shaped thing was that was dinner. Normally the place was packed, but shore leaves are few and taken seriously. There was only one other person here, tall and obviously like me, not Navy, with the long hair and flip-flops. He was pale, nursing his cup of coffee. The Percs worked as an excellent social lubricant, so I popped a few more, picked up my plate, and went over.

"This seat taken?" I said, goofing around. The man looked about the empty room from behind a pair of Ray-Ban bandoleros.

"No..."

I set my plate down. He looked at the food like it was a dead rat on my plate. Sitting I said, "My name's Jake, You are... new here." I extended my hand; he took it, his grip hard and cool.

"I am Johnny."

"And?"

"I have been assigned to do some research while the Salvor is in port. You the diver, yes?"

Word gets around quick on the boat. Who was this guy? I hadn't heard about him. My paranoid brain was starting to kick in again. He was dressed in black, a long leather overcoat. There could be plenty of guns underneath it. "What kind of research do you do, tied to the dock?"

"We will be taking one of the inflatables." He said, sipping the coffee.

"We?"

"You are the diver, yes?

"Yes," I answered slowly. I normally get the skinny before anybody. Something smelled fishy and it wasn't the cafeteria. "What's this all about? I haven't heard anything."

"Our work requires a minimum of advance knowledge and a maximum of discretion. It is one of the reasons I asked for you."

"So this is some top secret stuff?"

"Perhaps. It is just the way we operate."

"Who is the we you refer to?" I asked. John looked around the room then back to me.

"I believe I mean us." Johnny said with a conspiratorial smile that was beguiling.

I took a few bites from my plate, not being able to help but notice the look on his face.

"The food is pretty bad, you get used to it."

"Mmmm. How unfortunate. Tomorrow before we leave I will make you breakfast. It is not good to get used to bad food. We will leave at four A.M.; breakfast is at three. Nice to meet you, Jake."

"Yeah, likewise," I said with a mouthful of food.

I was up at two, took a shower and retaped my stitches, giving a fat layer of anti-biotic to the wounds before gauzing. Diving with stitches or minor bodily damage was routine. It generally took something life threatening before a diver takes his name off the active list and out of the money chase.

At three A.M., I entered the galley. The smell of high octane coffee was overwhelming. I stood there for a moment huffing the aroma, before finding out how to get some. A French press sat on a counter with a cup. I took it, savoring the first few sacred sips at the only table set up. A few minutes passed and Johnny emerged from the kitchen with one of those oval trays with a folding base, piled with breakfast: omelets, potato latkes, pancakes and more of that coffee. My taste for food was changed that morning. I had never known how good it could be; now that I knew, I could never go back.

We both pushed away from the table at the same time. I rolled two cigarettes, giving Johnny one. We smoked in silence and coffee.

"Man, that was great, and this coffee, I'm hooked."

Johnny smiled from behind his glasses. "You liked it then?"

"Do you do lunch?" I said, pouring more coffee. "So, what's the gig?"

"Basically I wanted to get to know you a little bit, before you get cut off at the neck."

I pushed back from the table, sliding my Big Chief out of my pocket and thumbing the blade open. Then I sat there sipping coffee with one hand, staring at him. He looked back from behind his glasses and allowed the moment to get really intense before cracking his engaging smile.

"Put your knife away, Jake, you will not be needing it yet. I like the way you dealt with the smugglers, though. They were two of Megacorp's best men. No great loss there, it was the drugs that the Coast Guard got that piss me off."

I still had my knife in my hand and could not believe what I was hearing. "How the fuck does a drug dealer get on a Navy boat?"

"I am a scientist, among other things. Megacorp needs me right now, so I get away with stuff. The Coast Guard only recovered three boxes, Jake. Any thoughts on where the fourth might be?"

I brought my knife hand to the table and started cleaning my fingernails with the blade, trying to give myself a chance to think. I had no idea what the fuck was going on here, so I decided to play dumb to see where it would lead. I shrugged my shoulder, wincing from the stitches. The guy had just read my mind, or was a good guesser; either way he knew more than I did, so I tried to change the subject.

"There is a rumor going around about guys like me disappearing, then showing up on the other side of the continent working again. You know anything about that?"

"That is perhaps something we should discuss in a more private situation."

Johnny's cell phone went off. He answered and hung up without saying a word. He then stood, looked at me and said, "Time to go, your gear has been put on the boat." He started to leave. I finished my coffee before following. He left his brief case sitting at the table; I took it and met him at the boat.

"You forgot this."

The sun was just coming up as we left Pearl Harbor and headed west. Johnny was driving the boat, the water was calm and he had the throttle wide open, enjoying the speed and salt spray. Once the island was a speck on the horizon, he shut the inflatable down. The silence on the ocean was inspiring. We both soaked it in for a few minutes, then Johnny pulled out and opened his case, withdrawing several canisters, narrow, made of stainless steel.

"What I would like are a few water samples, now that we are far enough away from Oahu to avoid the runoff pollution."

"From different depths?"

"Yeah, every one hundred feet until you can go no deeper, there are ten vials to be filled."

"A thousand feet, on SCUBA?"

"It is one of the reasons I asked for you."

"What is the other reason?"

"I want my box."

"You know, salvage rights are somewhat obscure. It is usually finders keepers."

"I am sure we can work something out."

"Can you help me with these tanks?"

The twin 120 cubic foot cylinders were the behemoths of scuba tanks. If you didn't have help, it was almost impossible to shoulder them. Johnny was stronger than he looked, hoisting the tanks and holding them easily while I slipped my arms through the vest. He had my mask and fins ready along with a pouch of the vials. He was a natural tender. Sitting on the edge of the boat, I finished a cigarette and cup of coffee before donning my mask, gave him the chin and rolled off the boat. The weight of the tanks pulled me down like a block of lead. Sinking fast, I continuously cleared my ears for the first few hundred feet, never taking my eyes off the depth gauge. At 900 feet I began filling my vest with air to slow my descent. At 1000 feet I came to a stop in the middle of the ocean. It was a black water dive. You could not see your hand in front of your face. I pulled the first vial and filled it, securing the cap before ascending 100 feet to take another. It was slow going and I could feel the current moving me; this was not good. I could drift for miles while working my way to the surface. Not good at all. But there was no use worrying about it. I still had eight hundred vertical feet to go.

At 200 feet, the black faded to blue as I checked my air supply. Shit! I was lower on air than I thought. One more sample to go, then push for the surface. It was going to be close. If the current moved me too far I would be lost; he would never find me and I would die of decompression sickness before the Navy could have a search underway. Fuck me, I thought, taking my last sample, I was set up and fell for it. What a fucking chump!

I kicked hard for the surface, dumping my tanks on the way. They were empty, it was time to blow and go. I was spitting mad at myself by the time I saw it. My lungs were burning for a breath that I thought would never come. But there it was, hanging at forty feet. A bottle with a regulator attached. Grabbing the down line with one hand, I put the regulator in my mouth with the other, breathing again.

Decompression would take a while, so I clipped myself to the down line and went into a state of meditation. It was something I routinely did while decompressing, plus I needed to think clearly. Something was going on and I was being dragged into it.

A fresh tank was lowered ten feet shallower, when it was time to move to the next stage of decompression. The guy knew what he was doing. Most scientists I've known are really smart guys, but couldn't put a blender together to save their lives. Apparently this one could.

After five hours I climbed the swim step, coming up over the stern, a towel sitting on the engine. Johnny was pulling the last tank aboard, looking aft when he finished stowing it. He poured a couple cups of coffee and came back, handing me one.

"Well, how did it go?" He said with a smile.

"A little deep for scuba. The current was running. How did you know where... "

"Followed your bubbles. You don't breathe very often." Johnny said with a questioning look on his face.

"Only when I have to."

"Lunch?"

"Fuck man, what are you doing? Reading my mind?"

Lunch was pasta, warmed by the engine, a baguette, and bottle of Chianti. Completely against Navy regs, it was fabulous. We sat enjoying the meal; the wine had bite, loosening us both up, which I think was part of his plan. Johnny reached into his pocket, pulling a little brown bottle out.

"Digestivo?"

It was apparent he was Italian, his accent, the food, and certain mannerisms, generally not found in Americans. I wasn't sure what he meant. However the wine had made me a bit more malleable than usual.

"Sure."

He produced a little straw, unscrewed the cap, took my hand, made sure it was dry, and dumped a pile of coke on it, handing me the straw.

"So you want me to talk, eh? Your torture methods are breaking me." I started laughing, stopping long enough to snort the pile, and begin again. "Just how did you get past the background check? Just to get on board the Salvor they want to know your asshole size."

"Yeah well, you know."

"No, no, I don't. Care to fill me in?"

"You will find out soon enough."

"Now, is soon enough for me." I said, going on the defensive. "Does this have anything to do with tech personnel going missing, or isn't this private enough?"

"You are a funny guy, Jake. Yeah, this is private enough. Megacorp will be taking you soon. They tried the other night. By eliminating two of their top divers you jacked yourself up on the roster."

"You mean what the Chief was telling me..."

"Is dead on. He could lose his commission for what he told you. Megacorp doesn't want anyone to know what they are up to."

"That's par for the course, but just what 'are' they up to?"

"In a nutshell, they are preparing for the future by having a trained workforce in place when the shit hits the fan."

"You're losing me."

"Okay."

We did another line. He continued.

"You notice how there are not too many new divers these days?" I nodded. "Well, the same holds true for most of the trades, science and med fields. People are so lost in the internet they have forgotten reality exists. And so, they quit preparing for it, assuming it would always be taken care of. It has not been, and it is falling apart. When the Golden Gate Bridge collapsed, Megacorp knew they had to do something to stall the decline of western civilization or their profits would tank. People like you and me will fill the void ... indefinitely."

"That doesn't sound too good. What happens when we die?"

"That is the kicker, we don't."

With that, the clouds opened up creating an instant monsoon on the open sea. The rain was warm but when it didn't let up, I knew we were in for a long ride home. The seas kicked it up a notch, too. Soon we were riding ten foot swells and having a blast. The inflatable was made for this kind of water and we pushed it to the limit. We would launch off the biggest waves of the set, catching air before plowing back into the surf, searching for the next big one. The problem with fun like this is either something goes wrong and somebody gets hurt or it is over before you're done having fun. In this case, it was the latter as we idled down coming into the channel for the harbor.

We had been having too much fun and it was dark by the time we entered the harbor proper. Johnny was driving and killed the running lights before we came to the dock where the Santa Maria was moored. She had been confiscated and taken to the East Loch for storage. Johnny passed the dock before cutting a hard left and disappearing underneath the pier. The tide was out and we did not have to duck to pass under the ship bumpers. Shutting the motor off, we sat there listening. For what I don't know, until Johnny said in a quiet voice, "Can you do this dive without your suit?"

"Yeah, I suppose."

"Good, slip into the water, I'll hand you a tank and rope."

I put my fins, mask, and harness on, easing myself into the warm polluted waters of Pearl Harbor. Several hundred years of cleaning hulls, and accepting the detritus of drydocking, left the harbor a dead zone. Countless divers died an early death after spending a few years cleaning Navy boats. Ablative paint systems are anti-life. Lucky for the Navy, nobody ever put two and two together. Now you didn't go into the water without a full spectrum injection of antibiotics and an exposure suit. I was up on my shots, and by the way Johnny was talking it didn't matter about the other hazards. My number was coming up. All I had to do was wait for it.

Swimming through the maze of pilings that support the pier came second nature. The piles were still covered with razor sharp barnacles, long dead, but they could still slice you clean to the bone if you weren't careful. At the edge of the pier I surfaced to get an idea where the stern thruster had been, submerged and began counting kick cycles. Slowly swimming along the bottom, I started a search pattern when I got to the right area. It was always possible the Coast Guard divers picked it up; they weren't the sharpest tacks in the box, but they have been known to get lucky.

A hand reached out of the gloom and wrapped around my face. I swirled, grabbing the arm and twisting it violently before realizing what it was ... part of one of the divers who got osterized. It was pretty freaky in the black water, but the encounter raised the odds the box was still there.

After a few more passes, I found it and quickly secured a line to it, then shackled a small lift bag to the box; putting just enough air in the bag to make it neutrally buoyant, not bring it to the surface. Following the rope and swimming back under the pier was just too easy. Then it got real loud, everything rumbling. I knew what it was and headed for the bottom! I was too late! With the tide out the bottom of the ship pushed me into the muck as tugboats nudged her into position. I started digging furiously for my life. My number may be coming up but I'd be damned if I was going to suffocate in the scum of Pearl Harbor. For all the effort of the next few minutes I was rewarded with that little click you hear in your regulator just before you run out of air.

'Fuck me', I said to no one and started to pull on the rope for all I was worth. I held that breath until my lungs felt like they were exploding as my arms screamed, pulling myself forward through the sludge. I couldn't see but could feel my perception closing down. I exhaled and sucked on my reg, trying to fill my lungs. I gasped, pulling with all my might. Then the lights went out.

I woke coughing shit up. Yellow fluid gushed from my lungs, like heaving after an all nighter but worse. I couldn't inhale! I was alive but dying. Something was stuffed into my mouth followed by a powerful rush of air, force filling my lungs. Opening my eyes, I could see Johnny holding a regulator in my mouth, pushing on the purge button. I began to breathe on my own.

When the sun rose we were out at sea again, not so far as before, but alone on the water. I sat up looking down on myself, covered in black muck. Johnny came forward with a cup of coffee.

"How you feeling, Jake?" He said handing me the cup.

"Bout as good as I look, like shit."

"You got some serious strong will, dude. Full on drowned and you still climbed the rope and did not stop until you reached the boat. A little CPR and voilà!

"Did we get it?"

Johnny chinned towards the stern of the boat where a box covered in the same black muck sat.

"Had to wait until the tide came in to retrieve it, got the bottom of that ship off of it. Good going, man. Now, you are cut up pretty bad, but you have to get in the water and wash yourself before I can deal with it, pretty rank."

He was right. I was wondering what the smell was. I didn't have to be asked twice, slipping over the side. The muck came off slowly only to reveal I was cut from head to foot by the barnacles. I was glad there was no memory of it happening; my imagination was good enough. Climbing back into the boat, the numerous cuts began bleeding all over the place. Johnny was there with a towel, needle and dental floss. He gave me a sniff of something that wasn't coke, so I wouldn't bother him as he poked the needle through my skin, pulling the floss through to close the gashes. It was noon before we motored back to Pearl Harbor. On the way in, he transferred the contents of the box to a duffel bag, tossing the box overboard when it was empty.

We hadn't talked much on the way back, I was stoned and Johnny seemed preoccupied. As we were tying up to the dock, I asked, "So, did I pass the test?" I was expecting some kind of smart assed remark or at least a yes.

"I needed to know there was someone I could trust. I'll be around." He gave me the chin, shouldered his duffel, picked up his case and left. I didn't see him again for another six months.

I played it cool getting back on ship. Getting busted by the Navy sucks. Being so wasted I forgot to ask him about my cut … 'I died for that shit!' What I didn't realize at the time was what an ironic statement I had just made to myself. Besides, I had just made friends with someone. In the future, I would find that Johnny would be the only friend I would have for many years.

My stitches healed and life went on. The routine aboard ship for the crew was never ending. As a diver there wasn't much to do when not diving. We were on call 24/7 so couldn't get deeply involved in any of the bigger projects going on. I worked out and swam, reading when not doing one of the other two, or did maintenance on our dive gear.

When our crane operator on the Salvor died of an apparent heart attack, it took a toll on our abilities as a salvage operation. Tommy was an asshole who would rather say 'fuck you' than 'good morning', but when it came to running a crane, there was none better. A union boy to the core, Tommy had worked his way up the pay scale since he was seventeen. At 72, he would have finally retired, full pension, bennies, a house on the ocean that was paid for and a wife half his age. Everything. But when they carried him out feet first from the crane, there wasn't much hope that he would ever get a chance.

Months passed as we went through operators like toilet paper. The new guys had no attention span. Generations of the internet and V.R. ruined one's ability to focus for more than a few seconds at a time. They could sit for hours, days, in front of a terminal, chasing dragons. Beyond that, the available workforce was becoming useless. Caldwell's advice about watching my back kept returning to the front of my thinking. Where were the new guys – any new guys – that had their shit together?

Chief Caldwell finally put me on the crane after the last union guy let a load slam into the side of the Salvor at the water line. It took a week of welding to patch her. It was no small task. With the loss of Tommy, the entire crane crew lost their drive. Tommy had been such a prick, everyone jumped for him. Now they just didn't care.

The steel plating we used to patch the hull was one inch thick, cut and bent to conform to the curve of the hull. Instead of tack welding pad eyes to the plate for the lift, the riggers used grips, meant for sliding a load, not lifting. It was easier for them, and it probably would have worked if they didn't tie the tag lines to the release mechanisms. I was in the water sitting on the bilge keel when they began the lift. Six tons of steel raised from the deck like giant curtain. As they swung it over the side, I was in position waiting for them to lower it.

Over comms, the radio operator yelled, "Look out! We lost it!"

He hadn't finished the last sentence when the six tons sliced through the water like a massive meat cleaver. It took my airline, dragging me along with it straight and fast to the bottom. It stabbed into the muck, parting the air and comm line before falling over, nearly crushing me into the seafloor. Having no bailout bottle, as it was shallow work, I began to rip at the latch securing my helmet in place; time was running out fast. Pulling that hat off and dumping my weights, I bolted for the surface, screaming inward with my first breath upon reaching the air. I regained my composure but could not reel in my anger, climbing the ladder to the deck.

Stepping onto the deck, I unstrapped my harness, dropping it and pulling back the top of my wet suit. My eyes scanned the deck for the riggers who were behind the crane trying to look busy. One of them was a diver, a Navy diver who rarely got wet, Rodney. Coming around the crane, I tried to look casual. It worked until I belted Rodney's rigging partner, knocking him to the deck. Rodney grabbed a slug wrench, swinging it, clipping me in the head, putting me down. He jumped on top of me, jackhammering my face with his fists until he was pulled off. Head wounds bleed a lot. I got up lunging after him and fell flat on my face, out cold and in shock. Rodney got what he wanted, a chance to dive. With a fractured skull, I was off the dive roster, indefinitely.

✱✱✱

The sound of surf and the smell of hashish opened my mind. The sunlight squeezed through my closed eyes. I opened them, slowly. Blue water showed through the open window as a trail of smoke wisped out. There was Johnny, in a wicker chair, smoking and reading a science journal. He looked over, sensing I was awake.

"Welcome back, Jake. Have a nice nap?"

"Where am I?"

"My place, you've been in a coma for a month."

"Huh? Wha? How?"

"When I heard you got hit, I contacted the Chief. He had you brought here instead of sending you to Crippler."

Crippler is the nickname of the V.A. hospital on Oahu, really called Tripler. They had a bad reputation and I was thankful Johnny and the Chief didn't let me become part of it.

"It is better if you are volunteered and put to work immediately than used for experimentation. After being a guinea pig, you are pretty much useless meat, winding up in the incinerator instead of the front lines."

"What the fuck are you talking about, Johnny?" He had me really confused now.

"I wish I knew. Jake. I wish I knew. Want some pasta?"

Garlic, Hawaiian chilies, olive oil, and pasta, with a garnish of parsley. How those few ingredients could taste so good was beyond me. On the ship, pasta came with red gravy. Wiping up the gubbins with a piece of bread I asked, "What ever happened with the dope?" meaning the box we brought up six months ago.

"It was not dope." Johnny said, getting up and clearing the dishes. I waited for a few moments expecting more. It didn't come. I was just starting to see that he never volunteered information. Whether it was a lack of trust or just his nature I wasn't sure, so I broke out my hammer and pick and started digging for it.

"Well, what was it?"

"A vaccine."

"What kind of vaccine?"

"For certain types of cancer."

"And why did it have to be smuggled in?" I was beginning to enjoy myself.

"Megacorp banned it."

"Why would that be? It's a fucking cure for cancer."

"Widespread use would cut into their profits."

"Could you just keep going or do I have to prompt you all the time."

"Okay, just this once." He started laughing, dumping some coke on a plate, using his long pinky nail to do a couple scoops. My head was still in bandages; hard as it was I managed restraint and kept my nose clean.

"You see," Johnny began, "there is a lot more profit in managing diseases than curing them. This is where it gets confusing. I am a Megacorp operative, as you soon will be." He held up his hand so I wouldn't interrupt him. "When the change happened, they did a first rate job brainwashing me, like they do everybody. Fortunately for me, it didn't take. I still follow my own agenda, pretending to follow theirs, because I have to. Long story a little shorter, I discovered it while doing research in Columbia for Megacorp. I was supposed to be developing a vaccine to give people cancer, not cure it. Profits come first. One of my associates reported the findings. Megacorp raided the lab destroying all the data, everything. All I was able to get before the raid was what was in that box.

"I do like my coke," he said taking another whiff, "and had made some connections while working down there. For a price, they would get it to the U.S. for me. For a price. I found you, you found it, and the vaccine, hopefully, is being synthesized, and disseminated. Who, what, where, how, I do not know and do not want to know. Knowing too much will get you killed or worse. I am just an innocent scientist in the employ of Megacorp." He started laughing, accidentally knocking the plate of coke to the floor. Johnny rubbed it into the carpet like one would a cigarette ash, thinking nothing of it.

Seizing an opportunity, "So, what was the price?"

"Yeah uh, been meaning to talk with you about that."

I could see it coming; there was no reason to make him explain. Working for a drug cartel was like working for the mafia: once you're in, there is only one way out. "Just tell me where and when you need me, I'll be there."

"Thank you, Jake."

I spent the next few days catching up. The bandages came off on the second day. The healing was good, just more scars to go with my collection. Then there was Johnny, an enigma. We'd hit it off on our first meeting. Getting to know him would take considerably longer. He led a private life, so he wasn't used to talking, especially about himself. I didn't force him to communicate and just let it come naturally. Not being much of a social butterfly myself, it didn't bother me. He kept alluding to some kind of Megacorp club that I would be joining, but never went beyond that, always changing the subject. Lucky for me Johnny was incredibly intelligent. When he would change the subject, I was never disappointed as he rambled on about quantum physics or molecular biology, always way over my head, but never losing my interest.

The morning of the third day the smell of rich, dark coffee woke me at three A.M. The living room was spread with dive gear; Johnny was out on the lanai. Coffee came first. I settled into a beach chair with cup in hand and a cigarette. We sat in silence for a half hour, each absorbed in our own thoughts. That first cup in the morning is like a moment of grace. Neither of us wanted to break it. The moment passed.

"What's the gear for?" I asked.

Johnny lit a cigarette, pointing his chin at the shoreline. A blue inflatable with twin 100 horsepower motors was nudged into the sand. It had not been there yesterday. Looking at Johnny quizzically I thought, 'Here we go again, another round of twenty questions.'

"We going for a dive?" He shakes his head no.

"I'm going for a dive?" He shakes his head yes.

"This have anything to do with the 'price'?" He shakes his head yes.

"When?" Johnny makes the sign language motion for sundown.

"I'll put the gear together and be ready." Getting out of my chair, "What are we doing up at three in the morning?" He shrugged his shoulders. It was then I noticed the pile of coke on a plate. Once again, I chose to keep my nose clean. Diving on cocaine is not a fun thing to do. Having done it a few times, I finally learned not to go down coked up. I'm a slow learner.

The gear was scuba, high-end commercial stuff, like those divers were wearing when they went through the mix master; even one of those pistol spearguns. The mask was fitted with night vision tech and had a welding lens that would flip into place when needed. The portable burning rig next to the lanai door explained that. Also a rebreather, a couple of lift bags, a wetsuit, and two big magnets with handles. After finishing with the dive stuff, I poured another cup and went for a walk on the beach to catch the sunrise, leaving Johnny to his thoughts and cocaine. Upon returning, he was gone. A note taped to the computer screen said he would be back by sundown, nothing more.

With the day to kill I made some more coffee and brought the carafe to a reading chair, picking up the medical mag Johnny had been reading. The opening article brought me up to speed about Megacorp's Reuseable Program. It was a real eye opener. This was what Caldwell had hinted and that which Johnny alluded to.

Since it was a medical material, they talked about the med aspects of the program, but you didn't need a PhD to read between the lines. The military was first to have access to the program since they provided the 'volunteers'. Megacorp's vision went beyond military use. They saw the future and unless they came up with something quick, profits would decline and the shareholders would be screaming bloody murder.

Megacorp created the problem, but it would not be Megacorp that fixed it.

The remaining articles dealt with how they created a reuseable. Here is where it went way over my head. There wasn't anything between the lines either. What I did glean is that the compound used for creation of a reuseable had been drawn from a subject. They could not synthesize it in a lab. There was only one source, and this source was never spoken of in any way. Apparently, the procedure involved an injection of the compound and required regular injections thereafter, the maintenance hit.

"Is this where Tommy, the crane operator, went?" I was thinking as Johnny walked in through the front door.

"Probably," Johnny remarked, answering my thought.

He had a bandaid on the side of his neck, his color was good, and the melancholia was gone. Johnny noticed the magazine I had been reading.

"Find anything interesting?"

"Is this shit really going on?"

"Yep."

"Are you one?"

"Yep."

"And you just went and got your hit?"

"Yep. Want something to eat?" Johnny brought a baguette, some mascarpone and bottle of wine out on the lanai. We ate as the sun went down.

The night was warm as the boat headed east, far from the island lights. It didn't take long for the 100 horse motors to bring us into international waters, beyond the jurisdiction of the Coast Guard. Running without lights made the journey that much trippier. Only the occasional readout from the GPS disrupted the black from its omnipresence. At midnight Johnny shut the motors down.

"Now we wait. Better start suiting up, we have to be ready when they arrive."

"Got an E.T.A.?"

"No. For the last 100 miles they have been running dead slow."

"You don't mean...?"

"They will not be stopping. Their speed reduction is so the Guard will not notice them slowing down just outside their territory. Slowing down would send red lights flashing to the Guard and they would have a chopper on us in minutes."

"So I gotta do this while they are running."

"Yep."

"In that case, I need to know where the packages are."

"Under the aft ends bilge keels. They are welded, so you are going to have to scarf the welds, without punching a hole in the boxes. Think you can do it?"

"If it was easy, anybody could do it, and you wouldn't need me."

"Here she comes." Johnny pointed to the south where a black curtain was being drawn across the stars.

I pulled the top of my suit into place and put a hood on. Then the weights, and rebreather. The torch was a hand held ultra–thermic. Burning at more than 15,000 degrees it could cut anything. My dive harness held an assortment of tools along with the magnets and torch. The lift bags were rolled up, stuffed in a goody bag.

A third of the sky was blotted out as the ship came into visual range, which wasn't very far away. Johnny started the motors, preparing to pace the ship. He had to keep the inflatable close lest the Coast Guard see two vessels on their radar. We were now with the ship, staying at the midship draft marks.

"It's showtime. The crew has dropped lines over the side. When you get it cut free, attach the line and fill the lift bag. When it breaks the surface, they'll haul it up. Good luck."

I gave him the chin, rolling backwards off the boat into the black water. The ship was moving about five knots. I could swim that fast and was doing it now, straight down to grab hold of the bilge keel before it passed me by. After grabbing it I stopped swimming, sliding back to the stern of the bilge keel. As the end arrived, I slapped a magnet to the hull, tied a tag line to it for safety and took a look at the underside. There were two metal boxes, just like Johnny said there would be. I retrieved the line that the crew lowered and secured it to the boxes along with one of the lift bags, pulled out the torch and started cutting. It was tight work but the diver that installed these knew what he was doing, which made my job that much easier.

The first boxes went smooth. When they cut free, I blew the bag and the package shot to the surface. With one side done, I gathered my equipment and with a magnet in each hand, used them to 'walk' over the turn of the bilge, across the bottom flats, then up the other side. Expecting an easy repeat, imagine my surprise when reaching the other bilge keel!

The aft third of the winglet had torn free from the hull, flapping and slicing the water with deadly power. Leaving one magnet on the hull with my tag line attached, I watched the movement of the wild piece of steel. At first it appeared chaotic, but there was a pattern in the chaos, which I watched for a little longer, to make sure of the rhythm. A wrong guess would get me killed. Timing was everything. With my back to the ship's hull I prepared for the moment. When it came I pushed off, swimming for all I was worth.

The timing was good, grabbing the steel as it came to the limit of its swing before whipping back. It was like hanging onto a pissed off bull, jerking me around like a rag doll. Slapping my other magnet to the wickedly moving wing gave me a solid purchase. The bull could throw me now, but I could get back on. Cold comfort, but better than none at all. The boxes were still welded on. I half expected them to be torn off by whatever the ship hit to do this kind of damage. Inching the magnet closer and tying on the lift bag to the boxes, I began cutting. It was crazy under these conditions. A couple tons of erratic steel is not something you want to be around. With the first one cut loose and hanging from the lift bag, I relit the torch and attacked the second with frenzy. I had had enough of this shit.

Suddenly the wild regular motion changed; something was happening and my sixth sense told me it wasn't good. But I owed Johnny one and was going to finish, even if it killed me. The drug cartel would certainly kill Johnny if this went sour.

The water started moving faster; you could feel it rushing past. Either the ship was picking up speed or I was sinking. In the black water, it was difficult to tell. When my eardrum blew, I had all the information I needed. I was sinking fast. The bilge keel must have finally ripped itself from the hull. There was no time for thinking. I had to act and fast. My tag line reel had 500 feet of line, and was paying out rapidly. I filled the lift bag to the max and continued cutting. What was easy on the other side was now a matter of life and death. I was almost through scarfing the last weld, when the torch died. 'Fuck me!' I thought and began to pry the box off. After a couple of bends, the weld broke just as the tagline reel ran out. I yanked the quick release holding me to the magnet with one hand, the other held onto the lift bags for dear life. The bilge keel section continued its downward spiral as I went the other way just as quickly.

On the way up I reeled in my tagline as fast as I could, not wanting to reach the surface 500 feet behind the ship. Surfacing at the stern,

I was still 200 feet from the pick up point. I was like a fish reeling itself in on the surface. There was the line dropped over the side. It didn't take long to secure a bowline to the packages and disconnect myself. They must have been watching because as soon as I disconnected they were hauling it out of the water.

Johnny had a clean towel, cup of coffee and a cigarette waiting for me.

"How did it go?"

"It went."

"Uneventful is the correct term."

"Yeah, I know, I was just trying to be clever."

"Try harder."

We stayed with the ship until the sun began to rise, parting company when the fishing boats heading out for the day created confusion on the water, at least as far as the Coast Guard's radar was concerned. We peeled away, heading back out with the fishermen. After an hour or so Johnny reversed course, making for the shack on the beach.

Back at the shack I showered, put some shorts on and made for the lanai and the lounge. I was beat. At the time, pumped with adrenalin, I didn't realize how hard it had been. Plus I never checked my depth gauge, figuring it at about 500 feet, give or take. Fuck! I'd felt it coming on earlier but blew it off. Getting up to go check my depth gauge, my legs went out from under me. I couldn't feel them. Fuck! I was bent and it was just going to get worse. Unable to get up off the floor, I yelled for Johnny.

"Johnny! Get the fuck out here!"

"I thought I heard something hit the floor," He said, affecting humor.

"This ain't funny man, I'm bent, bad. You got to get me to a chamber."

My arms started to cramp up, the pain becoming unbearable. I was able to grab a pillow and stuffed it in my mouth, biting hard, screaming into it. By now, I was locked in a fetal position. Every joint in my body was racked to a ten on the pain scale. It was unbearable. I was going to die.

When I woke I was wet and shivering. It took a few moments to realize I was under water. I checked my depth gauge: 165 feet. The number rang a bell, but understanding it was lost. I was in a hardhat. "Where am I and what am I doing...?" I said to myself just as the rope I was hanging from started pulling me up, then stopped. What the fuck? Checking my depth gauge again, 155 feet, it hit me what was happening. Somebody was performing an in-water recompression on me, using the Navy decompression tables, some of which begin at 165 feet. That realization kick-started my brain. It had to be Johnny.

Nobody in their right mind would do something like this, which is only done in extreme emergencies when a chamber is unavailable. In–water recompression rarely works except in mild cases of the bends. There are too many unavoidable factors, hypothermia being one of the biggies. I was shivering, which is good. When you stop shivering, the beginning of the end starts. Being in a hard hat...

"Hey, is there anybody up there?"

"Yo Jake, how you doing, man?"

"Do you have any idea how fucking nuts this is?"

"Yes I do. But it saves us from having to answer too many uncomfortable questions. Plus, Megacorp would have seized the opportunity to have you join the ranks of reuseables."

"You know, if I wasn't so goddamn cold I would argue the point with you. Got any coffee?"

"Yeah and its good and hot too." Johnny said, yanking my chain a little.

"You fucker. Hey, got a thermos or a bike bottle?"

"I'm sitting on the beach, Jake, enjoying a most beautiful day. I can get a bike bottle, lot of good it will do you though."

"Listen. Fill the bottle with hot coffee and duct tape a shackle to the bottle and send it down the line. Gotta get some warmth in me."

"But how you going to drink it?"

"Just leave that up to me."

Drinking underwater is something of a conundrum, but it can be done. Once a group of us dove on New Years Eve, to be under at midnight. Well, being commercial divers gave us license to do stupid things. We filled a dozen bike bottles with champagne and at the stroke of twelve we opened the valves, took our regulators out of our mouths and sucked on the bottles. An hour later we staggered from the water.

With a hardhat on the procedure is a little more complicated, but I was sure it could be done. Necessity made the seemingly impossible, possible. Hot coffee never tasted so good. Emptying the container then filling it with air, it made the return trip to the surface.

"Keep'em coming, Johnny."

As the hours passed the coffee kept my insides warm, while my pee helped to do the same to my skin.

When the tables were completed, successfully, Johnny dragged me from the water. I was physically spent and tipping the scales towards hypothermia; the coffee just stalled the inevitable. A nice hot beach was just what the doctor ordered. Unfortunately it was night. On the upside, there was a hot tub, complete with a couple babes and a plate full of coke. Johnny stripped me in front of the girls, who got a good laugh at what cold water shrinkage looks like. There was a shower he let me sit in for a few minutes to rinse off the pee smell, then set me in the tub like a paraplegic, blew a big snort up my nose, and jumped in with a bottle of Jack Daniels. When I came around the party was in full swing. Thinking with my dick, instead of my brain, I dove into the debauchery, not coming up for air until several days had gone by. And then it was to be rudely interrupted by a couple of Shore Patrol guys sent to bring my ass back to the Salvor.

It wasn't the first time the Patrol was called in to be my chauffeur, but it had been a long time since pulling a stunt like this. I was under contract with the Navy, what could I say.

"Sorry Chief." That first word was the most difficult, for a lack of ever being used. I respected Caldwell and he, me. I didn't want to lose it.

"Shore Patrol said the girls were pretty cute... Don't let it happen again. You able to dive?"

"You mean right now?"

"Coast Guard has a ship on pier 47 they need inspected."

"Smugglers?"

"They think so."

It was the same ship that I dove several nights ago. Talk about ironic. There were no drugs or other contraband. However, their Chief Engineer was grateful for the information concerning his bilge keel. He informed me they clipped a sunken ship that was floating just under the surface. In the daylight on the open ocean, he watched the flapping bilge keel when the waters were clear enough. I kept the fresh burn marks out if the vid, which got me a keen, if not thankful look from the Chief. Making points with the Chief is always good business. The Coast Guard would have noticed the burns and torn the ship apart.

The news brightened my burgeoning hangover. Our asses were covered. That they hit a sunken vessel was no surprise really. The high seas were becoming more difficult to navigate all the time. It was our garbage that was causing all the problems. The oceans and seas were a cost effective way of dealing it.

What began as a novel experiment of disposing our waste had turned into a nightmare of epic proportions. Back in the late 1900's, they began to fill old barges with trash, seal them up and sink them in one of the nearby ocean trenches over 10,000 feet deep. It worked. Once the garbage was down that deep, it could never surface again. Very clever, but we were always a clever species. Unfortunately, there was too much garbage and not enough oversight of the precedent that paved the way for a worldwide landfill in the deep. The sealed container idea was not cost effective enough. We were also a greedy species. Just take the trash 200 miles out and dump it. Better yet, and far easier and most cost effective was to dump your shit on the beach at low tide. Voilà - it is gone in the morning, like magic. We were also a lazy species.

The theory, if you could call it that, was 'the solution to pollution is dilution'. Well, we had reached critical mass. The seas were becoming more and more toxic. Which didn't make my job any easier. We were routinely given injections and pills to counter the effects of exposure to god knows what. There were no old divers. There weren't any retired ones either. Makes you wonder.

The party was over and work insinuated itself into the role it had always played in my life. It's what I did. Worked to live and lived to work. I didn't realize at the time how my work ethic would end up being my demise into the darkest realms of the soul. Until then, we pulled fishing boats off reefs, towed junkers out to sea, sinking them, along with routine in-water vessel maintenance.

There used to be any number of competent companies in the islands that handled this type of work. For one reason or another they all folded. The industry just sort of fell apart. Funny thing was that it was desperately needed. It was the cost of doing business that prohibited a thriving industry. Megacorp had created quiet monopolies of key businesses, primarily oil and water. Control these two systems and you could control the world.

Independent enterprise was becoming history. If you remained small enough you might survive a few years, even a generation, before a lack of growth caused stagnation and death. There were only a handful of big players. You needed money and resources to continue. Countries began to incorporate themselves, mimicking Megacorp tactics to carry on.

"Aren't all the armed forces under Megacorp?" I asked the Chief once, while recompressing in the chamber.

"Once Megacorp underwrote the National Debt, everything became Megacorp's."

"We still have a president, elections..."

"Puppets, Jake, the U.S.A. is a business as it always has been, along with about half of the rest of the world. Their lawyers are shrewd. When Megacorp assumes the debt of a nation, it gets the nation, too. A form of indentured servitude, but modernized and on a massive scale."

"No shit. And it's all legal?"

"Binding contracts that will take generations to pay off, if ever."

"That doesn't sound too good."

"It's not, but don't let anybody hear you say that."

I made like a zipper on my lips. Caldwell departed, but what he left in my head had me reeling. Just like all the little hints that Johnny kept dropping on me. The world was changing rapidly and had been for some time, but quietly. That's the way Megacorp worked, all legal but without the fanfare. They began as a small company, buying up personal debts and putting the debtors to work for them; sort of a microcosm of the way things are now. Small steps at a time, so no one would notice. Perfecting their methodology, Megacorp moved on to businesses, absorbing small but integral enterprises, without which the bigger companies would fall. Promoting themselves as benefactors, their practices proved just the opposite. The only one who benefited from Megacorp's acquisitions was Megacorp. They did what they did for profit, pure and simple. Megacorp had no heart, yet it would not let people starve to death in the streets. That is unless there was profit in it. No, they were building a workforce. The print in the contracts was so fine almost everyone signed before they felt the iron grip on their nuts. There was no appeals process. Megacorp had learned that from the U.S. penal system. Those that didn't sign were allowed to wither and die.

Megacorp was capitalistic, pure and unregulated, not that there is any thing wrong with that, just kind of cold and ruthless. Profits, dividends and growth were considered their prime directive, generally in that order.

With the business world falling in slow motion like a row of dominoes, Megacorp went after municipalities. Dried up towns, cities so far in debt they would never get out, even states, whose poor management left them in dire straits, wound up under the thumb of Megacorp. The procurement of an entire nation was the next stage of growth. Mineral rich countries in the heart of Africa, already deforested; suffering from famine, poverty, and nonstop rebellion. It was there the grand experiment began. The current ruler of the Congo eagerly signed over the country to Megacorp, in exchange for safe conduct out of the Congo to a new life far from the madness he had grown up in. And of course, what seemed like a large sum of money. Megacorp put him up in one of its subsidiaries, therefore all the money the deposed ruler would spend went right back to Megacorp. The ruler went through his cash rather quickly, leaving him deep in debt. Megacorp was happy to bail

him out. He now works for Megacorp and will – until the day he dies.
In a nutshell that is how all their arrangements work, more or less.

***

Seemed Johnny was going to be sticking around a while. A new
crane operator we need, we get an overeducated junkie instead?
Johnny said he needed someone he could trust, and by the way
accidents were suddenly heading my way, I would need someone to
trust, too. Chief Caldwell was old, would be retiring soon and had too
much to lose. I would not risk his tenure. To me he was somebody, but
to the Navy he was just another swab. Strange thing was, and it was
my own fault, I guess, that Johnny was about as close a thing I had as a
friend. I worked hard and kept to myself. Life was safer that way for me.
I did not harmonize all that great with the rank and file, nor did I fly
with the white shirts. Now, when I needed someone to watch my back,
there was no one. Like I said it was my own fault.

So, there I was sitting for breakfast reading a book when a shadow
took away my light.
"Excuse me, do mind getting out of my light?" I asked the shadow.
"You got to quit eating this shit, Jake." Johnny dipped his finger into
my oatmeal looked at it scowling and flipped it into the trash, forty feet
away, swished it.
"Nice aim. I was going to eat that." Nobody could have hit the bin
from this distance.
"Do it again." I said.
"What? This?" Taking a two finger dollop while pouring a cup of
coffee he, without looking, let fly a dead ringer.
"Let me try."
"Better not, Jake."
"Think you're the only one who can do it?" I took a good three
fingers worth. "A hook shot without looking."
"Don't..."
Too late, the shot went wide hitting another table. Actually Rodney's
table and it sent O.J. splattering all over him, of which I was unaware.
Johnny sat back with an, 'I told you so' smile on his face. A larger
shadow interrupted my light, again, and the hair went up on the back
of my neck. An arm of the shadow moved and I ducked, face into my
oatmeal. When I looked up, Johnny had hold of Rodney's arm.

"Get your fucking hands off me, you goddamned freak," Rodney yelled. Johnny held on just a little longer before dropping it. "Just fucking watch it, Jake, your bodyguard won't be around all the time." He looked at Johnny with disgust. "Touch me again and I'll report you. You leave normal people alone, like a good dog, remember."

"I touch you again, it will be to kill you," Johnny said under his breath. He toasted Rodney with his coffee before the big blonde, all pumped, went back to his table, confident he had bested the two of us.

"What was that all about?"

"I believe you hit that man with some of your oatmeal."

"That's not what I mean."

"I know. Let it ride, Jake. All in good time, my friend. What is your beef with him?"

"Ah, Rodney is all right. We just don't get along. No law against that. What'd he mean about you being around?"

"Let us take a walk. Got me a new assignment." Johnny topped off our coffees from the French press, took the coffee maker and went back into the kitchen, rinsed the carafe and came back out drying his hands. "Be here at five tomorrow, the cook has given me privileges." We left the galley, walked down the gangway and onto the pier. The morning sun was hot, winding through pier traffic out to the end where a Crowley Maritime tug was moored, providing ample shade.

"You were saying something about a new job."

"Well, two actually. I've been put on the Salvor to study the effects of decompression sickness on those of us with altered blood. Megacorp gave me an injection of something that I am not supposed to talk about, so I get to be the Guinea pig."

"You'd think they had enough studies by now. Is that why Rodney called you a freak? The injection?"

"Yeah." Johnny flipped his cigarette away angrily and lit another.

"What's the other?"

"You. I am to try and keep you from getting your brains bashed out, or damaged beyond repair. In the mean time, it is business as usual. You are going to be running me down in the chamber when not diving."

"You got me aiding and abetting a drug cartel and 'YOU' are supposed to keep me out of trouble? This is gold, pure fucking gold."

"Speaking of, we have to go out tonight. I would have let you know sooner but..."

"A minimum of advanced information and a maximum of discretion."

"I am surprised you were listening."

"How do we get it past the Chief?"

"Research, buddy. Makes all kinds of things possible. The pick-up will be a little different this time." Johnny pulled a locator device from his pocket. "You know how to work one of these?"

"Sure. What they gonna do, dump it?

"Yep."

"I hope someone reminded them it's a big ocean out there."

It was. By 9A.M. I felt like I had swum half of it. We had six bales sitting on the floor between the seats. The bales had the standard issue duct tape and black plastic outer wrap. Inside was pure something or other. I no longer cared about the contents and was getting tired of being the pickup boy as well. Whatever the debt was, it had to be paid by now, we had done this a dozen or so times.

The sky was going deep purple to azure, still dark enough to see lights on and movement at Johnny's bungalow. The motor idled down.

"Jake, there were supposed to be eight bales. The welcoming committee is going to be a little upset. I better deal with this." Johnny said quietly as he raised one foot, like he was tying his shoe, and booted me over the side. A moment later, a pair of fins splashed into the water. It was going to be a long swim in.

For me, the dope smuggling was a foreign affair. They were always half-baked and prone to failure even without the help of the Coast Guard. This last episode was typical of the bright ideas these guys come up with. Throw eight smallish bales into the sea in the middle of the night and expect them to be found. We were lucky to get six of them.

It was light by the time I swam up behind the inflatable. Johnny was arguing, in Spanish, with a man dressed in drug dealer black, who could not stop pacing back and forth, arguing back and waving a gun; typical big dog behavior. But when the man in black emptied the clip of his gun into Johnny's chest, the scene went from soap opera to murder. No one panicked, as if they were used to this type of thing. The leader reloaded and shot Johnny's corpse again and again, yelling a tirade at him. Every time a bullet hit the body, it jumped just a little from the impact. The four thugs with the leader were covering his back.

"Fuck me!" I said to no one, peering around the boat. When the man was finished with his tantrum, he started laughing. His lackeys joined in as they all got into their Caddy, bales in the trunk, and left.

Racing across the sand, I dropped to my knees next to John. There were no tears or great emotion, that is until I recognized the 'Happy

Face' appearing in red dots on his tee shirt. I started laughing. There was some sick humor at work here. I picked him up, carried him to the car and set him in the back seat. When his eyes opened, I jerked away – slamming my head against the doorframe.

"Goddamn it!"

"Jake, take me to the Megacorp..." he fell over in the seat, blood draining out his mouth and nose. A card fell from his hand. The card was like a hotel key ring, 'If found, please drop at any of these...', at least a dozen locations around the state. I drove to the nearest location, a post office, driving up to the back. When I got to the loading dock a man with a clipboard chinned me over.

"Only authorized personnel..." I hand him the card, "Oh, I see. Just one moment please." He leaves and I light a cigarette. To say that this was out of the natural order of things would be a gross understatement. I was pondering the idea of sending one's soul FedEx to either of the two final destinations, unaware that there was a third place you can go. I was pulled from my daydream by a postman with a gurney, body bag, and rubber gloves.

"Would you mind giving me a hand? We're a little understaffed." The postman said, handing me a pair of gloves.

"Sure. What you gonna do with him?"

"We have a chiller in the basement. A Megacorp van will be by in a little while to pick him up. UnHhhnhh." We lifted him onto the gurney and into the open bag. "Thanks, mister. Here, fill this out and send it back for your reward. It was your lucky day."

He handed me a post card form, the postman's fresh stamp in one corner. For being a good citizen, they were going to credit my account with 10,000 mega bucks, to use as I chose, with the exception of paying off existing debts. Pretty clever catch that one. To use it you had to consume Megacorp shit. I balled it up, trying a ten foot jump shot at the dumpster. I missed the shot. The dumpster's current resident did not. He/she/ it, climbed out of the safe haven to snatch up the card, withdrew a pen, filled it out, put it in the mail bin, then disappeared back into the shadows of the one man cave. I went back to the car. I didn't want to know any more about the lifestyles of the homeless. It was not to be.

From there a phone call to Caldwell gave me a few more hours. Knocking on the dumpster door, there came a noise like a rat makes when you disturb them and they push themselves further into a corner. I could feel him looking at me through one of many pitted rusty holes.

"You threw it away man, I saw you. Now get away from here before

I call the cops!" Came the voice from inside, screeching like a rusted hinge. It was a hollow threat.

"You're welcome to the credits, answer some questions and I'll give you some more."

"Liar! Get away from me." I threw a twenty into the bin, real cash, not megabucks. He had it before it hit the floor.

"Does the Megacorp van come here often?"

"No, but the bounty hunters aren't stupid like you. They take their money and run."

"So there is a trade in dead Megacorp employees?" I got silence in return. Another twenty hit the bin. When throwing money away, it seemed I couldn't miss.

"Just certain ones, like the one you brought in. Here they come now! Get away from here, you'll just bring me trouble." Walking away as the black van approached, I tried a shot with my half empty, cold coffee cup. A hand, barely visible above the rim, caught the cup in flight, not spilling a drop.

From the car I watched as the postman came out to greet the rig. Stepping out of the van was the biggest man I had ever seen. Tree trunks for legs and a head attached directly to a set of massive shoulders, arms like guys dream of having, with a pair of basketball-palming hands manipulating the tiniest of cell phones. If he weren't such a mean looking fuck, it would have been comical. They disappeared into the post office returning a few minutes later with the gurney and body bag. The big man tossed the bag into the van with a complete disregard for the contents.

I sank low in my seat as the van pulled out onto the road and followed a few cars behind. Traffic was heavy, so I wasn't worried about being pinned out. I was worried about losing the van in the mess. When the van took the exit to Tripler Army Hospital I kept going. Should have known where they would be taking him. Security is tight at Crippler. Thoughts of trying to sneak in were ludicrous. So I headed back to the Salvor.

Caldwell was notified of my return and called me to his office. In this case, it was 'Shaft Alley'. He was at the stern, inspecting the packing seal around the propeller shaft where it exits the hull. Shaft Alley was also one of the few places aboard to get any privacy.

"Hey Chief, 'sup?" I asked over the din of the engine room.

"You've been a busy boy, Jake. Have to admit I'm a little confused, otherwise I wouldn't be here expressing my concern over what my top diver has been up to lately."

I started to butt in and found myself talking to the hand.

"The scientist is going to be MIA for a while. I got a call from headquarters. Seems he got mixed up with some drug operation and found himself looking at the business end of a 40 caliber semi-automatic. You know anything about this, Jake?"

I was thankful for the poor lighting to help hide what slid across my face.

"Nah. We partied a little, but I didn't want to pull a repeat of my last performance, so I went surfing." God I felt like shit for lying. He knew it, too.

"I would never interfere with your personal life, Jake, but you are skating on thin ice, boy. You are one of the few people I can talk to and I don't want to lose that."

"You won't, Chief."

"Yeah? We got our crane operator back."

"I thought Tommy died of a heart attack."

"He did. Dead as a door nail and cold as ice when they came and took him off the boat."

"Who came?"

"Megacorp. A black reefer van with this big driver. Anyway, they took him and delivered him back yesterday. Trust me, it is not the Tommy you remember."

"What do you mean he's back?" I paused, mentalating. "The Reuseable Program?"

Caldwell nodded, a serious look on his face. "Just wouldn't want to lose you as a friend, Jake."

"They may come and haul my dead ass away one day, but you got nothing to worry about, Chief."

"I hope you are right, Jake."

***

For the next few weeks the Salvor was under contract to a local group of tree huggers, installing an artificial reef. Tommy and I studied the plans with the designers. A spin-off from the reef would be a nice surf break that the tree huggers could call their own. Since they paid for the installation they also had a say in who gets to use it. If it had been created 100 years ago it might, just might, have helped. Now it was a way to assuage people's guilt and get rid of thousands of junk cars. Was there profit in it? Absolutely. Surf enthusiasts with money could rent the break, by the hour, day, week, or month. The site had been researched years in advance of our arrival. Apparently the surfer crowd had deeper pockets than one would think.

Placing the flattened cars in a particular arrangement would create such infamous breaks as Cadillacs or the Hummer barrels. Funny thing was that, less than fifty years later we would be pulling them from the sea again for the steel and iron.

And Tommy, the crane operator, would be there for both. The Chief had been right about the change in Tommy's behavior. He had always been loud, boisterous, and full of shit. Now he was like a machine. If he had not been at one with his crane before, he was now. I was not sure whether he was an extension of the machine, or the reverse, the machine being but an extension of him. He ate alone; even his closest men gave him a wide berth. A darkness hung around his shoulders like an albatross. This darkness was impenetrable. The spark of life that is usually seen in the eyes had turned to a black flame.

At the end of Tommy's first week, a black Megacorp van pulled up next to the Salvor. When I saw it was the same driver, I decided to hang around. Tommy showed up and together they went into the med lab. Tommy was like a good dog, and the big driver was the master.

Hanging in the hallway was a stupid idea, so I came up with another and entered the med lab. The male nurse was behind a desk.

"Hey Jake, how's the head?"

"Been having some headaches and was wondering what the doc could..."

"He's not going to give you any more Percs, Jake," Jim the nurse said, looking over his glasses at me.

Just then came a scream from one of the exam rooms followed by the sounds of someone puking. I was into the exam room before Jim could stop me. There was Tommy on his hands and knees, puking like his life depended on it. The Megacorp thug towered over him. The doc was observing from the corner of the room, a look of revulsion on his face.

"Good timing." The thug said to me. "Help me get ahold of him so I can finish the injection. Your good doctor seems to have contracted a case of shrunken balls." The thug reached down, grabbing Tommy by the collar and lifted him off the floor, dropping him on the exam table. "Now, hold him down!"

I kind of spread-eagled over Tommy, pinning his hands and legs. He put up a good fight. The thug just let him struggle till he wore himself out. It doesn't take long for a struggling panic victim to wear down. Give them a couple of minutes and they are putty. The thug knew exactly what he was doing. When the spasms subsided, Megacorp grabbed hold of Tommy's hair, yanking his head sideways, exposing a clear shot at the jugular. I don't know how big the syringe was but it scared the shit out of me. He sank it into Tommy's neck, making sure he hit the vein before sending the oversized plunger home.

"You can let go now and leave – he won't be any more trouble."

"Yeah sure, glad I could help." I took one last glance about the room and at Tommy, a trail of blood running down his neck. He didn't have to ask me twice.

I chinned Jim on the way out, having just seen way too much. I was dumb with confusion. A cigarette out on the fantail helped to ease my nerves. What the fuck was that all about? It gave me the impression that there was more going on with the Reuseable Program than just being put back on line.

Building the surf break was intended to be an eight to ten week job. We finished in six. Tommy was indefatigable and accurate beyond description. With the barge of cars and the Salvor out there, he convinced the Captain to go double shifts. His argument was that you spend three to four hours a day just setting up and breaking down. Do a double or triple shift and the savings just mount up. The Megacorp rep couldn't argue with that logic.

On the fifth week of the job, Johnny returned. He came with the fuel barge that was to refill our tanks. When I saw him we made eye contact, but he swiped his nose with a finger, indicating to me to be cool. I played along. A half-dozen Megacorp suits had flown in just before the arrival of the fuel barge. They spent most of the morning grilling their new man, Tommy. The suits were grim when they arrived; afterwards, you could tell they were quite pleased behind their couched countenances. Johnny remained in his shell, even after the suits departed. It took a few days to break the ice. After the surf break was finished ahead of schedule, the captain caved to the whining of the crew. The Salvor was to remain in position for another day, surf holiday.

Longboards, shortboards, and boogies all shredded and ripped the new break. Lefts, rights, barrels, tubes, it had it all. After a few sets, Johnny and I found ourselves alone, drifting into shore.

"So what's happening, Johnny?"

"Ahh, you know." He mumbled.

"No, I don't. Otherwise, I wouldn't be asking."

"If Pablo had not shot a happy face on my chest things would be normal. It's his goddamned trademark and Megacorp knows it." Johnny pulled up his sunskin revealing a perfect happy face.

"No wonder he was laughing so much when he did it. So Megacorp figured out..."

"Yeah. They put their best boys on me and cranked up the mindfuck to the max. I should have died. I wish I had." Then in a more lively tone, "But not to be, so here I am. Takes a few days to come down. It is good to be back, surfing was just the cure. Ready for another?" Johnny chinned to the waves.

"Nah, go ahead. Gonna take my time and paddle back to the boat."

"It is good to see you, Jake."

"Back at ya." Johnny headed for another set while I took the long way around.

The paddle gave me time to think some. The last few months, what with Tommy and Johnny, have given me an idea of what my future might be like, if the heavy hints that Caldwell has been dropping are true. Johnny had been punished for being a bad dog. I'm sure if they had been cut in on the profits, the treatment would have been significantly different. Megacorp owned and operated one of the largest drug smuggling cartels in the world and didn't like small operations cutting in. There was too much profit in it.

At this time Megacorp had their hands in everything. They were still a young company reaching out, taking control just a little at a time, so no one would notice. Like a voracious weed, insinuating itself amongst everything; eventually overwhelming the native species until it was dominant. When Megacorp could not be in command, its tactics would change and become parasitic; an unshakeable cadger that was controlled from within. Either way, the system worked.

They had to have beaten Johnny with a pretty big stick. Even after the surfing session with his mock turn around in attitude, he was still shook. Underlying the smile and bravado you could see the fear in the back of his eyes.

Later that evening I interrupted Johnny masking his fear. Our rooms were connected by a shared bath. Noticing his side open, I walked in to find Johnny shooting up. My presence did not break his concentration. I waited patiently. Knowing the routine, I left, made a cup of coffee, rolled a cigarette and returned. Johnny was just coming out of it.

"Nice habit you got there."

"Yeah, well. You want?"

"No thanks, diving tomorrow. You're tending, remember?"

"Yeah, yeah. All the gear is ready for you to jump into and do your thing. More cars?"

"Nope, the Salvor is going to run all night. We'll be blowing a wheel off a tug, should be a blast."

"Blowing a wheel, a blast, haha."

"Just checking to see if you were in condition to tend; you are. Trust me, I'd rather have a junkie holding my airline than a drunk."

"Why thank you very fucking much, Jake. Have I ever let you down?"

"No, but..."

"But nothing, and I never will. It is in the unwritten code of user ethics." Johnny started laughing, more to himself this time.

Knowing the conversation was over I looked around his room for obvious hazards, blew out his candle and departed leaving the bathroom door cracked open. Any time now there should be a rush to urgently use the facilities. Next to the toilet, I left a couple of folded clean towels and a bottle of water. Then I went for a snack at the galley before it closed up.

The German chocolate cake was as bad as the coffee, but for comfort food it couldn't be beat. Tommy was sitting at what had become his table, reading the paper. After seeing what Megacorp had done to Johnny, I ambled over to his table to see how Tommy was in a social situation.

Pushing my luck, "Hey Tommy, mind if I have a seat?" He said nothing, just looked mean at me before returning to the sports section. I was never a sports buff.

"Who won the Super Bowl?"

"It's summer, Jake, just what do you want?"

"You really want to know?"

"No."

"I want to know why you're sitting here after dying of a goddamn heart attack and acting like nothing happened? Somebody from Megacorp shows up once a week and spikes you with a monster syringe... I was there, man, I saw him do it." A little voice in my head told me I had just crossed that line from pushing it to pushing it too far. I couldn't stop. "And now you walk around like some brainwashed automaton. What fuckin' gives, Tommy?" Here it comes, I had done it. Tommy came flying across the table aiming to grab my neck. I ducked but he got my arm, stood up and started playing airplane with me. Once he achieved escape velocity he let me go, sailing out of control across the cafeteria crashing into empty chairs and tables. Cut in half a dozen places and my shoulder dislocated, I stared up at the ceiling, reaping the rewards of my actions. Somewhere in the background someone was yelling, a dark shadow covered me. I put my hands over my face, figuring the worst was still to come. The next thing I knew Tommy was picking me up.

"They did this to me. I didn't want it." Tommy said in a quiet urgent voice. In a practiced move, he jerked my shoulder back into the socket. I collapsed in pain. Tommy made sure I landed in a chair, and then left me to my misery, as he left the galley in his.

We all have dark secrets, little shames and big, that we never forgive ourselves for having committed. Tommy kept his close, so no one would see it. I had only caught a glimpse because I cared enough to push him hard enough.

My shoulder hurt like hell as I got up and started putting the chairs and tables back in place. The cook watched from within the kitchen, through that little window that the food is passed. He didn't mind a fight once in a while as long as you didn't make a habit of it, and cleaned up after yourself. He gave me the look that I was on the verge of the habit thing. I shrugged my shoulders, instantly regretting it. The cook laughed, getting a kick out of it, saying, "You fucking divers, nothing but trouble," then continued on with whatever he was doing.

The cook was right, as a general rule. I spent the rest of the night packed in ice to get the swelling down in my shoulder, saving my remaining Percs for the morning which would come all too soon.

I woke to a sharp piercing stab in my damaged shoulder, "Hold still," Johnny said. I did, while he worked the needle into different parts of my shoulder, like a dentist giving novocaine.

"Precisely," Johnny said reading my mind. "That should give you a few good hours. We can re-hit when you take a break." He shoved a cup of coffee in my hand, "Drink up, Jake, we are running a little late today."

Arriving late to the jobsite is bad etiquette in general, but the gods smiled on us today. By the time we had the dive station set up, the chits and tag out procedures were just being completed. She was a Navy tug; twin screws, three rudders and a hull that had been patched more times than a hippie's jeans. The captain had run her aground during training exercises, leaving the port screw curled and torn. Finding a replacement was not in the plan. They had to repair it. Thankful it wasn't my problem, I hit the water. The propeller looked like a spoon that got left in the garbage disposal. Communicating through Johnny to Tommy the crane operator, I had him lower an enormous wrench, which I fought to get seated in the correct position on the propeller–retaining nut. Using the power of the crane to turn the wrench, the nut loosened. This had to be repeated several times before the next phase. It was not time to remove the nut. In my goody bag was one hundred and fifty feet of detonating cord, which I began to weave around the propeller hub, a sort of crazy figure eight.

Sitting on a pier bumper, drying off, Johnny handed me a blasting cap. A couple turns of electrical tape to secure it to the cord before dropping it into the water. Two wires now led up from the water from the blasting cap. A battery would work but the Navy likes to see us use the box. After connecting the wires I looked to the Chief Engineer who gave me the nod.

"This is the fun part." I said to Johnny, flipping the switch.

The explosion was loud and resounding, rocking the 150 foot tug and sending a plume of water just as high into the sky. The detonating cord acted as a big hammer, knocking the propeller loose on its tapered shaft. By the time the water settled, I was ready to go in. The hard part was over. I was on the home stretch. Attaching the crane's wire to one of the propeller flukes and floating the boss nut off the shaft with a lift bag, I gave the signal to take the slack out of the crane's wire. The explosion had destroyed visibility, so I waited for topside to give the okay.

When it came, I sat atop the stern tube with my back to the hull. Using my legs I pushed on the hub, getting it to slide down the taper. Once several tons of bronze starts to move, you better be out of the way. It slid off the end of the shaft and virtually disappeared, followed by coils of wire, followed by the crane. Tommy had not taken enough slack out. The resulting jerk pulled the mobile crane over the side of the dock. The crane hit bottom with a "whooomph", making zero visibility even worse. I forgot about the propeller, swimming through the murk to find the cab where Tommy sat at the controls. It was near impossible – it had to be here. Fingertips became eyes looking for glass.

The windows were shattered but intact, rapidly leaking air out and water in. I could just see Tommy sitting there, doing nothing. I scrabbled around the cab feeling for the door. It was then that Tommy moved. To keep himself locked in there, despite my efforts to get him out.

"Goddammit Tommy, let go!" I screamed even though he couldn't hear me. I couldn't believe my eyes. He was shaking his head no.

The fractured windows could hold no longer as they shattered inward, releasing Tommy's bubble of air. Climbing in through the glass I tried to grab him but he fought back. He was a madman now and I backed out and let him drown. There was just no other way. Visibility was slowly returning. His body hung motionless in the cab.

"Johnny, have a med crew at the ladder. I got Tommy." For me it was a race against time, we had to get CPR started immediately, but when his body was hauled to the dock, the med techs just backed away.

Dumping my gear on the ground, I jumped on Tommy and began chest compressions.

"What the hell is the matter with you people? Help me!" I was working like crazy now trying to save his life, when Johnny came up behind me and pulled me off Tommy.

"That is enough, Jake. They will take over from here."

In my excitement I had not seen the Megacorp chopper arrive. The big Driver had a helper this time to load Tommy into the bag, then into the chopper. I lit a cigarette and watched. The pain meds had worn off in time to help ruin my attitude. The big thug came back with a clipboard.

"What happened here, gentlemen?"

Johnny went dumb and the Chief Engineer wasn't offering anything either. My bad attitude just couldn't help itself.

"Crane went over the side. What's it look like to you?"

Johnny jammed me a pointy elbow. "The crane could not withstand the shock loading when the wheel came off the shaft." Johnny stepped in before I stepped in it any more. "It looked good then it just all went over. We were lucky nobody got hurt."

"You don't call Tommy drowning not getting hurt?" I burst out, unable to control my emotions.

Johnny looked up at the Megacorp driver. "Never mind him, he was close to the operator."

"Yeah, I see. Just don't let him cause any trouble over this." The driver finished, closing his clipboard. He looked me up and down, not recognizing me from the other day.

"He will not," Johnny promised. After the chopper left, he said "Jesus, Jake, that is one guy you do not want to fuck with. Believe me."

"Yeah, yeah. He was the same guy that picked you up after Pablo, uh..." I made a gun with my hand pretending to shoot.

"You were there?"

"I came up behind the inflatable just as he was offing you. How do you think you got to the post office? I waited there and saw your big friend come and get you."

Johnny spoke quietly. "Goddamn it, Jake, you got to cut that shit out. You get caught they will kill you. No second chance."

"Now we are getting somewhere. Is that what Tommy and you got, a second chance?"

"All right, poor choice of words." Johnny looked around the dock. Seeing no one, he continued, "Because it sure as fuck is not what you think of when the thought 'second chance' roams across your brain. So what happened down there when you yelled at Tommy?"

It was my turn to look around. "He locked himself into the cab. Would not let me help him. He wanted to drown. He deliberately left too much slack in the cable."

"Happens a lot with newbies. Sometimes it takes a while to accept what has been done to you. Tommy is having a particularly tough time. If he doesn't get a grip, he'll get his chance to die."

"And just what has been done to you?"

"I am still trying to figure that out."

Two tugs began pushing a crane barge in between the piers. The Navy wanted the crane out of the water. It was still salvageable and time was important if they wanted to save the engine. I started suiting up. The day's diving had just begun. We worked the day into night, and the night into day again before returning to the Salvor beat and tired. Swinging by the galley on the way to my quarters stopped me dead in my tracks. There was Tommy with a cup of coffee reading the paper. Johnny came up from behind, pushing me along the passage before I opened my mouth and strayed into deadly waters.

There were no more incidents with Tommy. He accepted whatever it was that was done to keep him running. He retreated into himself to survive. He spoke to no one and no one chummed up to him. This time around the mindfuck took. He was a Megacorp Op now. Strictly business. Johnny played like the brainwashing worked on him. It was scary to see someone who wasn't pretending. Megacorp salvaged Tommy like we salvaged the crane.

The world as a whole was already recycling just about everything. Recycling people seemed like the next logical step. For a consumer driven society, recycling was the plan to save the planet. It was not enough and never would be. We want more and more and once we have more, we assuage the guilt with the recycling panacea. What we needed was to consume less and be happy with what we had. But that would never happen. Megacorp made sure you were always one purchase away from satisfaction. It would be nice to say that the fallout from our lifestyle was the next generation's problem. That may have been true 150 years ago. We were the inheritors of a trashed world. Paradise lost in the course of ten generations. Any plan to salvage what we had left was wasted as we grasped for more. We recycled out of the necessity for more. The resources were now gone, or too inaccessible to profitably obtain. So now we all turn in our old shit for new shit.

Toys and gimmick gadgets had their run. Cell phones could be implanted now. The next great market was virtual. And Megacorp was all over it like flies on shit. Virtual real estate was a good one, setting a precedent. Now Megacorp had what they had always wanted, selling nothing and finding it quite profitable.

Johnny was good at fielding questions about the reuseables, but especially about himself. His deal with Megacorp was different than Tommy's, or the others that I had met. Maybe scientists rated more than tradesmen. We were all needed; some maybe just a little bit more. And there were perks that went along with it, too. Johnny was still himself to a certain degree. The Tommys were a complete wash, only the skills remained. The rest was lost or traded. It was similar to a junkie's relinquishing of reality for the pursuit of the dragon. If there was anything to the heavy hints that had been dropping like bombs, and my number was coming up, I didn't want a reality like Tommy's – a fucking zombie without all the drama.

The routine of work was the only thing that kept me from going completely paranoid. Diving always put me in the zone. For the duration of the dive, there was nothing else that mattered. Whether sealing through hull penetrations or polishing propellers, there was a singleness of mind, the workingman's nirvana, those hours when you are what you do. It is a unique experience worth all the years it takes to get there. Of course, getting there was no cakewalk. Bone necrosis, wasted discs, irreparable damage from getting bent too many times, broken bones, countless scars. Sounds fun, huh? It was part of the game, and it was enough for me. There were no great expectations beyond satisfying my work ethic, earning my keep and walking away at the end of the day. Had I been wise, I would have kept on walking long ago, before I became too good at what I did.

Johnny spent a lot of time on the Salvor. He helped on the dive station when not otherwise occupied. There wasn't much to it, but it had to be done right. Megacorp would pull him every so often to do whatever it was he did, always returning to the Salvor afterwards. Sometimes he would come back spent, mentally and physically, taking weeks to return to his sardonic joie de vivre. I'll say that for him. He was consistent with his attitude, respectfully punk and smart enough to get away with it.

Toward the end of each week he would, like Tommy, become depressed, withdrawing from what little social contact he did have. Like a hurt animal, he suffered in silence until the big guy in the black van came and 'juiced' the two. For the next five days, these reuseables were as good as they get. For the first couple days of their week, I would try and pick their brains about what they were going through. It was here the Megacorp mindfuck was particularly successful. Broaching the subject would cause considerable mental anguish, like being subjected to certain subsonic vibrations. Rodent control specialists use a device that emits a signal known to drive rats from the vicinity of the source of the sound. Crank it up and it does the same thing to people. Suddenly your heart rate increases, anxiety builds and nausea will get you running. Your fight or flight instinct goes into total flight mode. At any rate, that's how Johnny would react and I soon quit bringing it up. His discomfort was starting to bug me.

One morning, waiting for the tagout to be finished, I asked Johnny, "What ever happened to your friend Pablo?"

"He'll be around. He kills me. I kill him. It is a kind of game we play," he replied with his usual sense of humor. That is to say - dark.

"Some game. I take he is a reuseable, too?" I got 'the look' over the Ray-Bans.

"When he is not being used, he enjoys the drug trade in his spare time to keep his skill level up," I looked at Johnny quizzically. "He is a merc. Real high-end stuff. He wants to meet you but you are lucky you stayed in the water. Pablo is big on keeping his anonymity intact." Johnny caught my mentalating. "Go ahead Jake, ask."

"How come you and Pablo are like the flipside of Tommy?"

"Because we use the tool that was given to us instead of being used by it."

Vague as it was, it was an answer. The Chief Petty Officer approached with the tagout finally finalized. Hitting the water amidst a multitude of questions, one thing was for sure – for most of the reuseables, existence was a living nightmare. The remainder of the day until dusk was spent polishing a 30-foot diameter propeller to the 'A' grade on the Rupert Comparator Scale of roughness. The ship had a beard of marine life clinging to the hull, but fuel economy came from a clean wheel. Buffed to a brilliant sheen when done, the spotless propeller looked out of place. Fancy rims on a junker car.

I would find out soon that the odds of beating the mindfuck were infinitesimally small. Those that did guarded the secret desperately. Johnny masked himself with drug abuse and a brilliant mind to stay one step ahead of his controllers.

"Killing each other is not just a game but another tool we use, and the drug cartel is just a way to move the real product." Johnny continued our discussion after I got out of the water like I had never gone in.

"Which is?" I prompted, drying off my head.

"Meds to unincorporated countries."

"You mean those that aren't bought off, bought out or otherwise conscripted into the service of Megacorp..."

"Nice nutshell, Jake... they are allowed to die off. The system has grown into a beast. It no longer thinks in terms of years, but generations. Having outlived its founders, it now pursues its own agenda..."

"Which is?"

"Nothing short of world domination."

"A modest proposal."

"Very funny, Jake. Not all that far fetched either, it happens."

"And you think, with your doper friends, that you can stop it?"

"Maybe slow it down a bit."

"Sounds like a real win-win situation." My sarcasm dripped like water from the pier.

"Yeah, it is a riot. Want in?"

"I was wondering when you were going to ask." I half expected Johnny to pull out a gun and shoot me to hasten things along a bit. Instead he pulled a film can, dumping the smallest little pile on my dry hand. "That's all right, Johnny, I can live without a teaser."

"It is not coke, Jake. Just a little something I cooked up in the lab to help you weather the storm that is brewing. Now sniff it before Shore Patrol sees us doing drugs on the dock."

Without a second thought the pile disappeared into my sinuses. I could taste the heroin and whatever else was in it, pooled in the back, slowly dripping an acrid medicinal mucous down my throat. Nausea rose with my first cigarette; I tried to choke it back. Failing in that, the half digested burger and fries that was lunch burned up my throat, ejecting out over the edge of the pier, into the water. I lay on a ship bumper, succumbing to the reverse rush. Instead of blasting off, I sank, melting into the rubber bumper, no longer caring if the vomit made it to the sea or not. When the lights went out I am not sure, drifting as I was in review of my life. Spiraling down through the dreamscape came flashes, like postcards of past events, each one pointing to the next in the grand parade. Coming into view, crisply focused moments in time, before another image came to the lens. Soon I saw myself juggling the moments in an effort to keep a balance of goodness and shame. As the lifeline unfolded, the juggling became more frantic. The failures became too many, each bearing the weight of the world. I collapsed under the load, sinking deep into the ocean. Unable to free myself, I began thrashing in the cold water. Choking on my last breath, I woke underneath a public shower at a beach park. The full moon illuminated my surroundings. Surfers were taking advantage of a south swell and the big moon to do some night riding. Johnny sat with his board at a picnic table talking with some kids.

Picking myself up out of the sand, I let the water rinse me clean. I felt dirty; or was it still the dream and I was covered in the filth of my metaphors? I was just glad that Johnny wasn't hosing me down on the pier. The implications would have just been too much. The Freudian slip got me laughing. I shut off the water and went looking for a towel.

We returned to the ship late and wasted. Not being military had its privileges, few as they were. Waking early I jumped into a pot of coffee and began pounding out the report for yesterday's diving. It didn't matter that I had just joined an underground organization that was bent on saving a few lives and sticking it to the man, the Navy loved their paper and wanted it on time. When I knocked on Chief Caldwell's door at eight–thirty, he was already buried in a mountain of it himself.

"Evening, Chief," I said at the door.

"Morning, Jake, have a seat," he said without looking. Something was up, I could feel it and Caldwell was masking it. When he did turn to look at me, it was with the full Navy Officer gaze, that is to say he looked right through me.

"We have a destroyer that needs its intake screens cleaned. Need you on it today."

The coffee had barely cut the edge on my hangover. "It's an easy job, Chief, can't you let one of your boys do it today?"

"Are you questioning my orders, Jake? You and your new buddy are getting away with murder around here. It stops here and now! You got that report?" I handed it over. "Now get over to Bravo docks and brush your teeth, you smell like puke."

"Jesus, Caldwell, who put a burr under your ass?"

"Get out of here, now!"

When the door closed, Chief Thomas Caldwell opened the bottom drawer to his desk, removing a bottle of Jack Daniels. He poured a healthy shot and drank it before opening another drawer. Chief Caldwell knocked back another shot, staring into the drawer. After locking the door to his office, he returned to the desk. The phone rang. Chief Caldwell answered and hung up without saying a word. Reaching into the open top drawer, he withdrew his service weapon and put the barrel in his mouth.

He didn't have to ask again. I was out the door and gone. Johnny was loading the van when I got there. He was in a crappy mood, too. I was the one with a hangover and should have been shitting on everyone I ran into. Instead, I was the morning's toilet. We drove to Bravo docks in silence; it seemed the best way to avoid any more flying shit.

It was when I hit the water that I knew something was wrong. First thing was the tagout procedure was completed when we arrived, something of a miracle in itself. But after orienting myself in the water and facing the ship, I was stunned to see a clean hull, like she had just come out of drydock, which left me scratching my head. I knew the location of the screens that needed to be cleaned so I dropped down to the bilge keel, swimming forward. The screens were positioned 200 feet forward of the midship draft marks, just above the bilge keel. There were three of them, each six feet square with a thousand little holes to let the water through. Over time, barnacles and other marine organisms begin to grow in the holes, clogging them. Every so often they needed cleaning, but not these. Just then I heard a large electric motor turn on inside the ship. The water began moving! Someone had just started the intake pumps and I was sucked to the screen before I knew what had happened. I was fucked. The clock was ticking. Yelling into the helmet mike did nothing but give me a headache. Spread-eagled against the screen there was nothing I could do. Johnny would know it was taking too long, I hoped.

At the other end of my air line, a distinctly different scene was being played out. Johnny was sitting at Times Square, smoking a cigarette when the comm box barked with my urgent request. Just as he was getting up to answer, a big hand flipped the on/off toggle to off. Megacorp's big thug was standing there. He shook his head 'no' once, cutting off Johnny's outburst mid throat. Johnny backed away like a dog cuffed one too many times. The big hands pulled a loop of my airline and kinked it, holding it that way for fifteen minutes before releasing.

Picking up the ship's phone and dialing the engine room, the thug told a member of the black gang to turn it off. My body floated to the surface a few minutes later.

***

Floating in an ocean of depression so deep and vast, there was nothing else, only the shame of being. In the eye of the depression was the knowledge that you weren't supposed to be here. An intruder on the inalienable sacred lives of men. Every act against my fellow man, no matter how small or venial the incursion, was blown out of proportion ... or into proportion, depending on your point of view. Either way you cowered beneath them, scourging yourself with barbs of your exiguous humanity. You did not belong when you could have, now adding insult to the injury of your existence. If the eyes are the windows to your soul then do not look into mine. It fared no better than the picture of Dorian Gray. But if you want to, to see the depths of my failure, you need look no further. Hideous beyond belief, you will not see anything that comes close to human nature, only inhuman nature.

To be sure, you will never find me in a house of god. No, the sewers of men are too good for what has become of me. Deep and fetid, there was no place to hide, from yourself or the look from those whom were offended. Forced to watch as I hid from the eyes of god, naked and ashamed at my very existence. Clothes merely exaggerated my deformed nature, a beggar on streets of gold. Shit on the plate set for the deserving.

I was the evil one in children's stories meant to scare them into goodness. 'This is what will happen to you!' The fables were real in that they pointed at me. Unreal in that my description was always wholly inadequate; words cannot describe that which is beyond description. Only the nightmares of children come close to seeing what I have become. They run screaming from their beds into the arms of goodness. As of late I have returned to the dreams of men. Too old to cry, they cringe within themselves; for in seeing me they also see some wee tiny fragment of themselves. I have eaten the souls of my fellow man, dining on their excrement and setting them free.

I take from them but there is no return in the deed. A parasite, a leach, a vampire of the living. An antibiosis of the most despicable kind; only one benefits. If you understood the low form of my existence, you would see that there is no virtue in a life that only takes, a pitiless shame for my very being. If I could end it, I would, but I cannot. Being hell personified does not have an up side. It is impossible to face myself, but I am forced to, forced to oneness with my shame and failure. Repulsed by what I see and compelled to make it worse, hell finds no restraint especially when it comes to the weaknesses. I have become the shadow of men. In me there is only hell. In hell there is only me.

***

I woke to the aseptic surroundings of stainless steel and white sheeting. I was alone. That is not to say I was the only one in the room. The rest of the rolling slabs had their sheets pulled all the way up. They were safe. I could not harm them. Even the dead would not count me as one of themselves. What was I doing here surrounded by my betters who could not help but tolerate my presence? I did not belong! What am I doing here? Twisting the corner of my sheet into a garrote and cinching it tightly around my neck only added futility to the nightmare I had awakened to. My breathing stopped, nothing happened. My eyes stared wildly about the morgue, waiting anxiously for the darkness that would not come. My smeared reflection in the steel, ashamed and appalled by what it saw, would not turn away. Tears of sorrow and pity flowed from the steely eyes as they cried an ocean that would never wash the stigma away.

Brilliant white light seared my eyes. Hands used to dealing with the shit of men held me down, drove a spike into my neck, and then carried me into an empty concrete room whose sole adornment was a drain in the middle of the floor. They returned a few minutes later with a firehose and went to work. The injection had begun to do its job, too. The anguish and depression began to subside, only to be replaced with a brutal attack of high pressure water. Both orderlies struggled to maintain control over the nozzle as the jet of water knocked me viciously around the room. With no place to hide, my hands tore at the drain. It was too small. The reward for my efforts was to receive an excruciating enema of epic proportions. If their job was to clean me, they failed. On the other hand, if their job was to beat the crap out of me till every square inch of my body was black and blue, along with most of my organs, then they did a hell of a job. If the point of the exercise was to instill a deep respect for the medical personnel, well, it did that, too. No complaints from me.

The steel door slammed closed; I was alone with my pain, for that was all there was. The 'me' I once knew had been driven from consciousness by a freight train of agony. The slightest movement sent stabs into every nerve ending, igniting them, giving me the only stimulus I would ever know fully.

Before ... before I died, that is ... I considered myself a pretty tough motherfucker. Not the kind of bully that picks fights, not tough like that. But tough in the way of taking abuse, not giving it. The nature of commercial diving is, to say the least, abusive. That's just the way it is, hard work. But I was able to take it, day in and day out. Too many times I have ground my flesh to the bone, had meat torn from my body, only to continue on, finishing the job, declining medical care and heading to the next project. A rag and duct tape took the place of stitches and skin grafts. The sea was your hospital bed and work was morphine.

I thought I understood what pain was, how bad it could get and how to endure. Never had I been so wrong. There was no scale for the pain I was receiving. But there was a plan on delivering it. It always came after the injection. Kindness, for that's what the shot was. What else could you call something that unburdens you from mental torment, relieves, if but for a moment, the knowledge of what you have become? We reuseables were never told that either, just what we were, that is. But inside, deep in your heart of hearts, you found you no longer exist. The sorrow generated from that knowledge throws you into a pit of despair that has no bottom.

After the third session, I no longer tried to escape the blast of the hose or the cold-blooded way in which it was applied. Curled in a ball, with the heels of my feet covering my asshole, I learned to take it. The pain was unbearable for the conscious mind. You had to go deep inside yourself to protect your mind. The body was a lost cause. It soon became clear that death was not an option. To endure was all that mattered.

There were a few others like me, some a little farther along the curve, some a little behind. No attempt was made to isolate us from each other. It simply was not necessary. I had become a universe unto myself. Others did the same, or screamed endlessly. In time, the screamers would be taken away, only to be replaced by some other poor bastard. Once a man named Kim Tah broke our self−imposed silence, attempting to communicate with his homies in hell. He was desperate in his desire to talk to someone. No one responded to his pleas. When he came to me on his knees, pleading for recognition, I closed my eyes in shame, ignoring him.

I wanted to. To scream out his name, hold him, as I wanted someone to hold me. But the touch of human kindness was too good for us. Black

Megacorp jumpsuits pulled him away from my cot. He had grabbed my arm and would not let go, screaming, "Tell me your name!" A short club swung down on his forearm, shattering it and releasing his grip. They dragged him from the room, a wire loop around his neck attached to a pole, like a wild animal. A few hours later his body was brought back on a gurney. Kim Tah was black and blue from head to toe. His front teeth had been broken out at the gum line and left that way. He never spoke again. Kim Tah had finally accepted what he was.

Many years later I would meet Kim Tah again. He would remember me, repaying the kindness I had refused to give him.

Several months of relentless torture had sufficiently prepared us for the Megacorp mindfuck to begin. The sadism did not stop; it simply started to have a point. We were subjected to a streaming horrific vision of man's inhumanity to man. But not in the normal way, e.g. watching a vid screen. A probe was inserted into our brains. Its output brought more than visuals from which there was no escape. Pain and pleasure centers were also activated and shut off at critical moments during the non-stop screening.

We were being trained like dogs, to be good dogs, responsible and loyal only to Megacorp. And it was working. At least I think it was. There were some pretty tough hombres in our group. Kim Tah was what one would consider a nerd and the only intellectual. The rest were heavy industry, like me; miners, oilmen, welders, machine operators, millwrights. Every one of us bore the scars of training. Kim Tah had the added luxury of a ruined smile, although none of us smiled any more. There was no social interaction between us, even when it was possible. One glance at Kim was plenty reminder to keep your mouth shut. By the looks on my fellow inmates' faces, the training took. Washing my hands one day and looking in the mirror, I saw my face bore the same expressionless gaze. Deep into my eyes I peered. The soul was gone. My eyes went glassy but no tears fell. The training took.

But if it took, why was I still thinking behind the mask of Megacorp? It was explained that these were leftover remnants of a past that no longer existed for us, and that in time they, too, would pass. However, if the thoughts were persistent we should notify our superiors immediately for retraining. No one did.

My thoughts persisted. God, they were painful, but at least they were mine. I hid in pain meditation, reliving beatings to keep my thoughts from giving me away. Inevitably, if there is anything resembling human in you, it will show, eventually. We were experimented on a lot. You would wake in the morning, fresh stitches on some part of your body.

I was woken one night when they were bringing Kim Tah back from some twisted surgery. I dare not move, watching through slit eyes. Kim was unconscious, a blessing for him. He must have passed out during the butchery, for they never used anesthetics. When the orderlies left I rolled naturally, feigning sleep to stare at Kim. That he was in excruciating pain was obvious. He moaned and twisted in his nightmares, pulling his sheets away. Whatever they had done, they had done it to his stomach. The mound of gauze was soaked through with blood. The surgeons had done a piss poor job. The white tape securing the bandage in place was slowly pulling from the skin as the gauze absorbed more and more blood. Glistening full a large drop of blood began to form, wiggling and jiggling before breaking free. I watched it fall. Time stopped for one crystal clear moment as it splashed on the floor.

I will never forget when time began again. With the tearing sound of tape peeling from his skin, the bandage fell forward, followed not only by the weight of the blood but the entrails of Kim Tah, too. His insides fell out, mounding on the edge of the bed before slipping over and onto the floor with a splat, shining in the dim light. It was my own fault. I certainly cannot blame Kim Tah.

How long I lay there watching his life drip away gets lost in what happened afterwards. Against all training, against my own chances for survival, against everything that had been beaten into me, I got out of bed. Sweating bullets by the time I got to Kim's bedside made it all that harder to gather up his guts and return them to where they belonged. Intestines slipping through your fingers, squeezing compounds the issue. At length I filled the void, poorly. Covered in Kim and putting the skin back on top, I wrapped him in a sheet to avoid a repeat episode. I picked Kim up and with all I had, kicked open the doors of the unit and started running. Another set of doors; I dropped my right shoulder slamming right through them and kept running. My feet found pavement, shredding the soles of my feet down the highway. The pain was unbearable. I felt as if I was running on stumps. A hospital sign came into view as bloody stumps ground into asphalt. At the door to the emergency room I collapsed.

There was the black van and two big motherfuckers in black jumpsuits. I stood with Kim in my arms and was hit with 500,000 volts for my efforts. Kim fell from my arms as I twitched into unconsciousness. The last thing I heard was, 'what about Kim?' 'Leave him, he served his purpose.'

For the next month, solitary confinement. No food, no clothes, no light and worst of all, no injections. The pit I was kept in was but a physical metaphor for what I was going through. I thanked god there was no light, for I could not have faced myself. Foolish enough to think I was surviving; what kind of survival can there be if there is no death? Death had been taken from me. If they took the death, what else did they take? What was left behind?

I spent the time in a hell that had been created by Megacorp and myself. It takes two to tango. In my despair, I searched myself for whatever was left of me and locked it deep inside, where it would be safe while becoming whatever it was they had in store for me.

The end of my time in this particular hell, for there are many, came with a blinding flash and deafening crash, as the steel door was slammed open. My hands were not big enough to cover my filth, my self. Curled in a fetal position of total submission, the med tech had no trouble finding a vein to inject the offal. The tech left, the door was closed, but the lights remained on. The hypo kicked in a heartbeat, or rather several. The depression began to dissipate. Immediately my body recoiled in Pavlovian response, protecting itself from what had become a reality. The pleasure of the inoculation was never achieved. Unrelenting pain came before that dream ever materialized. The water's blast sent me across the room slamming into one wall before tumbling head over heels into another wall. My head cracked the wall loudly. Stars burst into view as I fell to the floor.

Semi-conscious, hands feeling for the jet that brought tremendous pain, nothing. It had stopped, the room was dry and so was I. Confused, I lay back and absorbed the juice like never before. The pall of gloom that had so enveloped me was gone. Through the pain, agony and despair came a nirvana of sorts. Anger, conflict, peace, joy, confusion, sadness, effort, and sloth all became one. Understanding of the way things were, beyond the limited scope of men, for a moment, became clear. The moment of clarity came with a caveat. Words become a useless tool when attempting to describe understanding of that nature. So, without trying to make a big deal out of it, the mantra of this nirvana was, 'Don't fuck with Megacorp'.

The door opened. Eyes unaccustomed to the light did not look away, instead maintaining a steady unfocused stare at the wall. When the two black jumpsuited techs approached, I brought my attention to them knowing they could no longer hurt me. Behind their rigid exterior and mirrored lenses, there was fear in their eyes. In my becoming what they wanted me to be, they had created, in their eyes, a monster. Megacorp knew from experience how potentially dangerous the survivors of death could be. It explained the response training. Years would pass before I could shirk the yoke of the training. Even then, the post traumatic stress syndrome would have a hair trigger. Until then I would be a good dog. Trust no one, survive, and whatever happens, don't fuck with Megacorp.

There was no welcoming committee when the black van dropped me at the start of the dock. My papers were checked at the gangway by the officer of the day. I could have sworn we knew each other, but he made no attempt at camaraderie. Instead it was 'by the book', holding my papers at the very edge and returning them to me like I had leprosy, making sure there was no physical contact.

My presence repulsed him. "Report to the First Engineer Mouse. You are to refrain from mingling with the crew. Insubordination will not be tolerated." The O.D. turned to a Shore Patrolman, "Take him to detention and search him, his duffel, too. Have a back up. Now get him out of my sight."

I looked to the black jumpsuit. No communication was required. He nodded his head towards the guard and like a good dog, I followed him up the gangway. Looking down from the deck and seeing the O.D. signing the receiving order, I began to realize what I was: a piece of meat, and Megacorp, my pimp.

After a strip search at gunpoint that left my orifices bleeding, I was led to the First's office. He was not there. I was told to sit and wait. Hours passed before Mouse, covered in grease from head to toe, returned from the engine room. The young man, obviously fresh out of the academy, was tired and, having a lot on his mind as usual, forgot.

He looked at me, stunned. "Excuse me, I'll be right back."

The First left and the yelling didn't stop until he returned. I wasn't able to catch much of it. Seems no one notified the First of my arrival, a breach of protocol that would not soon be repeated, by the sounds of it. When he returned clad in a clean white jumpsuit with hands and face to match, his face was set, a commander's face. No bullshit, no emotion, as firm as the hull of his ship.

Reaching out his young hand he said, "Hello Jake, welcome aboard the Salvor."

The hand, the words, were the first attempt at civil communication that I could remember. My hand came up, almost remembering what to do. He made the extra effort reaching a little farther to take a firm hold.

I did not squeeze back. I was afraid.

"That's all right, Jake. I was told it could take a while."

"A while for what?" My first words.

The First mulled it over before responding, "For you to come around."

"Come around to what?"

"Nothing, Jake."

In the back of my mind was a cauldron where my memory boiled. It was all in there, but too hot to reach. Every so often I would recognize someone, something in the roiling black water before it was pulled down into the miasma, lost.

Nodding to him blankly, I blurted, "Just awaiting my orders, sir."

"Yes. Just like Tommy."

"What, sir?"

"We will be shipping out tomorrow. Here is your room key. Take note of where it is. Don't forget it. You will dine before or after the rest of the crew and are confined to quarters when not eating or working. Do you understand?"

I nodded.

"Good. Make sure you do. Insubordination will not be tolerated. You can go now."

His eyes went to the pile of paper on his desk. Getting up quietly and hefting the duffel, I headed to the door.

"Jake," Mouse looked at me as I paused before opening the door, "I'm sorry."

"Me, too," I said, closing the door behind me.

A corridor of the officer's quarters had been vacated for use by the reuseables. The men I passed on the way paid no attention, inching to the far side of the passage to avoid contact. The room was empty, void of any personality, just the basics. A black video ball was mounted in one of the upper corners of the room. A red light moved back and forth as the camera continuously scanned the surroundings. I was numb, going through the motions of unpacking like an automaton. After clothes came gear, which was hung in a closet. Wetsuit, harness, booties, fins, along with a new, state of the art breathing system. Helmet design remained familiar; it was the air supply that was radical. Some part of me knew I should be excited about the tech; instead I stared at the equipment like a lummox. Everything was in order, except a small piece of paper was folded into the oral-nasal cup in the helmet. The hair went up on the back of my neck. Fear crept up my spine, loosening my bowels, shortening my breath. The paper was folded in the basic origami of a cocaine bindle. My back was to the camera, so it couldn't see my shaking, sweating hands unfold the paper. Easing back the last bend revealed handwriting and a little pile of powder. The writing said, 'eat this, trust me, Gee'. It made no sense to me. The fear of what was in my hands was nothing compared to the nightmare of being caught with it. Swallowing the bindle was the only way to dispose of it safely. It took every bit of strength I had to act normal for the camera. I was sweating profusely lying down on the bed, waiting for the door to be opened and the blacksuits to drag me away. I controlled my breath until consciousness left for the day. The active mind may have departed but sleep did not come and never would again. The sleep of the undead is anything but. It is more of a silent black scream that never stops.

I woke at three A.M. to the rocking of the ship. We were underway and it was time for breakfast. The crew rotation would begin at five. In the galley sat Tommy, nursing his coffee with a paper. He didn't look up. It would seem there was no camaraderie of the undead worked into the training, explaining the unease I felt when the urge to say 'good morning' stopped halfway up my throat. Instead, filling two thermoses, I headed up to the forecastle to be alone. With no one to talk to, I stared at the black western horizon. I lit a cigarette, drinking coffee, engulfed in the emptiness.

Someone came up to stand behind me. Knowing I wasn't supposed to be here, I downed my coffee, putting the cap on the thermos preparing to leave the presence of men.

Let me digress ever so slightly. There is a goodness in some men that regardless of their position, responsibility and duty, treated those around them fairly – like men, disregarding personal issues and judging by the job done. Of course there were not too many of this mindset. Their names have long been lost to time, all blending into one word. Smelling the night air and recognizing the cologne I could not stop myself, "Good evening, Chief, I was just leaving." I would always call him Chief.

"Good morning, Jake. And I am the First, not a Chief yet."

I started to get up.

"Stay seated, Jake, I just wanted to see you away from officialdom. How you doing?"

"Aw'ight, I guess." The fear of speaking brought an immediate nausea.

I lurched for the side, puking in powerful bursts and breaking a sweat. When it was over I sat down, spent, afraid.

"Jake, listen to me, you will never have anything to fear from me. If you have problems, come see me first. We will work it out. I will leave a standing order that the forecastle is yours at night, when we are at sea. When we are in port, the regular rules apply. You getting this?"

Tears rolled down my face, "Yeah, thanks, Chief."

"You're welcome, Jake. You got another hour, try to keep some of that coffee down, we got our work cut out for us. Be at the dive station at 0700."

Mouse left Jake to his meditation, thinking 'He was having a rough time but the fact that he called me Chief was a good sign. We don't need another Tommy; the training took too good on him. Jake was good at what he did because he had an active mind. He read instead of going brain dead watching the vid. If we lost that in the training he would be just another poor bastard that got fucked over by Megacorp.'

The black of night was shifting to deepest blue. It was just about time to go. Another cigarette and the last of my coffee dribbled from the thermos. Some one coughed behind me, causing me to spill my brew and dowse the smoke at the same time.

"Need a topper on that and a fresh butt?"

"No thank you, I was just leaving." With my head down, I turned seeing only a pair of black clogs. Johnny reached out and grabbed my chin - forcing me to look up. A penlight went back and forth across my eyes.

"Good, I see you ate it." Johnny said quietly, making no attempt to explain himself. "Have a seat, we still have some time."

Being a good dog I sat, empty as my cup of coffee, which was promptly filled by my tender. "Thank you." He lit two smokes and passed one over.

"You didn't tell me," I began.

"I could not. I can only hope you forgive me."

"For what?"

"Not killing you while it was still possible."

The morning sun was bright when I was escorted to the dive station. Johnny had injected me with something before we left the forecastle. It lightened the weight that bore heavily on my mind: clearing some of the fog of shame, dissipating the fear, helping me cope. He spent the next hour describing and explaining the functions of the new diving rig. Hoses were history along with all the weights, giving the diver more freedom of movement and near unlimited bottom time. He went all technoid, losing me in the digital details. All it meant was that I could be worked to death now. There was something in his delivery of the information that was setting a hook. The mind-numbing monologue of technical information was a cover. Between the lines he was saying something completely different. And I wasn't getting it ... or maybe I was. I just didn't know.

***

The Salvor was hipped to the listing 'Nimitz'. She was an aircraft carrier that had been recommissioned more than one too many times. The shipbuilders weren't making them anymore. They cost too much, many of the necessary skills required to build one were being lost, and besides, they generated no profit. Now she was a rotting hulk, on the way to China for recycling. Only she was taking on water faster than she could pump it out. There was no profit in a ship at the bottom of the sea, yet.

Armed with a mallet, a bag of tapered wooden DC plugs and a couple gallons of epoxy, I plunged into the open sea. At the stern on the port side of the carrier, I listened for the crew inside to begin tapping on the hull. Sound travels incredibly well underwater. The heavy blows of a hammer directed me to the first of the leaks. Choosing an appropriate sized DC plug, I jammed it into the hole using the mallet to drive it tight. And so the day went. Twelve hours passed before the first break. The sun was setting when the Chief informed us we were to work through the night. Johnny said they were testing the new gear under real-time conditions. What I heard was they were testing me, a stress test and to just be cool. Chasing my meds with a cup of cold coffee, I was back in the water less than five minutes after getting out.

For three days I pounded plugs and welded patches on the Nimitz before finally being pulled from the water. My legs were like rubber but I refused help – not that much was offered – gimping across the deck to the stool where Johnny took my hat off. I couldn't move. My ass was glued to the seat. The job however was unfinished. I needed a meal and a few hours sleep.

"Get up, Jake. It is time to go."

"I can't."

"You must! Suck it up, Jake, use the tool. Do not let these bastards see you give up. Dig deep man!" Johnny said, hushed and hurried while gathering up the dive gear. When he had the bag loaded, "We have one hour before operations resume. Come on, man, we are out of here."

Digging deep didn't do it. Sucking it up helped. I didn't give a flying fuck what the rest of the crew thought. In the end it was the training that got me to my feet. The Chief had given the orders yesterday, 'confined to quarters when not at work'. A wee small part of me did not want to let Mouse down. A huge part did not want to fuck with Megacorp. Giving all in that unforgiving minute, the monster they created rose, pushed back his hair, and, eyes on Johnny's back, followed him to our quarters. What got up off the chair wasn't me. At least not a 'me' I was willing to accept yet.

"You did good the last few days, Jake. They wanted to push you a little."

"They did."

"You just going to let them push you around? Or you want to push back? They want to see how tough you are. Well, show them the best way you know how. In fifty-five minutes they are going to throw you in for another three days. Why wait till the hour is up? Let us go back out there right now."

"Insubordination will not be tolerated."

"That is no shit and they get pretty fucking nasty about it, too. When has wanting to work ever been considered insubordination? You have to show them you are tougher than they think you are. Scare the shit out of them. The training continues after your first assignment. Unless you give them a show, it is back to the showers for you."

There was a knock at the door. "Coffee is here." Johnny got the door, cracking it only wide enough to snake his arm through to retrieve the carafe. "No thanks, got."

"What?" I asked, peeling down my wetsuit.

Johnny turned from the door, eyes going wide looking at my skin. "Goddamn, Jake, what the fuck is that? Looks like a bad case of diaper rash. You still washing?"

Turning to the mirror made me take a step back. "Fuck me."

Excess carbon dioxide in the atmosphere has been acidifying the oceans for centuries. The deep sea is a great sequesterer of the gas, but like most things can only hold so much. The mentality of the 'solution to pollution is dilution' worked for a while. Species adapted or died off.

Coral bleaching was first recorded in the late twentieth century. Acidification was the culprit. Localized in the beginning, it was considered an anomaly. When it went global, there was a catastrophe of epic proportions. Nothing was done about it, because there was nothing that could be done. Coastal industries collapsed; the food chain disrupted, starvation was rampant. It was not a particularly good time to be alive. We adapt. We survive. But what does that have to do with diaper rash? Long term exposure to ocean water caused it. Short term, twelve hours or so at a time was no big issue. I had it before, but never like this. I was being burned by the water.

"Here you go, pretty boy. Rub this on everywhere." He said, tossing me a tube of ointment, before returning to rummaging around in a waterproof case.

I peeled my suit down below my knees, applying the soothing goo when I felt a sharp jab in my ass. Moments later, Johnny withdrew a spent hypo. "That should help, too. Clock's ticking, Jake." I tossed him back the tube.

"Get the middle of my back. What was that?"

"No time to explain. Nots to worry, piss testing is a thing of the past for us."

I gave him a 'what the fuck' look as he pushed me out the door. At the exit Johnny said, "Showtime!"

The red-orange of sunset lit the deck, the hue camouflaging my sanguine face. The crew stopped, heads turned. We were a half hour early. I didn't sit as Johnny suited me up; instead I scanned the faces in that dying light; faces that wanted me to fail. Mouse came up to us.

"Morning, Chief."

He looked over at the western horizon, "Evening, Jake. You ready?"

"Yes, sir!"

Mouse saw the rash. The blisters were breaking, weeping blood. He shook his head, stopped himself from mentioning it. "You're cleared to dive. Men on board the Nimitz are waiting."

Flipping my cigarette, "Okay, Johnny, let's go." Helmet on; he walked me to the ladder, slapping the hat hard to let me know we arrived. I took a giant stride off the Salvor without looking back, into the open doors of hell.

The injection was crystal meth; he didn't have to tell me. Pushing it into a big muscle slowed down the delivery, so I didn't hit the deck tweaking. It was just enough to get me going. Purple water turned black. A long night stretched out ahead. A metronome of hammer blows punctuated the moment. Two hammers talking slowed the flow of water into the Nimitz. It was a slow and agonizingly repetitious process. The ship was 1100 feet long; there were a lot of holes. By dawn, the salve had worn off. Every square inch of my body burned. Every movement ripped swollen pustules open, exposing them to salt water. Wisps of blood trailed behind me, attracting all the wrong kind of interest.

The warmth of the two ship's hulls created a giant fish aggregating device. The dying ocean was still alive, just a lot hungrier. It wasn't the larger pelagics that were a source of concern. It was the smaller meat eaters. At first they were just a nuisance, getting in the way as they divebombed the trails of blood. A tear in my suit however, gave them a taste of my flesh. Little teeth ate a hole beneath my left shoulder blade. My rib cage kept the little bastards from eating a hole right through me. The pain I could live with. It was the maddening frenzy at which they went about their business that was driving me nuts. Like being caught in a cloud of ravenous mosquitoes – no amount of flailing helped. Feeling my sanity slip away, I tapped the hull for a five minute break, clipping my harness to the ship and hung there. With no way to stop the fish, I had to stop my mind.

There were hundreds if not thousands of ways to fuck with someone's head. Megacorp had used most of them during the training. I searched through the madness that had been those months for one of the refuges that my mind had created to survive. My situation was a little more complicated than simple, but the simple solution worked. Taking a dive slate, I unzipped my suit and slid it in position to cover my skin at the hole. One problem solved, temporarily. The greedy fucks were already tearing at the opening to get beyond the perimeter of the slate.

In the moment of losing my mind a practice I had learned as a young man took over, for I had lost control. My breathing slowed and concentration was focused on the in and outflow of breath. This was no small feat, but beat the hell out of screaming. A hammer blow brought me into the present, but not out of the nothingness. I went back to work, being the hole bunger. No thoughts entered my mind as the mallet drove the wooden cones into place. Time ceased to exist. I was oblivious to the fishes' continued onslaught. The fish were scavengers, only feeding on carcasses and the mortally wounded. The irony did not go unnoticed. The working meditation drove me on. Ambient light came and went. It no longer mattered. It had always been my habit to work without chatter on the comms. Johnny was hip to it, only checking in when my breathing became too shallow to hear.

Once after a long stretch of silence, he called in. "Jake, you there, you alive?" I responded with a blow from my mallet, "No." It was enough, he knew better than to inquire further.

At long length a staccato drum roll of hammers signaled we were finished, which was immediately confirmed by call from topside. "Jake, this is Chief Mouse. Come on in."

With each stroke, each kick, the meditation sank away like a stone in water. My teeth were clenched in pain when I reached the ladder. Johnny lowered a rope with a bag attached to the end for my tools. After the tools, I took off my diving hat and harness, dropping them into the bag. My wetsuit had become a close fitting torture chamber, which I shed with all possible haste. It had become as shredded as my flesh, torn and left bleeding from head to foot by the fish. What was left of my skin was swollen red, blistering viciously. Climbing the ladder left streaks of blood trailing down into the water, boiling with a frenzy of fish.

What stepped onto the deck of the Salvor was a nightmare beyond the imaginations of the crew. Some puked, some ran, all turned away. If they looked back, it was only to find me staring into their souls. I had every intention of scaring the living shit out of every one of them. They wanted a monster – I gave them one. The smell of feces wafted across the deck. Only the Chief approached, draping a towel over me while Johnny got the gear. The three of us left the deck in utter silence. A set of gore–clumped bloody footprints remained to remind them that evil had passed this way.

At the door to the room I collapsed. Mouse and Johnny carried my body into the room. "Into the shower. We have to rinse the salt water off." Clotted blood and chunks of flesh clogged the drain. They placed me in bed.

"Should I send the doc?" The Chief asked Johnny.

"No, I will take care of it. Just give me full access to the med facilities. We will keep him here."

Johnny left with the Chief, returning a short painful time later with a bag full of doctor stuff. Morphine came first, mainlined for a quick knock down, then an I.V. saline drip to end the excessive dehydration. Unknown hours were spent stitching skin together, matching muscle tissues and joining them again.

As the day passed, the healing began on my body. The rent in my soul however was unable to repair itself. This realization began the cycle of depression. After hours of tearing myself to pieces, all I wanted to do was get back in the water and let the fish finish what they had started. It would have been a blessing. Instead, I woke to the menacing presence of a black jumpsuit. I recoiled, shrinking away from him as far as the bed would allow. A smile crossed his face. It was not the smile of compassion or benevolence, but the wry smile of a torturer viewing his work in completion. My fear added a curl to the lips in satisfaction.

"Lie down flat and turn your head." It was not a request, not up for discussion, and not for me to question. I did as I was told.

Regardless of the stitches and open wounds, one of his big paws mashed down my face as he placed a knee heavily on my chest to keep me from moving. The pain of the syringe entering my neck was nothing compared to the chafing of raw nerve endings. Resistance was futile, making his heavy-handed treatment more of a symbol of control than it was necessary to perform the injection. My body was his. He would never have my mind.

I watched as he packed up his little nylon kit. A row of vials with dark fluid filled the top pockets with hypos lined up like little evil soldiers waiting to go to work. Zipping the case closed, he looked down hard on me. The juice was going to work. His piercing gaze said more than his mouth ever could. I closed my eyes, nodding in submission. When I opened them again he was gone and Johnny was in my room packing up my clothes and gear.

A dark joie de vivre came with the relief of the injection. The routine of my new life was becoming dismally obvious. "Hey, man." I said, quietly bringing my self up on my elbows.

"Jake, ça va?"

"You know."

"Yeah, I know."

"Am I being sent back?"

"No."

"Then what are you fucking with my stuff for?"

"We are shipping out."

"What?"

"You heard correct."

"Can you give me a little more?"

"Sure," Johnny said reaching for his works.

"Well, that too, but what I want is more information."

Johnny started to mix a fix, mentalating. When he had it together, he said. "Let me do you. You are a fucking mess." He hit me, then did himself. We sat there. As the pain shut down, I said, "Well?"

"Well, what?" He said back as I looked at him, screwing up my eyes. "Oh yeah. Cannot say you do not do as you are told."

"Was that a double or triple negative?"

"Our friend in the black jumpsuit did not drag you out of here kicking and screaming so I guess you did aw'ight. As far as the ship's crew goes, you scared them to death. Stripping at the bottom of the ladder and climbing onto the deck without any skin really freaked them. Hell, I was afraid of you. Half of the deck crew has applied for transfer, which of course will be round filed. So to mollify the men, we are being sent to another project for a while. Can you get up and walk around?" He came over to the side of the bed, giving me his forearm. I grabbed on; together we got me on my feet. Blisters popped on the soles of my feet when my full weight was put on them. It hurt like hell as I wobbled to the coffee carafe and poured a cup.

"Where we going?"

"We will know when we get there. It is the way things are done. Get used to it. Asking too many questions just sends you back to the showers. Learn by watching, listening, being aware, and acting dumb as dirt. In other words – be yourself, Jake."

"Hmmmm. Why thank you so very fucking much."

"You are welcome. Come on, get dressed, the chopper will be here in few minutes."

Socks and jeans felt as if they were woven of barbed wire. A silk aloha shirt, sandpaper. The loud overlapping colors of the shirt hid the spots of blood and blister juice that still oozed from open sores. Gloves on to cover my hands; a pair of big sunglasses hid my grotesqueness as we made our way to the helipad. Mouse was there, clipboard in hand and a couple of heavy jackets over his shoulder. He had our papers and orders.

"You're looking better," the Chief began. "For what it is worth, I'm glad you made it."

"I'm not. Just didn't want to let you down, Chief."

"Yes, yes. My thanks, Jake."

Taking a hint from Johnny, "You're welcome, Chief, any time."

The sound of a chopper broke our warm and fuzzy moment. It came in low and fast, touching down only long enough to let Johnny and I hop in and exchange papers with the Chief, who threw the coats in just as the chopper door was closed. There was no time for goodbyes as the helicopter lifted off, leaving Chief with a mouthful of words. Now that there was no longer time for it, I realized how much I had wanted to talk with him. Away from boats, salvage and death; spend some time with a man I considered destined for greatness. At least my version of greatness, that is. The moment lost forever, crushed beneath the great wheel of life and death.

I dozed and healed as the big transport jet ripped through the blanket of night. We were the only human cargo. Human as it gets anyway. Thoughts of what we are would not seriously be entertained for years. Unborn into a bleak world of work and pain, I had to focus on survival. Not life-sustaining survival. That apparently had been taken care of by Megacorp. But even so the I, me, Jake, the little bits and pieces that make me who I am, continue to be extant. I was now a Megacorp operative. I was also more than that.

Tommy, the crane operator, became the conditioning, the training. He had to, to exist. His mind could not cope with what he was or was not. Giving up his self was the only way to endure the personal torment that came along with the program, surrendering his humanity to continue being that which he could not end. Now he could only be a crane operator. Which was unfortunate for him and Megacorp as well. In him they got a functioning automaton. He may have been the best operator in the world, but now, that's all he was. No multi-tasking for Tommy.

I couldn't go there yet. Johnny's dope, along with his tutelage, kept me from bottoming out in the pit of despair. That, I now fathom, began when we first met. All the while he had been dropping hints and pearls of wisdom, most of which slid through my mind like quicksilver. Now at 50,000 feet, he spoke quietly about how I should conduct myself if I was to keep 'me' intact. And as I would soon learn, to help keep his cover in place, too.

"You could get away with shit like that in Pearl. We are heading out into the real world now, Jake."

"What, Pearl Harbor isn't a real place? Being forced to dive for six days and having my skin eaten off was real enough for me. Having every one I know shun me like a freak, shit, man."

"Not everyone. You have me. You have Mouse. Tommy has no one. You have no idea how lucky you are."

Looking at myself, "You call this lucky?"

"Give me a break, Jake. Life is a bitch, unlife even more so. But ... there is still opportunity."

"For wha ..." I was talking to the hand.

"To do the right thing. Remember, watch, listen, be aware." He swiped his nose. A member of the flight crew was coming. He was armed and none too happy about being chosen for the dirty work.

"You two gotta go?"

I went to stand. Forgetting about the chain around my waist I came up short. Catching a rifle butt in the forehead dropped me back into the seat. Stars swirled around inside my head as I lost control of my bladder. The warmth felt good, I dreamt I was diving. I woke to a sharp elbow in my ribs.

"Jesus, Jake! That is just the kind of move that will get you a trip to the showers. Speaking of – you need one." He handed me a towel.

"Oh man," I said, realizing I peed my pants.

"He unchained you. You are my responsibility now. There is a sink behind those curtains. If somebody shows up, just stare at your feet. Understand?"

"Yes, sir." I said flatly.

"That is the ticket. Talking like that will keep you out of a lot of trouble."

I appreciated his trying to help. I just didn't know how to show it. Standing up carefully, ready to be shorted again, I stepped from the seat. The chain around my waist had been exchanged for a pair of shackles around my ankles. My feet tangled. Unable to stop my momentum, I fell over into the aisle, face planting on the floor. Johnny burst into laughter. Figuring this was part of the lesson; I calmly got up, expressionless, shuffling behind the curtain. When I returned, I sat, folded my hands on my lap and stared at the floor, I received quiet applause and pile of powder to snort. The training was continuing.

I was a slow student. Apparently he saw something in me that I didn't see. I liked what I did for a living and went at it with all the gusto I could muster. Was there any other way? Not for me. Giving 110 percent every day was the rule, not the exception, but it came with a price. You sacrificed your body for the job. When every muscle and bone in your body aches, when there was no more to give, you gave. Cut to the bone, chunks of meat missing, swollen from jellyfish stings, you still showed up the next morning. Licking your wounds would only get you bumped off the dive roster. Once you've found your niche, you protected it by doing it better than anyone else. For me the price was worth it. Even when I failed, and I have failed often, it wasn't for lack of giving it my best shot. Sure we all want the glory, the prize, to be the one. Few of us, though, are willing to grind it out, day in and day out. The moments of recognition were few and far between. An old diver once described commercial diving as 'long hours of boredom punctuated by moments of sheer panic'. It was those moments that made or broke all divers. We all have our strengths and weaknesses; it comes with being human.

***

For the next year and a half, I crisscrossed the planet. My diving experience aboard the Nimitz was just a taste of what my life was becoming. It was worse than anything I could've possibly imagined and like a good dog I did as I was told. How many people died as a result of my following orders is anybody's guess. I don't want to know.

Johnny said it would be bad. How bad, I was just finding out. The S.S. Charlie Brown went down in the rough waters out of San Francisco Bay. The fog was in, the thick and heavy pea soup kind. The Charlie Brown was heading out to sea. Having been pushed sideways by the outgoing tide, the addition of a short in the bow thruster switch sent her into the north support piling for the Golden Gate Bridge. The piling sliced across the mid section well below the water line. She sank in minutes with all aboard.

Installed on the Charlie Brown was an emergency chamber designed just for this type of maritime disaster. When a ship wants to go down she can do it in the blink of an eye, or make the death long and painful. The chamber was for the blink. When the alarm sounded all hands dropped what they were doing and raced for the only thing that would save them on a one-way trip to Davy Jones's locker. From what I gathered during the briefing, most of them made it to safety and were now waiting anxiously to be rescued. The poor bastards did not know what hell had in store for them.

The water was black and cold as liquid ice. Fully suited, even with thermal heating going full blast, could not keep out the cold that penetrated my very soul. The dive plan was to use the slack tide intervals as our window of opportunity. The natural tidal flow through the Golden Gate was as treacherous as they come. Strong enough to sink a massive cable layer; it would certainly crush me like a grape, should I find myself at the wrong place and time ... again.

I fell deep into the blackness and unrelenting cold. Even at slack tide there was a cruel movement of water through the Gate. Attached to a weighted cable that acted as a sort of plumb line, the rapid descent came to an abrupt halt, giving me a chiropractic adjustment that I could have lived without. The H.I.D. lamps built into my headgear came on with blinding intensity. Panning 360 degrees, while operating a hand held sonar, gave me the location of the Charlie Brown. We were several hundred feet off our mark. Activating comms, I redirected the crane to set me on the stern of the sunken vessel.

My orders were to enter the chamber through the wet lock and retrieve a black plastic case that one of the crew had with him. My tools were a heavy machete-type knife and waterproof machine gun. When I asked (and was instantly rebuked for asking), I was told that it could get ugly and the box was paramount. Then the diving supervisor, in no uncertain terms, explained that if I didn't get the box, there was no reason for me to return either. So, when I stepped onto the slanting deck of the Charlie Brown, it was not without a significant amount of uncertainty. Before entering the wet lock of the survival chamber, I jammed a fresh magazine into the submachine gun and jacked a round into the pipe. There was no safety. After making sure the blade slid freely from its sheath, I spun the wheel that opened the door of hell. Just following orders.

Eyes filled the porthole from the main chamber as the wet lock drained. Half of them relieved, the other half crazed, all of them damned. Removing my helmet and life support gear, leaving it safely in the lock, I took a few deep breaths, calming myself into a state of clarity before entering a situation that could get ugly.

Releasing the dogs on the inner hatch and swinging it in, I was greeted with cheers and innumerable pats on the back that pulled me into the large chamber. The clamor was shouted down by the man in charge.

"I'm Chief Engineer Grimmer, we sure are glad you made it." He said extending a pair of large grease stained hands into the shake.

"I'm sure you are," I said freeing my hand from his paws, scanning the occupants for the one with the case. He was off to the side. "Got any coffee?" I asked, taking a casual step away from the big engineer. One of the men got the nod from the Chief and hustled to the back of the chamber.

Waiting for the coffee I wanted to keep it loose. "Where's the Captain?"

"Didn't make it." Grimmer replied.

"Wow. Went down with her..." my coffee arrived. "To the Captain!" I toasted and watched the lot of them mime a shot, respectfully. The formalities were over. I turned to the man with the black case, made eye contact and said, "I need that case, sir." It was not a request and the man knew it. He stepped forward, to my surprise.

"Thank goodness. Since I lost the key I've had to schlep this thing around everywhere," he said, raising his hand that was securely fastened to the case by way of hardened steel shackles. The kind you can't cut or break, or get out of.

It was then he saw the machete handle and sheath with the safety strap undone. He lurched backwards staring wildly at Grimmer. When Grimmer brought his gaze back to me it was to receive a cup of scalding hot coffee in is eyes. As he clutched his eyes, I stepped hard into a kick to his groin, bringing him to his knees as I brought up the gun.

"STEP BACK! ALL I WANT IS THE CASE!" this did little to ease the rising tension.

"You heard the man! He doesn't have the key!" someone yelled.

Pulling the machete, "I do." The silence was as grim and swollen as Grimmer's nuts, and ready to bust.

I pointed the gun at two burly balless deckhands, "Bring him over here and hold him down," I yelled above the confusion.

They hesitated, but fearing the gun more than their peers, the two moved towards the man with the case. They never got there. Grimmer lunged through the men, his hands aiming for my throat. They never got there either, as a burst from the machine gun dropped him in his tracks. The bullets were special: powerful enough for killing, but not enough oomph to punch a hole in the chamber. The ricochets, however, were another matter, as one tore through my calf, dropping me to my knees. The remainder of the crew chose this moments to lose their minds ... followed shortly thereafter by their lives. Squeezing the trigger, I sprayed death into a small room meant for saving life. The irony was not lost.

I waded through the men at my feet to find the only one left alive. He was protected by the case, hiding behind it next to a locker. My thought processes were no longer functioning. I was in shock from receiving a fair number of ricocheting rounds. Countless hours of training, pain, and fear dictated my actions. There can be no justification for what I did that day. Nor forgiveness.

I put the barrel of the gun to his temple and squeezed. Click. Empty. Dropping the weapon and pulling the machete I saw what fear looked liked as the blade came down, sinking deep into his neck. Nearly severed, his head lolled to one side, arteries spraying me with his life as I dragged him clear of his hiding place to 'unlock' the case.

I don't remember returning to the wet lock, donning my gear and securing the case to my harness. Nor do I recall the ride to the surface at the end of the down wire, which had been reeled in at a wicked fast pace in a race against the incoming tide. Nor dying on the deck of the salvage vessel. The diving skin had acted as a compress over a multitude of bullet holes. Once it was removed, my body bled out faster than a water balloon sliced with a razor. It was a minor setback in the grand scheme of things and just the beginning of my life in hell.

***

Waking to the realization of being a killer that could be counted on is not just merely unpleasant. It is devastating. Like a dog, I had been trained, abused, beaten and broken to become what they had made me. It was why I was alive, if you could call it that, because I was a good dog. There was no solace in knowing it was not my fault. Only guilt, shame, remorse, self-reproach, and a depression so deep and vast there was no escape, for you were always at the center.

Worst of all, I knew I would do it again. I had become a monster. Something to be feared. The rewards for a successful mission were no meds, no juice, for as long as it took to be sure I would not turn on the master. It took what seemed like forever. They knew what they were doing. Their job was results; mine was dealing with the fallout.

For reasons that, to this day, I still do not understand and have paid dearly for, my thinking mind was never shut down. Perhaps because there wasn't that much there to begin with. To survive this sort of living you had to escape, if but for a few moments, the horrors that engulf you. Reading gave me that evasion.

Megacorp med techs didn't give it a second thought. For them it was an archaic form of entertainment. They made note of it, mocking me. But for the techs, it meant they didn't have to deal with me. My folly was allowed. The Internet made mindless consumption of the shit it had to offer easy. The computer-speak used by the Net now was not really reading, so much as conceptualizing; a way of seeing the forest but not the trees. You could say more by saying less. Details became less vital. For Megacorp, that was the kicker. It was always in the details, becoming one of their greatest tools. The idea has always been easier to swallow than the shitty details. Megacorp was not original in its thinking, just incredibly adept at its application.

Taking the advice I had been given so long ago by Jonah, I read everything; text, advertisements, drama (what little there was of it), business reports, weather, billboards, menus, graffiti, anything to keep from reading the writing on the walls. Then one day that all changed. Folded into a clean set of clothes was a book. No shit, a paper book. The advertising said, 'complete, unabridged'. It was worn; the print tiny and the paper yellowed and brittle. The title, MOBY DICK, by Herman Melville.

Dry as the desert, the tale of the Pequod absorbed me and I it. You can logline the novel in a few short sentences but lose the glorious details in the glut of instant gratification. Real words, real reading. I wore the book out, frangible pages crumbling from one too many turns. Begging the techs for more was futile. When supplication failed, I would retreat into my self and bear the burden of what I had become. Any outburst would be met with a prejudice born of intolerance. I did not want to go there. Fear was the controller, the collar tight.

In time, which I had more than enough of, other books came. Some new, some old. Glossy mags to romance, mostly the stuff that came from the garbage; by the smell of some, it didn't matter. Read as if each was the last, learning to be careful and building a library. It wasn't much. It was everything. Then would come the call to work. God, the steel doors come down hard and fast. Being released, for that is what the experience has come to feel like – like a caged animal to be loosed among people for a while. 'Loosed' is not freed.

Some things never change. 'Stuff' will always be more important than the lives of many or just the life of the individual. The more important the stuff, the more lives became available. In our/my case that all gets a little confusing. Only rarely was there a call to save someone. And then only one of many.

***

The cold water bit sharply, snapping you awake with a sudden intake of breath. I used to love what I do. But when it is turned inside out and made evil, it takes some of the fun out of it. There was still the rush. Adventure is difficult to wash from a job like this and it's harder to rid your blood from its addiction. Unlike Tommy, the crane operator from the Salvor, whom I have not seen for years, divers were not machine operators. We knew how to operate them as a course of business, but were not stuck at the levers and buttons all day. No, we were a little more 'hands on'.

The cage sank into the green waters of the Gulf of Mexico. The once productive oil fields had been failing for years to produce a profit. The U.S. and Mexico had squeezed it dry. Now the oil companies were surveying for the last remaining pockets of crude. One of their teams had run amok while cruising through a cluster of old oil platforms, fouling itself in the rigging and garbage on the gulf floor. The cage hit the bottom hard, as I knew it would. Just as I knew I was the subject of far away laughter in the crane tower. They knew it hurt.

In the cage with me was a duffel with an emergency deep dive rig, for one. There was a crew of six. It could get ugly, I thought, as it usually does. People just wig out when their number is up, never knowing there are worse things. One of the worse things was just about to come through their door. The happy faces you are greeted with are one of the hardest images to get rid of when it is all over. Dr. Simon Brewer was the prize. The rest, fish food.

Swimming the length of the sub revealed the extent of her entanglement. Several loops of wire had snagged one of the steering fins. Why I did it is still somewhat of a mystery. I pretended to struggle for a moment, disguising my actions, freeing the sub from the snare. Video cameras in the dive helmet were beyond my control. They were always watching. The paranoid mind would not let you think otherwise. Then there were the faces.

"I am here for Doctor Brewer." Swiping the water from my face and pushing my hair back.

A young man stepped forward. "I am Dr. Brewer." He extended his hand. It was not taken.

"May I use your restroom?"

Palming an ink pen I followed a pointed finger. Breaking into a cold sweat, I had to sit and think. 'Think, goddamn it!" I yelled at myself, but nothing happened. Pulling a few sheets to make sure my hands were dry and pulling another I began to write. 'You are not Brewer. I will take him. Sub untangled. Disappear with your men or die.'

Standing, flushing and stepping from the head, "Can you help me with your gear, doctor?"

Out of sight from the crew I held the note for him to see. He read it twice before I ate it. Under my breath, "Do you understand?" He nodded, scared as shitless as he should be.

An old man, hunched over a computer terminal in an effort to blend in, jerked in little spasms as drips from my suit fell on his shoulders.

"Dr. Brewer, it's time to go." I reached down, firmly bringing him to his feet. I didn't want any resistance until the package was safe. If the crew played along they would at least have a chance. If not, I had no qualms about the only other alternative.

The man who pretended to be Brewer was quietly making the rounds to keep the crew at bay while I suited up the geezer. As soon as he was set, I backed us into the lock, allowing the helmet cams to capture the crew accepting what fate had to offer. Attaching a tether to the doctor, "Just keep breathing, old man, I will take care of everything else." He shook his head as the lock filled. Replacing air with water, light for darkness, pain for misery.

As we came out of the water, Dr. Brewer went limp. Unclipping his hat and breathing gear, dropping them to the floor of the cage, I picked him up, carrying him out onto the deck. Crewmembers backed away while security was preparing to engage.

"Where is a stretcher for this man?" The sound of a dozen weapons being jacked with a round was the only answer. I began to walk towards the med station. I mean, what else was I going to do with him? when the first shots were fired. Full metal jackets impacted my titanium knees, making a mess of both and dropping me to them. The steel deck met the jagged alloy, clacking noisily, as they were forced to continue, stump walking to the lab. The door to the lab opened just as I reached for it. And there he was – the same Megacorp thug that did most of the recruiting and training. I figured I was busted. I lowered my head, raising Dr. Brewer. The thug took the doctor from my arms and applied his boot to my chest, knocking me backwards onto the deck. Still conscious, I watched as he dumped the doctor's body into one of the black bags used for us, before slinging it over his shoulder, stepping over me, on his way to a waiting chopper.

'The bastards, not to an old man...' were my last thoughts as a rifle butt brought sweet oblivion.

I woke to a surprise. Hell is full of surprises. My knees had been fixed and I felt, well – 'well,' which was what had me. It means I got my juice on time, no begging. Something was wrong, or right, and I didn't have a clue. Was it that I didn't kill anyone? When killing them would have been just as easy, if not an act of compassion? A quick death beats suffocating on your own wasted breath.

Next to the bed were street clothes with a note stuck to the shirt. The sticky informed me of many things, but mostly that no one wanted to explain these things personally. I had been fitted with an exploding tracking chip, had 72 hours leave (DO NOT BE LATE!), and was not to fuck up. I dressed, following exit signs until finding uninterrupted sunlight. The harshness of the summer sun sent me scurrying like a rat to the shaded side of the streets. Sunglasses were in order. A cash card had been placed in the pair of jeans. Tracking me all the way, the fucks. Attired to a comfortable degree, I tried to be me; going into bars, having a few drinks, shoot the shit with the locals. It had always come with such ease. Now, after a few minutes, the homeboys would gravitate to the other end of the bar, like I was cutting big farts or something. The bartender must have seen my consternation.

"You either got big balls or are a really stupid mother fucker for coming down here. You seemed all right, so I served you. But your time is up. I'll ask you once to move along, before those boys you were talking to decide to tear you to pieces."

He didn't have to ask twice. The vibes in the place had gone from bad to deadly. It would take more than a handful of drunk rednecks to take me down, but if I killed one of them, I would wish I hadn't. Putting some distance between the wharves and myself, I tried to dissolve into tourist town but was unable to get into solution. Within 24 hours I was back at the facility. I had learned the lesson. This was where I belonged. They didn't have to beat it into me that I was now on the outside looking in. The neurosis that came along with being outcast dealt a near lethal blow, crippling me as a person, but not my ability to function. I wasn't quite ready for virtual suicide. Yet.

Going back over the last few years, it was easy to see how directed and single-minded life had become. Megacorp had been doing this for a long time and had it down, like any good business would. Investing only what you had to, to maintain a maximum of profit margin. Reuseables that were a pain in the ass, caused too much trouble or were

too inquisitive of their nature ran the risk of being put on ice between
jobs or worse. How ridiculous is that? What could possibly be worse
than what we have become? Nothing! That's what. This is as bad as it
gets. Yet, I was still young, relatively. Time and loneliness would teach
me that it does indeed, get worse.

Nothing was left to chance, with the exception of letting us out of our
cages. And even then, when we were free, they still maintained a solid
grip on us. A grip that crushed through to our souls, to the very core of
our being, annihilating it.

No longer a rookie, the perks for being a good dog began to accrue. The
pay was good but came in Megacorp credits, not real money. Needless
to say the exchange rate for real money was not in my favor. You could
throw parties, hire hookers, get drugs, and get lost. The credits however
all returned to Megacorp in a continuous loop of electronic transfers.
They sold what was bought, made what was sold and owned everything
in between. Paid the workforce in credits, which in turn was spent on
what was sold. It was a vicious cycle and somewhere within it a lot of
money was being made. I spent my share of it in all of the above with the
mentality of a disposable income. Mindless entertainment had its time
and place, but it grows old. I would find myself spending more time at
the facility on my time off, reading about debauchery through the eyes
of de Sade, than the eyes of a coked up tired working girl. Old habits die
hard. With credits came a library of sorts. Some books, antiques mostly,
were more for looking at than in. They were gold to me. The bulk came
electronically, which takes a certain ritual out of reading. The book
itself, the binding, cover and jacket. The pages' color, font, smell and
texture. The words, before anyone messed with them too much.

C'est la vie! Times change and then, there in the palm of your hand, a
thousand books. It is a trade-off, as are most things, in whatever life you
may lead. The electronic books bought me time to be more selective in
my purchases or at least the chance to be less impulsive. It took years to
fathom the limitless depths available, only to discover I was in a pond
of Megacorp's making, seeing only what they wanted to be read. A fish
caught in the shallows at low tide gasping for a breath of water.

Of water I saw plenty. Of death even more. The foolishness aboard
the submarine years ago was not repeated. Life had gotten good and
the thought of going back brought on a shitload of fear. So the good life
was perpetuated at the expense of the good lives of others. A raw deal
for them; I protected my side viciously. Therefore I was no different
than any one else. A model citizen.

That was being undermined, not surprisingly, by myself. In the desire to slake my thirst I stretched beyond my bounds, changed credits for real money – fucking gougers – in search of something new to read. Bookstores were few, off the beaten path in the old parts of town, rundown and something of a disaster, as a general rule. With no obvious system of order, or assistance beyond grunts from behind a counter from a graying head buried in a book, you looked around, found an area that seemed interesting and sat down amongst it all and immersed yourself.

I was awash in paper. Like a pig in shit, wallowing in the piles of parchment and vellum, I succumbed to the illusion of knowledge. It was a high of sorts, repeated at every chance. Like all highs though, it ran its course, leaving me empty. The substance, the grail I looked for was lost in the dream, a mental masturbation of millions of words.

"It's the folly of the young." A graying man in motorcycle gear said, looking down at me on the floor. "If you look a little higher, there is much to be gained from that which seems out of reach."

He reached his soft firm hand down, helping me to my feet. I judge people a lot by their hands and there is much to be read in a shake. "My name is Kale, you ride?"

I looked him up and down before answering, "Jake, never enough."

"Well, come on then, Jake, a little air will do you good." Without waiting for an answer, he turned on the heels of riding boots and left the shop. Outside sat a late model BMW, which sort of explained the expensive riding gear. Helmet on, he nodded to the bitch seat. Not the least bit embarrassed I hopped on and we left town.

The road wound through the local countryside. After an hour we stopped for gas and seemed to have left the world behind.

"Last gas for the next two hundred miles, you up for it?" Kale said, taking off his helmet and gloves.

"Who wouldn't be?" I replied rubbing the chill out of my arms.

Noticing, Kale said, "There is a sweatshirt in the tail bag. It will be getting a little colder til we reach my place. Just hang tough, but I think you're used that."

"I've had a little practice." We both laughed. He peeled off a few leaves of real money to pay for the fuel. "They don't take Megacard out this way," he finished, answering my thought as it rose to the surface. And I could swear he smirked a bit putting his helmet on. Three hours later, frozen stiff, hair frosted with a trail of tears streaming sideways from both eyes, we came to a house stuck far back off the road in a copse of trees. Deer scattered as the engine noise and lights spooked them from the evening feed. It was too dark to see anything beyond the lights of the bike. Then silence. The porch lights came on. An older couple came out into the light.

"What are you kids doing up? I told you I would be late."

"Just excited, Kale. It has been a while." The older Kale said. Young Kale says, "I know, I'm sorry," and gives them both hugs as they enter the house. Looking over his shoulder he says, "Come on, Jake, a little cold out, don't you think?"

"Yeah, little bit," I said brushing the frost off. Stepping inside, "Nice place."

"Thank you, it has been in the family a long time. Great-great-great-grandpa Kale had the place made a nature preserve so no one would cut it. It was his son Kale that started the biking tradition."

"I like them already." Jake said as he warmed his hands at the wood stove.

"Jake?" Kale asked. I turned. "This is my son Kale and his wife Helen."

"A pleasure, Kale and Helen." I said, shaking both their hands carefully, throwing a couple of questioning eyes in Biker Kale's direction. He indicated 'later' and to just go with it.

Dinner was waiting and talk was of the road, the gardens, the harvest, the deer. As sweet a conversation as I had ever heard between three people who obviously loved each other deeply. A casual lightness of banter I had never known, personally, and only seen rarely, existed here. It was one of those moments in time where you felt blessed just to be there and embarrassed to no small degree, surrounded as I was by the goodness of man. The pictures of family and professional livelihood along with the knacks of life scattered about loosely told the tale of their lives.

It was here that I saw what life is all about. It had a certain quietude and conscious way of living. After the kids went to bed, Kale poured some bourbon while I felt compelled to do the dishes. He pointed to a screen porch and pantomimed a smoke. I admired his discretion. It would have been a shame to spoil the smells of the home with tobacco.

I rolled a couple. The night was crisp but he didn't seem bothered.

"You are not so alone as you might think, Jake."

"I guess not. You're pretty smooth, Kale."

"You want to get to be my age, you'd better be." He smiled and tipped his glass adding a little more. "You like my kids?"

"They sure do love you."

"I love them too."

"It shows."

"That is good you can still see it. I wanted you to."

"It has been a while. Where I come from, well..."

"I can imagine. It is easy to see where you are in the system. And you are just starting to pick up on the fact that you have been played. Correct?" I nodded, he continued. "Just starting to spread your wings a bit, you cash in some credits and start looking for more."

"How did you know I cashed in credits?"

"I don't exactly know, just a few educated guesses. Which you will need to keep up on if you want to keep on keeping on." He refilled our glasses. "Come on out to the garage."

We crunched across the frosted grass, leaving green footprints in the glaze. The moon had risen and acted as a streetlamp, lighting the way. Drink in hand, I was entering another part of Kale's life. Half a dozen road bikes sat next to a tractor. A couple of newer ones, then each got older.

My "wow" was wholly inadequate for the moment. He liked BMW's.

"The old ones are granpa Kale's, the newer of course..."

"They all run?"

"Jake, please, of course they do. This one has a carb leak. Just can't find the right gasket material."

Jake looked at the aromatic drip that clung to the bottom of the float bowl. "We carry all kinds of that stuff on the boat. Gotta haves for repairs at sea. I could get you some?"

"Mmmmm. Just what I need, some gasket material." Disappointed. "What I could use is help with some deck repairs. The last few winters have rotted things up a bit and I don't want the kids hurting themselves."

"Yeah, sure thing," I said, knowing something had just gone over my head.

The night was quiet and I slept soundly. So much so, I hustled out of bed feeling I had overslept. Instead I was up first, watching sunrise with the deer. I turned to find young Kale staring at me sweetly.

"It's beautiful here." I said quietly.

"Yes, it is."

After measuring and determining the necessary lumber, the family took off for town to get it and groceries. It left time to dig postholes and tear out the rotted planks. Time for reflection on where this was going. How could I be here, surrounded by all this goodness. A murderer, a monster ... and I would do it again. The car must have come up the drive while I had been ruminating. Kale had come up quietly behind me.

"Don't think too hard about it, Jake. It's not about what you have done or will do. It's how you deal with it. Need a wheel barrow for the concrete mix?"

"Yeah, and a hoe. We get these posts in tonight they will be set tomorrow."

Hammers and saws went at the day. It was cool and the work wasn't hard, more a quiet, necessary busy. There wasn't much talk but there was a lot being said. By nightfall we were all tired. Sleep and friendship came easily. I woke shifting gears. Gearing up to head back, back into the nightmare of my life. Trying to keep the edge at bay, I worked quietly as the others slept in. The repairs were finished as a late breakfast was spread. Fresh jams and bread, hot coffee, eggs from the neighbors. Comfort food to the max, it made you feel good. And I did, for the first time in a long time, feel good. Young Kale and Helen cleaned up while Kale and I returned to the garage to put tools away, coffee in hand.

"Let's see. I figure this 600 probably fit you pretty good."

"Say what?"

"Say why don't you try this on, see if it fits. Weather report is you'll be heading into a cold front."

"I have to get back, but I don't know."

"Well, it's about time you did." Kale opened the garage door, letting the cool air in. "Go ahead, fire her up."

I expected a roar when the 600 started. Instead it came with a small puff of smoke, idling right down to a purr.

"On a cold morning you may have to use the choke." He reached over pulling a lever on the handlebars making the engine sputter. He pushed the lever back, making a slice across his throat. I killed the motor. "Let's see, one down four up. After that just don't goose it in a corner, these old ones get a little squirrelly. There are a few things I would like to talk to you about."

"I'm all ears."

"I hope so."

The next hour was a crash course in how not to be stupid, which I had apparently been doing a fine job of. Kale explained how to change credits, invisibly. And explained how I'd been busted for doing so by using the grey market instead of the black one. Megacorp knew and it would be dealt with when I got back. This sent a shiver down my spine and I expressed it.

"It should. I would not want to be in your shoes. Speaking of, try these on." Kale handed me a pair of boots.

Fully suited, the outfit felt like old style dive gear, the Michelin man effect. The thought, 'you don't really appreciate safety gear until you need it', drifted through my head. Stuffing my beret into an old helmet made the crushed foam fit snug enough. Kale pulled his shirt off to put on something heavier before stepping into his suit. In that moment I saw something I'd never thought I would see again; the scars of bullet wounds creating a happy face on his chest. He knew Pablo, the same guy that Johnny had been smuggling with.

"You met that guy?"

"Pretty much everybody that meets him is left with a little reminder of the encounter."

"I only saw him once. He did that to a friend of mine." I pointed at Kale's chest.

"I remember hearing something about that. An unfortunate consequence of not delivering in full." Kale stuffed a pair of earplugs in. The conversation was over. Pulling out of the garage I waved to his kids, wobbling the bike onto the gravel track that served as a driveway.

The road was dark with clouds close overhead. The cold worked its way in like an ice pick. Kale had peeled off hours ago indicating that I just keep heading west. I got gas at every chance, spending credits when I could, saving the real money for when it was needed. Long hours stretched into the night. Rain began, threatening to snow. Ignorance of the dangers paid off or I would have stopped. 'Endurance riding' he had called it. At the next gas stop I gimped, frozen and wet, into the diner for warmth and coffee. It was not to be. I was expelled before even having the chance to sit. I had left the milk of human kindness far behind; it was foolish to think otherwise. I shivered next to the bike, taking warmth from the engine. The gas jockey's glare and thump from his baton across my neck snapped me out of it. He knew I wouldn't fight back.

I was a reuseable. We had no rights and it was always open season on us when we entered the general population. Normally we would be left completely alone, shunned. Only our money brought us a limited access to civilized society. But it only took one redneck with a full load of the Megacorp mindfuck to get things going.

He could beat the shit out of me with it and the only thing he would get in return would be tired from swinging the club. Apparently that was what he was up for. A second blow crashed down hard on my temple, sending me sprawling into an oily slush puddle. The gelid rain that poured on me was a blessing compared to the cascade of brutal bashes that cascaded down. He knew where to hit, to cause as much damage as pain. One collarbone shattered, teeth broken, head lacerations poured blood across my eyes, I reached into my pocket. Withdrawing my hand came with a bone crunching home run that reduced the metacarpals to pulp. All the real money fell from my grasp as I crawled to the machine. I had to get out of there. But he wasn't going to let me off that easy. He stepped on the crushed hand pinning me to the ground. Through a haze of blood, gore and agony, I yanked my hand free inching forward. With my bad hand, I grasped the footpeg pulling myself closer. Not willing to risk the good hand, the broken one pulled me up. Slugger had stepped back; why he stopped I will never know. Why I said 'Thank you' through a mouthful of broken teeth is beyond me, too. Every movement screamed in rebellion. I pulled the helmet on but was unable to strap it up. The bike started, operating it was merely unbearable. The fuel stop was left behind along with all sense of illusion. I was home.

Blood dripped from the helmet as I pulled into dock security. The I.D. check was excruciating. Guess it was hard to tell who I was. The damage was worse than my imagination. I rolled up next to the ship, put the kickstand down, stepping into the position of submission and bleeding all over the place.

I was wracked in pain and remorse standing there. No juice, no meds, slipping into unending depression, just standing there. My head spun as the blood dried, caking my face and hands, wobbling unsure in the hot sun. Day turned to night then to day again, sweat melting the dried blood, stinging damaged flesh.

"Heads up Jake!" shattered the stillness, into which I had crept. The head would not come up. Not that it didn't want to; it couldn't – vertebrae had been damaged. The air whistled as a billy club caught me behind the knees, in exactly the same place as a blow from the other evening, collapsing the stasis of body, sending it to the ground in a heap. But not before I saw the look on the batter's face. I had seen it before. Hatred and ignorance. The Megacorp mindfuck.

Surviving without the shit they pumped into us, to keep us going, is a miserable existence of basic necessities, poorly executed. My room stunk of shit, rotted food and body odor. The one room domicile had been stripped; my library, grangerized, shredded like confetti. Not that I could read in my condition, the loss just added to the despair. Only those of us trapped in this nightmare can understand it. Even then, most succumb to the mindfuck to survive. Blank is less painful than thinking. A junkie going through withdrawal gets the misery level. A mother who had just lost one of her children understands the level of despair. Those of us who have failed, glom the personal implications of our actions.

There had been no communication since the smack behind the knees, no medical assistance. Food, water and a hole to shit in. That is, when you had the presence of mind to know what 'in' means and the ability to do it. I am not allowed to forget what 'all over the place means'. Each day's meal, a bowl of gruel and water, brought hope as a steel hatch was opened and tray shoved through. The small room was half full of trays. Time had become pointless, as had existence.

But they watch: waiting for me to cave, to break me, to give up and no longer be willing to endure. The wounds healed. That which didn't repair itself well, repaired itself poorly. The misery that had become my existence was endurable. Though how or why I could not tell you. Able to move now, I exercised as much as the meager food would allow and tried to clean the room. Wiping trays and bowls, stacking them to make more room. The stupid routines brought some sense into the madness that was settling in. With no books and my mind slipping away, I began meditating. How long this went on is anybody's guess. But one day the door opened. The big door meant for people swung wide, blinding light stabbing in before the glare was replaced with a silent silhouette.

"Hey, Johnny, long time no see."

"Yeah well. Come on, let us get you into a shower."

The shower was long and hot. As the steam lifted, mirrors revealed the lasting memory of that night. The scarring would be a constant reminder of what I was.

"Clean feels good," I said, making an attempt at levity.

"Smells a lot better, too," Johnny said, wrinkling his nose. He withdrew a kit containing my hypo and meds. After the procedure, "Come on, time for some food." He broke into a cynical laugh.

It was three in the morning, in between shifts, when we were allowed into the mess. Johnny sat me at a table with some coffee then disappeared into the stainless steel maze of a kitchen. I could hear him joking with the early cooks and preppers. There was something in his personality that let him transcend the boundaries that separate us from them. A something sadly lacking in me.

There were two other reuseables in the galley. They sat alone, talked to no one, looked at nothing. Their self-imposed solitude somehow buoyed me up. They had nothing, having given it all up in order to survive. Something I had not yet done. I felt sorry for them and sorrier for myself.

"Don't take it too hard, Jake. They had their chance, too."

"Chance to what?" I said bitterly.

"To keep control of their lives."

"You call this living?"

"Beats that." He chinned over at the two. Then served breakfast.

***

After breakfast came the briefing room. I was diving today. A twin screw ocean–going tug chewed into the breakwater when coming into port. Both propellers needed to be removed. The once smooth surfaces and tapered tips were now torn, shredded and gnarly. Nothing a little explosive wouldn't cure.

The cold water seeped into the suit. It had been too long, too dark a time since being in the water. It felt good. Taking several hours of 'bust butt' to remove the dunce caps and loosen the boss nuts, I called topside. It was deadsville. There are usually a handful of people around interested in what was going on. I climbed out of the water. A laborer lounged in the seat at the comm box. Johnny was gone. With helmet removed I walked quietly up to the chair, giving it a good kick.

"Hey, shit for brains, where is my tender?" The chair didn't fall over, but jarred awake the spaz and sent him sprawling onto the deck.

Coming to his feet with a chip on his shoulder and an attitude that you just wanted to poke in the eye with a stick, "They flew him out a couple a hours ago. You weren't around."

"I'm the diver, brains. Why wasn't I called?"

"Guess it wasn't none of your business," blurted the bad attitude.

"What do you want anyway?"

"I wanted my tender. When the radio wasn't answered... " He had stopped listening. It was then I noticed the radio was turned off. "It works better when you turn it on."

"Can't handle all that static, man." I looked at him coldly. "Hey man, I was doing my job."

"What's that, breathing?"

He choked. "I was told to watch this stuff. They didn't say nothin' about babysittin' one of you."

So that's how it was going to be. I took a moment to breathe deeply,

collect my self and my composure. Shit! It would be useless to activate
the chain of command to find out what had happened. Shit happened.
I had a job to do. With resources just cut to myself and a dumbass, there
was still a chance to complete the project. If they wanted me to stop,
they would have told me. I had to capture the kid's attention. Having
already blown it with my clever introduction, an option was available.

"Hey kid, you ever work with explosives?"

He looked me over with a scowl, shaking his head no.

"You want to?" I said being as charming as possible. It looked like he
was going to pee his pants or start jumping up and down, before the
hillbilly machismo put the clamps on. I could hear his gears grinding as
he shifted into something stupid to say.

Instead he sputtered, "Uh, yeah, sure." Wait a second here it comes. "I
know a lot about this stuff. We used to make bombs as kids." Ahhhh!
There it is. A pyrotechnic genius whose only fault was age. It was a stake
in my heart. The remainder of the afternoon was beginning to look
bleak.

"Yeah, this will be just like that. Except this time we go home with
all our fingers." The kid shifted a little uneasy, shoving his hands in
his pockets with an 'I didn't do nothin' look on his face. The next few
minutes were a crash course in why things go bang. He needed to know
why his job was to do absolutely nothing, something I thought he had
quite the aptitude for. Unfortunately for me he was as dumb as he
looked.

Dive gear on, I hit the water with a spool of detonating cord. After a
few turns of det cord around the hub and swimming back to the ladder,
he lowered the blasting cap, trailing out the two little wires that mean
so much.

His job was to hold the ends of the wire between his thumb and
forefinger of each hand, to keep the ends separated. After attaching the
cap to the det cord, I was on deck again, drying my hands. A fine bead
of sweat had formed on the kid's forehead. He thought the wires were
going to blow sky high, wanting nothing better than to let go. Lucky for
me he was too scared.

After calling the Chief Engineer of the tug to notify him we were
ready to blow the first wheel, and checking my watch, I rolled a cigarette.
Five minutes. They were big propellers. At fifteen feet in diameter it was
going to take a hell of a shock to knock one loose. At four minutes, I
pulled the small electronic detonating device from my dive bag, took
one end of the wire from his hand and shoved it into its designated

hole. "You ready?" Taking the second wire from him, I began inserting it. Relieved of his responsibility, his eagerness and stupidity returned.

"Can, can I do it?" he asked.

"Yeah sure, kid," handing him the black box with the cool toggle switch. "Just don't touch that till I tell you."

I had him. Given a few days with numb nuts, I could start to turn him into something. "Five, four, three, two, one – hit it!"

"Now?"

"Yeah, now." I started laughing, remembering my first time.

Kaboooooom. The explosion sent a shower of water erupting from the stern of the tug high into the air. All two hundred feet of her rocked from stem to stern. The kid's eyes got huge at the noise and visual. Followed by a shit-eating grin on his face. At least I had made somebody's day.

Disconnecting from the black box and pulling the thin copper wires out, I was back in the water, wrapping the second propeller. Back at the ladder again, I half expected to see the kid's grinning maw sticking out from above. Instead he was doing his job, the blasting cap dangled within reach and peeled off the spool clean, as I was swimming back to affix it to the det cord. Taping the cap to the wires raised the hair on my neck.

Calling into comms, "Hey kid, you there? Come on, man, pick up." I waited too long for a reply. I could almost feel the electricity racing down the wires. A pair of cutters almost did their job in time. The second explosion ended the day. The concussion ruptured my eardrums and shredded my lungs.

I woke in a hospital that services only our kind. How long had I been there was anybody's guess. There was not a whole lot of conversation. Answers to questions were even more rare. I used to be able to get a guesstimate of time's passage by checking when last I logged onto a computer. It no longer mattered. The less you cared, the easier it was to keep on breathing. I was way past not giving a shit anymore about anything by the time Johnny showed up again. It may have been months, even years, since his disappearance from the dive station. Like everything else, I could care fucking less. My hair was long; the dive gear, however, kept the beard cropped close, it being the last vestige of any vanity. That and the Aloha shirts I had become accustomed to wearing. The surprise on people's faces having to confront a wolf in sheep's clothing was something I had grown to enjoy. Happiness, face planting into fear, I loved it. To me they were sheep, just not on the list to be slaughtered, yet. And they saw their lives pass before their eyes, before their time. The smell of shit accompanied many encounters. Walking death has a way of loosening men's bowels.

The last incident did more than ruin my lungs. It tore my heart out. I consumed the cruelty that was given me and became it in return. Wherever I was sent to work, the reputation I developed always preceded my arrival. Not only was I despised, as we all are -- I was feared as well. It served me. Even the other reuseables would not tolerate my presence, which always gave me private quarters and beat the dorm with a bunch of dead heads.

Back on board, the name of the ship eluding me now, I went to use the shared bath in the middle of the night. When I opened the door, the bright light above the sink knocked me back, but not before seeing Johnny, sitting on the toilet, shooting up something.

"Sorry, man," I said closing the door. I had forgotten it was a shared bath that nobody had ever shared before. Waiting impatiently until I heard the other door open and close, imagine my surprise to see a loaded syringe sitting on a clean towel next to the sink. I availed myself of the house's hospitality, returning to my room to lie down and soak it up. Some time later, there was a light knock on the bathroom door.

"It's open."

"Eh, ça va, Jake?"

"Ahh, you know."

"Yeah, just a little bright spot in everyone's life."

"Something like that. Thanks for leaving me with a dumbass kid who couldn't concentrate long enough to do his job," I mumbled.

"Shit happens, Jake. That dumbass kid, by the way, gave his life trying to save yours. You must have touched him with your charm," came the sardonic sarcasm.

"Say what?" The dope kept me lying down. Johnny is always one step ahead on these things.

"He was just dumb enough to do what he was told. When Megacorp showed up, well, he got his head smashed in trying to buck the system."

"I was never told." I hung my head in shame. Not for what I had said about the kid, for I said nothing. But for what I let the thoughts do to me. The betrayal and anger was meted out on the job site, against innocents, far removed from the original incident.

"And you never will be. It would also be wise to keep this information to yourself. You start going after the perps in your own inimitable fashion, you can kiss your ass goodbye."

"So there is an out to this?" I indicated my current situation.

"There is always an out. The question is – is it really an option?" The interrogatory came with an impenetrable glare. I didn't have an answer.

"So, what brings you back? Just slumming, or you got something to smuggle in?"

"Actually, smuggling out was more what I had in mind."

The next twenty-four hours were spent in the drone of a military aircraft. The uninsulated cargo jet sent a hum through your body until every cell was vibrating, like sitting in a hall of chanting monks. Talk was minimal, as you had to yell over the engine noise. All I knew was we were traveling to warmer climes.

Johnny had packed my gear prior to our little party. We left shortly after the rush had passed, hopping a chopper to the nearest air base to catch the waiting plane. Ignorance of the job was bliss, along with whatever was in the injection. It lightened the long black night that my life had become, canceling my self-recriminations and dissipating the anger. By the time we landed on Oahu, my mood matched my shirt, sort of. The Megacorp van brought us to Pearl Harbor and the Salvor. For me, this was where it all began. The hair went up on the back of my neck, and then went down, something in the meds I figured.

Looking at the old salvage vessel, I realized for the first time she was old and I was not.

"How long has it been, Johnny? Since we first met. Quit paying attention after a while."

"More than sixty years, Jake. Time flies when you are having fun. Eh? "Fuck me!"

"That you were my man, that you were. Not much has changed."

"Yeah. The military really keeps up with the times."

"No doubt there. Cutting edge stupidity. You remember the First, Mouse? I think you will get along."

"That would be a first."

"Touché, Jake."

A short wiry blonde haired guy in a dirty officer's jumpsuit was coming down the gangway to meet us. He stretched out his hand to shake with Johnny.

"Good to have you back John." They shook and smiled, something I had never seen before in a 'them' and 'us' situation. Whoever it was, could cross the bounds between civilian and military, us and them, casually, and still maintain control.

Mouse stretched his hand to Jake. Grease packed the fingernails as calloused hands came together. "It's good to see you, too, Jake. You have quite a rep aboard the Salvor."

"Kind of goes with the territory, Chief," Jake retorted. He stared at the Chief. It looked like the man he knew, but there was a difference. Jake felt outwards with his darker nature to see if this 'Mouse' had been infected like himself. No, the man before him was as human as it gets, but it wasn't the Chief he remembered.

"Call me Mouse. That's what you used to call my dad."

"Yeah, I bet. Wait a minute! You mean your dad was Mouse?"

"He passed away a few years ago. He would be glad you remembered. I followed in his footsteps. When the old man wrote his memoirs he devoted a couple chapters to you. It was never published, but I read it. It is how I know you."

It's good to meet you again too, Chief... uh Mouse." I was being careful. I didn't want to blow it right from the start. When you are an asshole from the beginning, it is easier to control the way things go, but it creates a deep hole that's a bitch to get out of. Johnny had dropped the hint. I could always be an asshole. Here was an opportunity not to be one, so I did my best at being polite. Besides I still had that feeling that this man was meant for something other than running a boat.

"She looks good," I said admiring the ship. "Is Tony, from the Black Gang still around?"

"He retired."

"Tony was aw'ight. We had some interesting times."

"So I've heard. He never missed a chance to tell some of the stories. There are a few on board that have heard other stories, more recent ones. They resent your arrival, so all the rules apply. It would be best not to push it for a while. Good to have you back, Jake." Mouse turned and left. The life of a Chief is busy, eternally.

Johnny looked at me and swiped his nose. Mouse's last words were not to be taken lightly. We lifted our bags and slipped aboard trying to be invisible as we snaked the hallways to the dead-end that were our rooms. The vibes from the crewmembers that we did see were heavy with dread, making the air thick. Only after opening a porthole to get the seas breeze blowing in, could I get my brain to work again. It was the rebound of some of the Pavlovian training. When I would see people, outside of the work environment, my mind would shut down, becoming harmless. Then it would pass until the next chance meeting. You get beaten enough a trained response will develop.

"We are going to have to work on that." Johnny said, coming through the bathroom with a stainless tray in hand, reading my mind.

Morning came with a mild side to side rocking motion and the hum of the engines. We were underway. A look out the porthole put us heading northwest. Johnny had disappeared back through the bathroom door with his tray of goodies. I nodded gazing out at the circular view, cigarette smoke winding its way to the portal and wisping out. The motion and salt breeze felt good against my skin. It had been a long time since being out at sea. Most of my work lately had been in harbors, power plants or offshore oil rigs. It was all diving, but there is a difference.

The vast emptiness of the open ocean was but a reflection of my vacuous soul. For ages it seemed I had survived on the suffering of men. For me it was a razor sharp double-edged sword cutting deeply both ways, but never severing. No matter how hard I tried to separate the connection between them and me, a 'we' always remained. Whatever it was I had become, there was still a bond with what I had been. Human. Nor could the maltreatment by Megacorp rend one from the other. And they tried hard. In the end, what they got was a socio/psychopath that would work himself to death and god help anyone who got in the way. They got what they wanted. Did I get what I wanted? No. I wanted death. And no matter how many times I died, by my own hand, by Megacorps, or by the job, death would not come. Each time you'd hope it to be the last, but knew it wouldn't be.

Waking was like coming to from an alcoholic blackout. You felt like shit with an attitude to match. You knew you had done something awful but couldn't quite remember and no one would tell you. Ashamed, you masked it with negativity and a healthy smear of the attitude, a shadow in the brightest sunlight. A darkness men recoiled from like the cold. A civilized society would not tolerate my presence/our presence. So we were kept away from them for the most part, tolerated on the jobsite, just barely, and shunned by society as a whole. We were only allowed in when there was a sizeable, losable bankroll in hand. And kicked out when the roll was diminished.

Too many years had passed since the eyes and hands of warm friendship had been beheld. The few days with Kale and his kids were my most precious secret. What he may have tried to teach me had been lost in the rigors of hell and the profit margin. The seed he planted had fallen on fallow ground. Yet it was still there, waiting for a chance. A snowball's chance in hell that is.

***

The Salvor's first port of call was Midway Island. It was still a military outpost even though technology had made it somewhat obsolete. A little speck in the middle of the ocean that would wither away if the ships ever stopped coming. That is after a round of starvation and rat dinners, ending with a taste of human flesh when push comes to shove. The day was spent offloading food and supplies of canned goods, beer and fuel. Forklifts shuttled out of Times Square with military precision, under the watchful eyes of armed guards. They were not so concerned about what left the ship so much as making sure nothing boarded the vessel. Stowaways were as unwelcome now as they had been hundreds of years ago. The ways of dealing with them hadn't changed either. If the boat was still in sight of land when the hitchhiker was found the captive got a chance to test their swimming skills. If you were out to sea, it was handled slightly differently. The free loader was either put to work or, failing in that, there was always swimming. Of course if you were female there were perhaps other options. With a crew of three hundred, most women opted for a swim. The chances were slim, for anyone. It didn't stop them from trying.

As the sun slipped over the horizon, floodlights came on, the work continued. Johnny knocked and came into the room. "Evening, Jake, looks like you need something to do."

"Yeah, a little bit of cabin fever." I mumbled.

"Mouse will take care of that. The offloading crews are slow. We are going to be here another few days."

"These four walls still aren't getting any bigger."

"Yeah well, he is going to call in about an hour. Wants to clean the condenser while we are stuck here."

I perked up. Anything to get wet generally captured my interest. There was a look on Johnny's face. I had seen it before. "What's the catch?"

"Sharp as a tack tonight, Jake." He laughed a little under his breath. "In a break from the norm we are not going to take any lives. Instead we will try and save one."

There was a camel floating next to the Salvor at the stern on the inboard side. We would use this floating work platform as the dive station. Because of its location, under the raised dock, the camel was hard to see which was part of the reasoning behind using it. It would also be shaded during the day. Johnny always tried to make things as comfortable as the situation would allow.

The condenser is that part of the engine that pulls in cold seawater to help keep the engines cool. It is kind of like a radiator on a car where the air cools down the radiator fluid. Only on a ship, they use the cool seawater to chill the fluid. Any time you have seawater flowing through pipes, marine growth, barnacles and vegetative, clog the passages reducing efficiency. My job was to patch the openings where the seawater comes in so that the condenser could be dismantled, cleaned and put back into working order in the dry. After which the patches are removed. There weren't too many of us left who still knew how to do it in the wet.

Modern propulsion systems are less susceptible to this type of problem. The Salvor was old, but when it came to sheer power she was the strongest in the fleet. For this reason she was never retrofitted with pivoting nacelles. Whatever it was we were really doing out here in the middle of the ocean, besides not deadheading, would not require the incredible horsepower, just a wooden camel moored alongside. The first swim by of the ship was to verify the locations and sizes of the sea chests to be sealed off, to make sure we had all the right stuff. We did. My dive bags were crammed full of everything we could possibly need. Most of it completely unnecessary, but only we knew that.

By dawn I was installing the first patch. A straightforward, bolt–on affair, that squished the gaskets tight against the hull. The next two went smoothly as well. The patch over the scoop injection was payback. Big and heavy the patch had a tendency to do everything you didn't want it to. Using a dozen five gallon buckets upside down, filled with air proved to be the trick to holding it in place. Watching the sheet of aluminum plating that was the patch, I gave the word to go ahead and open the condenser, never taking my eyes off of it.

Inside the ship the black gang was opening a four-inch valve to bleed off the water. This caused all the patches to suck tight against the ship. I just had to make sure the scoop patch didn't shift while this was happening. If it did, the Salvor would be sitting on the bottom in a matter of minutes. After a final inspection of all patches, satisfied they would hold, I returned to the camel for a cup of coffee, a cigarette and the future.

Johnny was there, giving me a hand out of the water and out of my gear. A towel was stuffed in my face, followed by a cigarette. The first smoke after getting out of the water is always the best. I enjoyed it, staring at the side of the Salvor, still amazed after all these years that steel could float. Turning away brought my vision to a cup of coffee and the point of the exercise. Amidst all the gear dumped from my bags sat a shivering, smallish bundle of black hair wrapped in a fleece blanket. I looked quickly to Johnny and back again, trying to shake off the fear that rose from my stomach along with the coffee I had just downed. Lunging for the edge of the camel and leaning against a piling I puked a cold sweat. Little fish gathered to eat the bits of my last meal. Their frenzy matched the mental torment I was suddenly caught up in. I had no idea what was going on but knew how I would pay for it if we were caught.

Johnny came up behind me, palming a pill into my hand. After swallowing it and chasing the bitter flavor with the remainder of my coffee, I wiped my mug and turned to face my phobias.

We walked over to the shivering bundle. "Jake, Quan Yin. Quan Yin, Jake." A pair of black eyes emerged from the blanket, locked on mine. Her head bowed in salutation. Unsure of what to do I mimicked her motion. The introduction complete, her eyes however, examined me from head to toe. "She is the reason I had you flown in."

My eyes were spitting question marks while I poured another cup. Johnny refilled Quan Yin's cup. Pruney, waterlogged hands took it from him. Her eyes however were still on me.

"You are a little behind the curve on this one, Jake..." Johnny began.

"That's an understatement."

"Yeah well."

"I know, a minimum of advance notice and a maximum of discretion. Yeah, yeah, yeah."

"Sorry. Quan is a molecular biologist. She made some recent discoveries using deep water coral brought up by a trawler."

"How long has she been in the water?" Her shivering wasn't getting any better.

"A couple days, waiting under here."

"We need to rinse her off, get the salt water off or she'll never get warm."

Johnny went over to Quan Yin and began speaking in French. When he helped her to her feet, I turned away. She was quite the smallest adult I had ever seen. Quan was also embarrassed about stripping in front of me. I sat down on the edge of the camel, hanging my feet in the water, realizing I still had not been told anything. The water hose shut off. A minute later Johnny sat down next to me.

"So, I guess you are still wondering what this is all about?"

"Maybe just a little," was my snide reply.

"Megacorp wants her, to do the unspeakable, then use her brain. But it does not work like that and we would just lose her in the damnable process. Her work in developing new antibiotics would be lost at the moment of a breakthrough."

"The coral?"

"Yeah. The shallow water species are dying out too rapidly to be considered viable. The deep water reefs, somewhat of a mystery in themselves, still thrive. This is why the Salvor is here. Megacorp coupled a maintenance run with a shipment to here, and then we are off to get some coral. They know Quan dropped from sight, yet are confident she will surface. All vessels in the area are being thoroughly searched, that is with the exception of Navy boats."

"And that's where we come in. What am I going to do, stuff her in a gear bag?"

Johnny smiled his beguiler and lit two cigarettes. Handing one to me, "Yeah."

We were on stand-by for the duration of the condenser cleaning. When a ship is kept floating by patches, a diver is always suited, ready to go in should something go wrong. Food was lowered down to us, along with coffee and drinking water. Quan ate ravenously, everything but the meat, which left something for Johnny and I. The day waxed. Little waves slapped against the camel with unending regularity while Johnny and Quan conversed quietly in French. I sat on the diver's stool waiting for a call that never came.

Twenty-four hours later, the radio squawked. The black gang was finished and the patches could be removed. This proved as uneventful as the installation. Like most diving, overcoming the long hours of boredom was the biggest challenge. The water hit with a cold slap in the face breaking me from the ennui. It's not over till it's over and we were just beginning. A small crane raised the patches from the camel to the deck of the Salvor while Johnny and I broke down the dive station. Most of the extra equipment we had brought with us to make the bags bulky was dumped into the water beneath the dock. Quan Yin was warm and fed. A weak smile crossed her face at me as she folded herself into the largest of the bags. We piled the wet dive gear on top of her. Johnny gave her words of encouragement as he zipped the bag closed.

The crane wire lowered again. We hoisted the bag onto my shoulders. Once the load was secure I stepped one foot into the hook and held on with a free hand as the wire rose to the deck, ready to kill the first person that approached me. Once aboard, I kept my eyes down, heading for my berth.

"Hey Jake, hold on there!" It was Mouse. I turned on him, my free hand clutching a spud wrench. "Good job you did down there. Keeps us on schedule."

"That's why you flew my smiling ass in here." I deadpanned, not flattered in the least, with a death warrant on my shoulder and murder on my mind. "You mind if I go rinse off before we get all warm and fuzzy?"

"Uh, yeah, sure. Be in my office in an hour." His bubble burst, Mouse skulked away, not knowing how lucky he was.

The hallway was narrow. Not bouncing the package off the walls was next to impossible. Once in my room I set the bag on the bed and locked the door from the inside before opening it. Quan Yin popped out of the bag like a Jack in the box, her face red and breathing heavily. There was not a whole lot of free air in the confines of my dive bag. I got her a glass of water and hit the shower. By the time I got out Johnny had returned and the boat was rocking her way out of the harbor.

She sat with her face in the porthole, sucking in the cool night air. I dressed getting ready to head to Mouse's office. Quan Yin looked over at me, eyes wide as she focused on the scars that cover me. "Merci, Jake." She said quietly.

"Save it, honey, this isn't over yet." I smiled and left her with Johnny.

Mouse's door was ajar. I tapped, pulling it open, and looked into the empty office. Several huge stacks of paper were mounded on the desk. One of the piles wobbled, sliding onto the floor revealing Mouse hunched at his desk. "Goddamn it."

"I'll get it, Chief." I said, bending to gather the splayed paper into a stack again.

"I'm not the Chief, thanks just the same."

The guy bowled me over with a few simple words. Kindness, common civility was foreign to me. My first reaction was to be a smart ass, something that I just couldn't help. It never served very well either. I sat in a file–covered chair, dumb for a moment. What do you say when someone says thank you?

"You're welcome, Chief. What did you want to see me about?" I started to sweat it out. Remembering what Johnny had said, 'just be cool man, nobody knows nothing', I tried to play it casual, rolling a cigarette and lighting up.

"Your reputation doesn't do you justice. I was expecting some sort of nutcase you had to keep chained down."

"They do and don't put yours away yet."

"So I've heard. Let's hope it never comes to that." He said it like he meant it. "Tomorrow we will be in the Laysan Islands. A few hundred years ago it was designated a sanctuary. Now it is one of the few places commercial fisherman can bring in a good catch. With the net boats came trawlers dragging the bottom, ripping everything up. We need to get some coral samples before they are gone. Some scientist got a hit testing for pharmaceutical properties."

"And Megacorp doesn't want to pay an exorbitant finders fee..." I said sardonically.

"Or have anyone else produce it." Mouse finished.

"What does this have to do with me, other than I'm gonna bust off some coral heads for you."

"Just wanted to let you know you will be working tomorrow."

"Thanks for the heads up. Can I go now?"

"Sure. I understand conversations can make you a little uneasy."

"Just a little." I said, shaking it off and giving Mouse the chin before heading out the door. Mouse was fishing. He wasn't catching.

***

Deep in the ocean, sinking in a freefall, twenty pounds of extra lead speeding me to the goal, the bottom. At 1000 feet a strong current began pushing me sideways, still falling but now heading north and out to sea. The heads up display began winking when I was 100 feet from the bottom. I flared out to slow the descent but didn't dump the lead. If I had, the current would have swept me away. There is no fighting the ocean currents, just kissing your ass goodbye. Hitting the bottom hard, I tumbled along with the current until the lead weight dragging behind dug enough sand to stop. All around was black. The dive lights, though powerful, were not near enough to keep the darkness in check, a darkness that seemed to enter my very being.

The GPS indicated I was 250 yards off the mark, making it a long crawl against the current to the first outcropping of coral. Staying close to the sand to keep from being swept away by the current, progress was slow. When I got to the location there was nothing there but rubble. A trawler had been through recently destroying everything in its path. The next spot was the same. Just a few fish swimming around wondering where their paradise went. On the way to the third location, a cross current caught me off guard, sending me sailing across the plains of an underwater desert. The third location passed beneath me. There was no use fighting the water to get there, it too, had been wasted.

The fast moving water would bring me close to the final coral heads. Angling down the coral came into view at the last possible moment. I dropped the lead weight on a rope, snagging it amongst the coral and jerking me to a stop. There they were: smallish red coral heads and fan corals, creating a microenvironment, rife with sea life, an oasis in the heart of the desert.

I went to work chipping away at the coral heads, filling my ditty bag with as many fist sized balls as it would hold. Then, the strangest thing happened. A Hawaiian monk seal began vying for the same spot of ocean I was in. At first it was a nuisance, almost comical. That is until she tried to bite a chunk out of my ass. It hurt and I had had enough. The horseplay began to get frantic and rough. At one point she bit my arm and wouldn't let go. She swam hard, moving me from the outcropping. The more I struggled, the harder she bit and pulled. Suddenly the seafloor started shaking. What little visibility there was, was gone in an instant as the shaking and grinding came to a fevered pitch. Scraping along the seafloor was a trawler net, scooping up me and the seal into its one-way maw. Pulled into the swirling ball of trapped fish I fought to survive, from being battered to death by the stampeding herd. I clung to the belly of the net to avoid the onslaught.

Eventually the crew of the trawler began to reel in the net. The deadly ball of fish and seals pressed hard against me into the trailing end, crushing me with their combined weight, beating me almost to death in their struggle to survive. When the net surfaced behind the ship the fish went total frenzy. I had to escape, or die. Pulling a pair of side cutters I began to cut like mad, matching the insanity that swirled death so close. Clubbed by fish heads and tails slowed the work. Two more strands and I would be free. I wriggled through the opening, pausing long enough to watch the madness instead of being part of it. The seal that had tried to warn me stuck her head through the hole. It was too small.

The image of a small Chinese woman came to the surface of my mind. She was sitting peacefully and raised her right hand making scissor motions with her first two fingers. Then she faded back out again. In front of me were the big black eyes of a seal desperate for a breath. Free of the crowding, I attacked the net with all I had. The monofilament and stainless steel braid netting resisted, then parted under the cutting edge. The split opened up. The fish and seals began pouring out in a solid stream until the once full net hung limp. Feeling uplifted by my humanitarian effort, there was one more job to do. I grabbed a piece of the trailing end of the net, swimming just beneath the surface toward the trawler. The ship was idling, the propeller in jacking gear. In direct contrast to what I normally do, I fouled the propeller with the net. When they put it in gear, the net would ball up around the wheel. Swimming out from under the ship at the stern, I surfaced. There was the crew screaming and yelling at the lost catch. When they saw me it was all fingers and vehemence. I returned the single digit salute and began swimming on my back away from the ship. The Captain, or someone in charge, decided to run me over. They shifted into reverse and put the guns to it. As the ship charged backwards it caused me to reconsider the plan, albeit a little late. The stern grew huge, towering above me as the propeller chewed its way right at me. I dove straight down. Swimming with all I had to get below the meat grinder. Not fast enough! The whirling screw blades were sucking me into it!

With a groan the propeller came up tight to the net, knotting the prop to a dead stop, twisting the shaft in the process. There was no time to think. I headed down, away from the ship and into the current. Neutrally buoyant I let the stream of water carry me away. Surfacing miles from the incident and activating the homing beacon, I watched a group of monk seals swimming around me. Several dove from sight, returning a half hour later with a mesh bag full of coral. In all the excitement I had lost the bag of coral hanging from my waist. They stuffed it in my chest, keeping it there until I had a hold. The group of monk seals disappeared. I never saw them again.

Floating in the open sea, I half expected an epiphany of some sort after the encounter. It was not to be. Stranger things, by far, have happened in the oceans. The wheel was turning and for the moment I was one step ahead. One thing I knew was that there were more deep sea coral formations. And I knew how to get them.

The Salvor showed a few hours later, lowering a basket for me to climb into. Once on deck, the mesh bag went into a pail of deep seawater.

"You were out there a long time, Jake, thought we lost you," began Mouse.

"Just a little more to it than a grab and go." I replied. "The currents kept it interesting."

"So I've heard. A trawler east of here got themselves in a hell of a mess. Not life threatening so it was none of our business. You wouldn't know anything about that would you?" Mouse inquired.

"Me, Chief? Naw, I had my hands full of monk seals. Pesky fuckers, bite hard too. Listen, can we continue this later, I gotta shower."

"Nice haul, Jake. The scientists at the Megacorp lab will be pleased."

"Well, make my fucking day," I snided, heading for a bath.

Quan Yin was still sitting at the porthole, bowing her head slightly as I entered. I tossed her the smuggled coral head on the way to the bathroom. A small smile crossed her face. Johnny had still not returned by the time I was clean. Not being able to speak French or Chinese certainly curtailed our ability to communicate. After making a pot of coffee, I sat down, looking at her. After a time had passed which had not been uncomfortable I said, "I got your message," raising my right hand and making a scissors motion.

She smiled, nodding humbly. "Bien," she said. Her voice was soft and disarming, as if it came from a place of peace deep inside her self. A peace I would never know. Nevertheless, that one word let me bask in the glow of it. I wanted to become it, swallow it whole and have it become me. The door opened, breaking me from the reverie.

"Ça va, Jake? That trawler company is really pissed. Apparently one of the monk seals surfaced behind the ship and gave the finger to the crew."

"Wouldn't surprise me. They are killing them by the hundreds."

"Yeah. The species rebounded once they turned the whole area into a sanctuary at the turn of the millennium. It rekindled a once thriving ecosystem. Of course things change and when Megacorp acquired the sanctuary it was only a matter of time until they found a way to turn a profit. The eco-tourism thing worked for a while, but virtual everything kind of killed that industry, sooo... I see you brought Quan a sample."

"Yeah, strangest thing, man. The trawler is destroying their habitat, but way out here where you picked me up are more deep-water reefs. The monk seals followed me here, dove down and brought up that piece."

Quan Yin smiled again, got up and put the coral in the freezer.

"I think we may want to keep that information between us. If the research is positive, Megacorp will want all they can get and wipe out the supply. So if we have a stash..."

"Who is this 'we' to whom you refer?"

"Right now, the three of us. Later, we will see." Johnny saw the look of confusion on my face. "You were thinking maybe more?"

"Just a few. Got a joint, Johnny?"

After we got high and I came down from the dive, questions began to surface in my mind, reality insinuating itself into my buzz.

"Now that the fun and games are over, what are we going to do?" I inquired.

"About what?"

"Come on, Johnny, don't make me pull teeth here. My anxiety level is tweaked to the max."

"Aw'ight. Just fucking with your head. Good question though." Johnny poured a cup of coffee, offering Quan some. She declined but got up to make some tea in Johnny's room.

"So what's her story?"

"Quan was a big dog in Megacorp's biomed research facility. Long story short, she made some discoveries and Megacorp stepped in and canned the whole project. Proprietary rights and all that bullshit. She put up a good fight, called in Kale and his team of lawyers. They ripped Megacorp a new asshole but the corporation had it in the small print. So she split and started doing research on her own."

"And now she's a fugitive?"

"Technically, no. Practically, yes. They want her back."

"She don't want to go, I can dig that."

"Good, because there is a little more I would like you to do."

The 'little more' sounded like a lot more to me. "Why don't you call in your friend Pablo? Isn't he the man who likes to do this kind of stuff?"

"I don't like to use him for human packages. They have a way of dying before they get to the drop. But if he finds out what we are up to, however, both of us will have fresh smiley faces on our chests."

"This just gets better and better. How do you know Kale?"

"He defends us and helps to write the contracts. He used to be with Megacorp, but was clever in writing his own contract. Megacorp has to abide by the laws, too. Why do you think you got off so easy?"

"Easy! Fuck you man."

"You are still breathing, eh? Nice bike collection he has. I recognized the old R/60. It just went through a major overhaul by the way, so it will be ready when we get there."

Johnny was skipping ahead, smiling wryly as I struggled to catch up.

"Kale reworked your contract. You have a month off when we return to Honolulu."

"But what do we do with...?" I poked my thumb in the direction of Johnny's room.

"When we get into port she comes off the same way we got her on. Then into a cab and she is off your hands until you arrive in San Francisco."

"I had a feeling a month off was too good to be true. So what happens in S.F.?"

"You are going to take that motorcycle and ride across the country. It's about the best cover I could come up with, a husband and wife riding, touring the good old U.S.A."

"Say what! No way, man."

"Yes way. What could be better? You are all covered from head to toe, the perfect disguise."

"Someone with more experience maybe?"

"You rode that machine from Battle Mountain, beaten within an inch of your life, and the weather was the shits. I think you have enough experience."

"Quan will need some gear," I said accepting the challenge.

"Kale is taking care of it."

"I still can't believe you know him and that he is somebody."

"It is a small world, Jake. Especially when it comes to 'us'."

***

Fog smothered San Francisco like a grey wet blanket. The streets were cold and wet. The locals, layered in black, were as impenetrable as the sky, cups of steaming coffee held beneath their noses as they hustled from wherever they were to wherever they were going. Cabs, mopeds, bicycles and delivery trucks vied for space on the overcrowded streets. It was a madness of traffic that had been the lifeblood of the city for hundreds of years. A yelp, as a bike messenger T-bones a cab, sending him flying across the triple-parked cars, lost in the fog for a moment before crashing into the pavement. Back on his feet, he runs to tend his bike for a few seconds, then gone, racing away into the madness.

Since arriving all I had done was try and eat my way to heaven. It was not to be, but was worth the try. The city had always been accepting of those of a different nature. No one seemed to care. An island of compassion in a sea of hatred. That is, as long as you had money. I had enough. This morning I was outside my hotel having a cigarette and coffee, waiting for someone to pick me up. So it was with some surprise I saw the old BMW roll up. The rider was a punk kid in day-glo leathers. A Jap bike, all loud exhaust and flash of colors, came up next to the parked bike. The leather punk looked around and made eye contact. A glint of silver flew through the air. I caught the key ring on the fly.

By the time I looked back to the bikes the Jap bike was screaming away with two riders, and there was the Beemer. Saddlebags had been put on along with a windshield. Otherwise, she was pretty bare bones.

Opening the saddlebags revealed a black leather one-piece riding suit, gloves, boots and a helmet. Tipping the doorman to watch the bike, I returned to my room to change. The fit was good, creating the illusion of protection. It was a mental edge against the odds. Just what were the odds? And what the fuck was I doing here? One thing I came away with in the encounter with the seals was I had a choice. I could have let the trawler haul in their catch, much of which would have been tossed back into the sea, dead. I chose to cut the net. That one little act opened up a veritable Pandora's box that would not be shut. Although unsure of what I was about, I was here by choice. And that was all that mattered.

The world I lived in was that of total control. There was no real freedom, unless you consider an orgy in virtual reality freedom. And there never would be. The drugs in our weekly cocktail kept the chains firmly in place. I was learning now that there was still room to maneuver within the confines of Megacorp's iron grip. Just enough room to get yourself killed, if you weren't careful.

There were handwritten directions stuffed into the helmet that would lead me to a house in Oakland. The bike started on the first try, and I shot into the insanity of the streets of San Francisco. The city was the capitol of cool California. They meditate for hours on end, listen to the discourses of the current Dalai Lama, find a oneness within themselves ... but put them behind the wheel of a car and look out, man!

Crossing the Bay Bridge left the chaos behind, shrouded in its cape of grey mist. I emerged from the Treasure Island tunnel into the famous California sunshine. The house was non-descript, on a block surrounded by others like it. It needed paint and a new roof. I pulled into the driveway, parking in back, off the street. The motorcycle key ring supplied a civil, quiet entry to the house. Inside were piles of motorcycle mags on top of everything. The living room was a mass of computers, files, and riding gear. There was no apparent order.

I made a pot of coffee, did the dishes, got high and nodded out, thumbing through the magazines.

A jingle of keys pulled me out of it. Moments later the front door opened, and in stepped Kale followed by Johnny and Quan.

"Glad to see you made it, Jake." Kale said.

"Likewise. Your directions were good."

Johnny came into the room with take out food in a bag. Quan took it from him and went into the kitchen. Kale sat at his computer, fingers flying over the keys.

"Looks like you'll have good weather. At least through Cali and Nevada. This time of year it can get a little dicey."

"Just get me out of this state. You people drive like nuts."

"Yeah," Kale replied smiling.

Quan carried a tray into the living room while Johnny hastily cleared a table. After a quiet escape into the flavors of Chinese, another pot of coffee was made. Kale went to his desk, coming back with a small stack of papers.

"Here is the route I would advise taking. It keeps you off the main highways. You will have to watch your gas. Sometimes it's a long ride in between stations."

"Just 'where' am I going?"

"East, to the little town of Red Oak in Iowa. There's a school there which is a cover for the lab."

"Long ways away from the ocean."

"Wait until you're out on the prairie. It's a different kind of ocean, a sea of grass," Kale added. I looked at him with a Huh? expression on my face. "When you see it, you'll get it."

"When do we leave?"

"In the morning. We'll pack up tonight."

Within the explosion of stuff in the house there was a method to the madness. Quan tried her riding gear on. The suit was a little oversized, as she was a bit undersized. It would work. Street clothes were minimal to make room for the extra cold weather clothing.

"Buy what you need on the road. I've inked a map of your route and made notes of establishments that are friendlies."

I noticed the ink stops in western Nebraska. "What about from there on?"

"You'll have to wing it. If you get caught we don't want the location discovered."

"What happens if we get caught?"

"Trust me, you do not want to go there, Jake," Johnny interjected.

I shook my head and rolled a cigarette. "Fuck me." I mumbled.

Quan came up from behind and put her hand on my drooping shoulders. Her touch pacified my anxiety. It was a calming effect I had never experienced before beyond the consumption of drugs. It had a centering effect, too, that kept me from freaking when five pounds of steel was dumped in my lap.

"What the fuck is this?" I said astonished at the black metal.

"Just in case," Johnny replied

"Just in case what?"

"Just in case you run into trouble. That, my friend," pointing at the weapon, "is a Heckler and Koch machine pistol. 1200 rounds per minute of 12-millimeter cop killers. With three 100 round clips. Give you a couple seconds of fire time. At best you kill them, at worst you just scared the shit out of whoever. This lever gives you single shot, three round burst, or full auto. Plant your feet and hold on tight. There is a pocket on the thigh of the riding suit to hold it."

The gun was heavy with a clip in it, but it felt good in the hand and was balanced comfortably. This however didn't help with the weight of responsibility that came with it.

"So this is how it is going to go then."

"We don't know. The ride should be uneventful, then again?" Kale shrugged his shoulders. "We have been lucky so far, let's hope it continues."

This last sentence was said in such a way as to imply it wasn't going to continue. Kale was leaving out part of the equation. Which part I didn't know but I had a feeling I would be finding out.

"You two better get some rest. Tomorrow comes early and you have a long day ahead of you."

***

The smell of French roasted coffee roused me from an intermittent sleep. Stumbling into the kitchen and grabbing a cup and a smoke, I stepped outside into the light before dawn for a little peace with my first cup. There sat the bike. Someone in the middle of the night had affixed a sheepskin cover to the seat.

"You won't appreciate it until you've been riding for 16 hours straight," Kale said quietly from the open kitchen window before disappearing, leaving me to my thoughts and coffee.

Quan Yin was a quiet person. It wasn't just the language barrier. She seemed to spend her time deep inside her self, yet was constantly aware of what was going on around her. Johnny explained, that like all of us, she had been compelled by Megacorp to act unscrupulously in the quest of profits. Though she was not a reuseable, Quan had been used like one. Megacorp took her shame as a lever to have her commit further atrocities, for which she had never forgiven herself. When Megacorp put a lid on the discovery, she snapped, went underground and was now a fugitive.

Antibiotics had long been a boost to modern medicine. In the last few hundred years however, the bugs and viruses had evolved to become increasingly resistant. The flesh eating strain of staph was one of the first to gain an infamous reputation. It evolved into a pandemic affecting the coastal regions. The staph thrives in the devastated coastal habitat. As a diver I was one of the few who were given the antibi that works. The rank and file was allowed to die. Quan's discovery kicked ass on all the bugs and would evolve along with them, retaining its efficacy, a boon for people suffering all over the planet. It was not to be. Megacorp had designs far into the future. It was thinking generations ahead. For the corporation, it would be best to let some peoples die out, become extinct. It was an unfortunate consequence of being alive at this time. There were always cultures that could conceivably get in the way. Some didn't spend enough, others didn't produce, a few always looked for a handout. Then there were those who just didn't want to play Megacorp's game. Wiping them out in this generation would pave the way for the next. To be able to do it without violence and its expense was the kicker. Save those few who could afford it and those who would increase dividends – fuck the rest of them.

That, in a nutshell was the way it worked, the dark side of the equation. There were a few of us nutcases that want to throw a monkey wrench into Megacorp's machinery. This was something new to Megacorp. It was an infection of its own creation, eating away at the corporate inner framework. How they would react at the conspiracy of a few of its Reuseables had yet to be seen. It could get ugly.

***

Somewhere between Oakland and the Sierras, our moment of grace began to slip away. The last two weeks had gone too smoothly. Kale and Johnny had managed affairs until now. A cold rain slid down the jagged mountains through the trees, dumping its load of water in the foothills and right on top of us. The harsh chill and wet bit into us hard as we headed up the mountain grade. By the time we found a place to pull over it was already too late. We were soaked. We stripped in the pouring rain, pulling on long underwear and fleece before squeezing back into our suits and squelching into waterlogged boots. Three hours into the ride and I had already blown it. If Quan was aware of my fuck up, or cold, or miserable, she didn't show it. She accepted things the way they came, evolving to accommodate the new change rather than bitching. Besides, I was doing enough bitching for both of us. Her comfort within herself was catching and I soon found myself laughing at the situation. Hell, there wasn't a damn thing I could do about it anyway. With a change in attitude, it was time to get going and not stand there like a fool in the rain. We pushed on.

With the increase in altitude came the cold mountain air. The little arms that held so loosely were now shivering at my waist. If we didn't punch through the cold front soon she would be in trouble. We stopped in Tahoe for gas, another 50 miles and it was 90 degrees. Explaining this to Quan was futile but I went through the motions just the same, using the map on the wall of the gas station. At the end of my halting English explanation and ridiculous sign language she nodded, downing a cup of hot water. She refused the coffee I greedily gulped while sucking down a cigarette as if it would be my last. As I started the bike I thought, 'well, it can't get much worse.' How wrong I could be.

The next hour felt like ten as numb hands tried to maintain a grip on the handlebars. The grade was down hill now. We stopped for a vigorous rub down. The cold wouldn't be chased away. Getting back on was no easier than getting off. I sucked it up. The warm weather had to come soon. Quan's shivering became worse. Her whole body vibrated against my back, her helmet rapping incessantly on mine. The rain lightened, sunlight lit the landscape ten miles ahead. Tucked in and holding tight, I never noticed when the shaking stopped behind me, focused as I was on keeping the bike with the rubber down.

Ahead was an overpass, like all the rest we had gone under. I paid no attention. The road was icing up and took all I had just to keep her going straight ahead. The difference with this overpass was that a brick was hurled from the top. Smashing through the windshield didn't so much slow the brick as added a whole bunch of sharp shit into the impact, slamming me hard in the chest. The momentum pushed me back in the seat, ejecting Quan onto the frozen pavement at 50 miles an hour. Stomping on the brakes sent the bike sliding sideways, lifting the rear end off the ground. Stabbing my foot into the road to stay upright, handlebars cranked over away from the skid, the tires hit a dry patch and sunlight. The bike snapped straight again, locked rubber, screeching down the highway. The adrenalin rush was instant and timely. I turned around, racing back into the weather. A line of motorcycles stretched across the road. Quan lay still on the other side of them. 'Fuck me' I said and hit the gas. Lying down on the gas tank I shot the gauntlet. Rocks flew, belting me cruelly in the back. I didn't care. One took me in the head. I lost control. The BMW went one way and I the other. Scrambling to my feet before stopping, I pulled the one tool I never leave home without, my spud wrench, stumbling towards Quan. There was no time for the tender embrace and tears. I picked her up, heading for the sunshine. The gauntlet remained and they had reloaded. I stopped and reached for the machine pistol – fuck these bastards -- but an image of Quan unfolded in my mind. She was in meditation, raised her head and locked eyes with my mind's eye, shaking her head no. There was no questioning it. I held her like a big football, bent over and charged. This time clubs rained down. One with a screw in it ripped through my suit into my back tearing meat and skin with the threads. I tripped going down on one knee and received a series of vicious blows in return. Onward, against a rain of steel and wood, into the sunshine.

I took my helmet off and attended to Quan. The group of bikers circled us as I stripped her. One of them poked me with a piece of rebar. I grabbed the bar jerking it from his hands. "Come on, you mother fuckers." I swung the rod madly connecting with nothing. They stepped back and closed in staying just out of reach. One of them dropped low connecting a baseball with my left knee. I collapsed next to Quan. Fumbling with her helmet catch, I released it and pulled it off. Just then two things happened at once. One of them was a biker chick yelling 'STOP!' The other was the whistling of a big stick swinging through the air. It stopped when it connected with the base of my skull.

The air was thick, hot and it didn't move too much. Shafts of sunlight speared molten through gaps in plywood that covered the windows. I was alone. My suit was unzipped, boots and socks off. My right hand went to my thigh. The gun was gone. So was the spud wrench. Taking off the rest of the wet gear, in just my skivvies, I navigated rows of empty shelving to an open door.

There sat the bikers, a motley crew to say the least, all sitting quietly, facing Quan Yin. They were meditating! Slipping past and laying my clothes to dry on an abandoned car, I spied the bike, up in the air, on blocks. Fuck. I couldn't even get through the first day without killing the package and losing the bike to a chop shop. Standing a few feet from the bike it didn't look all that bad. The windshield had been removed; the handlebars were still bent, front fender mangled.

"It could have been worse. Usually is."

"How is Quan?" I said trying not to lose the calm of the moment. I could inflict a lot of damage but they had me way outnumbered and the gun.

"She'll be aw'ight. The ice kept her sliding. Tough little chick that one."

"She better be!" I exclaimed.

"Don't get yourself all worked. You were just in the wrong place at the wrong time."

"No shit and fuck you!"

A little hand took mine before it balled into a fist. I looked down into Quan's big black eyes, 'It will be all right. They will fix what they have broken.' The words weren't spoken but that is what she said. She pulled me into the sunshine and began to examine my body like a doctor. I let her, saving my machismo for those assholes. The stick with the screw had left a nasty gash. Quan rubbed something into it, stopping the bleeding. Her look said the pain was mine to deal with. Back at the BMW, the big biker was straightening the bars when we returned.

"You ground a hole in your valve cover when you went down. Mikey went to town to fix it. Should be on the road in a couple hours. Where ya headed?"

"The way I was going."

"Watch your ass, it don't get no better."

"Speaking of, where is my gun?"

"Now, mister, what you have to go and bring that up for?"

"Because I want it, and I will kill all of you to get it."

The biker looked over my body at the scarring I had earned and started laughing. "I do believe you would at that. Sure mister, here you go. He pulled the gun out of his jacket along with the extra magazines and handed them over. "Just didn't want you waking and going ballistic. Here's Mikey now." A fully chopped Harley kicked up the dust as it came off the highway into the abandoned truck stop. Dancing on the loose gravel, going too fast and fishtailing wild, came the group's mechanic.

Mikey had long hair braided into a tail, worn leathers and hands that were as gnarly as mine except his had a century's of grease caked into the nails and creases of his hand. People's hands tell a great deal about who they are. A shake even more so. His was hard and coarse, searching for a weakness in mine. Finding none in my hands or eyes, he busted a grin, using his smile to search more.

"Fucker sure can take a brick, Eightball," Mikey said to his partner.

"Good aim on a moving target."

"Lotsa practice."

"I'm sure. If you had killed Quan we wouldn't be discussing this." I finished, withdrawing the auto-pistol slamming a clip and racking a round into the pipe.

"Hey mister!" he said backing up a step toward his bike.

"Yeah I know. Wrong place, wrong time."

"Hey, I'm sorry about the rock. Risked my ass in town for the parts you needed." Mikey started to rummage through his saddlebags.

"Slow Mikey, really fucking slow. Wouldn't want you in the wrong place at the wrong time."

He dropped it into first and crawled along eventually pulling out a valve cover and gaskets for the BMW.

"So what stopped you from finishing the job?" I said. Mikey was a wrench, but he wasn't slow on the uptake.

"It was Cathy. She recognized Kale's bike." Mikey squatted, wiped the mating surfaces with a rag and began to reinstall the valve cover. My jaw must have hit the ground, he continued. "Everybody knows Kale, the dude is fucking legendary."

"Well, if you know him why'd you do it?"

"We needed the money. A guy shows up here a couple days ago. Offers us a bundle of cash to stop a traveling couple. Eightball took the offer and the rest is history."

"What were you supposed to do after you had us?"

"Call him, and hold you."

"Did you call him?"

"Yep."

"You gonna try and hold us?"

"Nope."

"You're in for a heap of trouble."

"Figures. All Eightball saw was, well ... an eightball."

"You poor mother fuckers. What changed your mind?" It was obvious Mikey was the leader. Eightball was just big.

"Well, it goes to figure, if you were on Kale's bike then you must be somebody. The wetback that made the offer, he'll be dead when he comes to collect."

"A wetback you say? Get a name?"

"No. Hell, never even saw the guy, he just talked from the back of a blacked out limo."

Pablo had put two and two together. Sort of explains Kale's last minute gift of the gun.

"Well, good as new, sort of." Mikey exclaimed topping off the oil. "Go ahead, start her up."

She roared to life, loud and obnoxious. Mikey doubled over slapping his thighs, and laughing wildly, eyes sparkling.

"Took the guts out of the pipes and tweaked the engine. She's got some go now!" He yelled over the noise. "Take it for a run, at four grand – look out!" The laughter didn't stop.

It was 90 degrees. In my shorts and bare feet I took to the road. At four grand she let out all the stops. Holding on tight and squeezing my knees to the tank I was barely able to keep control. At 140 M.P.H. the world seemed to be coming at me unnervingly fast.

Quan was gathering up the gear when I pulled back in. We dressed for hot weather; crossing Nevada and Utah was going to be a scorcher. There wasn't much to say to the bikers. I sure as hell wasn't going to thank them. Chins and nods were passed around. Before pulling away I chinned Mikey over.

"A word to the wise. I'd get the fuck out of here and don't come back. The guy in the limo gets a little upset when you come up short." I left slow, not wanting to spit Quan off the back again.

Pulling away, Quan gave a hug around my waist. Goodness washed through me, along with the knowledge that the bikers would not make it. Pablo would make an example of them. Word would travel fast. Too fast.

Nevada was a desolate stretch of dry mountains dotted with windswept towns where hulks of gambling casinos, like massive dinosaurs, were rotting to extinction. Broken windows, falling down signs, neon that never lit any more welcomed anyone who would think to try and survive here. And here they were. You never saw them in the sun. Just shadows, behind quickly closed tattered curtains. Human rats living in their own ruins.

Then they were gone, absorbed by the vast desert that lay behind us and stretched on as far as the eye could see. We stopped in Wendover for fuel, a small mining town on the eastern edge of the state. The once stately casinos stood empty, besides the squatters that is. Traffic still rolled in the streets. Megacorp company trucks. Like everything else, they had bought out the mining industry years ago. Running lean and mean, they ran it into the ground. Slave labor had overtaken good business practices. A weathered piece of cardboard on the ground, still clutched in the hands of a rotting corpse explained it all. 'Will work for food'

Dozers, excavators, monster–sized dump trucks and cranes were scattered everywhere. A patina of rust blended them with the landscape. Otherwise they were preserved by the dry environment like the relics of an ancient civilization. Soon, but not quite yet, another boom would boost this town from its decay. It would last only briefly before the high desert would return to scavengers. In the years to come the steel industry would slump, followed by the cave in of the mining industries that supported them. The iron and steel in the desert would wait. Wait until it was more profitable to melt down the tracks and buckets than dig it from the earth.

Ahead was Utah, the only state untouched by the hands of Megacorp. The Mormons had cordoned off their territory. The faithful had been called to return when corporate rule became evident. Their militia turned into a formidable army protecting the borders, with god on 'their side.' There is nothing funny about a bunch of religious fanatics with guns.

At the border was a checkpoint; I.D., marriage license, picture of the bike and license plate - don't ask me why but they even checked to verify I was circumcised. A large pair of shears hung on the wall. I imagined they were there if you weren't. We were stripped searched. My gun was noted and serial numbers taken, but was left in my possession; traveling armed was the rule, not the exception. Since Quan was unarmed she was taken away to a smallish building where they offered her a variety of weapons to choose from if she was so inclined. Passing on such an opportunity would have been considered a faux pas. She returned with a Benelli .410 semi-automatic pistol grip shot gun. The salesmen/guards were considerate of her size when selecting the weapon. She was street savvy enough to play along. The purchase came with an application to join the church. At the eastern end of the state would be another checkpoint to pick up the filled out app. We filled our water jugs and were just about to pull out when a guard approached, gun leveled.

My bowels rolled.

"Just wanted to remind you to stay to the road. Keep off the flats."

I nodded. The penalty was death, as the billboards bluntly stated.

Utah's ability to stay out of the corporate net was the abundance of lithium beneath the Bonneville Salt Flats. The element was still a key ingredient to electronics all around the world. Utah had one of the last remaining mines on the planet. Damn good leverage.

A blinding white landscape separated by a thin strip of asphalt. It was straight as an arrow and mesmerizing. Quan would squeeze me when I would begin weaving, succumbing to the hypnosis, and we would look for shade, pull over and walk it off. Kale had mentioned something about taking enough breaks. It was not my style, but once your ass starts wobbling on an unforgiving road, it makes a lot of sense. The air across the flats warped in the heat. After water and a cigarette we were back on the road.

The miles blazed on. The wrecks of sleepy drivers punctuated the ivory plain. Bleached skeletons blended with the salt, most had arms outstretched, supplicating the unforgiving pavement. Once you were out on the flats, you were not allowed back. By accident or design ¬– it didn't matter. With their vehicles trapped in a slush of semi-fluid salt, some headed out across the desert, hoping to reach the other side. There was no absolution for making it. Only the muzzle of a gun turning you around, sending you back the way you came.

It was also against the law to aid those unfortunates who tried to reclaim the road. Their fate would become yours. One of the 'gifts', definitely the wrong word there, of being a reuseable was excellent eyesight. Ahead was a family. Their car had blown a tire, forcing the car into a skid, putting them ten feet off the blacktop. It was ten feet too far. Quan squeezed for me to stop. It was one of the few times I could not give in. Slowing and reaching into the tank bag I pulled a bottle of water, lowered my arm to the side and dropped it. The plastic bottle bounced along the pavement into the dying family. We kept going. I did not help them, merely prolonged their misery for another few hours and probably signed our death warrant.

At this moment I wanted out of the state more than anything else. Another hour and we were cruising passed Salt Lake City, the first sign of active civilization since leaving the Bay area. The highway was busy and I was paying more attention to the traffic than perhaps I should have. Outside of town the cars and trucks dwindled, but we had picked up a tail. Quan squeezed and I pulled into the nearest rest area. The tail followed, parking at the far end of the lot. I lit a cigarette and checked the bike over, forcing myself not to look his way. When Quan Yin returned from the bathroom we pretended to have a casual discussion, snacked and drank before hitting the road. There was no use trying to outrun the tail. We had fifty miles to the border and another checkpoint. Any ground gained would be lost there. Plus I didn't want to get busted for speeding. There were no billboards about this. The penalty was probably life at hard labor. The state of Utah defended itself and way of life fiercely; I did not want to fuck with these people. Give me a biker gang any time.

The port of entry to Wyoming was really a port of departure from Utah. Fifty or sixty vehicles idled ahead of us in line. Each car in line was thoroughly searched, identical to the search upon entering the state. The inventory printout produced at the start was double checked at the end. If it didn't add up there was an enclosure you were escorted to. We were fucked. The water bottle. There was little to do but wait. Turning around and heading back for it was not an option. Chase cars and a chopper sat nearby on the ready.

It was our turn. The shade of the inspection awning was an unexpected relief after cooking on the hot pavement in the queue. We placed our guns on a table before stepping away to strip. The guard began with the weapons, matching serial numbers and counting cartridges. All we could do was stand to the side quietly as he emptied the saddlebags, tank and tail bags onto the tarmac. Each item ticked off with a pencil stroke and shoved aside. A tall burly man in official customs clothing stood just inside the shade watching the inspection from behind blacked out glasses. His stance indicated authority as he waited patiently for the inspection to be complete, with his hands behind his back.

When the inspector was finished, he rose from his squatted position and eyed us with an emotionless expression. He had seen it all before and I did not miss his quick glance to the shadeless penalty pen.

"We seem to have come up a little short." The inspector paused, taking in our reactions. "You are missing one water bottle. The report notes you filled up at the station. This is in violation of Utah law. I suppose you have an explanation," he finished drolly, having heard it all before too.

Before I was able to put my foot in my mouth Quan took a nonthreatening humble step forward, her head and eyes down. She looked up and in perfect English said, "It was my fault. I was trying to take a drink from the bottle when we hit a bump and I lost control of it. My husband knew better than to stop and turn around. I am sorry."

As she said this Quan reach out her hand with the filled out religious application. A small smile creased the inspector's face, then vanished.

"This may help during the inquiry." The inspector deadpanned holding the app. He looked to the big man silhouetted in the entry.

"Good afternoon, Captain," the inspector began. "I was just going to call an escort."

The Captain stepped forward, becoming visible. His face was cut from rock, creating hard lines of a man who has had a hard life. "There will be no reason to make the call."

"Sir?"

The Captain brought his hands out in front of him. In the right hand was the bottle of water, still full. "I was behind them. We had been notified to keep our eyes out for a traveling couple. These are not they. I witnessed her loss of the bottle; she speaks the truth. Here is the bottle. No law has been violated." Before the inspector could say anything, "Have the road crews sent out to repair a buckle in the asphalt at mile marker 111. Get on it, boy! We could have a real accident out there! Now let these folks, who have applied to our church, pass."

The Captain was not to be messed with. The inspector finished our form, stamping us departed. The Captain walked up to us and, loud enough for the inspector to hear, said, "Come back to our state when you are through with your journey and have your child here."

Quan bowed, "God willing."

To me, "Take care of her and your child." It was said with a lifetime of practice at telling people not to fuck up. My face was asking the questions my voice could not. He read it like a book.

Quietly he said, "A friend, and you will." With that he strode away in full command, leaving Quan and me to repack our stuff. The inspector had already moved on to another car in the next bay.

We roared out of there. It would be a cold day in hell before I voluntarily crossed that border again. The barren hills of Wyoming lay ahead. What wasn't empty was filled with huge corporate cattle factories. For more than a hundred miles it smelled of cow shit and rotting meat. The cows ranged amidst fields of wind generators. Wind was Wyoming's shield against poverty. Only a few prospered here but the spin off allowed many to suffer a slightly-less-miserable life.

Night was coming on as we pulled off the highway for a break. Sunset was a spectacle of orange and reds and it was damn near impossible to light up in the wind.

***

"Y ou speak English pretty good."

"So do you," Quan said smiling. "No one knows."

"That's why he let us go. When you spoke English he knew we weren't the couple."

"No, that is not why. We should be thankful, and back on the road."

"Trust me, honey, I am."

It was after midnight by the time we pulled into Cheyenne. A shadow of its former self, the only illumination came from the truck stop that spilled over into a hotel parking lot. I parked in the darkness away from registration. We were beat. The road had taken its toll on our asses. My shoulders drooped as I rolled a cigarette.

"Jake," it was the first time she used my name, "It would be best if I went in. The people here would not look kindly on your presence."

There it was. During the last few days I had not thought of what I had become or the destruction left in my wake. I had been living in the moment. The doors of reality crashed down with the sound of steel grinding into pavement. Without her foresight, we would have had to get out of town fast and be lucky to reach Nebraska before I became fodder for the meat grinder.

I lit a cigarette. "Yeah, sure," I paused. "Thank you, Quan." She bowed her head slightly, took one step backwards and turned. I looked down feeling like a jerk and leaned against the bike. Thoughts of a hot shower and a clean bed interrupted my misery. That is before two pair of silver tipped cowboy boots entered my examination of the oil stained concrete at my feet.

"Nice old bike ya got there. Sure would like to have me one." Cowboy # 1 said.

I stared at the ground, ignoring them.

"Where y'all headed, boy? Got a problem with your hearing, boy?" Cowboy #2 said.

"Yeah, nowhere." Still looking down, I flicked an ash.

"Nowhere, huh? Well, you found it." Cowboy #2 said taking a swig from his beer, laughing drunkenly at his cleverness.

"Sure would like me one of those. Can I sit on it?" Cowboy #1 asked, slurring.

"No."

"What, too good for an old poke like me? Why don't cha lookit me, mister."

When I did it was all over. "Holy fuckin' shit, Jasper! We got one!" Cowboy # 2 turned and began to yell to the truckers. I lurched from the bike, putting my weight behind a punch to the back of his neck, shattering the bones into the esophagus, stifling the cry. A bottle crashed over my head, shards of glass and backwashed beer cascading down my face. I spun grabbing Cowboy #1 by the throat and slammed him to the ground, fracturing his skull on the broken curb. I smashed the redneck's head over and over, pulping the back of his skull in my anger. Anger at what I was, at what he was and what we had become. Quan's hand on my shoulder ceased my obsessive compulsion. It took a moment to stop, another to let go, and another still before my mind reeled back the insanity.

"We should leave," she said simply and calmly, donning her helmet. Following her lead I glanced around only to see a group of truckers had gathered and headed our way. Quan was already on when I started the motorcycle up. With the noise of the bike the truckers put a little motivation behind their gathering. Beer bottles started to fly as we wound through the lot looking for the exit. The truckers had formed a human barricade. Fueled with beer and stupidity, they didn't realize who they were dealing with. Quan wrapped her arms tight around me, tucking in close. She could see it coming.

One last circuit of the lot had me on a straightaway for the exit. With speed bumps, there was no way to blast through them; it would be more like plowing. Over the last hump, I gunned the engine bringing her up above four grand in second gear. Hitting the bright lights and hugging the tank, we slammed into the knees and bellies as beer bottles and boards crashed down on us. It only lasted a moment before the entrance ramp to the highway came screaming at us. Slamming the brakes put us in a vicious sideways skid, the rear end squirreling and hopping till the brake was released and tires grabbed, scraping the pegs, then off into the blackness.

Waiting for the adrenalin to wear off was useless. I couldn't see the lights behind us yet, but sure as shit they were there. The truckers had to have found the bodies, authorities notified, blah, blah, blah. Cheyenne was the last big town to the border. Another hour and we could be there. Quan hugged me once and relaxed, settling in for a long night. It helped to cut the edge on my hyper-alertness.

Forty-five minutes passed. A sign: 'Nebraska, 22 miles – a Megacorp co-op.' A sweeter sign I never did see. Cresting a hill gave me a long look back in the rear view mirror. There they were, the lights strobing and closing in.

The motorcycle coughed, chugged and stalled. We ground to a halt just as the grade began to descend. We had not gotten gas in Cheyenne. Putting the bike in neutral, we started coasting down the hill while I fumbled for the reserve lever, and another two liters of gas. Fuuuuccckkkkk! It would take a few moments for the float bowls in the carbs to fill. All the while the posse is closing in.

The hair went up on the back of my neck. Lights came over the top of the hill behind us. The engine started. The posse was gaining momentum on the downhill run before heading up the next hill. It was a losing battle. I didn't know how long the engine would last when put passed four thousand rpm's. Kale hadn't mentioned anything about this, but I was sure it wasn't kosher. 'Not until we have to', I repeated over and over, watching the lights close the gap behind us.

A chase car pulled away from the pack, racing right up behind us, rear-ending the bike, sending us bouncing across the highway before regaining control. 'Wait' entered the forefront of my mind. I did, maintaining a steady speed. Quan was changing her position. It was impossible to ask 'What the hell are you doing!' The chase car held off, allowing the others to catch up, when four thunderous explosions jackhammered Quan against my back. 'Oh fuck, she's been hit.' Just before I stomped on the brakes I felt her moving around again. A tight squeeze and 'now' entered my head. I rolled back on the throttle, pushing the bike above four grand, shifting rapidly to keep up with it. The speedometer was pegged as a world I didn't like sped by in a blur. The lights behind us had stopped in a pileup.

'Port of Entry, one mile.' The bike chugged once. I squeezed the clutch and dropped her into neutral, coasting the last mile. We came to a stop just as the rear wheel crossed the state line.

Quan left her helmet on as the Megacorp border guard approached. My scowl stretched into an honest smile as I handed him my Megacorp I.D. He returned to the guard shack, swiped my identification and waited for the report. Looking at Quan behind her mirrored face shield, it was impossible to see that she was crying. Whatever she had done to stop the posse took a toll. This I could only feel. It was not the time to start asking questions.

"Mr. Strom, you have been cleared to enter the state of Nebraska."

"Would the state of Nebraska have a gallon of gas?" The smile returned.

The guard looked again at the report, like it would tell him if I could have it or not.

"Pull over to that pump. You'll have to pay for it." He indicated a fuel depot fifty yards away.

"Thank you," I said, actually meaning it.

With an hour until dawn we arrived in Kimball. It wasn't much but it had a motel. Quan had closed up shop, retreating deep within herself. She did not talk or make eye contact. I let her shower first while getting some take-out at the diner. The room had two beds and she was curled in one of them. Setting her cold eggs and toast on the writing desk, I jumped into the shower to wash the beer, blood and sweat away. But there was no way to wash away the stain of my existence.

I woke hours later to a warm body embracing mine. Quan had spooned me and was tracing my scars with her fingers. If only they could heal and dig deep to cleanse the festering of my soul. That they could not, but in the hours ahead, Quan mitigated my inhumanity. Her love was as soft and deep as that of the ocean. The comfort of our entwined bodies helped to assuage the coarseness of reality. The healing was reciprocal. As sunlight brightened the eastern horizon, we roused from the depths of our experience, hungry and ready to depart.

I never asked her what she had done to stop the posse. When reloading the bike however, the smell of fresh gunpowder from the .410 explained things pretty clearly. She was not a killer, I was. Not mentioning it, we rolled onto the road into amber waves of grain. A sea of wheat spread to the horizon. After an hour it still was endless. This was something Kale had talked about too. The great ocean of prairie parted before us into the night. Lights winked in and out of the tall grass. Housing for the labor force. Clusters of lights showed giant commercial silos surrounded by razor wire fences and patrolled by armed guards.

Dawn was blanked by a storm front moving south from Canada. Stopping in North Platte for gas, Quan thought it would be nice to eat down by the river and let the storm pass some more. I don't think either of us wanted to push through another biblical experience, plus the thought of swimming had me hooked.

To the east of town was a riverside park that had somehow escaped the ravages of the Megacorp harvesters. It was overgrown in the tall grass. The bike disappeared beneath the waves, coming to rest in the deserted parking lot. Parting the head high grass on the walk to the river we held hands for no reason at all. You'll have to understand that this was all new to me. Kind emotion, tenderness and caring were foreign to my environment, to my experience. I had seen it, read about it, saw vids that had it, but personally knew nothing about it. Quan was patient. We did not talk. It was more out of habit than inability. She communicated with her heart.

After a swim in the cool waters of the Platte and a lunch of fresh fruits, yogurt and granola, we stretched out on our riding suits and took a nap. The last thing I remembered was the blue sky, grass, the sound of the river and Quan's hand on mine. When she slipped away is lost in my dreams.

I woke to the barrel of a revolver stuffed in my nose. I mean really crammed in there. A dark skinned man with oversized shades and hat was at the other end of it.

The thin lips parted and spoke. "Buenos dias, hombre." He yanked the barrel out of my nose, the front sight ripping my left nostril into flaps. He spoke casually the way a man does when he is in control, thinking nothing of the blood that poured from my nose.

"I have heard a good deal about you. Most recent, of course, was your escaping the noose that was closing about you at the border."

"Fuck you, man," I said as he clobbered me with his gun.

"No, fuck you, Jake," Pablo replied, kicking me squarely in the balls with pointed cowboy boots. I doubled over, puking in pain. The next kick bullseyed my rectum. I had been rendered harmless.

Within the agonizing confines of pain, my right arm reached out for my gun. An explosion as the bone and flesh below my elbow burst into splinters.

"I heard you were quicker, and such a beautiful day." Pablo raised his pistol taking careful aim at my chest, the way he had with Johnny.

"Fuck you!" I spit leaping at him. Five rounds in rapid succession were fired before I hit the ground rolling and clutching my chest, screaming. But where was the blood? The dull ache of a bullet? My right arm hung limp getting up off the ground.

Quan stood there with the shotgun still smoking in her hands. She was not crying, a righteous set to her lips, justice and anger in her eyes. Taking the gun, I began to search Pablo. Three large caliber handguns, ammunition and a thick roll of real money was all he had. His car was equally as spartan – water and a cell phone. The keys were in the car and I drove it to the picnic site. Quan was gone, her clothes in a pile by the water. Just in case, I parked the car so that the front tire was on Pablo's chest. Just playing it safe. Then my heart sank. Stripping as fast as possible, I dove into the river, spearing for Quan's body. It wasn't moving. Putting all I had into it, for my right arm wasn't worth a shit, I was able to catch hold and pull her away from the small rapids into slower water. She kneed me in the chest before a blow to the nuts. Releasing her was only natural. Quan swam away to the shore, leaving me in misery. I gave her enough time to dress before exiting the water.

"Did you really think I was going to kill myself, Jake?" She asked tossing me the towel.

"Well, uh. I really didn't think at all, saw you floating and kinda went into rescue mode."

"Thank you then. When you grabbed me, I went into survival mode."

"You all right about this?" I indicated Pablo.

"No. I am not. Killing is never the answer."

"In this case..."

"There was no time. We should dispose of him and leave this place."

"I'll take care of it."

"No," Quan replied, "we are in this together."

Once the car was off of Pablo, Quan got hold of the feet and we placed him in the trunk. She was murmuring a chant as I put the car in gear, hopping out just before it drove itself into the river, floating for a few moments before sinking into the green brown water. It wasn't a hasty departure but we didn't waste any time loading up. Pablo's guns and money went into the saddlebags. Quan used what little we had in the way of med supplies to bind my elbow. Using dental floss, she stitched together that which had to be put together while my teeth bit hard into riding gloves. Making a bent splint from a tree limb and strips of tee shirts made for an adequate if unbearable position to ride in. I didn't complain; she wasn't.

If not for current events, the remainder of the day would have been spent in the pastoral countryside of Nebraska. I pulled off the highway onto the old Route 6, one of the first trans cons. It was pitted, potted and split, but passable. It was an effort to pacify the mind of madness without slowing our progress. We stopped at points of interest, reading the brass plaques of nowhere's historical moment in time. The road paralleled the original trans continental railroad, created in no small part by Chinese labor. After four or five stops of reading of the historical tidbits, I broke the silence, amazed as I was by the stories we read.

"There is no mention of the Chinese workforce."

"There rarely is. It is the white man's history. Not so much different than present times. You get no mention for your work?" She cocked an eye in my direction. Quan meant reuseables.

"No, no, we don't."

"The Union Pacific was just a paradigm for Megacorp. Don't you think? When the Union Pacific was through with them they were all sent back. Sound familiar?"

"Well, now that you mention it..."

A door was closing, no, a veil. Too much had happened. The kinds of things that don't bring people closer together. We had 300 miles or so to get to Red Oak. The sun was already low in the sky. The day had been long and eventful enough without adding a midnight run on country roads. It would have taken all my concentration and I had none left. We detoured south, coming into Lincoln through the back door.

In the hotel's café, with our backs to a wall, we eyed the front door never noticing the food. We were close to home and didn't want to take any more chances. Having Pablo catch me napping was beyond embarrassing. It was deadly. Quan explained that Pablo's demise would only put him off the track for a few days, a week at most. By then, well ... we should be there. But I wasn't banking on it. Johnny had left me some dope, just in case.

Back in the hotel room I booted a speedball while showering. My elbow was killing me and I didn't want to nod out on painkillers. Quan pinned me out, gave me a hug and went to bed. I pulled a chair and the auto-pistol, destined to sit the night on vigil.

The evening was uneventful. By nine A.M. the elbow was re-bandaged, we'd had breakfast, too much coffee and were on the road.

From Lincoln it was all backcountry roads. Quan had memorized the route off of Kale's GPS while still in Oakland. Rows of corn filled the undulating hillsides. Harvest was happening. The pavement turned to dirt. Road signs became non-existent. Quan would tap on my shoulder to get me to slow and point in the direction we were to go at a four-way or tee. Coated in umber dust, we came upon a harvesting operation crossing the road. By now I had a bad feeling about anything. We stopped in a cloud of smut. By the time it had settled, I had the auto-pistol in my lap, finger on the trigger, waiting. The big combine moved at a snail's pace. Out of the corner of my eyes shadows flashed amongst the corn. We were being surrounded.

Quickly raising the gun with both hands, I sprayed the cornfield to the left, dumped the clip and slammed another shooting into the field at the right. The bullets went high and wild as the splint broke. The recoil sent the gun flying, leaving my right forearm flopping there hanging uselessly at my side. I screamed in pain as blood began to run out the sleeve of my leathers.

Quan slid from the back seat removing her helmet and walked towards the combine.

"Nooooo!" I yelled losing balance and falling over with the bike. The hot exhaust burned into my leg as it pinned me to the ground. I could only watch as Quan stood humbly before the bike. The door to the combine opened, the face looked familiar, but the image began to blur, then the lights went out.

***

Chickens clucked outside the window, the screams of children playing were carried on the breeze that ruffled the curtains. My right arm was cast, left leg bandaged, and nose was stitched. A clean pair of underwear and jeans were folded at the foot of the bed. Something was amiss and I wasn't getting it. Pants on, I limped to the door of the room, listening before opening it. A grey head was intent on a computer terminal as fingers danced across the keys. The BMW sat outside the open front door, next to another, newer model. It was Kale's. The computer chair spun around.

The trip was over. We made it.

Coffee was on the stove but I had to smoke outside. The bike was a wreck. Somehow I didn't feel bad about it.

"Don't worry about the machine," Kale said coming to the front porch.

"I'm not."

"Noticed you let Mikey re-work it."

"I didn't 'let' anyone fuck with anything." Man, I had a lousy attitude.

"Lighten up, Jake. It was just your turn. You made it. Quan is safe."

"What do you mean it was my turn?"

"Your turn to balance the scales. Come on, I'll show you what I mean."

The house was one of a dozen or so structures amid a stand of tall red oaks, surrounded by corn and soy fields. "This is the grade school. We converted the milking shed into classrooms." Kale opened the door to one of the rooms. Quan was seated in the middle of a group of preschoolers playing Chinese word games. You would never know she'd pumped five deer slugs into a man's back yesterday.

"No, you wouldn't," Kale said reading my mind. "It's good therapy to work with kids after an experience like that. It kind of brings you back home."

Quan looked up from the children. Seeing the sadness in my eyes, she rose to her feet, bringing a boy with her. He was older than the rest of the kids. Melancholy hung on his shoulders like an anchor chain. Quan spoke in Chinese to Kale. While he interpreted Quan caught my eye, swiped her nose answering my questioning look.

"Jake, this is Tom," Kale said in his kind manner of speaking.

I stuck out my good hand. "A pleasure to meet you, Tom." He didn't take it, looking up at me with scrunched up eyes.

"You look like the man who killed my parents." Talk about a child's innocence crashing your soul. My eyes shot to Kale's. What the fuck did I deserve this for?

"He's not Tom, he is a friend." Tom looked me up and down, not quite sure whether to believe Kale. "Quan said maybe you guys could go dig some holes together or something."

"Not going to be much help there," I said lifting my arm.

"Well, maybe you could put the Beemer in the shop and start stripping her. You broke it." Kale started laughing.

"Yeah, guess I did," I replied with a chuckle, trying to keep things on the lighter side in front of the kid.

"You the guy who rode in yesterday?" Tom's eyes brightened for a second.

"Yeah."

"You looked pretty stupid laying under it." He started to giggle.

"Yeah, s'pose I did at that. How'd you like to help me push it into the garage and work on it?" The grin went ear to ear. Kale smiled and went back into the house.

By lunch, Tom knew the difference between a box-end and open-end wrench, how to find the right socket, and what a Phillips head was. Covered in black grease from head to toe, there were bragging rights to attend to while Kale and I had a private meal away from the rest of the farmers.

"You struck a note with Tom. First time he's smiled since being brought here. What happened out there, Jake?"

"Nothing, Kale. Nothing I ever want to talk about anyway. But I will tell you this. We ran for our lives. You gave me a few days of living. I don't know how to thank you."

"You have, Jake."

Tom came running up, white milk on his upper lip contrasting nicely with the smears of grease. "Can I show the guys the motorcycle?" A gang of wide-eyed kids had come with him.

"Sure man. Just don't spill the oil."

"I won't let them fuck with anything, Jake!" He gave me the chin and was off with his pals. I smiled.

"Giving him a real education, I see."

"It's a real world out there, Kale."

"It is at that. They have class all afternoon. Clean him up and ask him not to use that kind of language in school."

"Can do."

I left for the garage to make sure I had only one kid to clean and not six. Kale was right about working with children. It made me feel good to make Tom feel good. With school in progress, I sat alone having a smoke and coffee in the shade of the garage. Quan Yin came around the corner. I skooched over on the hay bale to give her a seat.

"It feels good to have you sitting next to me again. Kind of miss it. Aren't you supposed to be in school?"

"I only teach in the mornings. The kids, you know?"

"Yeah I know. So, what now?"

"You will have to leave soon. There is still nothing that can be done about the Megacorp pharma controls. I am sorry."

"Don't be. It's just the way it is. What about us?" The words fell. I felt like the pilot who dropped the a-bomb on Nagasaki. Was I that much of a fool?

"There can be no 'us', Jake," she paused, taking my hand and placing it on her stomach, "there is a we." My jaw dropped.

Just then a gaggle of kids ran by screaming, "The wagons coming! The wagons coming!"

"It's the first big load of corn this year. Come on, the children get a kick out of it." Quan got up reaching out her hand. We were the first adults to gather with the youngsters at the end of the road. Half a mile away, kicking up the dust, was a team of horses pulling a huge wooden cart heaped high with green ears. A driver sat holding the reins of the team, his head lolling back and forth.

I turned to Quan, "Get them out of here! Now!" I ran back to the garage, grabbed the saddlebags racing back to the road, passing Quan and a cabal of complaining children. On the run, I pulled two of the handguns from the bags while entering the cornfield, dropped the bags and sprinted towards the wagon. Five rows in, I dropped down and watched the harvest pass. The driver was dead, his head nearly severed. Jumping onto the back of the wagon and climbing through the corn to the front seat, I took the reins and stopped the cart. By this time, Kale and the men came running up the road. I climbed down, standing in the shade of a grim harvest and lit a cigarette. The farmers knew best how to deal with their own. The wagon jerked with the clip-clop of hooves and continued on its way down the Avenue Dolores. Kale came up to me.

"This was stuffed in his throat. I believe it is for you." He handed me a baggie dripping in blood. A note was folded in it.

'Time to hit the road, Jake, you can't stay where you don't belong ☺'

It was a long walk back to the farm.

***

The harvest party morphed into a wake. I was not invited. At the garage was Kale's bike with my leather suit, cleaned and patched, laying over the seat. The saddlebags had been recovered from the field and packed with the rest of my stuff. It was pretty clear the note echoed the sentiment of the farmers. I didn't blame them. A shuffle of feet sent me spinning, pulling a pistol. It was Quan with Tom in tow. The gun was stuffed back into my pocket.

"He wanted to say good bye."

Tom put out his hand. "Thank you, Jake."

I took the little digits and shook them in a manly way. "Thank you, Tom. Take care of that motorcycle. When you are a little older, Kale will teach you how to ride it." His eyes lit up, sparkling in the heavy moisture of mine. Quan reached out, wiping the drop that formed.

"We will miss you, Jake," she said, tasting my tear. We had a three-way hug. It would be the last for a long time. They turned, dissolving into the night. The motorcycle started with a thought and took me away from the fields and what might have been. My only hope was to take the evil away from my friends.

Staying south of the interstate, I headed west. Pablo was out here somewhere. Every place I stopped for gas or food had recently been infected by his presence. Paranoia, fear and hatred were the hallmarks. I was being led no matter which road was taken. Chased from everywhere, there was no place to go but onward. I road hard, getting through Nebraska and Colorado without a break. Utah lay ahead. The only reliable route was across the Great Salt Lake, again. With some one breaking my balls in every town, getting gas was almost impossible. I had to take it.

Border inspection in the middle of the night bore none of the activity of the daylight hours. I lay down in the inspection bay and went to sleep. Some time later I was brought to consciousness by the boot of the inspector. "Wake up, mister, you're cleared to pass."

Dawn was breaking. The brilliance of the flats was yet to be seen. I put the border behind me. By noon the reflection was blinding, but the end of the flats were near. After the final border inspection, which was completed without incident, I rode on into Nevada. A group of buildings at the edge of the road hinted of shade. I pulled over, not realizing this was the same place where Quan had befriended Mikey and the bikers. The still, thick air stunk of roadkill, a smell that hung in the still air as if it was around your neck. There were the bikers, crucified on the sign for the truck stop, rotting in the noonday sun. Each had been tortured before being left to die. Their desiccated and mutilated faces bore witness to the atrocity. Mikey's was not among them, nor Cathy's. It was wishful to think they had survived. Their bikes were not among the others, either. Perhaps he had listened. Eightball and the rest had a happy face shot into their chests, as if there was any question of who the perp was.

The remainder of the ride was lonely. A relentless reminder of what I was. How Pablo made sure I was unwelcome at each stop was a fucking mystery. Then again, maybe it was just me.

BLACK TIDE

PART TWO

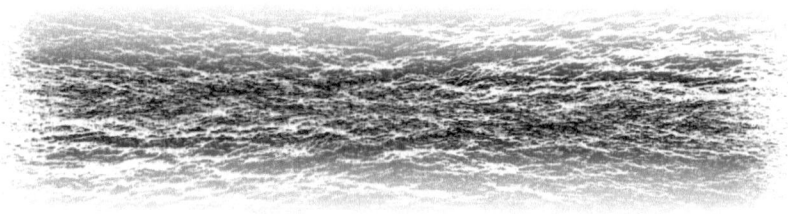

***

J ake returned to the Salvor in Honolulu. It had become his homeport. What happened during the next few years seemed a return to his chronic fate. Like Tommy the crane operator, Jake had become a utilitarian dark void. Unlike Tommy, he was waiting for another chance to live; that is to say, die. Then again, Jake thought, maybe Tommy was waiting, too. For another chance. It would have been a blessing if his fate had been a fatal one. Not!

The call came in one morning. A Japanese freighter had lost control of its stern mooring cable, which spooled around the hub of the propeller, knotting and weaving into a backlash of a mess. Mouse called Jake to the dive station, giving him the basic rundown of the situation. It was not an emergency but needed to be dealt with promptly and professionally.

"I also have a new tender for you."

"Shit, Mouse, I would rather do it myself with the portable gear than break in a new guy. They're such fuckheads."

"Can't help that, Jake. Just suck it up and do the best you can."

"Will do." Jake replied accepting his reality.

Mouse left and Jake began to load the van. Looking up from connecting the welding trailer to the van's pintle hook, he saw a familiar face looking down on him.

"Johnny! What the fuck are you doing here?"

"Mouse said you were to have a new tender, yes?"

"Yeah, but I didn't expect..."

"A Megacorp operative, or a scientist as your fuckhead?"

"Well, something like that. Help me lift the compressor into the van."

Van loaded, they left the base and headed for Honolulu Harbor. The two smoked a joint on the way and Johnny offered Jake some coke.

"Oh no, not again. No, diving on coke is a bad idea." It had been years but he never forgot.

Johnny shrugged his shoulders and put it away. Arriving at the pier, they pulled up next to the stern of the vessel. You could see the mooring wire over the side, tight as a guitar string. The Chief Engineer was there along with an interpreter. After introductions, Jake asked that they loosen the cable's tension. The Chief said they could not, the winch had frozen up. What that meant to the diver was that wire was under a lot of tension, and all hell was going to break loose when he started cutting. By the time Jake was done talking, Johnny had the dive station almost set up, with the exception of making a number of connections, air, juice, comms, welding ground, etc.

"Wow, dude! Thanks." Jake said seeing that he had done everything a tender was supposed to do and then some. Most tenders would have stood there with their thumb up their ass, or worse yet opened their mouths.

They finished setting up while Jake explained what Johnny was to do while he was in the water. It was to be a hardhat dive, traditional gear, with air hose and comms tied into the bulky headgear, which provided significant protection. Johnny took it all in. There was no need to reiterate anything. The guy was a natural. He set the hat on Jake's head, locking it to the yoke and did a comm check.

A crowd had gathered for the show. They would not be disappointed. Johnny guided Jake to the edge of the dock and after dumping a bunch of air hose into the water, slapped the hat with a shove to aid the giant stride into the thirty foot drop to the water. It had to look cool.

The propeller looked like a fishing reel that backlashed on itself; a real rat's nest. After looking the mess over, Jake called topside.

"Hey Johnny?"

"Yeah Jake, over."

"Better have those people back away from the boat a bit. I'm going to cut the down line and it could come whipping out of the water and kill somebody. It's got a mean fucking load on it."

Jake was busy making sure the ground lead from the welding unit was secure when Johnny came back on. A few moments went by while Johnny passed the word.

"Okay, Jake, all clear."

"Roger that. Make it hot."

Johnny flipped a knife switch, juicing the torch. The cable was four inches in diameter. It cut easily but there was a lot of it. The down cable was burnt through, only one strand of wire left to cut.

"Heads up!" Jake called over comms and cut the strand. The wire shot upwards so fast it looked as if it had disappeared. But it was now none of Jake's concern as he sat on a loaded coil of steel death. Jake looked at the insanely spooled wire like a bomb squad would. Which wire do you cut first? Cut the wrong one and it's all over. While thinking this over he asked Johnny, "Make it cold. Hey Johnny?"

"Yeah Jake."

"Just what are you doing here anyway?"

"My time is mine, when not in the service of Megacorp. One of the perks of my contract."

"Make it hot." Jake concentrated now on the first few cuts. Burning through a few of the cables relieved none of the tension. He was just trying to cut the snake into a few pieces before letting her loose.

"Here we go." Cutting into cable under monstrous tension in beyond thrilling: it's enough to scare the shit right out of you. The torch gouged through the final strands.

"Make it cold!" Jake yelled, backpedaling away from the propeller. He cut the master and the whole spool came alive like a compressed spring instantly released. It grew as the coils expanded, releasing catastrophic energy in the process. Jake couldn't move fast enough. The writhing, whipping coils hit him solidly in the head and upper body, knocking the diver from the stern tube. He sank into the tenebrous void and dreamed the dream of death. It was comforting. The working was over. This would not be the only time Jake would feel the bliss of passing away.

"Jake, Jake, come back buddy, we are not done yet."

"Yeah, uh, yeah man, I'm back."

"You okay?"

"Never better. What happened," Jake asked, trying to clear his head.

"You made a cut, the water started boiling and you got real quiet like. I could hear you breathing so I figured you were cool. The topside crew got pretty nervous so I just played it down like this is normal. Was I right?"

"Yep. That's the way the game is played," Jake said, swimming painfully back up to the propeller. The deadly rat's nest of cable was gone, leaving only a few turns of cable around the propeller hub.

"One more cut. Have them lower a line so we can pull this wire out of the water. The Coast Guard gets pissed when you leave stuff on the harbor floor."

A few minutes later, a Hauser line with a cable grip sank past the prop to the bottom. Swimming down and attaching the cable grip, he went back to the propeller.

"Make it hot and start pulling it out." Visibility had gone to shit when the cable hit the sea floor and got worse as they pulled it out of the silt. Jake cut the last wire.

"Make it cold. Is anybody close to you, Johnny?"

"No, they are all watching the show."

"Good, meet me at the ladder, I'm going to need some help."

Johnny was at the bottom of the ladder, reaching down with one hand, when Jake got there. He could see something was wrong and was taking off the dive helmet as blood dripped from the soaked padding. The left side of Jake's face was black and blue. He grabbed Jake by the harness, lifting him out of the water single handedly, climbing the ladder and laying the diver down inside the van. Johnny closed the doors, wrapped a towel around Jake's head, covered him in a blanket and took down the dive station. At least that is what Jake assumed happened.

Jake woke in the medical rooms aboard the Salvor. Mouse wasn't about to relinquish him to Johnny's care again. He had heard the stories. Mouse came into the room shortly after the diver woke.

"Morning, Chief."

"Evening, Jake. Just what in the hell happened to you? I get calls from the shipping agents and Guard concerning that wheel job and what a fantastic job you did. Pulling the wire out of the water was a nice touch, my thanks. Then I come down here and you look like a train wreck." Mouse raised his hands, palms up with a 'what' look on his face.

Jake looked down at the sheet over him. "Got hit by the cable, must've cracked the hat. Slowing down in my old age, Chief. Just couldn't get out of the way in time."

"But you rigged the cable for them to pull it out and did some more burning after you were hit. I had a little talk with your new tender."

"Pulling blank pages, Chief, but if it comes back to me, you'll be the first to know. What do you mean, new tender?"

"Megacorp rewrote his contract. When not working elsewhere, he will be here on the Salvor, 24/7."

'Kale must have had something to do with it', Jake thought.

"I don't think that will go over very well. He's not exactly military material."

"Exceptions have been made in his case. Don't ask me how. Ever since the Navy became a subsidiary of Megacorp, things haven't been the same."

Five years had passed since smuggling Quan Yin to Red Oak. Jake never asked and Johnny never offered. He had successfully built a wall around the memories. Like most of the work Jake did, it was best not to relive the experience too often. This one was particularly painful. There was never any mention of the discoveries that may have been made or of a child. Jake assumed this was part of the way things worked. The less you knew, the less you could give away under persuasion. Having Johnny around kept Jake from passing the point of no return, from giving himself into the darkness that crept from their veins. Johnny wasn't a shrink but had a knack for timely pharmaceutical consumption.

With a few days off for cracked ribs and a severe concussion, Jake left the Salvor to recuperate at Johnny's place, which came with a huge caveat from Mouse. The water was flat, the lanai shaded and the weed strong and pungent. With sand in his toes, a nice sea breeze and a cold beer, it seemed as good a time as any.

"So, the vaccine ever make it to market?" Jake asked, blowing out a huge cloud of smoke from his lungs.

"It would be nice if it was that simple. Suck out some juice, centrifuge it, and voilà, the cure for all that ails man."

"Not?"

"Not yet."

"How's...?" Jake found it hard to finish, so closed were the memories.

"They are fine."

Jake nodded his head in reply, relighting the joint. "Thanks for helping me out of the water. I don't get any real assistance anymore."

"Do not take it personal, none of us do. Just glad I was there. You know, you are crazy doing that underwater stuff, man."

"So I've been told. It's a little late to consider a career change, don't ya think?"

"Hmmmm, yeah."

***

It was December. Storms coming out of the arctic pounded the North Sea like Thor's hammer. Giant swells rolled angrily across the black water. Whipped by a cruel wind, they slammed into the drill rig, rocking the towering structure as the waves passed through the legs. Ice coated the cranes, winches and drill platform.

All active drilling had been stopped on the Goliath. One hundred men huddled in the galley, watching the storm through reinforced windows. Two Captains, a Chief Engineer and a handful of techs occupied the control room. Captain Stokke ran a tug out of Grimstad. The Big Brother, like the name implies, was one of the last and the most powerful of the big workboats. She was able to handle the towering 40-meter swells that assaulted the massive jack-up rig. In between sets, a lifeline was shot across from Big Brother to the rig. Captain Stokke and several rescue personnel were ferried from the boat to the rig in order to aid in coordinating the evacuation. The effort was timed well and the lifeline cut as the first wave in the set lifted Big Brother like a toy boat before swallowing her in the trough. How they were going to get a hundred men across was a problem her crew hoped Stokke had figured out.

Stokke was a big barrel-chested Scandinavian with a head full of white hair and a mustache that buried the lower half of his face. He had fingers like sausages, gnarled from a life battling the North Sea; his face red from the perilous rope transfer and anger.

"What do you mean, you are not ready, Captain Wallace?"

Wallace was British, a little taller than the norm with dark hair and the pasty unchallenged flesh of an Isleman. The righteous set of his face belied the torment behind spectacled eyes. Hands, like an oversized child's, worked themselves together in unease.

"We have to wait. I have my orders," Wallace said staring out at the angry sea.

"Wait! Wait for what? For one swell bigger than the rest to topple this rig with you and all aboard? We have already lost two men. Just what the fuck are you waiting for?" Stokke grabbed Wallace by the collar.

Two hundred meters below, on the seafloor at the base of the Goliath, a submarine came to rest in between the legs of the jack-up rig. Six divers sat in the wetlock, all heavily armed, as the hiss of air equalized the internal pressure to that of the deep sea. At a signal, the outer hatch opened, revealing a pool of black water. One by one they dropped into the icy darkness. At this depth the water was still; not even the surge from the tempest above reaching the divers as they swam to one of the legs of the rig, their lights panning the eerie darkness. One diver opened a hatch that led into the leg. The last diver through closed it, dogging it securely. There was no need for communication. Each man knew his duty. They began the slow climb up the ladder inside the water-filled leg, allowing the divers to decompress on the way. It took hours. The swaying of the rig becoming more active the higher they went until reaching the washing machine at the surface. Above the turbulence, the dive gear was removed and clipped to the steel ladder. The climb continued.

The door to the main deck was iced shut. A small torch lit the cavernous leg revealing the hard faces, grim with their task. The air grew thick with toxic smoke before the door was shoved open into the gale force icy winds as a wave crashed over the deck. Shoes set with crampons, the group split into two. One went to the galley, one to the control room.

The door to the control room burst open. Two rounds from a silenced weapon splattered Stokke's brains across the windows. Wallace jerked back from the hands that still held his jacket.

"That's what I was waiting for," Wallace said proudly as a bullet ripped into his open mouth tearing his jaw off. Another took him in the eye, ending an inglorious career.

The door slammed shut. The shooter pushed his hood back. His pale complexion and calm demeanor contrasted with the suddenly red and frightened faces of northern Europeans.

In carefully enunciated English the shooter spoke to the remaining crew. "If you have dreams of heroism I will crush them. On the other hand, if you want to live, clean up this mess. We have work to do."

The crewmen looked at each other. An emergency gurney hung on the far wall.

Harvey pulled his phone. When his call was answered, all he said was, "The Goliath is ours."

"Big Brother to Goliath – come in!" The ship-to-ship radio squawked. "Do we have an answer," came the urgent call from the waiting rescue ship.

Harvey picked up the microphone, "Here is your answer!" Hoisting Captain Stokke, Harvey carried him across the control room. One of his men opened the door to the outside. Blown by big winds and pelted with whipped water, Harvey stood on the main deck holding the half-headed Stokke above him. Eyes grew big with horror at the recognition inside the wheelhouse of Big Brother. Harvey hurled the body over the raging sea. It landed on the deck of Big Brother. He stuck a large magazine into his weapon, aimed and squeezed the trigger. The windows on Big Brother shattered but did not break. Moments later she peeled away from the rig heading east. Harvey reentered the control room as full of himself as a man can be, when he is in control of one of the largest oil rigs left on the planet.

Gurgles of breath still came from Wallace's body on the floor. Harvey picked him up and drank from the destroyed face, finishing with the final beat of Wallace's heart. He cast the body to the floor, wiping his bloody mouth with his sleeve. If there was any question as to what had taken control of the Goliath, there were a million more now. In the days to come, ransom demands would be issued. It was also necessary to kill a few of the crew to inspire the rest to go back to work. Seeing a man beaten to death with a pipe wrench is certainly excellent incentive.

The Goliath, along with the drill company that worked it, was not a subsidiary of Megacorp. The terrorists from Morocco did not want money. They wanted their country back. Megacorp had leveraged a buyout 20 years before. The servitude the state bore to Megacorp would last into the next century and beyond. In theory they would one day be free again. Harvey had figured out the theory was flawed and not in the favor of the peoples of Morocco.

Harvey had been a reuseable for Megacorp and at one point had become disposable. His talents had become obsolete. Twenty-five years earlier, he was a sub operator. During a survey of the old oil fields in the Gulf of Mexico, he had gotten his sub tangled in the debris at the base of an oil rig. With no diver they were doomed. Apparently Megacorp felt the same way. The corporation sent a rescue diver, but only for one man, a geologist named Simon Brewer. The crew and sub operator were to be left to die on the floor of the gulf. It was an old sub and Harvey was an old reuseable. The loss would be insignificant.

The diver that salvaged Dr. Brewer had a rep as a cold-hearted motherfucker. He left them as he was told, to die on their own fetid air. Why he disentangled the sub was still a question in Harvey's mind. A day didn't pass when he didn't think of it. He wanted to meet the diver and kill him for what he had done. After the rescue ship had gone, the little sub with it occupants were free to go. But go where? There was no safe port of call they could enter. Their identification was no longer valid and they had to keep out of sight. Remaining submerged during the daylight hours, they would surface at night. Food and water ran out quickly. It was scheduled to be a one-day survey. Trapped for three days and another five on their own, they were starving. Harvey hid deep inside himself as the withdrawal from the Megacorp pharmas kicked in his brain. The other men huddled away from him, fearing him now when they had barely tolerated his presence before. Harvey ate the fear, filling himself with hatred. In the minds of the starving crew, a demon grew. Their imagination was not betraying them.

Harvey breathed the night air sitting on the floating hull of the sub. The stench of the men below had been driving him insane; he wanted to kill them all for their whining and bitching. Sharks began to circle the sub, smelling imminent death. One of the crewmembers came topside. Harvey snapped with the sudden smell of body odor. Harvey did not know that it was not the body smells but the blood that drove him to what he did next. He grabbed the man by his hair, pulling him from the hatchway clubbing his head ruthlessly with his other fist until the body went limp. He dropped the unconscious body onto the steel hull and pounced like an animal, tearing into the throat and drinking from the fountain that pulsed, until it pulsed no more. The remainder of the crew watched this in horror through the portholes. When Harvey was finished, he threw the body to the sharks and jumped down the hatch in a frenzy not dissimilar to that of the sharks. Harvey had found a way to shirk the bonds of Megacorp and had searched all these years for the man who made him do it.

Harvey's plan was not a good one; he failed to do his homework. He used the Moroccans, who were fed up with their servitude. They supplied some fuel and manpower. When the journey to the North Sea began there was a crew of nine. Only six remained by the time they arrived at their destination. The idea was to threaten the world with a massive oil spill to gain the Moroccans' freedom. Harvey's motivation was purely to get the diver brought to the rig, so he could 'thank' him properly.

***

When the propeller shaft slid from the rear main seal, Jake slammed a DC plug into the hole, resealing it. His part of the project was over for now, as a crane raised the damaged shaft clear of the water. It was placed on blocks next to the rudder and propeller, which had to be removed for the shaft to be pulled. Beat and back on the Salvor, Jake had time for a shower before being called to Mouse's office. Mouse was out. Jake slumped into a chair and lit a cigarette. He hadn't budged by the time Mouse got back, drifting off to sleep, the smoke burning down to his fingertips.

"Evening, Jake," Mouse said sitting down.

Jake snapped out of it with burnt fingers. "Uh, ouch, morning, Chief. Sup?"

"Time to pack up your stuff again. You're heading to the North Sea."

"Kind of cold and shitty this time of year, Chief."

"That may be. A rig got highjacked. They want you to lead in a team of Megacorp mercs to retake the platform."

"Those guys have training, what the fuck they need me for?"

"It's not to be questioned, Jake. They've been checked out to depth but have no real experience."

"It was rhetorical. When do I leave?"

"As soon as you're packed. Good luck, Jake." Mouse stuck out his hand, searching Jake's eyes. Jake shook the hand and was getting the feeling things weren't quite right.

"What is it, Chief?"

"Nothing, Jake, just watch yourself."

***

A jet engine drowned all unnecessary conversation. Not that there was any to interrupt. Jake sat alone in the rear of a commercial airliner. A curtain separated the final rows from the rest of the cabin. He may as well have been with the luggage. Johnny had helped him pack. He was not going. The vibes were heavy between the two. Knowledge that was not being shared ate at the moment.

"Jesus Johnny, what the fuck is up, man? You're acting just like the Chief."

"Nothing, Jake, just watch your ass."

"Thanks for the straight answer, be seeing you around." That was 48 hours ago. Now Jake was on a landing course for Bergen, Norway, knowing no more than what Chief Mouse had said.

Bergen was the shipping capitol of Norway, a primary port for the North Sea oil and gas fields. What Jake found odd on the way to the port was the order in which everything was built. The architecture was conservative and conformist. Its character came from the anal retentiveness of lines and angles. Having been burnt to the ground many times over the course of its life, the city planners had ample opportunity to get it right. One would call it 'quaint nouveau' for its lack of older structures, of which only a few had withstood the flames of centuries.

The port was as orderly as the town; built for maximum efficiency. It too, had been put to the torch more than once, creating a chance for harbor evolution. It was one of the most active ports in the world and still is, relatively. Even the dead of winter didn't slow the traffic in and out of the harbor, of which Jake was soon to be a part.

Big Brother loomed over the commercial pier. The massive wall of steel that was the wave-breaking bow hinted at the power in the bowels of the vessel. A boom truck, its arm stretched over the deck, was dangling men who were busy replacing the shot out windows of the wheelhouse. A black flag hung from the stern, casting a pall over the mooring. Jake noticed the chevron. It matched his mood and the weather that pressed down over Bergen in monochromatic shades of his misery. Jake's papers were checked before he was allowed on board. Even then, an escort was required for him to move about the ship. Otherwise, Jake was confined to his room in the officers' quarters and officers' mess. It was a typical arrangement. Borders are crossed but protocol remains the same. Reuseables just bugged people too much.

Jake hung his dive gear and went to the mess for some coffee. He stopped cold outside the door, the hair going up on the back of his neck. 'Whatever it is, I'm going to have to face it sooner or later,' Jake said to himself, sucked it up and stepped into the mess. Six men, dressed in black with attitudes to match, were talking quietly in a cloud of cigarette smoke, undisturbed by the intruder. Jake kept his eyes on the coffee machine, poured himself a cup and lit a cigarette before approaching the table. Taking a drag Jake said, "You know if you guys want to be divers you should give up that smoking." He leaned on the end of the table rocking their coffees, spilling them just a bit.

"Hey! Watch it, motherfucker!" one of the mercs said swiping at his pants.

"Who the fuck invited you, asshole?" piped another.

"I did, now shut up! Buenos dias, Jake. Have a seat." The one head that had not looked up when he rocked the table now held Jake's eyes from behind a pair of oversized sunglasses. He stood extending his hand, "Pablito Escobar. Your reputation precedes you."

Jake took the hand and the squeeze was on. It's a guy thing. "It usually does," Jake replied, keeping a tight grip on his cool. It was no wonder the two men Jake could rely on told him to 'watch his ass'. "Been a long time, Pablo."

"Si, it has. But I have never forgotten your resourcefulness. It was one of the reasons I asked for you."

"And the other?"

Pablo looked around the table. "Another time perhaps. Just what have you been told about our mission?"

"Other than to watch my ass, nothing."

"Surely your Chief Mouse gave you the skinny, no?"

Jake shook head.

"You are a poor liar, Jake - que sera sera. We are to retake the oil platform Goliath. Terrorists have seized it and they threaten to blow the rig if we don't comply with their demands. Any frontal assault will be dealt with in a similar manner."

"So, I have to hold your hands and get you babies to the rig, so you can go kill some sand niggers to maintain the status quo?"

"Something like that. You picked up on that pretty quick. You also get the feeling my men don't like to be called babies?"

"Asswipes come in all shapes and sizes, keep' em in their diapers. We wouldn't want to have any messes made." Jake was pushing it and saw it coming. The merc with coffee on his pants pulled a blade, intent on poking a hole in Jake. Jake grabbed the hand and dumped his coffee in the attacker's lap. He screeched and let go of the knife. Jake spun it around and stabbed the knife through the man's hand pinning it to the table.

"Oops, Pablo, one of your boys shit themselves." Jake turned away to refill his coffee, when the new Captain of Big Brother stepped into the mess.

"I see you have met." The Captain looked at the man struggling to pull the knife out of his hand. "Escobar, keep your men in line while on board the Big Brother. Save it for the bad guys. You must be the diver. I am Captain Carl Draken." Draken was tall and broad shouldered. Command came naturally to a man with such a stature. Even Escobar nodded at the order he was given. "Come with me, Strom, these men have already been briefed." Then to the mercs, "We leave on the outgoing tide. Mind yourselves once we are under way, I won't tolerate any bullshit. There is too much at stake." He glared at everyone in the room, including Jake. "Let's go." Jake followed Draken to the Captain's quarters.

Another jack-up rig in the vicinity of the Goliath needed supplies. Big Brother was ordered to deliver. Since the route would take them along the undersea pipeline that lead to the Goliath, a plan was made. It was after midnight by the time Big Brother reached the open sea. With ten-meter swells rolling under the ship, the sound of puking was heard from the mercs' quarters. Jake laughed a small laugh as the smell of vomit drifted in the hallway. It doesn't matter how tough you are when it comes to seasickness. It brings everyone to their knees at one time or another.

Arctic wind burned at exposed skin in the hour before dawn, two days after leaving Bergen. Six men were busy suiting up on the frozen rear deck of Big Brother. One lounged on a winch, already bundled in rubber and smoking a cigarette. Crewmembers carried battery–powered sea scooters to the fantail.

Jake got up from the spool of wire and began to inspect the mercs. He didn't want to have to save any of them because they weren't set up properly. Each man was heavily armed, with the exception of Jake. His harness held only tools. 'That'll change', Jake thought as the call came through on the ship's phone. Jake signaled an 'Okay' sign around the deck; when he got it in return from each of the mercs he walked to the swim step, watching the swells. He was handed a scooter and a moment later, disappeared into the top of a wave right as it went under Big Brother. Swimming straight down for 50 meters to get beneath the surge action, Jake turned on his lights and waited.

The plan was insane. Perhaps that is why it was chosen. But there was more to it than that and Jake knew it. Pablo revealed little in the chance meeting in the mess. His handshake however, told Jake they still had unfinished business. Jake reflexively pulled his spud wrench, thumbing the adjusting wheel, as a string of lights descended from above. As the circle of death surrounded him, Jake started his machine and led the way into the depths.

Five hundred feet deep in the open sea is a test for any man's mettle. Once on the seafloor they gathered again. GPS readings were taken before heading west, single file, Jake in the lead. Hours passed as they swam along the pipeline that led to the rig. If they stayed close enough to the pipe the sonar from Goliath would not pick them up. When Jake got there he waited for the others to catch up.

The legs of the jack-up rig rose like giant redwoods from the seafloor. Jake saw the lights of the submarine and killed his. The others in line followed the lead. Pablo kicked over, saw the lights and sat down on the dark side of the pipe, pulling out a handheld computer. He scrolled to the blueprints of the legs. Ladders on the outside of the legs had been left in place after construction was completed. Jake had no intention of letting them know there was an easier way in. Pablo passed the computer around, getting the okay signal from each of his men. He nodded to Jake, who led the five mercs to the farthest leg. Five thugs began the long slow climb to the surface while Jake and Pablo stayed behind to deal with the sub. They did not want to destroy the sub and its occupants just yet, and thus alarm the terrorists. Just make it immobile. While Jake tangled the prop with a piece of Hauser line left on the seafloor, Pablo attached a remote controlled explosive to a darkened porthole. Satisfied with the trap, they returned to the other divers and the climb.

Hopelessly repetitive, the ladder was endless, requiring more concentration than one would think not to miss a rung. It wasn't until reaching the surface that things got exciting.

The sea swells were rolling at ten meters, making the climb through the surf zone impossible. There was, however, a way. He had been hoping for this and could lose a merc or two in the process. Jake let go of the ladder, swimming away from the leg on the surface. It was a roller coaster. Riding the waves, Jake waited for the biggest wave of the set. As the mountain of water rolled at him, Jake started swimming hard for the ladder, staying on top of the swell. As the water swept past the leg, Jake pushed for the ladder, grabbing hold and climbing like a madman to get out of the way of the next wave. He made it, breathing hard from the exertion and waved for the others to get it on. The next two sets brought two more men. The third missed his timing. As he reached for the ladder rung, the wave dropped away, sending him tumbling down the back face into the trough only to have tons of water crashing down on top of him and sweeping him out to sea. He surfaced a half-kilometer away becoming a shrinking bobbing speck on the huge expanse of ocean. Lost. No thought or effort was put into a rescue. The remaining three men in the water learned the lesson of the one. Six divers now climbed the gelid rungs. It was a sprint to the top; the frigid arctic air would have frozen them to the ladder had the pace been any slower.

With the rig shut down, there was no one on deck to see the mercs crawl from the hatch and hustle to the nearest heated enclosure. In the drilling office they stripped and redressed. Weapons were assembled and put at the ready. Jake sat back in the headman's chair. Dry and warm, he lit a cigarette, watching the mercs go through their little deadly rituals. Pablo finished his prep work and came up to Jake.

"Well, amigo, it would be best if you remained here. Since I know you won't..." Lightning fast, the butt of his machine gun cracked Jake in the temple, sending him to the floor. A second and third smash made sure he stayed there. Blood flowed from split skin as Jake's lights went out. Pablo and his men left the office. The four Mercs headed one way to find the crew. Pablo made for the control room.

Pablo had been one of Megacorp's finest recruitments. He took to the Reuseable Program with a certain unnatural ease. He woke from the initial injection like graduating from college with a masters in killing and PhD in cruelty. When crooked contracts and civil negotiation failed, they sent in Pablo. As an assassin he was invisible; as a persuader, de Sade. He was one of the reasons for Megacorp's success in recent years.

Fast as a shadow he crossed the deck, disappearing up a flight of metal stairs, around a catwalk and up another flight. Ducking low, Pablo circled the control room. At a corner window, he rose up enough to peer in. Crewmembers sat at their stations, sweat staining their backs and armpits. Terrorists #1 and #2 sat reading magazines, guns in their laps. Harvey stared out the windows at the angry sea. His eyes shot to the corner window. Pablo was no longer there. The latch that secures the entry door clicked loud above the hum of computers and sonars. #'s 1 and 2 dropped their papers and raised their guns while taking defensive positions. Harvey took hold of the communications officer to use as a human shield. The door kicked in, smacking soundly against the inner wall, and #1 and #2 opened fire, a spray of hot lead filling the opening.

Pablo popped up outside the windows squeezing the trigger of a hand cannon. The recoil rocked the shooter as the .50 caliber round exploded on impact, shattering the tempered glass inward. The tiny shards of glass traveling at nearly the speed of sound, shredded #1 and #2, ripping the flesh from their bones, painting the walls with blood and guts. The fleshless skeletons wobbled and collapsed to the floor. The machine guns silenced. The crew huddled together. All were speckled with the red dots that coated the walls. Harvey moved unnaturally fast. His shield protected him from the blast. The face of the communication officer, less his skin, screamed in lipless horror. The howl was cut short as Pablo rolled through the open door spraying a stream of lead death at the wailing skull, exploding brain matter over the cringing crew. Harvey shot the closest window, threw the body at Pablo and followed his bullets. He leapt from the catwalk to the deck below, losing himself amongst the machinery.

Pablo freed himself from the corpse in time to see Harvey jump. He was not quick enough to get a clear shot. Personally he was shocked to see someone move so fast, but to have lost the moment really pissed him off.

"God damn it!" he yelled, pulling his head back in from the destroyed window. He raised his gun and unloaded on the crew. The large caliber rounds tore them to pieces. It served no purpose other than being a cathartic for Pablo, like slamming a door in anger. Reloading his weapon and taking one last look around the control room, he left to go find his men.

He found the first one at his post. His throat had been torn open and there was a significant lack of blood in the frosted environment. Pablo continued on to the next post and froze just before rounding a corner. Taking a quick look, he saw Harvey bent over his man; wet, slurping sounds that were not waves, chilled Pablo to the core. His gun came around next, bullets flying. Pablo stopped half way through the magazine. Harvey was gone. The merc was lying on the ice bound steel, steam rising from the open neck wound. Pablo kicked the body. It was already freezing to the deck.

At the galley – mercs #4 and #5 – stood at the ready outside the doors. They nodded to Pablo.

"They know we are here?"

Mercs #4 and #5 shook their heads.

"Well there is no reason to stand out here freezing our asses off." Pablo knocked solidly on the door. When the knob was turned, he kicked the door with all he had, sending the doorman flying across the room. Pablo dove into the room, landing on his stomach. He shot at the feet. Anything standing went down. Screaming and gunfire battled to be heard. Mercs 4 and 5 came in behind and finished what their boss had started. More men wound up dead than was absolutely necessary, but that's the way it goes.

***

Jake woke after the sun had gone down. Not that he knew it. The room had no windows and the lights were out. At least it was heated, but just enough to keep water pipes from freezing. He stumbled around looking for the switch. His head ached and was swollen; vision went from blur to double to clear and back again at a nauseating pace. He retched, found the light switch, slipped in his puke, and hit the ground, banging the swollen area of his head on the corner of a crate.

"Fuck me, God damn mother fucking son of a bitch jesus fucking christ that hurt!" Jake clutched his head until the throbbing and spinning stopped. He got to his feet and stared blankly around the office. He found the thermostat and continued looking. The bastards took his boots and socks! Dive booties wouldn't be worth a damn in the cold.

Offices always have coffee. Jake made a pot, poured a cup and sat down with a cigarette at the engineer's desk. At the bottom of the neat stacks of files, Jake found diagrams of the rig. They depicted where everything was, what it was and whether it was currently operational or not. The prints were dated recently so the info should be reasonably accurate. He studied them closely. Having worked on other jack-up rigs, Jake understood the basic layout. All were similar but not the same. They evolved through technological advancements and differing environments. North Sea rigs were massive when compared to the platforms in, say, the Caspian Sea. They had to be, to withstand the winter's unleashed fury.

Survival is what Jake had on his mind. Having seen Pablo's face, Jake was sure he was at the end of a long list of the day's dead and dying. Jake had killed more than his share during the course of his unlife. It wasn't the killing that bothered him. For the most part, nobody was ever shooting back. The mercs, who probably were not much better than the terrorists, were at least trained for this shit. Jake was trained to withstand the mental impact of murder. He was not taught how to do it. So he made it up as he went along. All Jake knew was he would have to kill Pablo. What he didn't realize was he would have to open the doors of hell to do it.

Jake searched through the merc's gear for something useful, like a gun. Nothing. A spud wrench and screwdriver seemed a pretty weak defense against automatic weapons.

Years of diving had taught him to use what was available. You didn't always have the luxury of the right tool, but you generally had what you needed. Cutting the sleeves off a sweatshirt made for a passable pair of socks. Jake then wrapped his feet in newspaper before removing his booties from the warm air coming out of the heater. They were still damp but it would have to do. He jammed his feet into the rubber booties, and zipped them up. A little tight but once again, they would do. Putting on all the clothes he could find, Jake pocketed the tools, downed the last of the coffee and opened the door on to the frosted world of a frozen rig.

With the exception of the unending roar of the waves, the rig was dead quiet. Each step froze wet booties to the deck. It was slow going as the footwear slowly turned to blocks of ice. Like Frankenstein tiptoeing, Jake made his way through the maze of superstructure that rose above the deck. Each step added another layer of ice. By the time he made the stairway for the control room his feet had to weigh twenty pounds each. He could not stop, or risk freezing in his tracks, literally, followed shortly by freezing to death in the cold arctic wind. In an agonizing effort, Jake pushed himself up the stairs, feet clunking loudly, painfully, on the treads. The steel railing burned his hands as he pulled himself upward. The last flight was crawling on all fours. Jake could no longer put any pressure on his feet. They dragged behind him, useless clumps of ice. Jake had had no idea you could freeze this quickly and was paying the price of ignorance.

The door of the control room had been left open. A mean wind blew in through the broken windows, taking the heat away. Jake needed warmth. The heavy jackets that hung on the wall would not supply it. He looked at the pile of decimated crewmembers. The ones at the top were frosted over. Inching his way next to the heap of death, he jammed his hand deep into the bloody mass to be met with painful warmth. Withdrawing it, he watched in amazement as the blood and gore froze immediately upon being exposed to the air. Like a mole he began to burrow his way deep into the pile, the smells causing him to puke on himself. Jake's mind reeled as he pulled his feet into the wet warmth. He had read of hunters crawling into their kills to save themselves from inclement weather conditions. It had seemed like so much bullshit then. The warmth lulled his senses and he was soon asleep.

In Jake's dreams he was sitting before a fire, being held by Quan Yin. She was chanting softly, swaying gently like a breeze. He woke to her tender touch, looking up into her face. She smiled back, eyes full of love and kindness. Jake closed his eyes, smiling.

When he opened them again, all was red and loud. Deep within the pile, one of the bodies started thrashing. A primal scream of terror, muffled by flesh, ripped through Jake, as hands clawed at his face. He got to his knees and in a mighty surge stood, toppling the pile, grabbing the raking hands and bringing them both to their feet. She wailed insanely.

The cold hit Jake like sledgehammer. There was no time to deal with someone who had lost their mind. He let go of her with his right hand, made a fist and belted her soundly up side the head. She collapsed. Working against the clock and the cold, Jake raided the dead for their clothes, any thing that wasn't soaked in blood would do. When he had enough, Jake began to strip the unconscious woman, only to rebundle her in the deads' clothing. Jake was shivering badly by the time he got to do himself. Frozen fingers sealed Velcro and fumbled at zippers. He spied a thermos and grabbed it before sitting in a corner, away from the wind. Jake put the woman in his lap, and then buried them both in the heavy coats.

Steam rose from the thermos when he popped the top. He drank two cups of the blessed heat before waking the woman to get some in her. Jake capped the bottle before rousing her; he didn't want to lose the precious fluid.

"Hey, wake up." Jake said shaking her. "What's your name? Come on, snap out of it."

The eyes open and for a brief moment they were relieved. Then reality kicked in, with panic hot on its heels. She screamed and jerked to get away when the flight instinct took over. She wanted out of there, as did Jake, but not screaming like a maniac. He held on tight but otherwise let her thrash. Several long minutes passed while panic raged through the woman, leaving her spent and shivering, but still in Jake's lap.

"Where is the nearest warm office?" Her eyes looked at him in fright. "I am a friend."

It took a moment but the words unlocked one of the chains binding her mind in fear.

"The med labs, one flight down."

Jake already knew this but he wanted to get her mind working. His feet were black and aching and the thought of having to carry her down the flight of stairs was not exactly pleasant.

"Have you been shot?" It was hard to tell with all the blood and flesh bits frozen to their clothing. She shook her head no. "Can you walk?"

"I think so," she said weakly.

"Good. My name is Jake, let's get the fuck out of here." Jake stood, still holding on to her. His feet shrieked and he dropped to his knees, but not letting go of the woman.

"Oh Jesus! Fuck me." Jake ground his teeth in pain.

She slid out of his arms, running for the open door.

"No! Wait!" Jake yelled crawling after her. He stopped. There was no use. His feet were frozen. He scooted over to the skeletons, now welded to the floor with ice, using his screwdriver to chip their weapons free of frigid boney grips. Extra ammunition was in a bag on the floor. Jake heard a 'ding' followed by a sliding sound. Dumping an empty magazine from the gun, he slapped a new one in and racked a round into the pipe, spinning on his near-frozen ass to aim in the direction of the sound. A bloody parka came through the elevator door. Jake relaxed his finger just in time. It was the woman. She ran over to Jake.

"My name is Mirka. Come on!" She took the guns in one hand and grabbed Jake's parka with the other, pulling him with extraordinary strength to a small elevator. Once inside, Mirka hit the close button, then another. The lift jerked and started down, coming to a stop moments later. The door slid open with a 'ding', warm air flooded the enclosure. Mirka took the guns and ammunition into the room, setting them on a table. She returned to the elevator, stepped over Jake and keyed the lift to 'off'. Jake crawled into the blessedly warm room, relieving himself of the bloody outerwear.

"Let us get you up on an exam table so I can take a look at those feet." Jake nodded and raised his arms to pull himself up, when she took him from behind and lifted him right off the floor and onto a padded table. Jake watched her as she took off the extra clothes. Blood and grime smeared her face, however, not so much he didn't notice the scar on her neck, from repetitive punctures. He had never met a female reuseable. If Mirka noticed him notice, she didn't show it. Strong hands unzipped his booties and delicate fingers carefully peeled back his 'socks' revealing the blackened feet. Jake bit his lips.

All personnel aboard cold weather rigs are trained to deal with cold injuries. They are an occupational hazard. Mirka wrapped his feet in clean, wet, warm towels. On top of those she placed a mini electric heating pad and dialed it up. She slid the screwdriver and spud wrench from his belt and went to a cabinet. Driving the screwdriver between two doors, Mirka pried until the lock gave and the doors popped open. On the shelves were racks of 'juice;' the maintenance hit, along with boxes of syringes. Mirka stabbed a vial with one of the hypos, withdrawing a full load. With one hand she felt the veins on the side of her neck. When the spot was located, the needle was inserted through the skin. Mirka pushed on the plunger, sending the crap into her system. She pulled the point and threw it into a sink, falling into a chair to absorb the rush.

Jake watched in awe, as much as the pain in his feet would allow anyway. When Mirka roused she repeated the procedure, this time with a much bigger syringe, and put it into Jake. After Jake recovered, she hit him again.

"It is the only way to save your feet. When you wake we will talk." He dreamed a nightmare with no feet, in a place where people only ran. Stumping along on the bloody ends of his shins, he cried for help. The big feet ran by kicking up bits of brown dust that choked his nostrils. A hand came into view; Jake woke.

Mirka had washed and was now washing Jake's face. "I couldn't stand to look at you any more." A pile of red stained towels sat at the edge of the table. She wiped her hands clean, "You should take care of the rest." Mirka handed Jake a wet clean towel. Jake pulled himself into a sitting position, prepared for an agonizing protest from his feet. It came but was far less disagreeable than it should have been. Looking down, his feet were a pale blue with patches of black and flesh tones. He wiggled his toes. They didn't fall off, but it hurt like hell. Jake laughed. Mirka looked over her shoulder and finished up what she was doing before spinning around on her stool and rolling over to the bed. She shined a light into his eyes, fanning it across each pupil, then checked his pulse.

"You will be all right."

"How long have I been out?"

"Eight hours or so. I overdosed you on the juice. It's one of the side effects."

"And the other effects?" Jake asked, just a little concerned.

"You heal. Now, just who are you and what are you doing here?"

Jake wasn't going to lie to her. She had saved his feet and probably his life. "I am a diver. I brought the mercs in. Who are you? I never met a, uh, uh..."

"Megacorp keeps it that way. Keeps us separate and anonymous. There is some concern as what would happen if we started to breed."

"What the fuck?"

"Precisely." Mirka agreed. "But we have more to be concerned with than our little bastard offspring."

"What do you mean?" Jake said shaking off the imagery.

"The one who took over the rig is, well, not quite human."

Jake was sure she meant Pablo; Jake himself wondered about his humanity. "The guy is kill happy, really. I've dealt with him before. Shoots fucking everything."

"It's not your psycho friend we have to worry about."

"He's not what you'd call a friend, but if it's not Pablo then you've lost me."

"Ahh, one of the slow ones," Mirka said to herself. Jake considered it a private joke and let the dis pass. "The reuseable who took control of the rig is no longer one of us."

"You're going to have to do better than that. Speaking of – you got anything for the pain?" Jake pointed at his feet and raised his palms upward in 'well?'

Mirka reached into a cabinet and tossed Jake a blister of aspirin.

"Give me a fucking break, doc! Got any Percs in there?"

Mirka shuffled around in the cabinet, produced a large bottle and tossed it over, but not before taking a handful and stuffing them in her pocket. "I am not a doctor. I study anomalies in the seabed that would indicate oil. Take what you need, Jake. Going on a little vacation right now is not a good idea."

Jake dumped some pills back in the bottle and swallowed the rest.

"Don't make me play twenty questions with you, doc. My head hurts and I already played it with somebody else. Tell me what happened and we'll take it from there." Jake lay back and let the painkillers kick in while Mirka brought him up to speed.

"There was something about the alpha terrorist. You could tell he was one of us, you know what I mean?"

"Yes, unfortunately. What do mean by 'was' one of us?"

"I don't know exactly. How's this, he was, but he is not any more. I mean he is, but he has escaped the Megacorp controls somehow. I watched from behind the men that protected me. He moved so quickly you could hardly see him and there was something in his eyes. They burned hatred from a dark fire deep within him. I had never been so afraid in all my life. Life, ha, what a joke."

With the pain evaporating, Jake was able to hear what she was saying. "How could anyone break the conditioning?"

"I don't know, but it would have to be done out of extreme desperation."

"No shit, I have tasted what it is like to be without. I would have done anything to stop the despair. That is if I could have."

"Apparently this man dug a little deeper than you did," Mirka deadpanned.

"Why thank you. I suppose I did something to deserve that." The meds had kicked in. Jake was malleable. "Where is this going, Mirka?" Jake said, looking at his feet.

"We have got to do something! We cannot just sit here!"

"I can." Jake responded slowly, taking a long blink. Jake watched her through slit eyes. A moment of clarity expanded and he saw what was going on inside her head. "You have got to be fucking kidding me!" Jake said incredulously.

Mirka gazed intently at the floor. "No," she said quietly. "I want out."

"Take that gun and put it to your head. If it is what you really want, I won't stop you."

"I want out because I want my life back."

"It's not possible."

"It is. I have seen it," Mirka replied.

"Better to work with what you have been given. The scales can be balanced, hard as that may be to believe."

"Seeing is believing. I saw what came aboard this rig. The man was alive!"

"That man is insane! Otherwise Megacorp would not have called in Pablo. It takes one to know one, and I don't think that is the life you want to lead. By the way, you can live within the existence we have. I know. I've done it."

"But you are still a lackey of Megacorp. I want to be free of them."

"There is no freedom, Mirka, and no escape from the yokes around our shoulders. Only by balancing the scales do you get the chance to live. Even then it doesn't last but it's better than no life at all," Jake finished. There was something in his delivery that spoke of experience in this. Mirka searched his eyes with a thousand questions.

"You just do." Jake replied, answering a few. "When the opportunity comes you take it. Your stomach will turn and you'll think run, run fast and hard away from your fear. If you don't run, then from that point on, you will start living until it leaves you, spent, scarred, bleeding, and back in the hands of Megacorp. But for a short time you will have lived and helped make the world a better place."

"I don't know what the fuck you are talking about, Jake."

Jake laughed, "Me neither, honey, but you're right. We can't just sit here. Let's see if we can get me on my feet."

Mirka came up to the exam table, lending Jake a shoulder and arm to lean on. His feet touched the floor with such pain he would had fallen to his knees had Mirka not held him up. Jake sucked it up and tried again. Jake reached into the pain, breathing deeply as he put pressure on his feet. He let go of Mirka and leaned on the table.

"Can you put my boots on, please?" Jake asked through clenched teeth. Once they were on, "Fuck me! I gotta sit down."

Mirka slid the stool over just in time to catch Jake's falling ass. He reached into his pocket and downed some more pills. Just then they heard footsteps coming up the metal stairs. There was only one pair of feet that shuffled in the foyer. In the silence intruded sniffing, like that of a large animal, and subhuman growls. It paced back and forth before the doorway. Machine gun fire sounded just before the thudding dink of lead slammed into the steel outer walls of the med lab. The entry door was hit again as the owner of the footsteps absorbed some of the bullets. More growling as the feet ran up the stairs to the next level.

One of Pablo's men came up the stairs in pursuit. He had a member of the crew. With hands tied behind his back and a noose around the neck attached to a stick, they made effective human shields. Pablo picked up on things quick, but not before losing more than half his team. There were now two of the mercs left including Pablo. He left one to watch over the crew. After the team left, Pablo took one of the crew for himself. A small woman he could lift with one hand and throw if he had to. He duct taped her mouth, trussed her up and left for the workstations. The cold wind in the low light of late afternoon bit hard into exposed skin. Pablo slipped along the walls, staying to the shadows. His shield whimpered against the gelid spray from crashing waves that iced the rig. Pushing her on ahead of him, Pablo heard gunfire and jerked her back close. The shooting came from the control tower. Between two stacks of containers Pablo saw a shadow running across the roof of the tower followed by two figures strobed in the hellfire that rained from his man's gun. The single figure leapt from the roof, landing on the deck 100 feet below. The body crumpled on impact. It slowly, painfully, got up. Hobbling at first, it broke into a crippled run, away from the tower.

Pablo headed across the deck on an intercept course, his shield over his shoulder so as not to slow him down. Footsteps and panting came barreling down the alley of containers. Stepping into the narrow passage, Pablo crouched in a defensive position, holding his shield and weapon before him. His timing was off. The runner, too fast, bowled into Pablo going full out. The three tumbled away into the side of a container,

Pablo's head knocking soundly into the steel. Whatever it was crawled away from the collision, dragging Pablo's shield with him.

It took a moment for Pablo to clear his head, with blood turning to rime on his face. Through the glaze of red in the last light of sunset, he could swear he saw the face of his enemy buried in the neck of the woman, his teeth tearing at the flesh as it drank the blood of its victim. It glanced up to see Pablo aghast at the sight. It dumped the wasted soul and disappeared into the arctic night. Pablo pulled himself up, taking off in another direction, back to the office where he had left Jake unconscious. Finding it empty, he cursed himself and headed back to the cafeteria.

Jake and Mirka waited quietly until two pairs of feet raced back down the stairs. Jake stumped around the lab. The meds had finally kicked in. He went to the cabinet that held the 'juice'.

"Just what was it you said about overdosing on this shit?"

"It accelerates the healing."

"How do you know this?"

"I saw it done once. Locals ambushed our research team while we searched some long dry cenotes in the Yucatan. We had a Megacorp security detail that got shot to pieces before they blew the entrance to the cenote."

"So you were trapped, yes?"

"Yes."

"Well?"

"The commander of the squad pulled a pack of those vials you are holding and injected his men until there was no more. They nodded for a while. When they came to was when the nightmare started."

"What do you mean, nightmare?"

"They started digging us out. It was a maddened frenzy, ripping the flesh from their bones as they dug. Their strength was inhuman, but when they broke through to the surface it began."

"What began?"

"The opening had been surrounded by the local bandits. Bullets rained through the squad but did not stop them as they tore through the ranks of shooters. Jesus, Jake, they ripped the throats open and drank from the blood that gushed. It was horrible."

"I'm sure it was." Jake lit a cigarette. "How much did the commander give them?" Jake rolled a couple vials in his hand. "How much did you give me?"

"I don't remember. But I gave you a triple dose."

"Do it again." Jake began to unbutton his collar.

"No."

"We may not have the chance later, do it, or I will. Besides I'm American, we coined the Megacorp motto."

Mirka looked at him with a hint of confusion about what was just said.

"I believe it was first said by one Johnny Rocco. He was a gangster in the early 1900's. It was certainly the first time I've ever heard an adjective used as a noun."

Mirka gave the 'come on already' with her eyes.

Any way Rocco was trapped, holding a family hostage. One of the prisoners asked him what he wanted, since he obviously had everything money could buy. Well when questioned what he wanted, Rocco's reply was, 'more.' Therefore more of more is better and more of..."

"I get it Jake," Mirka replied, rolling her eyes.

"And people say I'm the slow one," Jake said with a slather of sarcasm.

They almost had a laugh. Under different circumstances... But it wasn't to be. A dark surrealism lay directly in their path.

Mirka hesitated before taking the vials from Jake's hand and a fresh syringe. Jake tilted his head to the side when she was ready to inject. Mirka pushed the point into the big vein and thumbed the plunger.

As she was doing this Jake asked, "What happened to the team that saved you from the cenote?"

"When we were safe and out of the way, Megacorp brought in a gunship and carpet bombed the place. There were no survivors." Jake perhaps should have asked the question sooner as he collapsed on the floor.

Jake swam in a blood red sea, a maelstrom, from which towering waves lifted him up before crashing down on top of him. Rolling in the crimson froth, he fought for breath but there was no air, only the viscous red fluid. Lungs burning, forcing the breath from him, Jake inhaled, choking as the fluid filled his lungs. As panic raced through his mind turning all sense to shambles he took in the blood, breathing in its richness and strength, exhaling all that was good. Goodness served no purpose in a world of madness rife with man's deadly sins. Witnessed through a sanguine lens, visions of horror assaulted him. Senseless acts of the mob mentality were no less terrible than the Inquisitions of Dark Age Spain, the concentration camps of the second world war, genocide in Africa, the slave trade in early America, sweat shops, prostitution rings, child pornography, the Christian crusades; all have the semblance of being orchestrated by a single mind of inherent evil. As events unfolded, Jake found himself no longer watching but the one behind the mask, with pointed hood ready to tighten the noose around a runaway slave's neck, or the torturer whose red hot poker vaporized eyes that saw what they should not have, the whip that split the skin of laborers, and the hand that turned on the poison gas.

Jake's mind writhed in the macabre imagery spinning about him in a crimson whirlpool. His struggles were futile as he spun around being pulled down into the depths. His eyes opened, all was darkness. The sound of the vortex merged with the open sea and the waves crashing against the oil platform. Little red lights of electronic devices blinked in the periphery of his sight. The visions of horror were gone. The feelings generated by them, however, did not dissipate into the blackness. Jerking himself into a sitting position brought Jake into the here and now. His feet no longer hurt and his head had quit aching. The swelling on the side of his head was no longer. Jake eased his feet to the floor not knowing what to expect but prepared for the worst. The full weight of his body did not disagree with them. A step, another, they worked. Somewhere inside himself Jake was sure he was pleased, but the feeling would not be found. Instead there was grim darkness that pervaded his consciousness, as if a door to his sinister self was somehow open and the shadow pouring out. There was no goodness here, not anymore. When he spoke her name, it was not the voice he normally heard. It sounded more like gravel being dumped from a truck. Not so much an animal, but definitely less than human. Jake felt Mirka more than actually seeing her. The feelings were dead on. He turned his head and looked at her before she replied.

"Good morning, Jake, you okay?" Mirka spoke hesitantly, uncertain of what she was speaking to.

"No, but I will be. I can walk. Is there any fucking coffee in this place?" Jake asked, trying to lighten up a little. In the back of his mind, piercing the blackness was something Johnny had told him: 'use the tool'. Jake was still a little unclear as to the full meaning, but what it meant right now was, don't take it out on Mirka. You asked for it, you got it, now deal with it. Something that is easier said than done when you realize you had just lost your soul.

"Yes, I was waiting for you to wake." In the darkness Mirka pressed the button on the coffee maker, adding another red light to the rest.

"Thank you. Dawn will be here soon, any ideas?" Jake asked.

"We should get out of here. Won't they be looking for medical supplies for the injured?"

"There won't be any injured." Jake said flatly.

Mirka understood. She did not have to inquire further. With two cups of coffee she walked over to the windows where Jake was standing, staring out at the coming dawn. Both cradled the hot cups, sipping in silence as real coffee drinkers are wont to do, while the night slipped away. Jake lit a cigarette. The sky began to brighten, dampened by heavy cloud cover. Mirka looked at Jake in the dim light. His skin was pale and tears of blood ran down his cheeks. Jake noticed her notice and wiped the tears away with his sleeve.

"You sure you're going to be all right?"

"Yeah. There is always a trade off. You get something, you lose something."

As if in response to Mirka's suggestion, an explosion ripped the morning a new asshole. Shrapnel immediately chased the blinding light. Jake grabbed Mirka and spun around, protecting her, taking the blast of shattered tempered glass in his back. They went down sliding across the floor. Maddened, Jake leapt to his feet, bringing up one of the machine guns with him. At the window, he sprayed 500 rounds, ripping into the containers and deck below. He was shooting at nothing.

Mirka came up to him and grabbed his shoulder. "Stop! Jake! We have got to go!" she screamed as the gun went still. Cold wind blew through the windows, freezing the spots of blood on Jake's back. She began dressing rapidly. Pulling on a coat she saw Jake just standing there at the window, smoking gun still at the ready. Mirka yanked his shoulder, turning him around and slapped him hard in the face, snapping Jake out of it.

"What the fuck's the matter with you! We have to get out, now!" Mirka yelled.

Jake mumbled something unintelligible, reloaded the gun and began to dress. Out on the stairs angry voices were heard followed by a burst from a machine gun, dimpling the steel door. Jake grabbed the guns and ammo and met Mirka at the elevator door. The lift slid open, they stepped in just as another explosion blew the med lab door from its hinges. Hot lead poured through the doorway as the elevator door whispered closed and dropped away. The lift stopped at the deck below the main deck.

The door opened into the machinations of the rig; machine shop, laundry, waste reclamation, and clean storage. As soon as they exited the lift, Jake jammed the door open with his screwdriver.

"They'll be climbing down the wire any time. Let's fill it." Jake laughed a little insanely and began taking anything that would fit and stuffing it into the elevator. He dragged a desk over and lifted it to the ceiling while Mirka used lamps and chairs to support it. Once the space was filled Jake pulled the screwdriver. Nothing happened, which was exactly what Jake wanted.

"Which way to the escape pods?"

"Down this passage." She took off ahead of Jake who stayed a moment longer to hear the men climbing down the elevator shaft. When he was sure he knew just where they were, Jake emptied a magazine into the sheet metal wall. Bullets hammered through the steel punching holes in flesh, screams as men fell the short distance to their death. Jake smiled, pleased with the effort, and chased after Mirka.

When Pablo returned to the cafeteria, he collected himself before entering. Covered in blood he made for quite a sight, which he intended to use to his full advantage. The crew sat at the far end of the room, waiting, which was something they were unaccustomed to doing. You had to be of a hardcore lot to work in these conditions. They were also company men. Raised in the oil fields, they lived for it. This mindset would also play favorably for what Pablo had in mind.

"Good morning, crew of the Goliath. We were sent by Megacorp to regain control of this platform. When we first arrived drastic measures were necessary to get an idea of what we were up against." Pablo was losing them. He himself had already killed a number of crew and they hadn't forgotten.

"Your anger and rage is understandable. But why focus it on me and my men, who are but servants of Megacorp sent to save your sorry asses." Okay he had their attention, now to use it. "We need to arm you men. Where are the munitions stored?"

A big Swede in a supervisor's jumpsuit stepped forward.

"What's your name?" Pablo barked in a commanding tone.

"Sven Larson, drill crew chief. I can take you there."

"Better yet, Sven," Pablo tossed his machine gun to the man, "Pick a few men and take one of mine. Get all you have and bring it back here." Sven caught the weapon, checked it for ammo and pulled six men from his group, using only his eyes. They left as a pack. The merc took point with Sven bringing up the rear. Regardless of the appearance of trust,

Sven was still not convinced these were company men. More likely this 'Pablo' and his men were the terrorists. After five minutes of walking the merc in circles. Sven raised his gun and put a bullet into the back of the merc's head. His men were shocked but Sven was their leader; they acted accordingly by relieving the dead man of his guns and ammo.

Sven was no fool. He had been working the Goliath since he was a kid, when the rig was privately owned. Sven never fell for all the corporate bullshit. The money was good and they left him alone. You don't get many shirts out on an active drill platform and that's where he kept himself. He couldn't speak for all of the crew but the six he picked were 'his' men. The nature of the work involved a deep trust of the tight knit crew. The skills were hard to learn and not everyone was cut out for it. It's why they call them roughnecks. Not a man in the crew had a full set of digits. Stay in the biz long enough and you're bound to lose one sooner or later. Your hands were your union card.

The rig had a brig of sorts, for drunken sailors, strung out wildcats, and those who just lose it, going rig simple. It was next to the Purser's office, which held the guns. After forcing the doors, they loaded crates of munitions onto a skid. They were mostly small arms, handguns and machine guns. There were no anti-personnel hand grenades, RPG's or incendiary devices; after all, it was an oil rig. There was a case of concussion grenades; no shrapnel, but enough whack to incapacitate most people. He passed these out among his men. Industrial explosives were kept at the far end of the platform, cantilevered off the end in its own storage. Sven wasn't about give it to Pablo.

The morning was still black as the drill crew made their way back to the cafeteria. They went by one of the frozen corpses that Harvey had fed upon. The torn neck had frosted at the edges; snapping, when poked with the barrel of a gun.

"What would have done this, Sven?" Karl, a quiet machinist asked. He voiced what the others were thinking.

"I don't know, but I think it best we evacuate the women and shirts. This was one of the mercs and there doesn't appear to have been much of a struggle. Karl, you and Lundquist go back to the purser's office. Lock yourselves in. Use the computer to monitor energy draws all over the rig. Nothing can survive this cold. We should be able to get a fix on whatever else is on board. Call the cafeteria in fifteen minutes. We should be there by then." Sven ordered.

There was no questioning the directions. "Come on, Lunds!" The two men beat a path back to the office.

"What are we going to tell that Pablo about his man?"

They heard footsteps coming down a passageway toward them. A motion sensor activated a hall light. What ever it was, was suddenly hurtling towards them. Sven was able to get off a few shots at the shadow before it bowled into them, snatching one of his men from his feet and carrying him away. Adolf screamed as he was slung over the being's back. Sven and the other men could not shoot without hitting him. In the few moments, Sven turned, sighting on the running figure and emptied his clip into the thing's back, killing his man in the process. The phantom stumbled, going down on his knees. It howled a blood curdling cry as it turned upon the men. This time four guns came up, drowning the howl with a deafening roar of automatic gunfire. Red eyes glared before it hurled the dead body at the shooters and disappeared around a corner.

Adolf's perforated body hit the ground, blood splattering from multiple wounds. The droplets froze in the air pelting Sven and his men like rocks that melted again on contact. They loaded Adolf's body onto the pallet of munitions.

"I guess we don't have to tell him anything, now."

"What the fuck was that, Sven?"

"I don't know, but god help us."

When Sven and his men entered the cafeteria what had been a cackle of voices went dead quiet. Sven glared at Pablo carrying Adolf to cold storage.

"Why didn't you tell us?" Sven said coldly to Pablo.

"Would it have been useful?" Pablo condescended.

Sven's phone rang.

"Sven, it's Lunds. We have a power draw in the med lab. It's not much but somebody turned something on."

"Stay on it, keep the doors locked." Sven closed the phone and said to his crew, "I need ten to the control tower." A dozen men stepped forward.

The group kept a tight circle, all facing away from the center as they wound through the maze of passageways. Dawn was still waiting in the wings as they scuttled onto the main deck below the control tower windows. Sven watched from around the corner of a shipping container.

A spark, a flame. His eyes widened as the glow of a cigarette burned behind the glass. Sven nodded to his second and picked a concussion grenade from a pocket. He looked it over, found the pin, pulled it and threw the damn thing at the windows. The grenade clipped the railing of the catwalk, falling to the expanded steel before exploding. The blast sent his men diving to the deck for cover and knocked Sven back a few paces. Moments later machine gun fire poured from the windows into the containers below. When it stopped, Sven made his move.

"Let's go!" He yelled. The crew were back on their feet, running for the tower. Up the stairs, past the med lab landing, then up another flight into the control room. Heavy breathing filled the room with utter silence as they gazed on the massacre of the previous day. Familiar faces were twisted in fear at the time of their death, frozen now in a macabre greeting. More than a few felt their breakfast rising too fast to stop. The steaming puke turned to ice, shattering on the floor.

Sven pressed the elevator button. Getting no response, he forced the doors and looked down the shaft. Three men stepped forward, slinging their guns for the climb down. A minute later, they were dead.

***

A wraith, pale, translucent, swirled at the end of his gun. Jake smiled at the veil of madness. Mirka watched the dementia growing in Jake. He was changing just as the mercs in Mexico had, losing their minds in an ever expanding narrowing of perception. His actions were devolving along with his rational mind and it wouldn't be long before it was gone all together. When the moment came there would be no thought, only action.

At the end of a long passage below decks, Mirka and Jake stopped running. Before them were the escape pods. Each was capable of handling six passengers. Jake felt his mind slipping away. All he wanted to do was get Mirka off the platform before he lost it all together. He pulled on the lever that opened the hatch to one of the pods. Ducking low, Jake looked into the ovoid, verifying that it was fully equipped, when he heard quick footsteps from behind.

Mirka put both feet into the kick, hitting Jake in the lower back, sending him flying into the vessel. Jake hit the far wall in a hard way. The door slammed shut and was locked down before he could respond. A look of compassion filled the port in the door looking in on Jake, as her right hand reached for the big red launch button.

Jake took too long to assess the situation while staring into the big eyes on the other side of the port. He was not strapped in when Mirka's hand came down. The pneumatics kicked in, the escape pod was launched and Jake was slammed into the trailing end of the projectile, cracking his head hard against the steel wall. He fumbled futilely with a harness in a desperate race to be locked down before impact. It was not to be. The pod slammed into the North Sea, a kilometer south of the Goliath. Jake had one arm in the harness when it hit the water. His body vaulted to the other side of the pod. His arm, however, remained in the harness. Unconscious on the floor of the pod, the gaping wound at his shoulder spurted his blood and injections until there was no more. The hum of the bilge pump could be heard sending the excess fluid into the sea. Jake died on the floor, never knowing that his life had been saved.

Mirka had lived on Goliath for the last nine months and knew the rig inside and out. She also knew a few other things she never told anyone about. Only Mirka knew she had been suicidal since the incident in Mexico. She wanted out. Mirka considered Jake's balancing of the scales and continuing on. No, she was too far gone to see the whole picture. She did not want what Pablo or the other had, as she told Jake. She wanted out, period. If she could do a little balancing act on the way...

The route was bitter cold. Mirka used the structures of the rig to conceal her movements to the cantilevered storage. She swiped her pass and the locks disengaged. Inside was as cold as out. Mirka had done her homework, knew what she was looking for and where it was. She had schmoozed her way into the social network. She was a reuseable, but she was also a woman. On a rig where 99 percent of the personnel is male, well, you go figure.

The detonators were digital, operated by remote, and could be set to go off one at a time or all at once. The explosives were new generation. When compared to C4, half the volume yields tens times the destructive power. It was a lot of bang for your buck. She filled four rucksacks with blocks of the stuff, punching detonators through the explosives' plastic wrap. Mirka worked rapidly but lost the battle to beat the sun.

✳✳✳

In the steel grey light of dawn, a lone figure could be seen scuttling across the deck. No one saw Mirka dump the first bag of explosives into one of the legs of the jack-up rig, or the second, or the third. On her way to the final leg, she froze in her tracks. It was not light enough to see clearly but whatever it was made her skin crawl.

It sat atop a stack of containers and machinery, like a gargoyle perched at the end of a flying buttress. Slowly the head turned until its black glare rested on Mirka. It breathed in her scent. The stony figure rose from its haunches and faced Mirka, toes curled over an edge of steel. A sharp high-pitched cry came from the creature's maw that pierced the coming dawn. Then there was a short silence before it leapt towards Mirka.

Machine gun fire erupted from the top of the drill platform. Bullets hammered into the hurtling creature, changing its trajectory and slamming it into a steel support. More bullets poured into the prostrate figure. When the shooting stopped, another demon took to the air. This time it was Pablo, swinging on a rope from the highest point on the rig to the deck below. He let go while still in the air, unslung his gun and landed feet first on the deck. When he got to where his bounty had fallen, it was to find a blood splotched smear on steel. He swung around. 'Where was the woman?' he thought. She had been excellent bait and her arrival serendipitous.

Pablo had left the men hours before to secure his post at the best vantage point, atop the big drill. A frigid wind bore into him as he kept vigil. He saw the woman first. She lit up bright green in the night-vision goggles. Pablo could not exactly see what Mirka was doing but could tell she was doing something. She was not just wandering aimlessly and walked with a sense of purpose. He had hoped to discover her purpose when another movement caught his eye. Sitting fifty meters away was what Pablo was looking for. It stood and leapt. Pablo did what came naturally under such circumstances. He opened fire. Thirty bullets found their mark before he replaced the magazine and dumped another thirty into its body. It took him three seconds to get to get to his victim.

In the moments after the final shots, Mirka made up her mind on a course of action. She scrambled to the human form that had flown at her and stuffed a slug of explosives into its shredded pants. Turning to run, it grabbed her pant leg. Mirka was no pansy chick. She worked out. Panic and adrenalin gave her the extra 'umph' she needed to break free. Such close contact scared her shitless as Mirka streaked through the endless maze of machinery and equipment. Tired calves pumped her across the deck to the final leg. The dogs to the access hatch were frozen over. Using her machine gun as a hammer, Mirka beat at the globs of ice, freeing the dogs. She tossed the bag in, slammed it closed and locked the hatch in place. The hair went up on the back of her neck. She turned quickly dropping to one knee while shouldering the gun. When Mirka saw a form she squeezed the trigger. Click.

***

Even with night-vision goggles Pablo could not track the thing. It was cool, not warm like most humans, so the glasses were less than useful. The female, however, was winding her way to the far side of the platform. Pablo followed her. He wanted to see where she was going. He came upon Mirka just as she was slamming the hatch closed. He missed it. Damn! As she spun around and brought up her gun Pablo realized what he was dealing with. She was another reuseable. When her gun jammed, he took a good look at the battered weapon and the shattered ice chunks at the foot of the door.

"That's what happens when you use them as a hammer. They can shatter a man's skull and remain operational. But steel, ahhh, no. My name is Pablo Escobar. It is a pleasure to meet you. You are?"

Mirka recognized the man as the maniac who shot up the crew in the control tower. She threw her gun down, muttering something angrily under her breath. "I work in the research department, Mirka Vladisova." She said clearly with no emotion.

"I do not remember seeing you in either of the two groups of crewmembers. Where could you have been?" toyed Pablo.

"The men in the control room used their bodies to keep me alive." Mirka was not playing.

"And they say chivalry is gone. Come, let us get out of the cold. The cafeteria should have breakfast ready. By the way, what were you doing out here?" Pablo waved the way with the barrel of his gun. Mirka played it cool. She clutched the detonator tightly in her hand as they made their way across the deck, saying nothing.

All heads turned as the cafeteria door opened. Some ducked. When she pulled back the hood to her parka, Sven was out of his chair to snatch her from Pablo.

"Dr. Mirka! Where have you been? There has been no word from the men trapped in the control tower!"

Mirka shook her head slowly, glancing towards Pablo. "There will not be any word from the tower."

"Come, come, my girl! Away from these men and have a cup of hot coffee." Sven shouted to the far side of the room, "Greog, some fresh coffee, short stack and some eggs! Mirka is back!"

There was shuffle and banging of pans followed by an apron-clad cook bringing out breakfast as ordered. Mirka gave him a grateful eye as she wrapped her cold hands around the steaming mug. Sven was checking the scene out, watching his men with one eye. The other never left Pablo. The merc was alone now and therefore that much more dangerous. Most of his men were armed, but they were wrenches and fitters – more accustomed to bar fights than gunfights. No, too many would die if Sven gave the order to kill Pablo. This required patience and Sven was not a patient man.

But he was father, brother and confessor to all the men aboard. That included Mirka. He fussed over her eggs making sure everything was okay and topped her coffee after a couple sips. He was usually worried about her interactions with the men. Having women on a rig is kind of nice as long as everyone is on their best behavior. Every once in while though, guys will be assholes, thinking with their dicks. This would usually happen after booze was smuggled aboard. Sven would get a call in the wee hours to quell a disturbance, only to find Mirka standing over a couple drunken sailors that she had just kicked the shit out of. She didn't mind a little flirtation but she reserved the right to choose rather than be chosen. When push came to shove, she could flatten any man on the rig who went there. That didn't keep them from trying.

In his years, Sven had heard the disgusting bragging of men who made it with a reuseable female. It's a really unfortunate guy thing. You know, forbidden fruit and all that shit. They don't call us dickheads for nothing. He never spoke of his experiences and busted the heads of those who did. Mirka generally saved him the effort. He admired her ability to handle the men and she liked his fatherly attitude without the groping.

"How did you get past that thing out there?" Sven inquired.

"I didn't. Pablo shot it full of holes just before it reached me."

"Here, let me take your coat." Sven offered.

Mirka hesitated, palming the detonator before letting him have her coat. Sven may have been a fool once but that was long ago. He had since learned to keep his eyes and ears wide open. Her hand was too small to fully conceal the red plastic housing. Mirka noticed him notice and swiped her nose with a free hand. Sven nodded and shouted to the kitchen.

"More eggs and homefries, Greog. Make sure they're hot, this girl is mighty cold!"

"Bring Mirka back here, Sven. You know what they say about heat and a kitchen." Greog shouted back over the noises of the galley.

"Ya, ya! The cook is right! Why didn't I think of it before?" Sven hustled Mirka through the stainless swinging doors heading straight to the far end.

With a few moments before Pablo would come in, Mirka wasted no time. "You must get your men off the rig. If they stay they will die. I have set charges to blow the Goliath to kingdom come. It is the only way to get rid of that monster."

"You can't! The oil!"

"The spill will be minimal. There is no more oil here, Sven. It's all gone." Sven's jaw dropped. "You must make a plan and do it quickly. There is no time!"

Just then Pablo came around some pantry shelving. He spoke casually. "Ahh, here you are. Conspiring, I see. Do not be concerned. It is only natural. Let's see... I imagine you plan to rid yourselves of the madness that waits outside that door and if a few bullets find their way to me in the process, like you did to my man on the way to the armory, all the better, eh? But how could you rid yourselves of such a thing? I guess you would have to blow it to kingdom come. Eh, Mirka?"

Mirka cursed herself. How could she have been such a fool? Deciding to disregard the remark, "I need some more coffee, Sven?" The two walked away from Pablo. There was no use wasting time. Unless wasting time is what you wanted to do.

After another pot of coffee went empty at Sven's table, he got up and approached Pablo who was having an animated discussion with Mirka.

"We need to bring in more food supplies. We were not anticipating a terrorist attack. Cold storage is down two decks."

"Bring up some steaks. And while you're at it, go to the explosives shed. Bring me back fifty pounds of your best and some detonators." Pablo ordered.

All of Sven's men got up, checked their weapons and made for the door.

"Whoa, Whoa, Whoa! What's up, Sven? You're making me a little nervous here." Pablo said, not nervous at all.

"With that thing out there, we will split into two teams. At least one may make it back."

"What's to keep you from coming back at all?" Pablo eyed Sven.

"I'm not going anywhere, Pablo." Mirka pitched in.

Pablo may have been a cold-blooded killer but he didn't miss the little things. He saw the warmth that poured from the men when he had brought her in, shivering in her boots. They would be back. "Good luck. May your Viking gods protect you." Pablo laughed and waved them away. Once they were gone he put his feet up on the table. "Mirka, could you get me a cup of coffee?"

Mirka bristled, making a tight smile as she got up and went to kitchen. She needed some anyway. Yeah right. She needed time and was buying it.

"So how did you pick up on my thoughts?" Mirka asked feigning openness.

"I've been working at it a long time. Unfortunately I missed the real information."

"Being a reuseable and with the thing outside being somewhat less than human, Sven figured I would know about such things," Mirka explained.

"Says a lot for what they think of us. And do you? Know about such things." Pablo prompted.

"Not nearly as much as you."

"Perhaps you know what happened to the diver that brought us aboard this rig?" He asked.

"He is no longer aboard the Goliath."

Anger rose inside Pablo. "Where is he?" He demanded.

"I launched him out in an escape pod." Mirka smiled.

Pablo got up to strike her but pulled himself back just before letting fly. He sat gripping the edge of the table. "Why would you have done that?" He asked calming himself.

"We have one monster aboard. Do we really need another?" Mirka smiled again.

"I had plans for that man."

"He seemed quite a capable individual. I am not surprised you wanted him. To answer your question of why – it's because I think it is time to balance the scales. By the time Jake found the med lab, his feet and hands were horribly frost bitten. He would have lost them. I used a cure meant only for emergencies. I've seen it done once. I got him off the platform because there are also the side effects."

"Jake without his hands or feet is something I wouldn't mind seeing," Pablo said slowly, enjoying a little creative visualization. "At least I know where he is, which is better than not knowing. Finding him again should not be much trouble."

Mirka got up and refilled her coffee. Bringing back the pot, she set it next to Pablo. She felt like throwing it in his face. She was planning she knew not what. The weight of the detonator in her pocket gave Mirka the confidence to continue.

Pablo topped off his cup, chuckling darkly to himself at the dis. He knew she would conspire against him but he had been playing this game a good deal longer. Funny thing was Mirka didn't appear to be bluffing.

She had not made any threats or even hinted at such. She was playing it cool. A little too cool. Beating the shit out of her would prove a waste of time. Mirka was a reuseable and so understood pain and torture to an extremely intimate degree, making pain a useless tool. Pablo decided to go fishing instead.

"You seem to have developed friendships aboard the rig. It is rare to see the bonding between an us and them. But... you are a good looking woman. I imagine sucking the right dick now and then could make life quite nice," said Pablo.

And Mirka knew it. Her early days in the Reuseable Program had taught her just how cruel men can be. Having no tenure, reputation or clout made her an easy target for every lewd bastard she would meet. The abuse began verbally and before long she was being repeatedly raped. She had to take it. There was no other way. As long as the job was not interfered with, it was open season. After a few years the abuse began to take its toll. It was, of course, her own fault. Some suits decided a little education was called for.

Mirka was flown from a workboat to corporate headquarters. She was cleaned and coiffed, and dressed before being thrown to the wolves. The wolves were corporate lawyers with an insatiable need to do physically in the night what they do with words during the day. That is to debase, degrade, humiliate, and of course get their rocks off in the process. What drunken ignorant fools did in bar rooms and parking lots with pool cues and worse was nothing compared to the disgusting acts of highly educated men.

One lawyer, usually left out of these affairs, for he was a reuseable too, was invited on this occasion to partake in the ruining of one of his own. She was dressed like a whore and treated like a slave. Shortly after it started, Kale waded into the circle of men viewing the action and waiting their turn. With a letter opener, he quietly opened the onlookers, like wet letters. Intent on the activities, the lawyers never noticed the dwindling of their ranks until it was too late. The drunken suits were no match for a man who knew what he was doing.

Kale dressed Mirka and took her to his place. While she cleaned up he rewrote her contract so this sort of thing would never happen again. He could not repair the damage that had been done. Who could? It would, however, make her existence that much more bearable. That was a long time ago. She was forever grateful for what Kale had done, though she never saw him again.

"I imagine you are quite right about that. But then again, you would know more about such things than me. Sven is the father of the crew. I work hard and mind my own business. It took a long time to earn his respect."

"But just a couple minutes to make him your dog. Is that what you were doing out on the deck when I found you? Minding your own business?"

"After I got rid of Jake I figured to take a look around and see how the rig was holding up. You have everyone in the galley."

"God I love a good employee." The sarcasm dripped from Pablo.

"Yeah? Good employees pay your salary so don't go around killing them all."

"You're good. Real good."

The door to the galley opened quickly with a gust of frigid wind that blew napkins and paper cups across the room. Sven Larson filled the doorframe, pushing a cart stacked with explosives and dead men. Behind him came more carts pushed by more men with more dead. Behind them came more carts with food and more dead. Sven had left with twenty men. All twenty returned, but only six were walking; the rest got a cart ride.

Sven and his men were grim as they unloaded the bodies and put them in cold storage. The weather outside would have kept them frozen plenty solid but the old drill chief wanted to put on a show. He and his crew were splattered in frosty blood and their guns reeked of fresh gunpowder. The fourteen dead were stacked before Sven approached Pablo.

"I guess there would have been enough food after all," Pablo stabbed sardonically.

"We procured the explosives you wanted. Now if you don't mind." Sven turned away, but not before catching Mirka's eye and giving her a blink of affirmation. He went to sit with his men by the heating duct and have some coffee.

Pablo did not miss the little communication between the drill chief and science officer. He just didn't know what it meant.

Indeed Sven had gotten the explosives for Pablo and food for his men, but he had also completed a few items of his own agenda. Mirka had been clear about what she intended to do. Sven had no doubt that she could and would keep her word. When the teams left the galley they headed straight for the escape pods. Sven asked for six volunteers.

The six silently stepped forward. The rest boarded escape pods and were successfully launched. Sven ordered his men to then gather up fourteen crewmembers who had died earlier in the week.

***

Jake woke to the stainless surroundings of a Megacorp Reuseable ice room. Rows of rolling slabs filled the room, only about half were full. Gray sheets covered the lumps of flesh leaving only the feet visible with a toe-tag dangling. A few days earlier Jake was given an injection to bring him around from limbo to purgatory. He may have been on ice for days or years. There was no way of knowing; besides it really didn't matter. Everyone he had known was dead. The Stiltskin effect. Jake assumed Stiltskin was an early model reuseable who first noted the anomaly.

The doors of hell opened with a resounding crash, jolting Jake from the reverie of the damned. Light speared into eyes unaccustomed to it. Jake clenched them shut in Pavlovian response – whatever came next was always unpleasant, to put it mildly.

"Ça va, Jake. Put these on. We are headed back to the Salvor." There was none of the camaraderie usually present in his voice. It was strictly business.

That was all well and good as far as Jake was concerned but he couldn't help it as a smartass remark worked its way up his throat. "Well fuck me up the a... I'll be right with you, sir." Looking passed Johnny, Jake saw the big Megacorp recruiter, his massive paws empty and waiting for something to do. Jake knew he didn't want to be that something and acted accordingly. His shoulder ached like a motherfucker when he went to put his shirt on. There was no time to inspect it now. In short order he was ready enough, standing at the foot of his slab with his head down. If it was going to come it was going to come and there was nothing he could do about it. But he didn't have to ask for it all the time.

In single file with Johnny in the lead they wound through the painted concrete hallways. All the doors were exactly like the one they'd just closed. It was mind-numbingly utilitarian and monotonous, void of any décor or personality. When they reached the corridor that led to the exit, an elevator that would have gone unnoticed chimed. The door opened, and a man in a hospital gown, cut and bleeding, came screaming from the lift. The inmate bolted for the exit door leaving bright red footprints on the drab linoleum.

The Megacorp thug moved like a cat. A really big fucking cat. Dropping low and extending his leg, he tripped up the madman. The momentum sent the flailing body sliding into the exit doors, leaving a red smear on the floor. The bleeding man reached for the door handle as the thug walked up to him, towering blackly over his crumpled form. The inmate looked up, dread filling his face and contorting his body. He sprang away from the door, towards Johnny and Jake. The thug let him pass. Johnny sidestepped the madman, who plowed right into Jake. The poor bastard grabbed at Jake's clothes screaming, "Help me! Don't let them take me!"

Jake was a little slow on the uptake, sometimes. The little voice in his head was screaming, 'TEST!' For once he listened. Jake took hold of the man's gown at the collar and lifted him off his feet with one hand. The other hand made a fist and Jake clobbered him hard with a right jab. The inmate went unconscious. Jake's shoulder went into pain overdrive but he wasn't going to give in to it. He walked over to the Megacorp thug, still holding the inmate.

"I believe this is yours." Jake dropped the man at his feet, took two paces back and resumed his position. He had become neutral inside, mimicking the décor.

The elevator chimed again. This time an unhurried med staff with a gurney in tow came to fetch their stray. Jake had been right. It was a test. The next two days were spent traveling from wherever they were to wherever they were going. Jake asked no questions and paid scant attention to, well, anything. When Jake and Johnny stepped aboard the Salvor, the Megacorp thug signed the paperwork and left. Until then they had been inseparable.

Jake lugged his gear up the gangway with Johnny leading the way to their rooms. There was no talking. Anyone they happened to pass looked away from them.

Jake dropped his bags on the floor of his room and sat on the bed staring blankly at the floor. He was cold and empty. Something had happened during the last job and he hadn't the slightest clue as to what it was. The unknown was pressing down on him as the bathroom door opened. Johnny stepped in with the usual tray of heroin-filled syringes and a pile of coke, neither of which would help mollify the void of anguish that Jake had created for himself. Johnny made a pot of coffee while the medicine took effect. When Jake roused from a nod he was handed a cup of coffee and a question.

"What happened, Jake?"

"I don't know. Happened to what?" Jake replied trying to shake the fog.

"You are going to have to do better than that, man. What happened aboard the rig?"

"I did my job. The mercs got aboard."

"Uh huh. Not good enough, Jake. Okay let us start again. What happened to you?"

"No! What happened to my arm?" Jake winced rubbing his shoulder.

"All right, we will work backwards then. Med techs put it back on. Lucky for you no one put the heaters on in the pod. You died in there, Jake. The best the lab could figure is you were not fully in the harness when the escape pod was launched. Your arm was torn off on impact."

"Oh man."

"Which brings up my next question. What were you doing in an escape pod?" Johnny finished his coffee and poured another cup.

"I don't know." Jake returned his focus to the floor.

"God damn it, Jake! There is going to be an inquiry! The Goliath sits on the sea floor and you are the most likely suspect. Your life is on the line, man. You just going to give it up?"

"What about the crew? Any women?" Jake asked snapping out of it.

"No. Only fourteen survived of a crew of about 100. Mostly shirts."

"They sent fucking Pablo! Just what did they expect!" Jake exclaimed.

"Pablo doesn't exist as far as Megacorp is concerned. And neither do you but they want someone to take the fall. The corporates in the North Sea want to crucify you. Frankly Megacorp would just as soon throw you to the wolves as defend you, so you have got to defend yourself. This is our chance to go over your story."

"I want a lawyer!"

"There are no lawyers for this kind of thing. You will be brought before a maritime version of the Spanish Inquisition, fucked royally, then they will decide whether you live or die."

"So it really doesn't matter what I say. I'm fucked." Jake hung his head and shook it.

"Yup. But I would like to know."

"You know I wouldn't jump ship, Johnny. And I didn't. I just can't remember what happened. My job was to get the mercs aboard. I did that. Then they clubbed me and went about their business. Nobody said anything about saving the crew. Besides after Pablo was through with them, there wasn't much left to save."

"I see, I see. I am going to make a leap here. So, after you woke up you went around the rig seeing Pablo's handiwork? What did you do then?"

"Discovered what freezing to death is like." Jake saw the look on Johnny's face. "I needed clothes. Pablo took mine."

"Did you happen to see the hijackers? "

"That is something I'd rather not think about. It was total freaksville."

"Why do you say 'It'?"

"Because it wasn't human. One of the crew and I deduced that it had been one of us, a reuseable. But it sure wasn't one anymore."

"That is why Pablo was sent. Megacorp wanted it captured."

"Fat fucking chance that. You'd have to catch it first but it moves too goddamn fast."

"Who was the crewmember you met?" Johnny kept the questions coming. Jake was lucid, sort of, and Johnny knew how quickly memories can fade.

"A reuseable. When Pablo gunned down the control room personnel, the men shielded her with their bodies."

"What was her name? What did she do?"

"Science officer of some kind. Her name was... Mirka."

"Hmmm, the name rings a bell." Johnny wondered aloud.

"She saved my hands and feet. They had become frozen solid."

"No shit. And just how would she have done that? The medical community might be interested, just a little."

"No they wouldn't." Jake said sadly.

"I am sure you are right about that. Just what did she do?"

"She way overdosed me on the juice."

"There have been some studies done..." Johnny began.

"Studies my ass! Megacorp uses it when things get tight. Then they waste the bastards cause they can no longer control them."

"You seem like a good dog."

"Yeah well, don't push it."

Johnny looked his friend over and decided not to push it. "We are diving tomorrow. Figure getting you wet will do some good."

"No arguments from me."

The Salvor was tied to one of seven mooring buoys off Barbers Point on Oahu. The mooring system was meant to hold oil tankers in place while they offloaded the crude through a twenty-four inch pipeline. The last two hundred feet of the line was flexible and needed to be replaced.

In the old days a crew of divers would be sent out to work round the clock until the job was finished. At 120 feet in depth each diver had twenty minutes to do as much as he could before his bottom time ran out. At best it was an extremely inefficient process.

Now it was Jake and a crane. He knew when he hit the water that it was for the duration. New diving technology afforded management something they had always dreamed of, unlimited bottom time. Jake didn't mind. It would take the better part of thirty-six hours to complete the project. With a three-pound maul and a slug wrench, Jake went at the sixty-four nuts and bolts that held the first flange. There were four flanges. Tap, tap, tap. It was the kind of mindless repetitive work that sets the mind free, allowing it to wander.

He wondered about Mirka. Jake had successfully shut her out of his thinking until Johnny brought it up. In fact he had done a good job of blanking the whole affair. But now as the metronome of slug wrenching counted the time, it all started to come back.

***

While Sven's men gathered up fourteen dead, he attended the carts of explosives. Sven added detonators to several of the packets of explosive then buried them deep in the pile so they would go unnoticed. Mirka had given him the code she used for the leg charges and he set his the same. The day had given way to sunshine. Sven used what little time he had to say goodbye to the rig he had given so much of his life to. Now in the end he would even give it the rest. The rig had become a graveyard. The dead were like so much litter strewn about, their frozen corpses a ghastly reminder of the nightmare that now lived here. Tears froze on his cheeks as he placed more charges to fuel storage and critical structural components. If the rig was going to go down he didn't want anything to survive. That was the point, after all.

Mirka got up, leaving Pablo, and headed to the kitchen for another pot of coffee. Sven followed her in.

"Did you see it?"

"No," Sven replied.

"What are you still doing here?"

"This is my rig. I go where she goes."

"In that case you're going straight to hell, Sven."

"C'est la vie. The sun is out. Perhaps the monster does not like it," Sven added.

"Perhaps. Let us use it. Use the men to close the sub sea BOP – (blow out preventer). I'd rather not waste what little oil is left and spoil the water any more than is necessary. Then get your men off."

"They will not go."

"Then have them say their prayers. When the time comes there won't be any notice. Thank you, Sven."

"That's what friends are for. I hope you find what you're looking for."

Mirka hugged the older man and returned to Pablo's table and poured him a cup.

"The sun will not be around much longer. This time of year we only get a few hours. Sven said he did not see the thing so if you want to look around now's the time."

Pablo got up and stretched, picked up his guns and headed to the door. Mirka was right with him. The sun was already setting, the horizon a blaze of red and orange that bled into the darkness that followed. As the sun winked away, the hair went up on the back of Mirka's neck. Whatever it was, its alarm clock had just gone off.

The two were caught off guard when it came at them. They had been looking up when they should have been looking down. A low growl came with the shadow. Pablo swung his weapon, firing into the darkness. A hand emerged from the shadow and ripped the gun from his hands, using it as a club to smash Pablo a cruel blow to the side of the head. The merc went down for the first time in his long career. The creature picked up Pablo by the feet and slammed him into a container, opening a gash in the merc's head. Blood poured from the wound. It then raised Pablo above its head and let the blood drain into its mouth.

Mirka watched from behind a shipping container. In the dim light she could see the slug of explosives still attached to the thing's belt loop. As it held Pablo high she toggled the detonator. Nothing happened. Mirka screamed.

Suddenly the night was alive with automatic gunfire. Sven and his men had followed them out. When the gunfire stopped there were two figures lying on the deck. Sven dropped his gun and reaching into his pocket, pulled a second detonator and tossed it to Mirka. He then grabbed the two evils, dragged them to one of the explosive carts and began lashing them to it.

Pablo came to, thrashing violently against the ropes. "What the fuck are you doing? Let me out of here! You don't know what you're doing!" A rope caught his flailing arm and pinned it to his side. "Goddamn it –

we're supposed to take it alive!"

Sven stood after securing the line. "I think not." He turned his back and walked over to Mirka. "It is time to balance the scales."

The lines securing the load began to strain and pop like guitar strings. The creature still tangled in the lashings lurched toward Sven; a wicked clawed hand took the man by the neck. Sven turned to face it, and with his last breath before his throat was crushed he yelled, "NOW!" Mirka flipped open the red safety cover and pushed on the toggle.

No one heard the explosion that destroyed the Goliath. The darkness was vaporized in a blinding flash of light, followed by the remaining charges set by Mirka and Sven. The massive drill platform exploded into the night. Its legs buckled as the superstructure collapsed. Containers and equipment went high in to the sky before falling into the North Sea. Ten minutes after a little spark jumped the gap between two wires, igniting hell on earth, nothing remained. The sea absorbed the evil as it had always done and returned to its natural state.

Mirka was behind the container when she flipped the switch. The shipping container was blown clear of the rig. It took Mirka with it. When it sank, it left her on the surface. Her body floated upon the icy seas. Sharks would circle and leave without sampling. Some things just aren't fit for consumption.

***

Thirty two hours later Jake climbed the swim step onto the Salvor. His body was blistered from extended exposure. 'It could be worse,' he thought as Johnny removed the dive hat.

"Goddamn I needed that. Thanks, Johnny." Jake said it in a way that suggested he had been relieved of a burden.

"Thank Mouse. He was the one who made it happen. The guy likes you. Do not ask me why," said Johnny wryly.

"Yeah well work is over and we better get the fuck out of here." Jake meant off the deck. They were starting to get the look from the crew. The look that said 'what the hell are you still doing here?' Jake and Johnny stood, nodded to the C.O., and left for their rooms. Never once were they allowed to forget that they did not belong with normal men.

After a shower and getting high, Johnny handed Jake a cup of coffee and a letter. "By the way you look, I believe you had a moment of clarity while playing 'erector set.'"

"Didn't think it showed," Jake responded. "What's this?"

"A letter from Megacorp stating the charges against you and when you are to appear."

"Well fuck me!"

"Indeed. Care to fill me in? All I got is you can not remember shit."

"It was probably better that way 'cause you sure as fuck ain't going to believe this." Jake described the last few hours aboard the Goliath – from waking after the overdose of 'juice' to having his arm ripped off. Jake shuddered with the last description and rubbed his shoulder.

"Ow, it is a push, Jake. I believe you and it helps to explain a few things. While you were working I did some research on the overdosing thing. You were right. Megacorp keeps a tight lid on it. If reuseables knew they could beat the system, well, it would be a bad thing. Be best to leave that out of your story. The knowledge alone is enough to turn your ass to ash."

"Too much truth, huh?"

"Maybe just a little," Johnny deadpanned.

"So, did your research tell you why I'm not a freak that needs to be destroyed? By all accounts I should be."

"No. But I am a good guesser. Want to hear it?"

Jake raised his hands palms up and shrugged his shoulder

"You bled out. All the crap that you injected drained out through your shoulder. Of course only time will tell if there was any permanent damage."

***

The proceedings were held at Megacorp Corporate Headquarters. It was a mammoth structure of grey granite and mirrored glass, as heartless and cold as the men within its walls. The basic design was similar to ancient Mayan ruins, that is, a stepped pyramid appropriately named the Madoff. The small joke was lost on the current generation. Jake saw the name engraved in stone as he was wheeled into the building. He laughed knowing the history. The Madoff scandal was a symbol of the crumbling empire from which Megacorp would rise like a Phoenix. The man himself was heralded as the forefather of modern economics.

But that was long ago and the money game had gone through some radical changes since his time. Bernie Madoff would have been crushed by the current system, even though he was the embodiment of the spirit of the times. What went on now must have been in his wildest imaginations.

The wheels of the rolling chair squeaked incessantly and one had a flat spot. Jake could do nothing about it even though he was not shackled or restrained physically; an injection of neurotoxin had rendered him unable to move. He could hear, think clearly and talk, breathe, and apparently pee his pants if the thick underwear were any clue. He had been briefed on how to play his end. Johnny had put it simply. 'Just be cool, Jake. Do not be a smartass, call them names or use 'fuck' too often and keep your anger under control.' It was pretty good advice for heading into a situation like this. Jake had one ace up his sleeve.

After getting his juice and the extra injection Jake was wheeled back to his room to wait. He was left alone. The med techs fully relied on the neuro injection to keep him harmless. Johnny came through the bathroom door to see his friend hanging limp, head down in the chair. It was hard for him to see such a capable individual rendered helpless. Jake raised his head. When his right hand reached out for a pack of rolling papers and tobacco on the writing desk, Johnny's tray hit the floor, dusting the commercial grade carpet with high grade pharmaceuticals.

Jake glanced at the floor then up at Johnny. "What?"

"How did you do that?"

"Do what?" Jake smiled.

"Move your hand, raise your head!" Johnny replied with dismay in his voice.

"Well, I thought gee I'd sure like a smoke and decided to roll one."

"Goddamn, Jake. You are not supposed to be able to move. Why do you think they left you alone? They did this to me before and the only thing I could do was shit my pants."

"Got a match?" Jake licked the paper and finished the roll.

Johnny was thinking while Jake was goofing around. "Jake, you think this is one of the side effects of the O.D.?"

"I've always been pretty much average. That neuro should have hit me the same as any other guy. Wow! You mean I'm special? I've never been special before!" Jake said like a kid.

"Well, this kind of special could get you some extra-special ed or special dead, if you catch my drift." Johnny didn't think it was one bit funny.

"So what do I do now?" Jake's smile sank away seeing the look on his friend's face.

Footsteps were heard coming down the corridor. "I'd say put your chin back on your chest and keep it there." The door opened without a knock just as Johnny was pulling the fag from Jake's lips. Jake blew a thick cloud at the intruders but otherwise played along. As the guards backed the chair out of the room Jake said, "Hey, I think I gotta pee. One of you guys want to hold my dick. No? Okay, here goes. Ahhh, sweet... Never mind. I probably wouldn't have held yours either." Jake laughed hard. It was all he could do. Johnny watched him from the doorway, shook his head, had a laugh too and went back inside.

The wheel stopped lopping before a pair of dark red hardwood doors that matched nicely with the granite floor and walls. Each door was four feet wide. Jake guessed they would be ten to twelve feet tall but couldn't risk a look without giving himself away. Two big knobs turned from the other side and the doors swung silently inward. Jake suddenly had the urge to pee. He had been joking before. Authority could do that to people and Jake was people. The wheel began to turn. Each thump on the flat spot jiggled his bladder just enough so that by the time he was before the huge semi-circular table where the inquisitors sat, he had to relieve himself. Jake could be a little slow on the uptake sometimes. He now saw that wetting yourself in front of others would have mortified another person, psyching your game. Jake was a diver. It didn't bother him in the least. He just smiled and relaxed.

The seats on the other side of the conference table were mostly filled with suits. The Navy was there. Well, actually two. The U.S. Navy reps were complete with scrambled eggs and enough shiny medals to sink a destroyer. Then there were the top dogs of E.U. North Sea division, who bore no small resemblance to a group of pallbearers. Their black wool uniforms were tailored severely, as was the cut of the silver or blonde hair. Only the mustaches had any flair, and that was to inspire dread. There was no adornment on these men's coats. Only brass buttons, each in use despite the conditioned air. Half a dozen seats were empty; their occupants were still enroute. Some critical eleventh hour evidence was being flown in.

Jake listened quietly to the scuttle while he surveyed the room. His field of vision was hampered what with his chin on his chest, but there was little he could do about that now. When they entered the room he could not help but notice a heavily armed tactical force acting as security. They had all key points of the conference room covered with the focus on the accused. That is to say – Jake.

A gavel came down on a table off to the side, disrupting the silence and making Jake lose count of the granite bits in the floor tiling. A round little man with hunched shoulders put the gavel down and stood. He placed his hands on the tabled before him and admired his manicure before addressing the assembly. Roger Stimple looked over the curved conference table at the suits and uniforms. He knew all of them by name. Each one was a Megacorp board member and lawyer. The North Sea delegation was another matter. Those men had an axe to grind and he knew them only by reputation. Bastards, each one.

Roger Stimple was told to begin the proceedings as scheduled despite the delayed arrival of a few of the Norwegians. All parties agreed to start so here was Roger, mediator between Megacorp and the accusers. Traditional courts were a thing of the past. Megacorp's methods were quick, painful and quite cost effective. If you were busted, your name would be entered into the database. Within moments everything about you would be brought up. Good deeds and bad ones, even ones you had no idea about. The computer would chew it around for a while and give a verdict. Its decision was final and there was no appeals process. Rest assured justice will be done and your life irrevocably changed. No, you would not go to prison and find out just how big your asshole is. You went to work. What you think, Megacorp is stupid and going to pay your keep? They learned long ago that if you work a man hard, eighteen hours a day and feed him just enough to keep him going, you are not going to have any trouble with that individual. Of course there were always a few who would push back. Death solved that issue. And if you couldn't work, well death was there for you, too. This situation was, however, a little more involved than most blue and white-collar crimes.

"If everyone is ready we should start the proceedings." Stimple watched the conference table until he received nods from all in attendance. "Commodore Skru, you may begin."

Skru was the commander of the North Sea delegation. Unlike the other Norwegians, he was short, thin, with black hair and wimpy mustache. He had a high forehead and eyes that looked through slits. His voice however was strong and sharp, each word clipped neatly at the end. English was obviously his second language.

"As all of you know the Goliath went down one year ago today," Skru began. "The man that sits before us, if you can call him that, is the one responsible for the destruction of the largest oil platform ever built and the death of 130 men and women who worked aboard her." Skru paused, eyeing the group narrowly. "Fourteen men survived the nightmare of an experience. It is the only way they can describe what they lived through. I will not repeat the tale as all of you have read the depositions. The loss of the rig is bad enough, for there will never be another like it. It is the expiry of 130 trained personnel that is the real diminution. The privation of their experience will cost the North Sea region untold amounts in revenue, now that we are unable to tap the remaining reserves."

Megacorp understood the loss of seasoned technicians. The creation of Reuseables was theirs alone. They did however lease them out as Mirka had been. Jake and the team of mercs were also leased.

Jake sat listening to the opening remarks. It was full of information he did not have. Skru was no fool. He knew exactly what he was doing. Two things were key here. Jake realized he had been on ice for a year and the whole thing was about money. Skru could give a rat's ass for the people that died. He wanted to be subsidized for the North Sea's loss of imaginary capital. Jake saw things simply. There was no reason to muck it up with so many words.

Mirka had told him the seabed was dry as a bone as far as oil was concerned, or mostly anyway. Apparently this was not common knowledge. Everyone knew they would run out sooner or later but the North Sea kept producing, at least on paper. Huge in-water storage tankers near the shore of Bergen were being filled as fast as they could make them, at least on paper. The tanks were anchored to the bottom 200 feet below the surface.

For the North Sea delegation the loss of the Goliath could not have come at a better moment. There was a lot on the line and Jake would be the scapegoat for one of the biggest payoffs of all time.

Skru continued. "Jake Strom was leased to us by Megacorp. We asked for their best diver. What we received was a coward and saboteur." He let the words hang in the air. The silence was pregnant with possibility. All eyes turned to look upon Jake who could not help himself.

"Bullshit!" Jake said loudly in his defense.

"I do not understand the English slang. What has the waste of an animal have to do with anything?" Skru responded sensibly. Any number of the Megacorp guard and a few at the table laughed quietly to themselves before covering their mouths and finishing the chortle.

Stimple stepped in at the breach of protocol. "Mr. Strom. You will be given ample opportunity to speak in your defense. Any further outbursts will be dealt with severely. Now, before we return the floor to Commodore Skru, perhaps you would explain to him what you meant. I am sure we would all like to hear."

'This guy should have been a fucking teacher', Jake thought, when he should have been thinking about what to say. "I apologize for not making myself clear. What I meant to say was, Fuck You, you lying little bastard! Is that clear enough?" Jake had been removed from the debating team in high school for generating similar responses. Unlike his schooling, a cattle prod was applied to the back of his neck, contracting every muscle in an agonizing spasm. Jake gritted his teeth but did not cry out. The electrocution was for what he said. He had been asked to speak. Johnny had mentioned that such language would get him into trouble. Jake, however, could be a little slow on the uptake.

Jake slumped into the chair, his body spent for the moment. A weak smile crossed his face along with a silent, sick laugh. An involuntary urge caused him to shake his head 'no', to himself. He felt it happen and simultaneously felt the bottom of his stomach fall out, the urge to puke, and his bladder relax. 'How am I still thinking? I should be dead by now'. By rule his brains should have been splattered across the floor from a barrage of bullets. Simply for moving his head. If silence could get more quiet it did in the conference room of the Madoff. Not a peep. Jake wondered if the big dogs at the table had peed their pants, too. Jake concentrated on keeping perfectly still. Even his breathing was imperceptible. Jake's senses were heightened at the proximity to death. He could smell the sweat and feel the fear that closed the room in claustrophobia.

"SHOOT HIM!" Skru screamed, shattering the moment.

Fortunately for Jake, Skru was not Megacorp. The order would have to come from Stimple or one of the corporate lackeys at the table. Jake didn't move. The guns did not fire. There were any number of reasons why this was so. As mentioned earlier, any reuseable under the scrutiny of the board could not move, with the exception of to speak. Period. Any who did would be shot without provocation. Now this had been a standing order for more than a century. Fifty years ago the drug that was injected into Jake was introduced for the first time. Since then no one had been shot for moving. Three generations of guards had been through this room. Since none of the current security was an actual witness to what happens when a reuseable goes berserk, they froze at the triggers and waited for orders.

Another reason, despite the accusations of the North Sea delegation, was that Jake was a Megacorp Reuseable with an undeniably horrific track record. That is, he got the job done, all the time. Megacorp was always willing to overlook a few personal defects or bad habits as long as the job got done. Besides they had no intention of paying the North Sea dime one for the disaster. Megacorp would not defend Jake, nor would they condemn him, but allow this thing to play itself out. They did not trust the North Sea or have any evidence against them. Megacorp knew they had ulterior motives. Hell, Megacorp was nothing but an ulterior motive.

The gavel came down hard again. "Commodore Skru, you have no authority here. Be reminded that you and your entourage are here as guests and should conduct yourselves as such." Stimple enjoyed putting the man in his place. It masked his own fear. He, too, was second generation. Prior to convening, Stimple had watched the vid of a trial that went awry. Growing up in a virtual reality kind of numbs you to vid violence. But when he viewed the trial, he grew weak and felt an embarrassing moment warmly in his pants. All present at the proceedings were killed in a matter of moments by one reuseable with no weapons.

When Stimple saw Jake's head move, he relived the experience, imagining it to be here and now. By the time the daymare was over, his seat cushion was absorbing the moisture from his pants and Skru was yelling.

"Commodore Skru, you have called this man a coward and saboteur. Do you have any evidence to back up these statements? Let me also say we are not interested in subjectivity. Keep to the known facts please. You may continue." Stimple sat back and stared at Jake. One more move and he would give the order to kill.

"This, this man, as you wish to call it, began showing his colors as soon as he arrived in Bergen. After he boarded the Big Brother he met with the men who were to retake the Goliath. In the galley he pulled a knife and stabbed one of them who was drinking coffee. There is no doubt in our minds that this was the beginning of the sabotage. By eliminating one of six men the odds were more in his favor. We have the deposition of the Captain of Big Brother, who was there at the time." Skru remained standing while papers were being shuffled all around the arc. Stimple took the moment to reread the deposition before continuing.

"It says on page four, paragraph three and I quote, 'I entered the galley and watched from the door. I didn't like the mercenaries and had decided to keep an eye on them. Jake was having words with their leader. When I approached the table, one of the men had a knife stuck in his hand and was desperately trying to pull it out as the point had become embedded in the tabletop. When the knife was pulled free, the mercenary returned it to the sheath in his sleeve.' It seems there is a slight discrepancy between your story and the deposition. I imagine the truth was lost in the translation. Please continue."

"Yes, well I believe you are correct, Mr. Stimple. Only five of your men made it to the Goliath. One was lost on the way. Unfortunate to say the least. But most convenient for your diver." Skru paused and Stimple stepped in.

"Mr. Strom, do you have anything to say regarding the Commodore's statement?"

"What's the point?" Jake responded with little interest.

"An excellent observation. However the board would like to hear why the sixth man did not make it to the Goliath. Tell us, now." Stimple leaned heavily on the last word. It was an order and Jake was sure if he did not comply there would be recompense.

"It was a rough swim. He didn't make it."

"Was it the same man you stabbed in the hand?"

"I didn't take notice," Jake replied. He did not like playing this game.

The day ground on inexorably. Skru did his best to malign Jake's character. It was not hard and seemed to be the bulk of Skru's argument. He had scant few facts concerning Jake's actual involvement. He wanted someone to blame, a name to pin it on it.

"Commodore Skru, you had mentioned yesterday that you would have substantial evidence concerning this inquiry, today. Where is it?"

"My colleagues should have been here by now." Skru began but was timely interrupted by the chime of his implanted phone. "May I answer this? It is from my people."

"You may." Stimple relented.

Skru nodded. "Commodore Skru," he answered. Skru's face went serious before it paled and the muscles sagged. Moments passed while he listened intently. Shaking his head he said, "Thank you" and broke the connection. Skru tried to regain his composure before addressing the assembly; he failed. An elbow from the man seated next to him brought the Commodore back into the moment.

"Yes, yes. Mr. Stimple. The helicopter that was bringing our team has just gone down in the waters off the coast. The work tug Big Brother is en route to the site. The helicopter holds not only our investigative team, but another survivor. This is the substantial evidence I had referred to."

"Is Big Brother equipped to retrieve the chopper?"

"Its cranes are large enough. However we lack a capable diver.

If Megacorp could lease us one for a day..." Skru paused, the irony weighing down upon him.

Stimple had already been tapping away at his console. All available information on the crash was at his fingertips before Skru stopped talking. The lost helicopter was a marine rescue model. Basically it was designed to remain intact after an in water emergency landing. The fuselage was water tight and held several days worth of air for crew of eight. It was the location of the crash that caught Stimple's eye. It was right in the middle of the North Sea's underwater oil storage facility. Megacorp knew where it was but had never seen it. The North Sea had been using it for years. By creating a substantial oil reserve they were able to remain independent in a world dominated by corporate control. 'If somehow Megacorp could get a look at it', the mediator thought, 'it just might do me good'. Now that, my friends, is a good company man.

Jake had not fallen asleep. He had been listening, too, although his body was aching from the jolt and from not moving for too long. "You need a diver? I can do it." Jake braced himself for speaking out of turn.

It didn't come. Stimple had raised his hand. "We appreciate your offer but under the circumstances..."

Jake cut Stimple short. "Under the circumstances you don't really have another choice. You can't get another diver here in time. Unless that was the idea, in which case I should really apologize..."

"Mr. Strom, the pharmaceutical restraint lasts for 72 hours. There is no antidote. It must wear off. Commodore Skru, I am afraid there is little we can do. You should call Big Brother and have her return to port." Stimple crossed his hands on the desktop and stared at Jake.

"This is outrageous! For god's sake man! People's lives are at stake!" Skru's voice cracked.

"Unfortunately Mr. Strom is correct. We cannot get a man here in time. Now, let us return to the proceedings."

Jake admired Stimple's back-to-business attitude but he could also tell Skru wasn't about to let it drop. The man was tied emotionally to the crash. It was in Jake's nature to empathize with the pain of others. Even though Skru wanted to hang Jake for something, Jake felt sorry for the guy. He was hurting. True to his nature Jake opened his big mouth.

"Hey Skru, you really want to save those people? What are they to you?" The cattle prod came down sending Jake into agonizing seizures. He bit his tongue in order to not break his teeth. Blood and saliva drained from his mouth onto the floor. The dark grey hues of granite contrasted nicely with the crimson splattering. Jake heard Skru controlling the emotion in his voice.

"Yes, we must save them. My son is aboard the helicopter."

"Then I'll get him. You willing to back me up? Not that it matters. It's just nice to know if somebody is on your side." Jake didn't wait for a response. He raised his head. The cattle prod came down. Jake grabbed the hand and forced the guard to drop it. He stood, taking the man by the collar. There was a moment of grace after the sudden action. In that silence, rows of brass buttons were unclasped and machine guns pulled from deep within the wool jackets. Jake released the guard's collar and brushed at the wrinkles he left on the uniform.

"Sorry about the hand." Jake turned and walked over to Stimple's table. He leaned on it with both hands staring right at Stimple. "Stimple, there isn't much time. I haven't read my contract in a while and I'm sure I'm pushing it. You have had a fair offer for me. Emergency pay, you can't beat that." Jake was close to being finished and bent close to Stimple's face, their noses almost touching, speaking so only the two of them could hear. As Jake started to speak, the smell of shit rose up from around Stimple's chair. Jake knew the rest would go just as smoothly.

"The wreck is in their oil storage. While I'm there I can take a look around and report back to you. I would imagine this information has some value; here are my terms..."

A North Sea helicopter waited atop the Madoff. Jake was hustled to the chopper surrounded by black wool and machine guns. Once off the ground it headed west to rendezvous with Big Brother. The wool coats dissolved into the flight seats. It was only Jake and Skru sitting across from one another. Jake examined the man. He was just that, a man doing his job. It was probably not what he really wanted to do, but was what he ended up with. Skru was normal; Jake realized they were more alike than different. Fate doesn't take everyone the same way. It is more cruel than that.

"Thanks for backing me up," Jake offered in an attempt to break the ice.

"Your timing was good. How did you beat the drugs? We almost shot you." Skru put his gun aside.

"Shit happens. You got dive gear aboard Big Brother?"

"They said it should do."

"Good enough. We can make it work," Jake replied, keeping his concerns to himself. Over the years he had dived every piece of shit hat that was available and considered himself able to dive anything.

"Mr. Strom," Jake could tell something serious was coming. They always preface it with Mr. "You will be diving in a very sensitive area for the North Sea."

"Save your breath, Skru, I know all about the oil reserves. I also figure the reserves aren't as full as you would like people to think. My guess is you ain't got jack."

Skru squirmed, "Jack?"

"Nada, squat, zilcho!"

Skru twisted his face in confusion.

"You have no oil."

The commodore went ashen, nodded his head and looked at Jake. "We have enough for our own needs and some to share with neighbors. That is all." Skru was not ashamed. It was just a statement of fact.

"I figured as much. And you're just bluffing to keep Megacorp off your back."

Skru shrugged just as the helicopter banked in preparation to land on Big Brother. The pilot was good and timed the landing well. When the cargo door opened, Jake was the first out, reaching a hand to the shorter Skru, helping him to the rocking deck. An iron clasp latched firmly to Jake's shoulder. Jake turned his head to see who belonged to it. A huge Norwegian, a veritable incarnation of Thor, was at the other end.

"My name is Hans. I am your tender. Follow me, please." Hans dragged Jake away from the helipad and below decks. After a maze of stairs, elevators and passages they arrived at the dive ops. Jake's head was bruised in another dozen places from not ducking in time to miss a pipe flange or overhead valve. He didn't care. Goddamn boats were always like this.

When the door to dive ops was open, it reminded Jake of every station he had ever entered. Limited space created an organized mess. Only one thing was out of place: a full model Mark V diving suit was assembled on a dummy and was being worked on. When there is no wasted space you don't have an antique taking up valuable real estate.

His tender had been standing silently next to Jake. "Hey Hans, where is my dive gear?" Jake asked, for there was no modern gear in sight. The big tender nodded to the Mark V.

"You kiddin' me right? Testing my balls, a strange sort of hazing?" Jake was fishing. He didn't realize he caught on the first cast.

"No, Jake, there is no time for that. You must begin."

Jake took the hint and walked over to the suit. He inspected the rubber seals, connection between the breastplate and hat, communications and air hookups. Satisfied, he began peeling off his clothes and dressing in the fleece underwear that would keep him warm in the drysuit. Hans, the tender, was right at his side.

"So when do we go?" Jake asked.

"Thirty minutes. We are just approaching the crash site and want you in the water as soon as the ship stops."

"Well, let's get me into the suit." With the faceplate open, Jake was able to talk to Hans. "How deep?" Jake started.

"Seventy-five meters." Hans was busy tightening the breastplate bolts and securing the hat.

"What's the bottom like?"

"Ten meters of visibility and more gnarly torn up steel than you can imagine. We have lost several divers surveying the area."

"Was it the storage facility?"

"We thought we built deep enough. We were wrong."

"Diver! Report to the moon pool! We are ready to go!"

Jake got up from the chair unassisted. Hans offered but Jake declined. The breastplate and helmet only weighed eighty pounds and the weight belt another mere 108 pounds. Each step required a monumental effort and god forbid you stop before you get to where you are going. Chances are you wouldn't get started again. Twenty-two steps later Jake arrived at the edge of the pool. His airline was hooked up as was his comm line and safety line. The speakers in the hat crackled. "Comm Check 1, 2, Jake, you got me?"

"Loud and clear, Hans, let's do this."

"One thing, in your pocket is an explosive device. Use it if you must. Your hose is in the water, whenever you're ready."

"Gonna be dropping fast so just play the line out as quick as you can."

Jake tilted his head to look down at the surface. He vented the excess air from the suit and took a giant stride into the angry water. He disappeared and the air line sped through Hans' hands. The markings on the air line were going by too fast to follow. At 90 meters the air line stopped.

"Topside, this is Jake – I am on the bottom, all okay."

"Any sign of the helicopter?"

"Negative. Big fucking mess down here though. This what's left of the storage facility?" Jake asked.

"Yes."

"Roger that. I'm going to get oriented and start a search pattern. Have your guys run all the side scan sonars you got. See if you pick up any thing out of the norm. Jake out."

The seas' floor was scattered with debris. Cage frameworks and broken storage cylinders made for a junkyard of epic proportions. With the antique dive gear, walking around was not an option. You would tangle your hose, or worse, cut it. Swimming didn't work so well either and was a hopelessly slow process. So Jake figured flying was the best option. He climbed to the high point of a twisted structure and looked for another he could jump to. The first leap sent him right to where he wanted to go but he was slowing down too soon. Pulling for all he was worth with his arms he was just able to grab an outcropping of steel. He scrambled like a madman to gain a purchase to avoid sliding down to the bottom.

He scanned in all directions. If the helicopter were near he would see it or at least see the emergency beacon. From the top of the steel hill, Jake looked down into a deep cavern. Pulling a spool from his harness, he rigged a weight to one end and tossed it over, letting the line run free like a fishing reel. At around 110 meters it stopped. Jake turned off his headlamps and was enveloped in black water. You could not see your hand before your face. He sat and meditated allowing his eyes to adjust to the darkness. He stretched his arms and stood again, peering deep into the cavern. Was it his imagination, sparkles in his eyes, or was a regular flash being emitted from deep below? Jake closed his eyes and shook his head and tried again. There it was, in timed intervals.

"Yo Hans, Jake here. Over."

"Ja, Jake, been waiting for an update."

"Well, I got one for you. Couple hundred meters north of your position is a trench. Looks like the chopper is at the bottom. Move Big Brother to my coordinates. Then I may need all the line you got. You copy?"

"Roger Jake. The captain is relocating ... now. Call you when we get there."

"Thanks Hans, Out.

Moments after Big Brother began moving, Jake got the feeling things weren't kosher. He felt a slight tensioning of his airline. The ship was moving. This seemed normal until he was yanked from his perch only to slam into a piece of steel right behind him. The airline went tight.

"Hans, stop the boat, stop th... ' The air line separated along with communication and the safety return line.

Hans was on the horn with the first call. It was too late. Jake's air line parted effortlessly as it was scraped along a length of torn steel. There was nothing Hans could have done. Jake had maybe two breaths to decide what to do. Dive down the trench and hope to find some air or race back the way he came, hoping to find the airline before Hans pulled it up. His feet pushed him back the way he came, his eyes searching for a stream of bubbles that would mean the hose. There it was, 15 meters away. The air in the helmet was foul; his lungs ached as he grabbed for it. At the last second it pulled out of reach. Jake screamed "FUCK ME," and in one mighty surge, jumped at the receding line. His right hand grasped it while the left pulled his knife. Jake stabbed a hole in the dry suit just below the breastplate and shoved the air hose up into his helmet. He gave the airline one sharp pull. If Hans was doing his job he should feel it. Jake got one pull back. The old time signal means, okay.

Jake paused for a few moments to flush the dive hat with fresh air and to figure out how to move around and get the job done. There were no comms now. Jake could only hope Hans was old school. After considerable effort he was able to return to his vantage point above the abyss. Using the safety line attached to the air hose, Jake secured the airline in his hat. It was fucked up but at least it gave him air. Jake gave the line two sharp tugs, letting Hans knew to let out line. As soon as Jake felt it, he jumped out as far as he could, plummeting to the depths. Jake was thinking, 'Man, this is deep' just as he slammed onto the top of the chopper.

"Son of a bitch that hurt!" Jake said to no one. He climbed down, taking care not to dislodge the air hose. There wasn't much silt and he was able to peer into the portholes of the rescue pod. There sat six frightened people in the dark. One was covered with a sheet. There should be one more, Jake thought. He tapped on port, instantly getting a response. He gave the okay signal and got one in return. Now he moved to the cockpit. The windows were smashed in and the pilot still strapped in his chair, dead as any who venture into Davy Jones' locker unprepared. Jake looked him over and almost cried. The facial features were dead ringer Skru. It was the man's son. He didn't cry because he wasn't sure if it was for the kid or for himself. While Jake was testing the waters of self-pity, someone started banging on the porthole. He went back to see a note held against the glass.

'CRANE LOWERING WIRE, GIVE THREE PULLS AND UP YOU GO!'

Jake knocked after reading, giving the okay signal. He pulled his own slate and wrote, 'just sit back and relax folks', and held it to the port.

With time to kill he thought to take a look around. This trench had been a dumping ground for centuries. The wrecks were numerous and untouched. It was a salvage diver's dream. A 'thunk' broke his reverie. The crane's shackle had hit the bottom. On the way back he checked the safety harness of the pilot to make sure it was secure. He didn't want to lose him on the way up. He hooked the shackle to the lifting eye, gave three pulls on his air line and hopped in the copilot's seat for the ride. He felt the chopper lift off the bottom. They were on their way home. Jake closed his eyes and relaxed. 'Fuck that was close' he thought, when he was jerked from the passenger seat and began sinking like a rock. He had forgotten about the hose. It had once again tangled with some of the crap on the seafloor. He still had air but there was no swimming up with all the gear. When he hit bottom, he dropped the 100 plus pounds of lead and made a jump up, only to come down again, too fast. The drysuit already had a hole in it where he made an incision to insert the air hose, rendering it useless for buoyancy.

This was not a good situation and he knew it. Jake felt a strain on his line again and was relieved Hans was at it. It stopped a moment later along with his air. The line parted again.

"Well fuck me up the ass again!" Jake pulled his knife, cutting with purpose at his drysuit. If he could get out of it and slide his head out of the hat and still have one breath he might make it. Blow and go from five hundred feet down. Jake squatted and pushed off the bottom, no clothes and swimming like hell! At that depth the body is negatively buoyant. Any pause in kicking or strokes would send you dropping back down. Jake pulled for all he was worth.

Thousands of hours of dive time seemed to have prepared him for this moment. But soon the strain was taking its toll as the oxygen in his blood was being used up rapidly with the effort. Jake closed his eyes and pulled. Each stroke had to be as strong as the first. He began meditating to shut down his screaming mind.

The color of the water began to change from black to deepest blue. Twenty strokes later he could he could see his hands. A punch of adrenalin surged through his hypoxic blood supply. His body said STOP! Jake would not. It was light now, he was close. Just a few more strokes and his peripheral vision began to close. Moments later tunnel vision. 'Fuck! Not yet!' he thought. And those were his last. Jake succumbed to shallow water blackout. He almost made it.

Big Brother had already set the chopper on the deck and was just getting under way. Hans was coiling up the parted airline. He and the captain had agreed no diver could have made it back. They had lost three divers in the last six months. They never came back up either. The decision to leave was still a heavy one, even though this diver was a reuseable. After hanging the hose, Hans took one look back to where they had been. Was it wishful thinking or did he see something? He ran to the nearest ship's comm.

"Wheel house! This is Hans, turn around I think I saw something!"

"Hans," said the Captain, "You sure? We got hurt people."

"Yes, there it is again, please Captain!"

Hans heard the P.A., "Prepare to come about. Lookouts - scan the dive site. Sound off if you see anything." Within seconds three of the lookouts confirmed one man in the water, face down.

Hans donned a survival suit and was ready to hit the water when the workboat was in position. Captain Krull idled the vessel giving Hans the go ahead. Hans lowered the ladder and secured it to the gunwale. He looked before leaping.

Reaching out with his arm he yelled, "Take my hand!" Jake was unresponsive. Hans surged ahead taking hold of Jake's hand, locking the grip. Lucky for Hans, he had big hands and a body to match. He hoisted the naked Jake from the water single-handedly and climbed the ladder. Once on deck Hans cradled Jake in his arms and made for the med lab.

At the door was a guard. "Sorry Hans, people only. You know the rules."

"Goddamn it, Lex, he saved all those people." Hans pleaded.

"I know, but I can't." Lex had his orders.

"Could you at least get me a bottle of O2?"

"I can't now. Get him back to his quarters or I will have to call security." Moments like this made Lex hate his job. Hans turned and left muttering under his breath. Just before he exited the corridor, "Hey Hans, once you get him in bed go to the machine shop and get a bottle of O2 they use for the torches. Cut the hose and stick it in his mouth."

"Thanks Lex!" Hans double timed it to the sleeping quarters.

A half-hour later Jake was in bed, wrapped in a heating blanket and sucking on a green tube from the welding supply. He was still unconscious. Hans had called the Captain and notified him of the situation. Captain Krull ordered him to stay with the reuseable and to restrain him. Hans gladly fulfilled the former and disregarded the latter. He had hot food and coffee brought up from the galley and prepared for an all-nighter. It would take another day to get to Bergen.

Not long after Big Brother reversed course, heading east, the ship to shore radio buzzed.

"Big Brother, Communications Officer Lundgren speaking."

"Lundgren, get me the Captain. This is Commodore Skru."

"I am sorry sir, Krull is also a surgeon and is busy in the hospital right now."

Skru understood and kept his cool somehow. If Krull was in surgery then the salvage must have been successful. "How many survived?"

"Six, sir."

"And my son?" His voice was cracking.

"I do not have that information, sir. Captain Krull will be calling you just as soon as he is out. We are doing our best and returning at full speed."

"Good. If you get any news call me immediately." Skru was a bastard, not a prick.

"Will do, sir. Big Brother out." Communications Officer Lundgren did know what Skru wanted to know. He just didn't want to be the one.

Skru knew Lundgren knew too. After all, he grew up in the Navy and understood. His heart was too heavy and he felt the worst was yet to come. Until Big Brother arrived he had to figure a way to deal with the debacle of pulling weapons on the board of Megacorp. It was no small breach in protocol. In fact, he had never heard of it being done before. It was precedent setting.

For Skru and the North Sea delegation it all depended on whether the diver would keep his word. If he talked, and Megacorp could force it, the North Sea would be under Megacorp control in a matter of a few short years. 'We are of Viking heritage... ' Skru was thinking when the phone rang.

"Skru." Answering.

"Krull here, sir."

"Well, don't keep me waiting man!"

"I am sorry, sir. Your son saved the lives of his passengers by staying at the controls."

"Then he is dead." Skru said solemnly.

"Well sir, there seems to be something of a grey area here. The diver survived and would like to talk with you." Said Krull.

"Put him on."

"Cannot sir, he is in a coma."

"But you said..."

"He came out of it briefly, asking to speak with you, and only you. He was very specific."

"Thank you, Krull."

Jake woke to the warmth of an electric blanket and the smell of rich, dark coffee. Hans sat in a chair across the room reading a book. At Jake's first movement the book was closed, coffee downed and a fresh one poured. Jake pulled at the tape holding the tube in his mouth. Hans finished it for him and pulled the tube out and shut off the O2.

"My god, you're alive!"

"Yeah, that is one of the unfortunate aspects of being me," Jake wrylied. "Sure would love a cup of that coffee." Hans poured a new cup and handed it to him and was just about to barrage Jake with questions. Jake raised his hand indicating silence. "Hand me my small black bag, will ya? Then give me a few minutes. I like my first cup alone."

Hans handed Jake the nylon bag and left, the wind gone from his sails.

Jake drank the coffee like it was a gift from the gods. He then mixed a speedball, heavy on the heroin, which truly is a gift from some demented god. Not that Jake minded. The works were put away and Jake was on his third cup by the time Hans returned with Captain Krull. The tender opened the door allowing the Captain to enter first.

"It is good to see you up, Mr. Strom. We are very thankful for what you have done," Krull stated sternly. Captains can't help it.

"Number one – it's Jake. Number two – you are welcome. Number three – we need another carafe of coffee, Hans," Jake said in the slow rambling babble of a junkie. Krull nodded, Hans left. Jake sat up straight and put his hands on his knees. "Where's the kid?"

Krull looked at him like, Huh?

"Skru's kid, the pilot."

"He is in the hospital under a sheet."

"Shit. Get him out on deck. You have got to keep him cold. His injuries were not that bad."

Krull looked at Jake incredulously.

"Now!" Jake yelled, making for the door. He yanked it open only to run into Hans, dumping the coffee. "Forget about it. Take me to the hospital, Hans. Let's go! No time to lose." Hans headed down the hall. Jake ran past him and together they sprinted to the infirmary. Jake bowled the guard aside bursting through the double doors. There were two gurneys with fully covered bodies. Jake yanked both sheets revealing the son and a woman. He grabbed the dead man along with the sheets.

"Quickest way to the deck, Hans, NOW!"

Hans bolted for the door, holding it for Jake and led the way. Once they were out in the freezing cold Jake could relax. On the lee side of the tug there was a small enclosure out of the wind and ocean spray but still cold as a witch's tit.

"Hans – get me some cushions, coffee, tobacco and a survival suit, I'll wait here." Jake was near naked, bare footed and shivering by the time Hans returned. They laid the kid on the pads and covered him with the sheets. Jake slipped into the suit. "I ain't leaving this kid. Tell the captain to call Skru and have him chopper out to meet us before we get to port. You got that?" Hans nodded, "Then get movin', man!" Jake lit a cigarette and poured some coffee. It was going to be a long night.

The silence of dawn was broken by the whack-whack-whack of a single engine Sikorsky. The sun was not quite awake yet. Jake yawned, stretched and poured some coffee before rolling a cigarette. What was he going to tell Skru? Johnny was the scientist, not Jake. But today, to save his own life he would be a mad scientist and just maybe save someone. Hans interrupted Jake's reverie to let him know the helicopter had arrived. Although Jake was generally the one taking orders, today he felt like the man in charge. The adventure at the bottom of the sea; a near-death experience and a sleepless night; he was punchy and at the top of his game.

"Get the kid into the infirmary and don't let Skru see you. Then have Skru meet me in the officer's lounge. I'll be there in fifteen minutes. Thanks, Hans, now move it!"

Jake got up off his haunches and took a while to get vertical. Everything hurt. It meant he was alive and alive felt good. After a quick shower, Jake mixed a little concoction of Johnny's and booted it. In black jeans, workboots and an aloha shirt, he ran his fingers through his hair, looking in the mirror; he figured it about as good as it gets. Leaving his room, he pinballed down the hallway as the ship rocked. Jake arrived at the officer's lounge first. He poured some coffee and savored the aroma. Officers drink better than crew. This he would always remember. Disregarding the no smoking signs he rolled one, lit up and had his feet on a table by the time Skru arrived, with an escort.

Jake didn't move. Simply chinned to Skru before looking at the others.

"Get rid of those men. It is just you and I, Commodore." Jake stubbed his smoke and put his feet on the ground. His body language said 'I mean it.'

Skru read it instantly. "You men go to the galley and wait for my call. Don't be hanging around the corner either." At the least his men were obedient. He turned to face Jake.

"Cup of café, Skru? Sit down. You make me nervous." Skru sat and sipped from the cup Jake gave him. Jake learned that once you take the control of a situation it's your job to keep the ball rolling and, of course, maintain control.

"So, what have you been told?" Jake began wasting no time.

"I should ask...?" Skru was cut short.

"I am asking the questions today. Now what do you know?"

Skru swallowed his anger. He was used to being at the other end of the stick. "You found the helicopter and with complete disregard for your own self, rescued all aboard. I know that two are dead, my son and a woman. Despite my demands there has been no word about his condition. That is all I know." Skru raised his hands palms up. "Perhaps you have the courage."

Jake could tell he was being truthful. Well mostly anyway. Now came the tough part. The drugs he shot earlier eased anxiety, made him lightly euphoric, empathetic, and helped him to speak honestly from the heart. Johnny had many such mixes for different occasions. Jake smiled kindly at the old man and took his hands in his. Jake's eyes got glassy as he spoke.

"Your son was a fine captain. He stayed at the controls to control the crash so that the others would survive." Jake squeezed Skru's hands gently. Tears fell from the old man's eyes splashing them. "I wish we had time to mourn, but time is not on our side. Megacorp is surely on the way."

"What do you mean?" Skru pleaded.

"Your son died of drowning. His physical injuries were superficial. I checked his record. He was a top gun pilot and from my point of view one of serious conviction and loyalty. You must have done a fine job raising him."

"I'm still missing something. Thank you for the kind words."

"Okay, pilots like him are hard to come by. Megacorp will take him for the Reuseable Program. A drowned man is relatively easy to revive. If he had been all smashed up well..." Jake dropped the ending.

"What can we do? I would die before letting that happen! No offense."

"None taken. There was a reason why the pharmaceutical restraints did not work on me. Long story short, my blood had been altered beyond normal parameters. I believe if we do a transfusion, mixing my blood with your son's it may be enough to bring him around." Jake was dead serious but had no idea if it would work.

"Good god man. Are you insane? What would be the difference if he becomes like you?"

"He won't. And if he does, at least he will be with you. The only other option is to make him unusable."

"How?" Skru asked with some trepidation.

"You use a sledgehammer. We will call that Plan B." Jake had given Hans orders to have the med staff on standby with a transfusion rig and pump ready to go. On the way to the lab Jake asked Skru, "Are all you North Sea guys together on this?"

"We stand in agreement." Skru replied.

"No man, I mean really together. You ready to fight and die for your independence?"

"Yes we are. To a man."

"Okay then. I'll back your oil storage stats. By the way, I didn't blow your rig."

"I know."

The med lab was busy and the two men were directed to an office down the hall. Desks had been shoved together for beds. The pilot was already there; he was naked but covered with a sheet and a red fleece blanket that went well with his blue face. Skru was at the bedside, oblivious to anything but caressing his son's head. Jake took his shirt off and lay down. The hematologist was a wee tad on the hesitant side.

"We don't have time for you to deal with the moral implications that are stopping you. Hans said you were good. If you don't start soon, a Megacorp guard is going to come through that door and splatter your brains all over these four walls." That was all it took, a little fear to overcome another fear. The blood guy was good. In under two minutes the fluid began exchanging in a continuous loop. Jake felt the cool enter his body bringing down his core temp. "Could you get me a heated blanket, please?"

"How long will this take?" Skru asked.

"To be honest I don't know." Jake sensed the tension rising in Skru. "Listen – ask the blood guy how long a complete transfusion normally takes and we will go from there." Jake reached into his pocket and pulled out a couple blue pills. "Here Commodore, the next few hours will be a little tense. These will help cut the edge. Can you get me something to read?"

Skru looked at the pills and took one, pocketing the other. He returned a few minutes later with the latest issue of the Maritime News. The cover article concerned the anniversary of the Goliath disaster. Skru settled in next to his son, holding the cold, lifeless hand with fatherly love. Jake saw the goodness in a man who several days earlier would have been happy to see him hung.

"Commodore, who was the woman?" Jake meant the other dead.

"She was our evidence, we hoped. Her name was Mirka and worked for us under lease from Megacorp."

Jake about shit his pants and was immediately thankful for the drugs constipative side effect. They also helped him be cool when he wanted to jump out of his skin.

"Skru, you have to get her here NOW! Or all will have been for nothing. Bring some big syringes." Jake was still maintaining command. The pitch and delivery created a near autonomic response in the Commodore, who was out of his chair and out the door by the time Jake had finished. For once Jake was thinking fast and clear. His life, Mirka's, the kid's, hell – he didn't even know the name of the pilot, anyway – it was all on the line. Megacorp likes nothing better than to catch you when your pants are down. You're just that much easier to fuck.

Skru returned followed by the squeaky wheels of a gurney. He was alone and a pile of 25 cc syringes lay atop Mirka. Skru closed the door and locked it. Turning to Jake, "What do you want me to do?"

"Have you ever drawn blood?"

"I have seen it done."

"Ever shoot up?"

"I had an I.V. once."

"Okay cool. It is just as easy as it looked. Unwrap one of those." Jake pointed to the pile of points. "Remove the protective cap and come here." For the transfusion, Jake had the blood guy insert the catheter into his neck so his arms were free.

"Hand it to me." Skru did. "Squeeze my bicep on the left arm." Jake made a fist and began to pump it. When the vein stood proud he ran the point like a pro. As the blood leaked into the hypo, "Okay, let go now." Skru released his grip and watched Jake fill it.

"Here comes the hard part. Roll her next to me." When they were side-by-side Jake reached over to feel where her heart was. "Remove her shirt." Skru choked. "Ahh fuck it." Jake held the syringe firmly, reached up and stabbed Mirka in the chest and depressed the plunger. When it was empty, he pulled it out and dropped it on the floor as he fainted.

Jake woke to being slapped hard in the face. Skru was yelling, "What do I do?"

Jake's head lolled back and forth, saliva running from his mouth. "Do it again! I cannot." The lights went out; this time for good.

In Jake's dreams he traveled the road of good and evil eventually finding himself at the crossroads. The reasons to take one direction were as many as the ones for the other. The road to goodness and freedom would be nothing but a life on the run from what he had become. Evil, however, offered life and the killing that went along with it. It also made for moments like now where being here meant something. Jake took his first steps along the highway to hell.

He woke to the sound of soft crying and the hushed tender words between father and son. The catheter was gone. Jake brought himself up on one elbow to look at Mirka. Her chest moved rhythmically. Closed eyes opened to stare at Jake. He smiled then swiped his nose with his finger. Mirka smiled back, touched her heart and mouthed thank you before closing her eyes.

Jake turned and swung his legs off the table facing Skru. But it was not Skru Jake was inspecting, it was the son. He eyed him closely and harshly, feeling out with his mind for that telltale signal of the presence of another reuseable. If you were one, you knew when you were in the presence of another. Head to toe, twice. When satisfied he reached out his hand. "The name's Jake. I don't believe we've met." The handshake would make Jake certain one way or the other.

The strong hand of a young man took Jake's. "Captain Thor Skru. It is a pleasure to meet the man who rescued us. My thanks."

"You're very welcome. Luckily I was with your father when the call came." Jake smiled a thousand watter. "How did it happen? The crash I mean."

"That is the embarrassing part."

"Come on man, I fuck up all the time, now give." Jake was just trying to be nice and poured himself a cup of coffee, "Want one, Thor?"

"Sure sure. We were on a routine run, a post-storm inspection, when we saw her body floating near the trench. We lowered a man into big swells. He had a hell of a time but eventually got her. That's how we got Mirka. Flying here yesterday, a down draft pushed the chopper right to the water. I powered up, racing along in the trough and we beat ditching but a rogue wave blindsided us. I did all I could."

"You are one lucky and brave man. Your father should be proud."

"I have one question for you," Thor began. "How did I survive? I remember the cockpit windows imploding."

"Perhaps the one you are named after had a hand in it." Skru offered, "And I am very proud of you my son." Neither Jake nor Commodore Skru had any intention of telling Thor, or anyone else for that matter what had been done. A regular reuseable would not have been able to revive a dead person by transfusion. The residual essence left in Jake's system after the overdose not only helped him beat the pharmaceutical restraints but get the kid going again, so it would seem. Now he was spent. The evil within him had done good. He was, however, used up; used up like the syringes on the floor.

"Commodore, why don't you take Thor for a few laps, get his blood flowing?" Jake opened the door for them and locked it behind them. He started a pot of coffee and rolled a couple cigarettes while the brewing was doing. Mirka had not opened her eyes again. Jake looked her over. She looked like a train wreck. Burns over bruises, broken nose with the customary pair of black eyes, eyebrows and hair burnt away, and that was just her face. Normally she would have been put on ice since she was a Megacorp op. So what was she doing in the ship's hospital? The same one that denied him care.

Jake held a steaming cup of java beneath Mirka's flattened nose. The swollen eyes hardly parted just enough for her to see the cup and take it, just enough for Jake to see the liquid windows to her soul. She took a sip, then another. Jake gave her a few moments of peace while he rummaged through his personal bag looking for his works. He mixed a gentle speedball for two. No meth, just a little coke and downtown. They were living in a moment of grace, but Jake knew it wouldn't last. Megacorp would be arriving soon. As yet they considered Mirka dead along with the crew of the Goliath. Jake would like to keep it that way. But how?

"Welcome back. I think of you often, like every time I bend over. Got me a nice ruptured disc." Jake laughed, "It's good to see you."

"Sorry about that, but you were going over the edge so I gave it all I had." Mirka mumbled through her puffed up lips.

"What I meant to say was thank you."

"You're welcome, but I believe you have balanced the scales with me. Your gift was unprecedented. I don't believe it has ever been done before."

"Don't go giving me any awards just yet. I did something else a little unprec ... extreme, and am unsure of the fallout. Now here," Jake handed her a syringe, "Just a little something to help with the near future. Can you do yourself?"

"No."

Jake was sterile and doctor like. Mirka hardly noticed the injection but Jake noticed why she could not do it herself. Her right arm was broken and her left hand was, well, gone. Jake poured some more coffee in an effort to shake off the weirds. 'Fuck what happened?' he thought. But there was no time for a trip down memory lane. The drugs were kicking in, easing the pain and lubricating the jaw.

"I would love to sit and talk and hear your story and tell mine. So we'll save it for later." Jake took a slug of coffee and lit both cigarettes and stuck one in Mirka's mouth.

"We are on the workboat Big Brother. One year has passed since the Goliath went down. You have been floating in the North Sea all that time. A gyre brought you in closer to the mainland and a rescue chopper spotted you. They saved you. The two men you saw leave were the pilot and his father. They will be the ones to get you out of here."

"What's the point, Jake? Megacorp will put me back in service with a new hand, so unless I'm missing something here..."

"Megacorp believes you are dead. A write-off in the aftermath of the Goliath. Nice job by the way. Blew it to smithereens."

"The dream is nice, Jake, but there is no way to live outside the system. Without the weekly 'juice' it would be just misery with no end. I've seen men punished that way." Mirka said sadly.

"Me too, but there is a chance. If you can get to the USA, Kale and I can arrange to take you somewhere. There is also another option and perhaps better."

"You know Kale?" Mirka said with eyes as wide as they could get.

"You know him, too?"

"A long time ago he saved me." Mirka saved the details for herself.

"Me too. Taught me about the balancing the scales thing." Jake explained.

"I wondered where you got it from. It didn't exactly seem like your idea."

"Why thank you very much. I'm going to call the Commodore." As far as Jake was concerned Skru owed him one. Jake made the call, and a cigarette. Commodore Skru returned to Jake and Mirka. He left his son under the care of the ship's doctor.

"Why was it you requested that I be alone?" Skru was armed and the pistol loose in its holster.

"Because of the delicate nature of the situation," Jake said exuding compassion and hoping it was being picked up.

"Mr. Strom, not only did you bring my son's body back from the deep, you also brought him back to me. You have no idea how much this means to me." Skru was near tears but they did not flow.

"Well I suppose we will find out just how much." Jake replied as Skru cocked his head, eyeing Jake questioningly. Mirka too roused when she heard the Commodore's statement. Skru froze. The movement from the dead woman scared him and he reached for his weapon.

"No Commodore, please." Jake was ready to beg.

"Mirka was one of your scientists aboard the Goliath. She is also like me." Jake let it sink in, "Do you understand?"

Skru nodded, "So that is why you injected her. To bring her around."

"Yeah. I wanted her cognizant before Megacorp arrived. You see they think she is dead along with the rest of those unaccounted for. I'm not a big fan of Megacorp but I'm caught in one of those Catch-22's. So was she. Now is her chance to try and break free."

"Excuse me, Jake. I am not a 'she' and why are you making decisions for me?"

"I just naturally assumed you'd want out and I am in the process of using my one favor to do it for you."

"You know it's not possible, Jake. We already talked about this." Mirka hung her head and shook it.

Jake rolled and lit another cigarette and poured some more coffee. He was on a roll. Whatever the concoction was that Johnny had created, it kept him three steps ahead.

"There is a way. Sort of. But for this I have to lay my cards on the table. Skru, when I brought your son back I did not know what I was doing."

"YOU DID WHAT!" Mirka snapped.

"I was simply happy for the chance to have my son back. I was not thinking either. It was a desperate affair and I think any father would have done the same." Skru was calm. Jake wanted to keep it that way but ...

"I am glad you feel that way. In not knowing what I was doing, I do not know what I have done."

"Jesus, Jake, what did you do?" Mirka asked with a gimme for the tobacco and papers. She reached for them with the phantom hand. "Could you roll me one?"

"Let me," Skru offered.

"I gave his son a transfusion. We mixed our blood rather than the way you got yours. You however did get a dilute dose as it was already blended with Thor's. I've got a good feeling about this but that don't mean jack. What this means is I don't know what the future holds for Thor, or for you Mirka. The only solution I can think of is to have you watch over him."

"But how? Megacorp will ..." Mirka began. Skru was wrapped in what was being said.

"Let me finish and you can ask all the questions you want. Megacorp will have my ass back in the grind. You, however, don't have to." Jake raised his hand to stop Mirka. "You're history as far as they are concerned. Now, the North Sea uses us all the time. They are given an ample supply of 'juice', generally a lot more than is actually needed. The stuff is useless to anyone but us and is impossible to replicate." The listeners were looking at him like he was either crazy or a genius and they were not sure which. Jake saw this and filled them in.

"A friend of mine is a scientist and fills me in on all this shit. Anyway there is more than enough. Swiping some now and then shouldn't be a big issue. In the meantime, Mirka can keep an eye on Thor and deal with stuff, if there is any."

"You mean Thor might now be a reuseable?"

"I don't know. If he is, at least he will be with you. On the upside, he doesn't know he died. Most don't handle it too well."

"Since you seem to know it all today, Jake, what do I get after being a shrink and a doc? At some point I will no longer be needed."

"That's where your nose for oil comes in. You know the North Sea is in deep shit, perhaps deeper than you realize." Jake looked over at Skru, who lowered his eyes and nodded. Mirka didn't miss it.

"I'm going to go out on a limb here Skru, stop me if you want to. Mirka, the North Sea delegation is one of the few remaining independents in the world. And they want to keep it that way. The oil reserves are the one thing that keeps them from being absorbed by Megacorp. Here's the catch. There are no reserves. Well, not near what they report anyway."

Mirka's jaw dropped. When she recovered, "I had suspected the numbers were artificially high. Goliath wasn't producing and the other rigs were just slurping the bottom."

"She is right, we have been altering the books for some time now. The underwater storage tanks were mock-ups to keep up appearances.

"The question is, are there more pockets of oil, or have we sucked her dry?" Jake was directing the conversation. "Mirka?"

" My research indicates yes, there are. Of course nothing like it was in the day," she replied.

"Would it be worth the effort?" Skru asked.

"How could it not be? And you need somebody to find it. There you go, Mirka. You wanted something to do."

"Unfortunately my records are at the bottom of the sea."

"Got that covered, too! While I'm here I am supposed to verify by visual inspection the storage facility and log the capacities. My gear should be here in a few days. We should be able to find your stuff, too. How did you blow it?" Jake asked.

"25 kilos in each leg. Sven, the drill chief, added more in different locations and your friend Pablo was tied to that thing with another 50 kilos. As far as I know the control tower was not set with charges." Mirka stunned Jake.

"What, how, tied to it?" Skru was in the dark.

"Pablo grappled with the monster. Sven was quick with a rope and lashed them to pallets as they fought. He piled on the explosive. Pablo never realized until it was too late. I hit the detonator not two meters from the insanity. We had to be sure. Sven was a good friend." Mirka finished with a dose of melancholy.

"Excuse me, may I call you Jake?" Skru asked.

Jake nodded. "Well, Jake, what is this monster Mirka speaks of? We were under the impression terrorists had hijacked us."

"I don't know. Mirka spent more time there than me. I will give you my guess. It was a reuseable Megacorp lost control of, or he escaped somehow and found a way to survive. It was madness. Mirka?"

"Hopefully we will never really know. But Jake is close to the mark."

Jake felt Johnny's magic wearing off fast. A crash was coming on. "Are we all good?" Jake never heard the responses. He fell forward off the desk he was leaning on, faceplanting on the carpet.

Mirka looked at Skru and raised her arms. "You should call some orderlies and have him taken to bed. He's all right. All he needs is some rest. What is your name, Commodore?"

"Sigurd."

"Ahh, the dragon slayer. May I call you Sig?"

"Of course. It has been a pleasure to meet you and I look forward to working with you. Unfortunately I have other duties that I must attend to if we are to keep up this charade."

"A very real charade, Sig. I will dress. Find Thor and arrange for adjoining rooms. We will work this out." Mirka began undoing her hospital gown. Sig left for the bridge and communications office.

A fully armed Megacorp assault helicopter landed on the rear deck of Big Brother. A dozen SEALS hit the deck moments later. Once the position was deemed secure, three suits carefully navigated the steps to the rocking deck. They were not seamen. Captain Krull crossed the deck with the sure footsteps of a life at sea. His credentials were checked before he was let past the circle of guards.

"Good afternoon, gentlemen. Welcome aboard Big Brother. I am Captain Krull."

"It sure is a lot bigger than I thought it would be," exclaimed one of the suits.

"IT is SHE. SHE is the largest of her kind and in a class of HER own. SHE is more powerful than anything Megacorp will ever have, Mr. Stimple."

"I meant no disrespect. However, she may, one day, be ours," Stimple stated plainly, in an attempt to catch the captain off guard.

Captain Krull was nobody's fool. "Commodore Skru is waiting for you in the officers' lounge. Your men are not allowed inside."

Stimple raised his hand to an objection that was about to be blurted by the C.O. "Lead the way, Captain." *It may end messy*, Stimple thought, *but it doesn't have to start that way.*

The officers' lounge was like an old library; dark mahogany bookshelves lined three walls, all full. Overstuffed chairs and ottomans, a large teak conference table, thick oriental rugs and red velvet wallpaper. The room was opulent in direct contrast to the huge workboat. Skru was seated with his feet up, smoking a cigarette and reading the history of the Spartans' battle at Thermopylae. He closed the book and stood slowly as the men came into the room.

"Thank you, Captain. That will be all." Krull nodded to Skru, giving him an imperceptible wink before turning on his heel and closing the door on his way out. Skru was pleased Megacorp had come to meet him. They were on 'his' turf, the North Sea. Two of the suits Skru had never seen before. "Mr. Stimple, I believe introductions are in order."

"Yes, Commodore Skru, just getting my sea legs." He laughed uneasily. "To my right is Jack Hisiger, our top oil specialist. Jack, Sigurd." As they shook hands, Sig was forced to pull away abruptly and snatch the nearest rubbish bin, to catch the lunch Jack was in the process of disgorging.

The others ignored the minor disturbance.

"On my left is Benjamin Goldstein, our numbers man. Ben, Sigurd." Goldstein didn't have the curse his associate was dealing with. Stimple wasn't all that perky himself, but he was hanging tough. This was his show. Skru wasn't about to let him have the floor yet.

"Something to drink? Vodka, scotch, bourbon, and we have an excellent wine cellar. I myself am having coffee." Just the names and memories of hangovers brought another round of puking from Jack. The smell of vomit paled Stimple. Sig knew it wouldn't be long till he went over the edge, too.

"Water, please," requested Stimple.

The commodore complied and made Jack comfortable on the bathroom floor, closing the door. He deliberately left the pail of puke in the lounge. Skru topped off his coffee and lit another cigarette.

"Mr. Stimple, I believe you are here to check on the status of the suit we had brought against Mr. Strom. And then there are the things you don't want me to know about. Am I warm?" Skru blew a cloud of smoke in Stimple's direction. Not at him mind you, just close enough. The lounge with all the furnishings was closing in on Stimple. The lack of air movement and now the smoke...

"Yes, you are war..." Stimple dove for the trash can and added his lunch.

Skru smiled. Seasickness is for the duration.

Goldstein sat down in one of the big chairs like he had done it all his life. A cultured life of leisure, that is. He smiled slyly at the Commodore. "Well done, Sigurd, and I believe I would like a scotch. Make it a double."

Sig called for some orderlies to take the two men away and for someone to clean up the mess.

"I was pleased to hear of your son's survival, along with the rest of the personnel. Quite amazing really, since you were accusing the diver of being a coward. It makes me wonder if the rest of your allegations are as founded." Benjamin rested his scotch on his belly and smiled benignly.

Skru had the feeling he was about to be screwed. He couldn't divulge any of the new information without revealing Mirka. Sig was just going to have to take it.

"The near death of my son has changed the way I feel about a great many things. I believe the North Sea would rather put this behind us, cut our losses and move on." Sig was playing it cool.

"But what of the evidence that was so important?" Goldstein was not so easily appeased.

"We were bluffing. You know, we lie so much to each other it is sometimes a relief to tell the truth." Sig actually believed what he said. Goldstein didn't.

"I don't buy it. You have a reputation going back forty years for being one of the biggest debating pricks we have ever had to deal with. You've been a pain in my ass for thirty of them. Now suddenly you roll over and get all warm and fuzzy with me. Give me a fucking break, Sig."

"Ever married, Ben?"

"No. My career."

"No kids then either?" Sig pressed.

"No."

"Then I wouldn't expect you to understand. Imagine losing your portfolio and finding it again safe and secure. It's a poor analogy."

"No doubt, though you did hit a tender spot. I imagine you are wondering why we are here. There is another chopper on the way with more suits, as you call them. We knew you were yanking our chain so we thought to take this opportunity to check out the rest of your story. With our diver here, we are going to take a look around at your facility."

"Are you strong-arming me, Ben?" Skru assumed a more dominant body language.

"It shouldn't come to that, unless you have something to hide."

"No. Ben, you will see that everything is in order. When do you want this done?" The bluff had been called.

"As soon as the gear arrives."

Jake was dreaming he was in Mirka's arms. His erection was close to doing what erections do, the dream was that good, when he was whacked with a baton right in the nuts. The fantasy was ruined along with one of his testicles. There he was, the Megacorp thug that was wherever Jake was. Like a shadow, with pain. No locker room humor accompanied the blow; only the sardonic smile of a man who knows he is in control. Jake clutched his groin, sitting on the edge of the bed.

"Give me your left arm." The thug demanded.

Jake wanted to say, 'but it's still attached'. Instead he raised his arm. The big man examined the inside of Jake's elbow and shook his head at the tracks. With a brutal methodology the thug stabbed an empty syringe into the inside of the elbow. He worked the needle around a bit before hitting the crimson flow. When filled it was yanked out. The procedure was over. Jake knew better than to complain.

"Lie down face up and turn your head to the right." It was not a request either. Jake was getting 'juiced'. Now this, the thug was good at ... sort of. "Be on the back deck in two hours." He tossed Jake's gear bag on the floor next to the bed, turned and left. Jake fell back into bed and let the 'juice' do its work.

Jake had no idea how long he had been out. But one thing was for sure. The alarm clock had just gone off. A knock on the door roused him from the last of his dolor over his busted balls. Standing and walking to the door was merely excruciating. An orderly with coffee and Danish stood there holding the tray out forward. Jake took it along with a slip of paper that trembling fingers held against the bottom of the plastic tray. A Megacorp guard sat on a chair net to Jake's door.

"Thanks, and could you bring another carafe, please?" Jake asked, "four cups is hardly enough to start the day with."

"Ya sure, anything else?" asked the wait.

"Make it strong." Jake looked down at the guard, smirked and went back into his room. He poured a cup and unfolded the paper napkin. On it was a rough sketch of the basic layout of the storage facility. Of the forty-eight ten million barrel tanks, only six had been completed and half of those were destroyed. Jake committed the locations to memory, sopping up some spilled coffee with the napkin to destroy it. After two more cups, he began to come up with a plan. Megacorp wanted to see 48 tanks. Jake tried to think of it as a regular inspection. It was something he did routinely. Rarely was an inspection unbiased. You were told before you hit the water to make, let us say, a ship look as good as possible or the opposite. Whoever was paying the bill made the decision. This time it was to make a few look like many. It could be done.

More coffee came. Jake knocked back a cup before his door was rapped on again. Johnny was leaning against the jam having an animated conversation with the guard. He finished, said 'ciao,' and came into the room.

"Shit," Jake said, spilling his coffee.

"Well good fucking morning to you, too."

"Ahh just kinda hung over. What was that shit?"

"I call it 'Lucidity.' Takes a few days to pull out of it. But for a few hours you are sharper than a razor."

Jake rubbed the stubble on his chin. "What the fuck are you doing here?"

"You are diving. I am your tender... What?" Johnny asked at Jake's questioning look.

"It just that Hans will be bummed. He tended me when we got the chopper."

"Oh. You have not been told and the Lucidity has worn off."

"Told what?" Jake asked.

Johnny laughed lightly and shook his head. "You get no more contact with the North Sea delegation. Whatever deal you swung with them better be tight."

"They want to keep their freedom. I intend to help them."

"And just what is it you need me to do?" Johnny inquired, backing his friend without question.

Jake explained about the storage tanks. He would need Johnny to cut the video feed from time to time to aid in the deception. "I also need you to talk with Skru, find out how his son and Mirka are doing. I kind of pushed things a little and I'm still not sure what I have done."

"Some things will never change. You are going to get us killed before this thing is over." Johnny laughed.

"I seriously doubt that my friend. Time to suit up. Have to be on deck in 20." Jake pulled his dive suit out of the gear bag.

"See you there." Johnny took the bag and left for the dive station. Jake was disappointed. At the very least he had hoped to get high. He took it as a sign that things were more serious than they appeared. Jake stretched into the dive suit. It fit like a second skin. He put on his booties and donned the dive harness. There was a knock at the door.

Armed guards led Jake along the companionways to a storm door that led out onto the main deck. A temporary enclosure made of vinyl sheeting stood next to the port gunwale at the stern. The sound of propane heaters, like jet engines, kept the tent a comfortable 80 degrees. Outside was a cool zero degrees under leaden skies. Hans leaned against a winch bundled in fur, looking like a Viking. He wanted a moment with Jake, who knew better than to even acknowledge his presence. At worst Hans would be killed. At best ... there was no at best.

"Jake! Hey Jake, it's me, Hans." He stepped forward from the winch into the trio, an empty hand extended. It was not rewarded with a shake but with the butt of a machine gun to his head. Hans took the hit but didn't go down. He was a big man with a heritage of tough guys behind him. Jake lurched forward and caught the second butt behind his ear. It saved Hans a broken face. Jake grabbed the gun that hit him and threw it over the side. He spun around and did the same with other guard's gun.

"Get out of here, Hans!" Jake yelled as four hands grappled with him, taking him down and pinning him to the deck. Jake had not hit the two guards; he had merely relieved them of the long guns. Now a nine-millimeter semi automatic was pressed painfully into his temple. Jake didn't move a muscle. The two guards were yelling something at him but he wasn't getting it. Suddenly the weight of the two men on top of him was doubled as somebody started to play pile up. The pistol went off as 400 kilos was jerked up off of Jake. The bullet grazed his temple before ricocheting off the deck and heading out to sea. He looked up in time to see two bodies being hurled over the gunwale.

Flaps from the tent were flung open at the sound of gunfire. Johnny, Benjamin Goldstein, and a still-green Stimple rushed through the opening to see the guards flailing in the air before splashing into the icy seas thirty feet below. Jake was on his feet as blood poured down his face obscuring his vision. All he got was a nod from Johnny, indicating now would be a good time to save the lives of the guards.

Passing Hans, Jake said, "Drop a ladder and get ready to receive a couple of pissed off Megacorp dickheads." At the side of the ship Jake took one look and dove over. The shock of the cold water was less invigorating than it should have been. It hurt like hell but there was no time to fight it as the three-meter swells smashed him against the side of Big Brother. One guard was close. Jake got hold of him and made for the rope ladder that Hans lowered. Jake tied the guard to the ladder and went for the other who was sinking fast. Boots and bullets were not meant for swimming. The water was as black as the guard's buscus jumpsuit. Jake swam downward, reaching out with his mind. His eyes were useless. Material met his hands and Jake locked on, reversing his direction. The man had drowned but that didn't slow Jake. Something grabbed the dead guard and jerked the body from side to side. Jake couldn't see it but it had to be a shark. 'Son of a bitch!' Jake felt for the holster, no gun. 'This was the motherfucker that was going to kill me'. He was still swimming up against the attack of the shark. The water was getting lighter. He pulled his spud wrench as the grey shark came again for another attack. Jake stabbed the spud into the shark's eye just as the meniscus layer began cover the huge black eye just prior to biting. The shark rolled, diving into the deep taking Jake's wrench with it. By now his lungs were burning for another breath. Jake almost took it. Instead, he reached the surface.

He had drifted a good 30 meters from the ship in the struggle. Hans spotted Jake first and hurled a life ring attached to a line that landed next to the diver and the dead guard. Jake secured the man to the ring and touched the top of his head. At the signal Hans pulled on the line and hauled the body from the water. Jake followed, climbing the ladder. He found Hans performing CPR on the drowning victim. Jake looked the body over for shark damage. The Kevlar jumpsuit had saved his life. Now if only Hans could. The tender's life depended on reviving the man who clubbed him. Together they went at it until yellow fluid was puked from the lungs and a gurgled foamy breathing began. Only then did they allow the Med Techs to relieve them. Jake put his hand on Hans' shoulder and squeezed while looking deep into the tender's eyes. Jake smiled, nodded and left the cold and warmth of friendship for the heat of the tent and the cold hearts of men and their greed.

Johnny handed him a cup of coffee and sat him down in front of one of the blowers. "Jesus, Jake. What was that all about?"

"Yes, do tell. I'm sure we would all like to hear," Goldstein began. "You were told no contact. What do you have to say for yourself?"

"What would you like to hear? Your goons would have killed that kid," Jake spat.

"They had their orders. Why did you save them?"

"Seemed like a good idea at the time. Now I'm not so sure." Jake was mad and busy digging a hole for himself with it.

"You are going to need some stitches to close the hole in your head. Do I have permission to take him to the hospital?" Johnny asked Goldstein. The sight of Jake's blood had rendered Stimple useless again, his head buried in a bucket.

"Will he be able to dive?" Goldstein was not in the diving business.

Johnny looked at Jake and shrugged his shoulders.

"Do I really have a choice?" Jake said sarcastically.

"No."

"That's what I thought. Let's get the fuck out of here." Jake left the tent leaving an unhealthy trail of blood back across the deck.

The hospital was having a busy morning. The two guards took up the remaining exam rooms and the doctor was busy with them. Jake was busy bleeding all over the waiting room floor when a nurse entered with a tray of sutures. A soft hand pressed gauze against the wound.

"The seawater cleaned the damage so we won't be needing to debride the wound. Would you like a local anesthetic?"

"No thanks. Just close it up…" Then it hit him. The touch, the voice … he raised his eyes to see Mirka. She swiped her nose with an index finger.

"We are a little short handed today. You sure about the local?"

"No. Nice pun and just how are you going to do it?" Jake replied as Johnny entered.

"Better give it to him. He is a glutton for punishment. How are the two guards?"

"They will live, but one will be limping for a while."

A white curtain parted as a man leaning heavily on the arm of an orderly wobbled into the waiting room. Mirka was fishing a needle through the skin on Jake's head when he approached. His free hand reached out to Jake.

"I, I wanted to thank you. I have a wife and kids." Moisture welled up in the man's eyes but didn't spill. "If there is anything you need, just ask for Waldo, that's me."

"Just go easy on the kid you butted with your gun. He is a good man and doesn't deserve any shit from Megacorp."

"That can be arranged."

"How's your partner?"

"Mad and embarrassed. You will have to watch out for him."

"Thanks for the heads-up. You better stop him if he decides to cross me again." The guard nodded and returned to his room. "Ouch!" Jake squealed as Mirka pierced his skin with the second stitch. They couldn't risk talking for fear of being overheard. Nine stitches later she put her tools away and for the first time looked Jake squarely in the face. In sign language, as her hand and wrist were free of the cast she answered Jake's unvoiced question. 'We are okay.'

Jake nodded and said, "Thanks doc. Best one handed stitcher this side of anywhere." Mirka shrugged her shoulders. "Time to go to work", Jake finished. There was much he wanted to discuss with Mirka but now was not the time. He gave her a brief hug and left with Johnny.

"Who was that?"

"The woman who saved my life and blew up the Goliath," Jake replied.

"Why did she sign that 'they are okay'?"

"Because I saved their lives."

"Who is the other?"

"Skru's son."

"You are being a bit cryptic here, Jake. Just how did you save their lives?"

"Transfusions."

"And it worked?"

"Apparently. She is a Megacorp op. Skru's son was not."

Johnny was not sure how to respond to such a thing. There wasn't time for it anyway. They entered the tent.

Stimple had regained his composure with the use of modern pharmaceuticals. It just took a while. Every time he ate a pill he would puke it up shortly afterwards. Eventually he got enough of the drug in his system to beat the seasickness. With the nausea stopped, the businessman prick resurfaced with an axe to grind.

"You know, Mr. Strom, we received the results of the blood test that was taken earlier today. How are your balls by the way? You want to keep them, it would be best if you stick to our agreement. Do you understand me?" Stimple made to puff himself up, expanding his chest and taking a dominant stance. It made for good comedy but it was a poor time for laughter.

"Yes sir. I'd love to sit here and split hairs with you all day. However diving in shark infested waters is probably a little safer for me at this point in the game."

"Any time you've had enough of the game, just let me know. Percy told me he would gladly let you, how do you say, live the dream of death."

"Percy, huh? Well I do appreciate the offer, really, but I have work to do. Maybe when I'm done we could talk about this some more. Let's get the hat on, Johnny."

Johnny had been waiting with the dive helmet in his hands, ready to slap it on Jake's head if he went too far with Stimple.

"Comm check one, two. You got me, Jake?"

"Roger that."

"I doubled up the battery pack. You can run the suit heaters full time. Camera comes on as soon as you hit the water. Ready when you are." Johnny stood up from the radio and guided Jake to the step off point. He palmed Jake a syringe before patting him on the hat. Jake wrapped his hand tight around the little plastic device and took a giant stride into the North Sea. When he got himself oriented in the water, he blindly stabbed the point into his thigh, pushing whatever it was into the big muscle.

"See you sissies in a few hours." Jake began his descent.

"What did that bastard say?" Stimple was out of his chair, taking the remark personally.

"All the divers say that. Nothing personal." Johnny said, reading Stimple.

Stimple had every reason to be nervous. During the inquisition, Jake had paid little attention to the proceedings. Instead he had been focusing on Stimple. He was not sure if it was his imagination, inspiration, or comprehension. But one way or the other he saw that Stimple was homosexual. Not that there is anything wrong with that. Hell more than a few big dogs in Megacorp were closet queens. But that was the kicker. You had to keep it in the closet. The morals in politics and religion were as twisted as ever. Anything goes as long as you don't get caught. Business was business and the bottom line was all that really mattered. But get caught with your pants down and your dick in some boy's ass and you'll find out very quickly that keeping up appearances is just as important as the bottom line. Stimple had been cool. You don't get to his position without some serious vesting. He covered his tracks well by being discreet and wearing a condom and flushing the DNA. He wasn't going to go down just because a prostitute didn't floss.

But even in the freezing north, Stimple was losing his cool. The diver, whom he had never met before, pinned him out. No one had ever caught him masturbating in conference before. He was afraid of losing it all. Luckily it was part of the agreement with Jake. Jake would keep his mouth shut if he was given immunity. It was in Megacorp's interest to let Jake walk. Admitting fault is something Megacorp is not wont to do.

Jake sank into the cold darkness. Not straight down mind you, but at an angle to land on the seafloor next to the nearest intact tanker. Visibility was a poor ten meters on the way down and a good fifteen at the bottom. Strong currents and large volumes of fresh water from glacial activity kept silt to a minimum. Jake hadn't noticed the gravelly seafloor when he salvaged the helicopter. He had been counting on the silt to help obscure the quality of the video. Fanning the bottom with his fins when he touched down raised a cloud of coarse sand that sank quickly back to the seafloor. Jake was shit out of luck with plan 'A'. Plan 'B' was to keep his distance and not allow too good a look. After swimming the tank and giving a good overall view he headed to the next tank. Or rather, Jake swam in a large circle to create the illusion of a straight line, only to arrive back at the same tank from a different angle.

"Okay topside that was our first tank. Taking a heading of 120 degrees. E.T.A to the next tank five minutes."

Johnny was monitoring the comms and the video. He noticed the silt issue, or lack of it, right away. He also saw the way Jake was going to play it. On the plus side was the halocline effect created by the influx of fresh water. It created an oiled image on video. There was little that could be done to make it better. But there were half a dozen ways Johnny could adjust it to make it worse. He sat with headphones on, absorbed in the little dials. Shouting erupted behind him. Another little dial upped the headphone's intake of ambient noise. He made like invisible, intent upon the video monitor.

It was Skru pleading with Stimple and Goldstein. Thus far he had kept silent about his son. That is until Thor began to suffer. Skru may have been the top man in the North Sea delegation, and a ruthless bastard at that, but it was being a father that broke him. Thor toughed it out in the beginning and his father stood by him. But when his body was racked in pain that would not be killed with pharmaceuticals and his mind in despair when realizing what had been done to him, Skru ordered Mirka to give him an injection of the 'juice'.

"I will do it this once. If he does not begin to cope you will have to deal with him."

"He was fine yesterday! Did you tell him? Why did you tell him?" Skru was just beginning to lose it.

"I did no such thing. None of us are ever told, but we become aware of it. He must get control of himself!" Mirka knew the worst was yet to come.

"How can he when he suffers in so many ways."

Mirka looked hard at Skru. Her voice of experience said, "This is nothing. You cannot imagine what it is like," she finished contemptuously. Her experience also let her instantly regret what she had said. "Perhaps the injection will help. We will know soon enough." Mirka spoke this softly and placed her hand on Skru's shoulder.

"He is my only son. I thought, I thought ... my god, what have I done?" He turned and left the room.

Mirka prepared the injection and mainlined Thor in the neck. All the hell on earth was unleashing itself upon the mind of the young man. His sanity was ripped from its mooring in his conscious mind and spit into the maelstrom left behind.

Skru returned to his office and began to unravel. The false garment of power and superiority had fallen away at the sight of his son. Something inside him said there was nothing that could be done. He did not listen. All that was left was a frightened little man unable to bear the consequences of his actions.

He slipped into the private quarters where his son was kept. Mirka was gone. A note on the tabletop had his name on it. It held all of three words, 'I am sorry'. Thor was on the bed covered by a sheet. His wild, staring eyes saw nothing. Skru pulled back the sheet to see the boy's hand and feet tied securely to the bed frame. He set down the stack of papers and prints he had brought with him and sat on the edge of the bed. When he stroked the face of his son the boy went animal, tearing at the flesh of his father's hand with his teeth. Skru pulled his hand away, bitten to the bone. His blood ran freely across the clean white sheet, then across his pants as he reached for his service handgun. Resting the barrel against Thor's temple he closed his eyes and squeezed. He sat this way for some time. Unable to bring enough pressure to bear on the trigger, he put the gun away and picked up the bundle of papers. On the way out the door Skru said, "Forgive me." He was not sure whether he was saying it to his son, himself, or his people. Perhaps all, for Skru was about to do the unforgivable.

"Mr. Goldstein, Mr. Stimple, I have a favor to ask."

Goldstein looked at Stimple. This was highly irregular, especially from a man who asks for nothing and demands everything. They nodded to each other.

"What's in it for us?" asked Goldstein, seeing his pound of flesh.

"Everything," was the little man's reply.

Johnny was listening to every word. Commodore Skru was spilling the beans for the life of his son. He was selling out the North Sea delegation. He couldn't call to Jake. Everything was being recorded. There was a chance. If Jake was paying attention he might get the message. If not it was his ass. Johnny began to tap the touch pad that opened and closed the comm link. It was silent at Johnny's end and looked like a nervous twitch. In Jake's hat however, a click was heard at each tap. Johnny sent the message three times. Goldstein got up out of his chair and came up behind Johnny to look over his shoulder.

"How's our diver doing? Could be he has gotten in a little over his head." Goldstein's sarcasm dripped all over Johnny.

"He has just finished the swim by of the fifth tank and is heading to the next. It is his nature." Johnny answered both questions.

Goldstein didn't miss it. "Indeed. Have him continue. We are very interested in his findings."

About halfway through capturing the essence of an underwater storage tanker -- Jake was proud of his ability as a cameraman -- there came an incessant clicking in the hat's speaker. He missed the first attempt by being annoyed. And the second by laughing to himself. It was the oldest trick in the book, almost. When you couldn't talk you used the Morse Code. It was ancient tech and had more than once saved his ass. On the third attempt he got it, but took a few minutes to process it.

"Fuck me!" Jake said aloud in the dive hat. The note read: 'Skru caved. Cover your ass!' It did not say 'watch your ass', but 'cover'. This was key information.

"Come again, Jake."

"I said, fuck me. I just swam in a circle and wound up where I started."

"Clever, Jake. The big boys behind me really think you are a sharp tack now."

"Oops, back to work. Taking a heading, 120 degrees, again." Jake knew it was lame but the truth beats lying. Keeps it simple.

Five minutes later Jake spoke into the comms. "Coming up on tanker number..."

"Yeah, Jake. Come again. Lost you. Steel interference."

"Maybe so. But you better bring Stimple and Goldstein to the monitor. They will want to see this." Jake panned the length of the tank. Steel girders, like the ribs of a ghostly whale skeleton loomed on the monitor.

Stimple's jaw dropped. Goldstein smiled in smug satisfaction. Skru remained seated and hung his head in shame.

"We had suspected something like this." Goldstein said to no one in particular. "Have the diver continue. We want the entire complex documented," he said to Johnny while donning his parka. Outside the tent stood the Megacorp thug, Percy. Goldstein had a decidedly one-sided conversation with the big man. Goldstein left the rear deck and dive station for his stateroom and some privacy. One man's grief was another's – well – whatever makes him happy.

Jake spent the next twenty-two hours creating a legally binding survey of the storage site. He had done many of them. You either got it right the first time or did it over and over until someone's anal retentiveness had been satisfied. Jake could be called in to qualify the video. Cover your ass was the name of the game. The mind-numbing hours of repetition took its toll after a while. He would stop and clear his head before starting a new vid sequence. It was not difficult to lose track. Johnny helped when he could by logging the tanks on his laptop. In the end perseverance wins the day by sticking it out, not saying fuck it, and doing your best. Jake just couldn't help himself. It was the way he worked.

It was night when he climbed the ladder. Johnny was standing there to take the camera from a weary Jake. He removed the dive helmet and harness before stepping away. The deck floodlights had silhouetted his tender and created hot spots in his line of sight. When Johnny's thin form stepped away, a big blot of blackness came forward blocking even the lights. A voice came out of the darkness. Jake knew it all too well.

"Come with me," said Percy. It was not a request and never would be.

There was nowhere to run. He saw Johnny watching from the door of the tent before falling into step behind Percy. Jake was cold by the time they entered the superstructure. They passed the hospital, galley and stairway to the wheelhouse. Jake didn't know the layout of Big Brother all that well but he had a pretty good idea of where they were going. Percy paused at the door to Thor's room, keying the lock. He waved Jake in and closed and locked the door behind them. The room smelled of sweat, piss and shit. Thor's. Jake could not help but stare at what he had done.

"That's right. Look at what you have done to this poor man," Percy stated with true compassion.

"I thought ... I don't know what I thought," Jake admitted.

"We could have used him. Now even that is not possible." Percy reached into a fanny pack and withdrew a large caliber single shot pistol. He loaded it before handing it to Jake.

"Normally I take care of these things myself. Yours is a special case and I need to insure you will not do it again. I know you better than you know yourself. For you there is no other way. Take your time. I am a patient man. But do not try it."

Jake looked at the gun, at Thor, then into what was left of his soul. He stepped to the bedside and stuck the snub nose into Thor's eye and dropped the hammer. Blood, brains, bits of bones and skin blew back from the sockets. The pressure needed somewhere to go as the round spent itself smashing through the inside of the skull. Jake took the splatter full in the face. What missed him, wound up on the walls, ceiling and floor. He dropped the gun onto the bed. His mind was as empty as the spent, hot shell casing still smoking out the barrel. He wished there was another round. Not for Percy, who had avoided getting sprayed by placing his chair directly behind Jake, but for himself.

He had killed men before but never like this. In a senseless act of kindness, he had ruined not only a man's death but his life, a father, and a nation. If he had only done what he was supposed to and left the rest to Megacorp. Jake would say god at this point but Megacorp is more appropriate. Besides when was the last time god got his hands dirty? Jake watched until the heart stopped and the eye socket quit pulsing like an overflowing toilet. He hung his head and said some small futile prayer from his childhood before turning to Percy and the Pollock he had created on the clean, empty surfaces.

With his foot Percy kicked over a bucket and rags. Jake waited a moment for a haranguing of some kind. Something like, 'you got to clean up your own messes, boy. You really think I was going to ask one of the staff to clean up your shit? Now get down on your hands and fucking knees, start scrubbing and pray to god for your soul.'

What Jake got was, "When I come back I want this room clean and the body ready to be taken to the morgue." Percy carefully avoided the splotches of grey matter on the floor as he left the room. Jake looked at Thor's body, at the mess he had made of everything. Blood would flow in the streets of every Norwegian town and city as the news of Megacorp's corporate takeover was released. He peeled his wetsuit off and dumped it in the shower stall before dropping to his knees.

Jake cleaned everything, but no matter how hard he scrubbed, the stain over his soul grew no smaller nor did it lighten by any discernable degree. There was a rap on the door. It was still night. A glance to a porthole verified a few more hours still hung in the blackness before dawn. Mirka slipped in. The door was not locked. She gaped at the uncovered face of the pilot. Of gore she had had enough, and was numb to the sight. But contempt came to her eyes when she spied Jake scrubbing a baseboard, looking pathetic. Tears of self-pity ran down his face when he looked at her.

"I did the right thing, didn't I?" He begged.

"No Jake. You did all the wrong things, but for the right reasons."

"How are you?" Jake was hoping for some compensation.

"You should have just left me. What do you want? Jeez... thanks Jake for bringing me back into this miserable excuse for living? What in the fuck did you think you were doing?" Mirka knew what Jake had done to pay for his sins. It was the same for all of them. Forced by the machinations of Megacorp or by circumstance to do the unthinkable. More often than not it was the former, for little happens without their consent in one form or another. That the whole thing was a Megacorp set up from the beginning would not necessarily be paranoid thinking. Didn't Percy drop a hint in that he knew Jake better than he knew himself? She spoke again in a softer, more conciliatory tone. "Jake, do not let anyone see you as you are. Suck it up and put it away. It does not and will not serve you." The doorknob turned, stopping Mirka.

Percy did not wait for permission. He had been listening outside the door. When he stepped in, he locked eyes with Mirka for a long intense moment. During Mirka's lifetime she had more than once been afforded the presence of Percy, Megacorp's thug that did all the recruiting, whose simple heartless methods led to understanding. She broke the stare down and glanced at Jake. His body language said he 'got it'.

Mirka turned back to Percy. "Excuse me, I was just leaving."

Percy had been blocking the door and sidestepped to let Mirka pass. The door clicked shut behind her. Jake emptied the bucket for the last time. He picked up the cleaned gun and handed it back without saying a word. Besides, he didn't know what to say after what he had just seen.

"Get your wetsuit and return to your room. There will be a meeting tomorrow. No drugs. To answer your question, she is, as yet, none of my concern."

Jake wrapped a towel around his waist and grabbed his stuff. He left without saying goodbye but strangely enough wanted to say thank you; both of which would have been inappropriate. On the way through the maze of companionways and stairwells to his room, Jake found out the hard way that he was no longer welcome aboard Big Brother. He ran a continuous gauntlet of being hit, kicked, clubbed and stabbed the entire way. Covered in spit and feces, he fell into the shower and let it bleed.

***

A Megacorp chevron was whipped taut by the wind as Big Brother headed East to Bergen. Jake didn't notice as he scuffed along against the bitter cold storm. He was due at eleven hundred hours, sharp. Johnny had sedated him to control his impulsive nature and let Jake go with the flow. Jake argued against it, having been told beforehand 'no drugs'. The explanation was simple. No Lucidity. Jake didn't balk and took the dose. He was having a tough enough time keeping up with Mirka's advice as it was.

When Jake opened the door to the ship's lounge half a dozen pops nearly sent him diving for the floor. The dope kept him on his feet just long enough to see champagne issuing from bottles all around the room. Jake wavered, taking in the room full of smiling faces. Goldstein ambled up to Jake. He was already working on a good hangover with a bottle still foaming and two glasses in hand.

Ben poured and handed Jake a glass. "Well done, Jake." He reached out and pumped Jake's hand. "You have expedited the inevitable. The corporation wishes to express its thanks."

"I'm afraid I don't know what you mean." Jake said quietly, buying himself some time as he eyed the room. Top dogs one and all.

"In one year you have done what would have taken a decade. The North Sea delegation was already dying a slow and pitiful death. Many lives were saved this way, if that is any consolation. Their oil is gone, but that is just one of many resources the countries have. We will capitalize on this and the peoples of the delegation will be better off for it..."

Jake set down his full glass and balled his fists. Through a tight jaw he said, "Glad I could help." He turned and left the room before he started to kill them all. At the door Jake paused. Already the room was laughing behind his back. The little voice in his head was screaming 'KILL THEM'. He turned and faced the suits. Their laughter abruptly ended and the smell of fear engulfed the room. A smirk crossed Jake's face as he eyed them all. He nodded his head and stepped out into the fresh air on deck.

Jake's moment of superiority crashed with waves that hit the bow of Big Brother. He slipped on the rime and slid hard into the bulkhead. He just sat there as the salt spray pelted him. The door to the lounge opened and someone stepped out. Jake remembered Mirka's advice and was getting up, but slipped again on the ice covered deck. A woman's hand reached out to him. He followed the arm up to the face before taking the deceivingly slender digits.

"What are you doing...?" Jake slurred.

"I'm sorry you had to go through that Jake. They are not happy men and take pleasure at the discomfort of others. Your reaction was by far the most honorable. Come on." Mirka said pulling Jake to his feet.

"I didn't see you in the lounge. How were you even allowed inside?"

Jake had fallen into a puddle and was soaked on one side. The dead of the North Sea winter sent a chill through him. He tried hard not to shake but found it impossible. Mirka put his arm over her shoulder and walked him back to the guest quarters.

"Seems like old times, Jake." He leaned on her and fought the cold. "I turned myself in, Jake. That is why I was there, so they could watch me squirm as well."

It took a moment to sink in. "You did what!?"

"Life on the run sucks, Jake. You will find out one day I'm sure, the way you go at things." At the door to Jake's room, Mirka knocked while Jake fumbled for the keycard.

The entrance opened into shadow. The curtains, drawn across open portholes, muted any bright spots that would disturb the gloom. Mirka navigated around the coffee table and set Jake on the bed. She started with his jacket while Johnny undid the shoes. Once they had Jake in a fleece jumper his shivering began to subside. The two had stripped Jake in silence and it wasn't until all three were holding cups of steaming coffee did that Johnny introduced himself.

"Thanks for getting him back here." he said.

"It was as good as an excuse as I could find to get out of the room. It was cruel, the way they mock. I saw what they did to him a few days ago and knew I could not take it." Mirka was talking to Johnny but it was for Jake's benefit as well. Jake had saved her life. Or at the very least given her a choice in the matter. "He helped me get through a very difficult personal time and showed me there is a way to live with it. I knew he would crash when he left the lounge. So I helped. Besides, I could be of better service working on the inside."

"That could very well be so. We have about 24 hours before reaching Bergen. Want to check out for the next twelve or so?" Johnny unveiled a stainless steel tray with three loaded syringes.

It wasn't often you could take a mini vacation while under way. The party in the lounge was just beginning and wouldn't end until they docked. Johnny locked the door and the three sat in the subfusc atmosphere and injected the heroin. It wasn't just to get high, but it was that, too. It gave a chance for the mind to digest and come to terms with their existence. As far as Johnny was concerned, their lives were intense and needed extreme measures to cope effectively. Mirka disdained recreational use but didn't balk at the offer. She, too, was having a tough time coping.

The afternoon slipped into evening. The never-ending rising and dipping of the hull through the waves along with the drone of the engine had lulled the three into dream. Jake snapped out of the nod when the pitch of the engine changed. 'We picked up a net,' he said to himself. Ten minutes later there was a knock at the door. Johnny was back in his room and Mirka was still curled up on the top bunk. Jake had the bottom half of his suit on and was zipping up the booties when he got up to answer the door. It was the captain of Big Brother.

"Good morning, Captain," Jake said lighting a cigarette.

"Good evening, Mr. Strom."

"It's Jake, Captain. And by the sound of it, you got a net fouling your propeller."

"Hans is at the stern setting up dive station."

"Be there in twenty minutes. I'll use my own gear if you don't mind. How come your lookouts didn't see the net?" Jake asked.

"It must not have been a floater. It is surprising the net got by our anti-fouling system. We usually power right through them, leaving shreds in our wake."

They were called ghost nets. Lost at sea by fishermen, they were the bane of navigators and captains around the globe. When the nets began interfering in maritime traffic, a massive effort had been put in motion to keep the shipping lanes clear. After twenty years and countless miles of poly netting had been removed, there was no discernable effect. The flotsam and jetsam just kept coming. So much had been lost over the centuries that it was decided it could never be cleaned up and so the project was abandoned.

The problem with the nets was that they floated, sometimes just below the surface. The ghost nets had created a life cycle all their own. The nylon and polypropylene were buoyant and didn't break down in sunlight. It was the reason the material was used – because of its durability. Once allowed to drift freely upon the surface of the sea, marine growth in the way of barnacles and seaweeds would engulf the netting. Eventually the weight of enough growth would sink the tangled mass of rope and monofilament. Down it would sink into the depths. Away from light, away from nutrients and warmth, the life died and was fed on by the denizens of the deep or decayed. Released of the many kilos of living organisms, the nets would rise to the surface and begin a new the cycle.

What this meant for Jake was job security. There would always be a need for men with skills. 'Lucky me', Jake thought pulling on the rest of his suit. Johnny came through the bathroom with Jake's helmet and life support batteries.

"You are sure Hans can handle this?" Johnny asked referring to Jake's choice in tender.

"There wasn't really much of a choice in it. Keep your ears open though, and your eyes on her," Jake asked, nodding to the upper berth and pulling on his harness. He put the helmet and batteries in his gear bag and hoisted it to his shoulder. Johnny had a cup of coffee to go for his empty hand.

"Take it easy out there, Jake. Just do your job and come home."

"Yeah. Right on the first, and I'll see what I can do about the second."
Jake was out the door on his way to the rear deck. He passed the lounge
on the way. The party was in full swing, apparently undaunted by the
crippled vessel. Jake laughed to himself. He couldn't put his finger on
it, but there was definitely something funny about it. 'It must be the
drugs', he mused, giving himself a good shake before stepping out into
the frozen night.

The warmth of the enclosure setup on the lazarette did little to melt
the icy stares that greeted him when he entered the temporary dive
station. Riggers and deck hands went silent and backed away to avoid
contact in the confines of the small warm space. Hans looked up at the
movement of the others. He had been intent upon wiring up the comm
box and hadn't seen Jake enter.

"Diver on station. Everybody head to the galley for coffee and a
briefing. Jake, have a seat and I will bring you up to speed." Hans didn't
have to ask the crewmembers twice. The men were eager to kill the one
they thought had sold out their country. They were also not fools. A
vessel adrift in the North Sea in winter is a disaster waiting to happen.
Despite the anger they all wanted to get home to their friends and
families.

"Thanks, Hans. The vibes were getting pretty intense," Jake said,
unloading his gear bag.

"They think it was your fault."

"Its not the first time I have been accused. What do you think?" Jake
pushed the helmet yoke around his neck and pulled the neck dam over
his head. He had a flash of putting his head in a noose.

"I think you are a victim of circumstance, as we all are. At one time I
was on my way to being a professor in the University at Stockholm. Life
takes its course, Jake." Hans bent to a table and produced a print of the
hull at the stern.

Big Brother was old school. A steam turbine powered the shaft
that turned the propeller. The propeller itself was cordnozzled. The
cordnozzle is a short tube slightly larger in diameter than the propeller,
which surrounds the propeller and maximizes the thrust. Two oversized
rudders helped to turn the boat, and a pair of hydraulic cutters were
the first line of defense against ghost nets. The cutters ran on tracks
mounted to either side of the keel. The whirling hydraulic blades
shredded everything that was destined to pass through the propeller.
A time-tested system, the cutters had saved many ships in inhospitable
seas where divers were not available or not an option. For one reason or

another, Big Brother's system had failed to operate.

Jake stared out the vinyl window at the open sea. Waves were running about six meters with occasional larger sets. With the huge support vessel at the whim of an unforgiving sea there was only so much time until a bad situation became worse.

Jake began adding tools to his harness. "Ready when you are, Hans. Where is the rest of the crew?"

"The captain asked for volunteers. I was the only one who stepped forward. The rest are at their emergency posts." The ship rocked hard to starboard. The men steadied themselves.

Jake laughed darkly to himself as Hans snapped the dive helmet in place.

"Jake, testing one two." Hans spoke into his headset.

"Gotcha Hans, let's do it. Keep me posted on what's happening topside. If you need help call my room. Johnny can be trusted. No crane?" Jake asked stepping out into the freezing wind.

Hans helped Jake up the guardrail. "Not tonight. Good luck, Jake."

Jake gave Hans a thumbs up and stepped off into the winter gale. Falling into a sea as cold as black ice snapped Jake into the moment. The waves slammed him into the rudder as he struggled for a handhold. There was a gap between the fairwater that surrounded the gudgeon and the hull. He pushed his gloved fingers into it, holding on for dear life, while he got oriented. It was like hanging onto a raging steel bull, jerking Jake one way before abruptly changing direction. He was facing the propeller but could not see it. A huge ball of netting clotted the cordnozzle and tied the flukes of the propeller.

Timing with the waves, Jake pushed off the rudder toward the writhing mass of monofilament. He clutched a handful and pulled himself around the cordnozzle until he was sitting behind the propeller on the shaft. This way he could wrap his legs around the shaft to hold position while freeing up both hands for cutting.

"On the stern tube, Hans and starting to cut."

"Roger that. The captain would like you to look at the cutters if you can get a chance."

Jake shook his head and laughed sardonically. Just when you're putting out all you got, they ask for more. "As soon as I get a handle on this rat's nest." Jake put the guns to it, working his way around the propeller and cutting away as much loose netting as he could. It was important to get the excess away so that he could work without getting tangled himself.

***

"**W**ell Stimple, quite the coup, don't you think?" Goldstein remarked drunkenly as he held onto the arm of an appropriately clad prostitute named Regina to keep from falling down.

Stimple stared at the floor. He was plastered and his focus on the carpet was all that kept him from puking. He looked up at Goldstein, glazed over and turned green. His response was more visceral than vocal: a fountain of champagne and appetizers sprayed Regina like a firehose. She staggered back, taking Goldstein to the floor with her. Goldstein was uttering a series of expletives when the sound of gunfire exploded from the entry door. The woman wearing Stimple's caviar and crackers now wore his brains. The little man's body was hurled against the bulkhead by the impact of the bullets and crumpled to the floor.

A ragged and rabid Pablo stepped through the doorway. What was left of his face bore an insane smile, a skull to which some flesh still adhered.

"Good evening, Ben. I failed to receive your invitation in time to change." He fanned his gun at the torn jumpsuit he wore. The lidless eyes gawked the room. "I see all the old familiar faces." The bloodshot orbs stopped at the sight of Stimple's corpse. "I have saved you another embarrassment, Goldstein. Why, thank you for offering." Pablo grabbed a bottle of champagne and tilted it into his face. What was left of his lips and cheeks failed to contain the flow that effervesced from holes and tears.

Deadly fear filled the room for the second time that day. Twenty-five pairs of eyes tried to make sense of what they were seeing. The ruined human face laughed loud and ugly at their dismay.

"Do you not recognize me? You, who sent me here in the first place to do your bidding? Think now! Think goddamn it!" he yelled, before pouring more champagne across his face, and rinsing his eyes.

"And now you celebrate without the one who gave you the North Sea!"

Pablo was a little out of the loop on this one.

"I see," Pablo said, affecting hurt feelings at the silence. "There was once a time when you held these little celebrations in my honor."

Goldstein could hardly grasp what had just happened as he stared at the gruesome countenance. Bile came to his lips. He was choking on it as the ship rolled to starboard 45 degrees before righting and tipping to port. The party tumbled with the deck, grabbing at anything or anyone to keep from falling. Only Pablo maintained his stance. It was hard to tell but he seemed to smile beyond the permanent smile he now wore. His wide eyes rolled from side to side, watching the bureaucrats try to save themselves. It was a comedy that only Pablo appreciated.

Benjamin Goldstein found a stable perch by hanging on to the edge of a grand piano that was bolted to the floor. The ship continued to rock and the blare of a klaxon signaled 'red alert'. The lights went out and were replaced with flashing red strobes, a shuffle of bodies, and flashes of gunfire that echoed painfully in the confines of the lounge. When the lights came back on, Pablo was gone. The only reminders that something had gone horribly wrong were Regina, stripped, crying at the bar sink as she tried to rinse her dress clean, and, of course, what was left of Stimple. One of the men from the other side of the room screamed, painfully yanking Ben into the moment. He looked over to see the man cringing away from the pool table. Spread-eagled and face up on the green felt of the pool table was Stimple. Blood from what was once his face puddled around his head, creating a crimson halo on the verdant field of play. His shirt had been torn off to reveal a happy face in bright red dimples on his torso. When Goldstein focused on the man's chest and read the message, reality raced back into head as quickly as the vomit bolted up his throat. 'Pablo!' He regurgitated into the open piano. The puked falling onto the strings created music for the damned. His life passed before his eyes as the ship rocked hard to port, dislodging the piano lid's support strut and slamming the lid down on Goldstein's fingers. His scream was the crescendo for an ominous minuet.

***

The wave sets had been getting bigger since the sun went down. A gale came out of the north, pressing down upon the Big Brother. Johnny was pitched from his bunk onto the steel floor by the last set of waves. He steadied himself and worked his way to Jake's room. Mirka had loosely tied herself to the bedrails to keep from being thrown.

"You okay, girl?" he asked.

"Yes thank you. What about Jake?" Replied Mirka with genuine concern.

"He will be aw'ight. It is a little rough but he has seen worse."

"I hope so. It's going to get a lot worse." Mirka tossed Johnny her phone. On the screen was the forecast. The storm had started north of the Arctic Circle and was barreling south. In the next few hours they would be in the center of it with 150 mile an hour winds and 60 to 100 foot waves.

Another set of waves rocked the ship. Johnny grabbed the ship phone and dialed the wheelhouse. The red alert siren went off just as the call was answered. "We have taken on a net and lost power. All non-essential personnel to the life tank!" The line went dead.

"Better gather up your stuff. We are ordered to the tank." Johnny said this without urgency.

"This is all I have," Mirka replied.

"Oh yeah, right." He remembered she had only been pulled from the water a few days ago. "If you want to go, do not let me hold you up. I have to hook up with Jake."

"For all his faults, I'd rather be with Jake when it gets rough," Mirka replied firmly.

Jake was making good progress removing the net. The problem was there was so much of it and the ship's movement kept him holding on half the time to keep from getting thrown. With a length of netting, he tied himself to the propeller shaft and kept at it. At the base of the propeller where the blades meet the hub, the poly line of the net had been put under such pressure and friction; it had fused into a solid plastic block. Jake put the knife away and withdrew a hacksaw. He worked until his arms felt like rubber. Rather than stopping for a break, Jake went to look at item number two on the day's agenda. The cutters.

Jake hugged the shaft and inched his way forward. His lights illuminated the wheels that held the rotating blades. They were free of debris and appeared functional. Remembering the prints Hans had shown him, he continued farther forward to where the shaft enters the hull. Recessed into the hull on the port and starboard sides were the hydraulic lines that powered the cutters. Dangling from the indentations were the disconnected lines. Timing it carefully, Jake jumped from the shaft to the port hydraulic line. He struggled against the surge to reconnect it. When he made the jump to the starboard side he caught the shape of something out of the corner of his eye. It had distracted his attention. Only by sheer luck was he able to grab hold of the hydraulics. As he snapped the connection in place he was wondering how they could have come apart.

Jake turned around and looked for what had caught his eye. There it was. It wasn't big, compared to the ship, and it just sat there. The prints had shown nothing like this attached to the hull. His curiosity got the best of him and Jake pushed off swimming for all he was worth to get to it. He grasped a handle next to a hatch at the bottom of the submarine. Jake recognized it. It was the same sub that was docked at the base of the Goliath when he'd led Pablo and the mercs to it a year ago. Jake punched the codes to open the hatch. When the light went green he swung the door open and secured it to keep it from flapping as Big Brother pitched from side to side. Jake crawled into the wetlock, sat down and took off his helmet. A communications headset hung on the bulkhead. He put it on and reset the frequency to hail Hans.

"Yo Hans! You there buddy?"

"Ja, Jake. The Captain has been calling every fifteen minutes. Any progress?" Hans replied.

"Some. Can you patch me in to my room? I have to talk to Johnny!"

The Velcro that kept the door to the dive station closed ripped loudly followed by a gust of wind and salt spray. Johnny and Mirka stepped through the flap and quickly resealed the door. Hans looked up at the two and removed his headset and handed it to Johnny. "It's for you."

"Call the Captain!" Goldstein yelled, cradling his broken fingers. The call was greeted with the same curt response Johnny had gotten. There was no explanation, just the orders to evacuate to the tank. Goldstein sat on the floor with his legs wrapped around a leg of the piano to keep him in place while trying to protect his hands. The rest of the men in the room began to show their true colors after the phone call. Panic rose from their guts and bowels were loosened. There was a mad rush to nowhere before they realized they had to go outside to get to the chamber. The fear this knowledge produced froze them in their tracks. Each one was snapping under the weight of not knowing what to do. They were business men. The hookers, on the other hand, understood that survival was a more hands-on kind of thing. When the entourage had come aboard Big Brother, all were given a briefing in the lounge concerning what to do in an emergency. This briefing is standard aboard a vessel of any size. While Goldstein and Stimple were busy posturing in front of their associates, the girls were paying attention to what the Purser was saying. Regina forgot about her dress and stumbled across the rocking deck to the closet that held survival gear. She started tossing the insulated buoyant jumpsuits to her associates, but not before throwing a couple to the wolves to fight over. Regina understood this type of man. She had been with many in her time. Their only concern was for themselves and their precious portfolios.

Her girls were dressed while the men fought each other. She watched the pathetic flailings until her eyes fell to Goldstein. He didn't even try. He had skooched himself under the piano to avoid the fracas. Regina worked her way around the room by holding onto the walls. At the piano she reached down for Goldstein. Not thinking correctly he reached out with a busted hand. Regina knew there would be only one chance. And she took it. She grabbed the hand with all her might and pulled. Carpals and metacarpals were crunched together as the swollen hand buckled under her grip. Goldstein was screaming again as Regina dragged him out. Her sisters pitched in to give her a hand and soon they were stuffing him into a survival suit.

Regina was no fool. Goldstein was as bad or worse than the other men, so it wasn't out of compassion that she aided him. He was footing the bill. Before opening the door to the howling wind and raging sea, the women clipped themselves together with short tag lines. Goldstein was right behind Regina. They looked at the emergency route map attached to the wall one last time and opened the door. Regina stepped out onto a deck covered in black ice, pulling Goldstein along. He balked at the door, refusing to go outside. Regina took one step backwards, raised her elbow, smashed it into his face and then yanked on the tagline. Dragging Goldstein now, they moved aft to the stairway that led to the main deck. The steps were iced over and Ben took a fall, taking all eight women with him. If it wasn't for the thick insulation of suits they probably would not have survived. From the bottom of the stairs they crawled to the chamber.

A foyer protected the access. Out of the weather Regina was able to read the instructions and open the door. Once her girls were inside she closed the door and faced Goldstein. Regina unzipped his survival suit and reached into the breast pocket of his jacket. She withdrew Goldstein's checkbook and a pen.

"Write me a check for what you owe us!" she yelled above the storm.

"I can't! My hands!" he screamed back.

"Write it or you die out here!"

Goldstein fell to his knees and wept. Regina shoved him out of the way, entered the chamber and locked the door behind her.

"Jake, ça va?" Johnny said into the mike.

"High and dry, my man. Guess what I got for you?"

"A chopper to get us out of this mess?"

"The next best thing. All fun aside, I think you better listen. There is no way I can clear the wheel. But, we have a sub stuck to the hull about 50 feet forward of the prop shaft. You have to get off the ship. Your friend Pablo has returned and I got a feeling this ain't no social call."

"I will assume you are serious. How do you recommend we do this?" Johnny asked with his usual dose of sarcasm.

"Jump ship. I'm sitting in the sub's wetlock. When I leave, the hatch will be left open. If you and Mirka jump over the side you should be able to find it and get in. It's going to get ugly, Johnny. Take Hans with you. I don't need him any more. Get the sub away from the ship and hang out. I'll catch up with you." Jake turned off the comm.

Johnny took the headset off and looked at Mirka and Hans, shook his head and started to laugh. "You want to go swimming?"

As they made a plan in front of the tent's heater, Hans felt a shift in the deck. He had worked Big Brother for ten years and understood her. It also helped him make up his mind concerning what he had just been told. "Big Brother is taking on water."

On the bridge all hell was breaking loose. A detachment was sent to the lounge to check on the passengers. They were never heard from again. With only a skeleton crew at the helm, no one noticed the small red diodes that began flashing at the corner of a panel full of red flashing lights. Petcocks were being opened in the engine room and holds throughout the ship, letting the sea in.

When Pablo left the lounge he went below decks to the engine room. With the crew in emergency mode, he went unnoticed wriggling through pipe mazes and machinery to open some valves and close others. He did not want to scuttle the ship quickly but slowly and painfully. Pablo was fully versed in emergency procedures and able to stay one step ahead of the crew and avoid detection. The incoming water would further distract them while he went about his business.

Jake turned the exterior hatch lights on and dropped back into the raging sea. He fought his way to the stern and took one last look at the fouled propeller. It was hopeless, he thought, popping up behind the ship. Hans had thrown a line overboard for Jake to climb. Without it, he would have been lost to the sea. He grabbed hold of the line and waited for the stern to dip low in the trough of a wave then climbed like hell as the next wave lifted the stern clear of the water. The resulting upward jerk sent Jake flying over the guardrail. If he had landed on the deck in that moment, it would have been a blessing. But the deck dropped away into the trough on the backside of the wave and Jake plummeted fifteen meters to the frozen steel. He landed face down, knocking the wind from his lungs and breaking half a dozen ribs. The rolling deck tumbled him to port then back the other way. The ship was beating him to death by the time he woke and latched onto something solid. Looking aft he saw no one. The dive shelter had been torn away by wind and wave. Jake hoped Hans had made it to the sub as he pulled himself vertical. Everything hurt, breathing most of all. Red foamy spittle dribbled from his nose and mouth. He tasted the blood and figured he had punctured a lung. 'Fuck me', Jake said to himself.

He began to make his way forward, blindly searching his way in the night towards the wheelhouse. Screams came from the catwalk a deck above. Moments later, bodies of crewmembers were falling like rain from the sky. Jake scowled; Pablo was on the move and so was he. Up three flights of stairs and the light from the open door of the wheelhouse made all too visible the remains left in Pablo's wake. The steel door resounded deafeningly as it banged against the stops before slamming shut, only to open again as the vessel rocked against the mighty waves. After securing the door, Jake entered the slaughterhouse. A sense of déja vu surged through him. The carnage was nearly identical to that aboard the Goliath. The crew and Captain were dead. All were riddled with automatic gunfire.

Jake searched for the control panel that would actuate the cutters. Their original purpose, that of cutting up drift nets, was not what Jake had in mind. He found the switch and flipped it. After a few moments the red light went green. Jake smiled and cracked his knuckles. He would now follow the crimson trail left by Pablo. Giving the control room one last look, he spied an antique whaling harpoon mounted above the windows. It was beautiful in a vicious sort of way, and with a line attached, it just might serve his purpose adequately. Jake hefted it, smiled darkly and headed aft.

Goldstein huddled in the entrance of the survival chamber whimpering like a dog. His hands ached. Fingers swollen like sausages were barely able to clutch the pen. After three tries he gave up trying to write the check and concentrated on just signing his name. His scrawl was nearly illegible but it was there. Ben got to his feet and held the little piece of paper to the porthole on the door.

Regina saw the damaged hand and went to get a closer look.

The check was blank but the signature, stained with blood, was readable. She opened the door and Goldstein fell into the chamber. Once the money was safe in a watertight envelope the women bent to Goldstein and gave him water.

Soon other knocks were heard at the door. The men from the lounge had begun to migrate to the chamber. Some had survival suits on – others did not. They did not come as group but rather one by one. The camaraderie that once existed between the men was gone in a fight for survival. Fifteen of the party made it, five never would. A deadly silence engulfed the chamber.

"Okay, Hans, go! You heard the man." Johnny yelled above the sound of the sea.

Hans tied a rope to the guardrail and threw the rest of it overboard.

"I can't leave my crew!" Hans yelled.

"You are not the captain! They are probably dead anyway!"

Hans radioed the wheelhouse. There was no response. He tried the engine room. Nothing. The sound of the wind increased. The Velcro seams began to separate and in a matter of seconds, the roof and walls of the tent flapped wildly before being torn from the deck mounts and flying off into the blackness. The three were pelted by rock hard rain and thrown to the rolling deck. They scrambled to the lee side and battled against the elements to reach the midship draft marks. Mirka and Hans hung on to the railing for dear life while Johnny scanned the sea, timing the wave sets. Ten minutes crawled by before Johnny turned to Mirka, shouldering his briefcase.

"Ready?" he yelled, "On three. One, two, three!"

Johnny grabbed Mirka and Hans by the collars and jumped the guardrail. When they hit the freezing water Mirka and Hans convulsed in shock, expelling their breath. There was no time to surface and let them catch it. Johnny swam straight down, following the draftmarks. At the turn of the bilge, he headed across the bottom flats with his dead cargo in tow. The glow of the sub's hatch lights loomed ahead. Johnny put his head down and swam for all he was worth.

The wetlock wasn't big enough to perform CPR. Hell, it was barely big enough for the three of them. He closed the outer hatch and opened the inner. Hans was blue and deader than a doornail. Mirka on the other hand revived with only a few rescue breaths. When she was in the here and now, Johnny said, "You do him. When he wakes, it will be better if your mouth was over his than mine." The two laughed briefly before

Mirka went to work on Hans. Johnny set about to find out how the sub worked.

Two minutes into the CPR, Hans began to cough up yellow liquid from his lungs. He gasped for breath while Mirka held him in her arms. The fit began to subside and reality rose up around him in the shape of the sub. Mirka smiled down on the innocence, knowing what a wonderful feeling it is to find out you are alive. Of course she no longer felt such things, but she had, long ago.

The interior lights flashed once and the steady hum of the sub's electric motor brought a smile to Johnny's face. "Here we go kids! Hold on!" He toggled the vacuum switch to release the hold on Big Brother and power dove away from the impending nightmare. Mirka held on to Hans and kept him from rolling forward into his puddle of vomit. Johnny circled Big Brother once, leveled off at 50 meters in depth and put it in neutral.

"Now we wait."

When the madness began, that is to say when the party in the lounge popped its first bottle of champagne... Actually the incubus began more than a hundred years ago when Megacorp rose from the ashes of a destroyed economy and started the 'Reuseable Program'. But for the sake of the story...

Percy had been sitting in the corner of the lounge. His buscus attire blended him into the folds of sanguine curtains and shadow. He sat and watched the debacle without interest. With one hand on a weapon beneath his jacket, Percy waited for his time to come. When Jake turned on the big dogs in the lounge before he left and scared the shit out of them, he thought it was time, flicking the safety off the seventeen-millimeter submachine gun. It was not. Percy was thankful. To be certain he would have blown Jake through the side of the ship with thirty high-velocity, exploding tip rounds, if it had gone any farther than the evil eye. It was his job to ensure those in his care acted appropriately. That is to say not go on a killing spree. Jake was one of his charges. Mirka had been, until her contract was rewritten. And Pablo, one of the first Percy had brought into the world, had been out of control for years. His way of expediting the downfall of profit killing situations for Megacorp had made him indispensable in the short run. But for the last twenty years, Pablo had been pursuing his own agenda and had become a 'profit killer'. His manipulation of the South American drug trade had omitted a cut for Megacorp. For this reason alone Pablo had been put on the Most Wanted list. The ironic part was Megacorp still used him for contract work, in the hope he would be killed in the venture. When Goliath went down and no word from Pablo, Megacorp thought they had finally rid themselves of the parasite they had created.

All that said, Percy had come to like Jake. He had never cut the man any slack and Jake had never asked for any. Of course Jake didn't cut himself any slack either. It was one of the reasons Percy had grown fond of him. Jake dealt with his misery himself and did not plague those around him with it. Percy saw a lot of himself in Jake.

Percy had been brought into the system during the early stages of the Reuseable Program. He had been a drill sergeant in the military. That and a Master's in psychology had proved a brutally useful combination. At that time, the foul injections that ruined a man's death and gave him hell everlasting were done in groups of ten men. Control groups. Percy's grasp of modern psychology helped him come to grips with the unnatural realities of a life after death far sooner than his cronies. Instead of sitting back and watching the other nine men suffer he aided them in the transformation. Percy did not hold and coddle them, letting them know it was "all right" in a soothing voice. Instead he devised his own ruthless training of physical and psychological abuse that forced the men to suck it up and come to terms with reality. Megacorp watched and learned, eventually recruiting Percy to apply his skills to all the new inductees. Jake's own training had been designed by Percy and only differed slightly from the original.

When Pablo appeared in the doorway and dispatched Stimple, Percy had been in the bathroom. When he returned the damage had been done and the killer was off making his rounds. The scene in the lounge was pandemonium. Twenty drunken button-downs were fighting over a couple orange survival jumpers. Percy sat back and laughed to himself at the comedy. It was none of his business. His ignorance of Pablo's return was temporary bliss. When the piano lid crushed Goldstein's fingers, the urge to laugh out loud at the foolishness was barely containable. His butt rose off the chair then settled back down. It had always been his rule to follow orders to the letter, period. And his orders had nothing to do with helping a bunch of drunken fools. Percy didn't fear any backlash that might come from his lack of action. In his time he had seen seven generations of Megacorp CEO's and their cabinets come and go. Each was more ridiculous than the one before it. He had watched greed and the men that lived for it for three hundred years. He had seen enough to know that the current regime would not last long.

When the ruckus had subsided in the lounge, Percy got up to survey the damage. Only four men remained in the room. Three were passed out, their faces battered with numerous indentations left by oversized class and business rings. He squinted to read the embossed skin dimples. Most every blow had come from a different person. There was Oxford, Harvard, Washington and Princeton along with the various regional Megacorp insignias. Percy pulled four more survival suits from the closet and dropped one next to each man. It was funny. When he opened the closet there were at least 50 more suits.

Percy recognized Stimple on the pool table before he read the message shot into his chest. When Megacorp lost control of Pablo, Percy took it personally. As far as he was concerned, Megacorp had not lost Pablo, he had. Some how, somewhere, he had slipped under Percy's radar. It was something in Pablo's personality or early life that evaded the big trainer. Pablo had been an orphan with no papers or checkable background before the age of sixteen when he joined the Columbian Army. At seventeen he was recruited into a black operations unit. By eighteen, his ruthlessness and aggressive approach to warfare was legendary. At nineteen he led his squad into an ambush. No one survived. Hours later he was drafted into the service of Megacorp where his talents were put to a more constructive use.

Pablo's signature, ☺, had always disturbed Percy. It wasn't the irony. It had to be something from the past. Something had driven Pablo, and Percy wanted to know what it was. Percy had taken it personally. In a twisted way he cared for the men he was forced to ruin. It was actually by accident that he discovered the meaning behind the ☺. Percy had researched the time period of Pablo's youth to find the causal link. He came to dead ends on all accounts. Columbia and its neighbors lived in a perpetually tumultuous political and economical climate. Couple an ineffective government with dysfunctional but powerful drug lords, along with the wars against drugs and the wars for them and you find a chapter in a country's history filled only with death. Just to survive until you were sixteen was a miracle. Of course you were one mean motherfucker by then, too. It explained a little.

Years later three fighter jets aboard the USS Nimitz went down during training exercises off the coast of Columbia. The Nimitz was stationed in the South Pacific along the western seaboard of South America. Over the past several decades the Nimitz had serviced both sides of the drug wars with airstrikes. Percy had been called in to 'recruit' the drowned pilots and prepare them for service in Megacorp's forces. It was there he started to put two and two together. The insignia for the Nimitz's squadron was the ☺ . It explained a lot.

Percy returned to his room and gathered his personals to be ready when the time to abandon ship was announced. His bulk filled the doorway to the lounge when he entered to get a survival suit. Jake, in dive gear, was leaning on the harpoon taking in Stimple, when a gust of cold air whipped the room. He turned to see Percy and for the first time felt as if they were on equal terms. He crossed the room unsure of how amenable Percy was to the new disposition. Jake took the harpoon in his left hand and extended the right.

"Boy, am I glad to see you!" Jake exclaimed.

Percy took the hand and nearly crushed Jake's fingers before he released and said, "It is good to see you, too."

An unusually large set of waves assaulted Big Brother and the brief moment of bonding as the two dove for the nearest stable support. Jake grabbed the bar and Percy a nearby cocktail table. "Listen, big guy. I have never asked for anything, but tonight I think I need a little help." Jake sucked it up. He never liked asking anyone for help, let alone this guy.

"Desperate situations call for desperate measures." Percy deadpanned.

"Funniest fucking thing I heard all day. You got any more guns?"

Percy opened the flap of his coat to reveal the submachine gun. Jake's jaw dropped. The gun was small but the chamber and barrel were the size of your big toe. Jake hefted the harpoon. With a hickory shaft and line it had to weigh ten kilos.

"Wanna trade?" Jake laughed tossing the 'poon' to Percy.

A huge hand snapped out and caught the dart. At least that it was it looked like when held by a 150 kilo man. Percy found the balance point and scanned the room. On the far side adorning a partition was a life-sized image of Megacorp's current CEO, Benjamin Goldstein. Holding the spear at shoulder level, he reached back to the limit of his extension and let fly. Jake was sure E=MC2 had something to do with it as the harpoon flew straight and fast as an arrow, impaling the picture of Goldstein between the eyes.

"Better than I could do. Hey man, Pablo is here. He is scuttling the ship and killing everyone he crosses."

"I know." Percy replied.

"Then you know we have to do something about it. He has already been to the wheelhouse. There is no one manning the ship."

"He works his way aft to where he has allowed the party to corral themselves." Jake looked at Percy with a 'how do you know this' expression n his face. "I know how he works. I trained him."

Jake nodded, remembering when Percy had said, 'I know you better than you know yourself.' Jake agreed with the statement.

While Jake had his little moment of clarity, Percy withdrew his gun and when Jake raised his eyes, he tossed it to the diver. Jake looked it over and smiled. It's a guy thing.

"Use both hands and..." Percy began when the ship was struck again by a mountain range of water. "...the gun to give me a clear shot. I will take the starboard side." Percy coiled the rope that was attached to the harpoon, slapped Jake hard on the back and headed for the door. Jake was still trying to fill in the blanks as he opened the door to the port side. 'What was I supposed to do?'

The men that made it to the survival tank shivered just inside the door. Upon receiving the blank check, Regina sat with her girls and discussed surviving the foreseeable future. After an inspection of supplies it was agreed a certain amount of compassion be cast in the direction of their clients. Goldstein had been the first to be allowed in. He was a shambles of his former self. Nursing his hands and hangover, cold and forgotten in his corner of the chamber, Regina saw him for what he really was. Oh she had seen how low Ben would go during her years servicing the Megacorp elite. His ass still bore the little scars of a dominatrix whip that had forced him to beg for mercy. But that had been merely play-acting to the extreme. To see him begging now for mercy, pain meds from the locker, and booze for his head was far too real and saddening. He struggled to force them to do as he said, only to be beaten back into the corner. Regina had searched the chamber when they first arrived and taken anything that could be used as a weapon or used against them, stowing it in their end of the survival unit. She was determined they would survive.

The other men in the Megacorp group stumbled drunkenly one at a time from the lounge and were allowed inside the chamber, if they made it. Only one had a survival suit on. The rest were frozen, cold, and wet. They had been loud and obnoxious when they arrived but the backlash from drinking all day subdued them after a while. That, and having a few of their heads bashed by a brass spud wrench, that is.

Jake headed aft along the port gunwale. He would drop and take cover behind support gussets any time he heard anything out of the ordinary. More often than not, he hit the deck by stumbling over a corpse. They were littered everywhere. Coming around the stern end of the superstructure, Jake was able to get a look over the aft deck from behind the mahogany guardrail. Dim lights glowed from the ports of the survival chamber. Every once in a while a shadow crossed the port. It would seem some had made it. How many was another question.

A dark motion caught Jake's eye on the starboard side of the upper deck. The big shadow leapt and landed on a container below, spun about and was gone. It was too dark to really see well and the crashing waves didn't help any but Jake was sure it was Percy. The reason Jake saw it all, was that it was too big to miss.

Percy was on the move, taking the fight to Pablo. Catching the hint, Jake went to jump to the top of the survival chamber when the mahogany railcap splintered into a thousand wooden shards, impaling Jake and knocking him back into a steel wall. He jammed himself between the wall and a hard place to keep from being tossed around before looking at his thighs that burned like fire. Punched through the wetsuit sprouted big, red gnarly toothpicks.

"Son of a bitch that hurts! Aww god!" He pulled the largest spears of wood out before attempting to stand.

Gunfire lit the deck with strobe light effects. Pablo was running forward and shooting behind, a tactic that was definitely not his style, but there was a plan. He headed to the desal ¬¬– the filter unit for the desalinization of seawater. It was a three-dimensional pipe puzzle that would limit the effectiveness of Percy's weapon. Percy stalked the cage like a lion making occasional thrusts to keep his prey on edge. Pablo did likewise. When an opening in the pipe puzzle became clear, he would fire harmlessly into the night.

Jake moved forward on the upper deck before tossing a rope over the side. Percy was keeping Pablo's attention on the stern, giving Jake a chance to come from behind. Over the railing and quietly down the rope, Jake dropped to the main deck next to the control booth for the desal unit. The panel that powered the unit held rows of gauges, knobs and toggles, all labeled in Norwegian. Some buttons were green, others red. With no time to lose, Jake's hand came down on all the green switches he could see. With nothing to lose, he hit the red ones. The clatter and roar of a diesel motor blended with the cacophony of the storm. Gauges that were pegged at zero sprang to life as the different filter stages came on line. Jake dialed the throttle full on and stepped from the booth, pulling the over calibered little gun Percy had given him.

He flipped the safety off and set the gun to fire a three round burst. He aimed at the crazy pipe puzzle and did a triple tap, sending nine 17 mm rounds into the maze, smashing through piping and filters. High pressure water blasted the area. As long as the diesel engine kept running, the spraying water would continue.

The machine gun's recoil sent Jake flying backwards and dropped him hard to the deck. 'No doubt I missed some key instructions', he said to himself as stars spun in his head. Blood trickled down into his eyes, "Shit!" Jake's dive helmet had been hanging over his shoulder on a lanyard. 'I'm sick and tired of banging my head on every damn thing!' He put on the helmet and locked it to the neck dam before jumping over the side and swimming like hell to the stern.

Percy's body had absorbed a half-dozen rounds from Pablo's erratic firing. He was big and his body could take it, but he was unsure how many more he could withstand before his abilities became compromised. He had chased Pablo down and almost had him in his sights before the snake of a man crawled into the piping of the desal unit. He would wait. With Pablo trapped, Percy checked on the survival chamber to get an idea of who made it and how they were. Some part of him was thankful the women had made it. The men he could care less about; there would always be others like them. He did a double take on Goldstein's hands as the man begged for some first aid. He smiled when none was given, but the huge purple hands...

Percy dropped to a crouch when the howling night exploded nine times and burst the pipes of the desal unit. The sheer volume of water expelled at over two thousand P.S.I. created an epiphenomenon, that of blowing Pablo from his lair out onto the open deck that was cleared by the powerwashing. Freezing water shot viciously and wildly across the stern from loose piping that also sent a downpour of epic proportions. With the ship out of control in the heavy seas, whipped by the wind and now the water, you would think things couldn't get any worse. Percy moved slowly within the shadows of shadows. Pablo lay still crumpled against the starboard gunwale. It was impossible to tell whether he was breathing or bleeding. Percy didn't drop his guard and crept along the perimeter to get close enough for a kill. It was hard going against the elements but he persevered. Once in range he searched for his quarry. Pablo was gone. Percy tucked next to a forklift for protection and went into a deep meditation.

He had practiced this technique for years and it was part of his daily

routine. It had saved his life? many times, and came in handy when
tracking down strays and escapees from Megacorp. Because he trained
most of them he knew them extremely well. In the meditation he could
lose himself and sometimes tap into the mind he sought. Or at the very
least, think like his enemy. This was one of those times.

Pablo had not hidden in the pipes because he was afraid. He was
planning and now knew there were two after him. Pablo's approaches
were never subtle. He loved a grandstand exhibition or at very least an
excessive display of overkill. Nevertheless, Pablo was Megacorp and
had been through the training, the Pavlovian response to pain. Surely
the blast of water from the desal unit brought back a series of quite
unpleasant memories.

Pablo was close. And waiting. Waiting for the other party to show
himself. He had never had much patience or practice in waiting. When
you are a natural reborn killer, it is action that makes things happen. If
the timing were wrong, terror would generally make up the difference.

Jake found the trailer line left by Hans and began to climb it again.
He was careful and quiet and thought he had timed it so the waves
wouldn't send him flying onto the deck. Wrong again. A massive swell
pitched the ship low on the port side, almost swamping the deck. Then
it shot upwards, raising the port side and dropping the starboard.
Jake saw it coming and braced himself for the impending crash to the
hard steel desk. The impact was worse than he imagined. Bones broke,
absorbing the shock. Which ones didn't matter at the time for they all
felt shattered. If it wasn't for the rocking of the ship, he would have been
an easy target. Jake tumbled to port helplessly then back to starboard,
when a bullet passed through his dive helmet. It entered from the back,
chewed a path across the right side of his head just above the ear and
exited through the faceplate. This snapped Jake into the present. Peering
from the corner of a container, Jake surveyed the deck.

The night was pitch black with wind and wave making it impossible
to see well. Jake was sure Pablo was on the starboard side next to a
winch. Percy for all his bulk was invisible behind a forklift on the port
side. Jake was thinking they could play hide and seek around the ship all
night or until she sinks, whichever comes first. A catalyst was needed.
Someone foolish enough to expose himself and draw out Pablo and
let Queequeg have at it with the 'poon. Jake unhooked his helmet and
set it down. It was useless now. Without it, well suffice to say, it would
make Jake's plans a little more interesting. He held a rag to his head,

scanning the deck. Next to the container he was hiding behind was one of the ship's inflatables. He slipped over the tubular side and found the emergency flare kit. Jake loaded the flare gun and took a couple extra rounds and shoved them in his pocket. He laughed to himself. In the vids the good guys are always shooting the bad guys with one of these. It's a stretch. Jake just wanted the light that would come from it.

It was time to add part 'A' to part 'B'. In the pilot's seat, Jake fired up the boat. With no mufflers the roar was deafening. He turned on the siren, lights, and pushed the throttle to the stops. Out of the boat and on the run around the stern on the starboard side, Jake closed his eyes and fired. He had aimed in the direction of Pablo. Not to kill him, though that would have been nice, but to blind him momentarily. With the starting of the motor, Pablo would have been all eyes. On the run, Jake shinned a gunwale gusset, tearing through his suit and peeling back the flesh.

The first flare pinballed wildly about the starboard side. Dodging the flare, Pablo had to move himself into the open. Jake pumped the last three steps with all he had and leapt at the momentarily blinded Pablo. His sight might have been compromised, but his other senses were wired. Reaching up, he grabbed Jake in mid flight and used the momentum to slam him savagely to the deck. He followed through, dropping a knee to the groin and a fist blow to the throat. Jake hoped the steel doors to unconsciousness would come down to stop the pain. They didn't but he had achieved what he wanted; to get Pablo out into the open. Jake choked up blood and puked in pain as he struggled to get to his knees. A heavy boot caught him in the stomach and sent him crashing into a bollard. Stars once again burst into view but only for Jake. Pablo was back in form. He strode to Jake's supine form, lifted Jake and head-butted him, snapping his head back with the crunch of bones before dropping him to the deck.

From Jake's position he could see Pablo reloading his weapon. At the edge of his peripheral vision, the big dark shadow of Percy stepped out into the open area. Ever alert, Pablo jerked his head around at the movement. Neither man could see the other but they knew each was there.

The disembodied voice of Percy defied the storm and echoed from a half-dozen places.

"Your job is done! It is time to go!"

Pablo sprayed the deck with machine gun fire with no apparent effect other than getting hit by one of his own bullets that had ricocheted. He didn't flinch but a hole in his thigh pulsed blood. 'That's what you get for using such a big gun', Jake thought morosely, pulling another flare round from his pocket.

"My job has just begun, old friend, and your time has come to an end." Pablo yelled back but not as effectively as Percy. He emptied the magazine, shooting in an arc to try and get a glimpse of Percy. The funny thing was, Percy was not hiding but standing stock still amidst the equipment on deck. He is so big and visibility was so poor, he looked like a machine. Pablo dumped the empty magazine and reach for another. There wasn't another.

This Jake could barely see but it was enough. He snapped open the breach to the flare gun ejecting the spent casing and was in the process of reloading when Pablo's foot came down, crushing the bones in Jake's left hand. He kicked Jake in the head for good measure. As Jake rolled from the blow, Percy's monster sub machine gun fell from Jake's harness. Pablo didn't see it at first. Jake fumbled with busted digits to get a shell into the flare gun. This Pablo did see. He stepped back to put all he had into the steel toe, when he saw the gun. The weapon did not distract him and a pro football kicker would have appreciated the follow through. Pablo dropped to his knee after the kick to Jake's midsection and brought up the gun. He could feel, by weight, that only a few rounds remained. As he stood bringing the machine pistol to bear on Percy, Jake fired the flare gun.

Percy had been patient. And patience was its own reward. By nature Pablo was impulsive and overconfident. The moment would come and when it did he would be ready. Pablo's first blast of gunfire shattered Percy's kneecap and tore a hole in his calf. He did not move. The second burst impacted stomach muscles and dimpled his oversized pecs. He held tough. Hearing the magazine from the gun hit the deck, Percy shifted his grip on the harpoon and reached back as far as he could. He was strung tight as a guitar string. The pop from the flare gun was comical in the face of gunfire. The small bright orange sun lit the deck with a wiggling, wicked glare. Because the harpoon was pointed directly at Pablo and the strangeness of the illumination, it looked as if Percy had no weapon and was simply striking a pose.

Pablo began laughing, the insane jeer of a man who knows he has won and enjoys the moment victory. He picked up the biggest little machine gun ever made to bear on a man big enough to justify its use. In the blink of an eye, Percy's posture changed. The harpoon flew across the distance between them. Pablo never saw what hit him. The harpoon struck Pablo just left of the sternum between the ribs, bullseyeing the heart. The muscle exploded on impact. The force threw Pablo back a good twenty feet against the gunwale. The tip of the barbed spear pierced him through, penetrating the steel.

Pablo sat there, 'pooned in place. A look of amazement worked its way across his face, like a child who had just seen a magic trick, a real good one. Cupping a handful of blood that ran from his chest, he raised it, watching it dribble from his fingers. He felt the wooden shaft of the harpoon, caressing the well-worn smooth surface. The steel shaft of the barb extended from the hickory. His fingers followed the hammered metal to where it penetrated his chest. The barb was fully imbedded. He could feel the barb just inside his rib cage. It would not be coming out of his body.

With all his might Pablo pulled on the shaft to extricate the tip from the steel wall behind him. His howling rivaled the storm, adding another element to the symphony of the damned that had seemed to be playing ever since this whole thing began. The wailing brought Jake and Percy back into the moment.

After firing the flare Jake assessed his injuries. Besides the broken fingers and ribs, and the forest of mahogany splinters still in his thigh, he was relatively intact. Blood ran down his face from the grazing of the bullet, obscuring his vision. When he stood his head spun around until he had to vomit from the disorientation. He spit the last of the bile and was grateful for the big hand that helped him up and kept him from falling down again.

"Did you get him?" Jake said exasperated, wiping the spittle from his mouth.

"It would seem so." Percy chinned to the starboard gunwale where Pablo was amusing himself.

"How'd you fare? I see a few holes and suspect there are more. Thank you, Percy. It could not have been done without you."

"Nor you, Jake."

"Listen, man, you have to get into the survival chamber. The girls will take care of you and you can take care of them. It will be a few days before a salvage team is here."

"What about you?" Percy asked with a cock of his head.

"You aren't losing me yet. I have a ride waiting. Unfortunately it is not big enough for you. We'll hook up in Bergen. Trust me, Percy, it's not time for me to skip out just yet."

"I do," Percy replied, when Pablo let out a blood-curdling scream. It was a wail that rivaled the cries from hell. For that is what it took to pull the tip from its stab into the steel. Pablo stumbled to his feet, eight feet of hickory shaft protruding from his chest and six inches of hardened black steel from his back. There was something sickly funny about the sight, except for the gun that came up along with him. Pablo was on overdrive. Jake could just see his finger curling around the trigger as the gun was brought level. With all his might he jumped into Percy on a flying tackle. Percy wobbled as Jake got hold and kicked his legs out from under him while pulling down on his collar. As the two fell the staccato of the final rounds of the 17mm machine pistol shattered the night.

Neither Jake nor Percy was hit but they were now partially deaf from the explosions. Nor had they taken their eyes off of Pablo. He had used both hands when firing but, like Jake, had failed to secure his footing. Jake had been thrown up and back down the deck behind him when he had fired. There was no deck behind Pablo. The recoil of ten rounds lifted him off his feet and blew him back over the gunwale into the sea. All that was left was the line attached to the harpoon, which was trailing over the gunwale in fast pursuit.

"GET IN THE CHAMBER!" Jake yelled, running after the line. The bitter end had gone over the rail when Jake got there. Without hesitating he dove over the side grabbing the line just as it went under. He wrapped the end around his hand a few times so he couldn't let go, surfaced for one breath and dove down the side of the ship to the turn of the bilge. Jake swam forward beneath the bilge keel until he reached the midship draftmarks. From there he headed under the ship to what is known as the 'bottom flats'. At the centerline keel Jake began to inch his way back toward the stern. Without lights it was impossible to tell where the cutters were. He had turned them on when in the control room. Now they would be whirling at 5000 revolutions a minute, ready to shred to bits anything that passed through.

Jake knew they were close. He could feel the movement of the sea, changed by the wash of the cutters. Suddenly Pablo was in his face. He had climbed back along the line and lunged for a death grip on Jake's throat. Jake dropped the line he had been holding and grabbed the wooden shaft forcing Pablo away. Eight feet away Pablo writhed like a madman. Wasting no time Jake swam toward to the blades. Several kicks later he heard a crunch and the pole was yanked from his grip. Pablo was on his way through the most devastating osterizer ever made.

And so was Jake, if he didn't do some thing quick. Swimming away was not an option as the cutters created a vortex that pulled debris into them. Jake dove down, his only chance.

Percy held up for as long as it took. Jake was now on his own. He dropped to one knee and began crawling towards the survival tank. His lifeblood leaked through the sieve his body had been turned into. Bare hands stuck to the rimy deck, ripping skin away each time he moved forward.

Never in all his life had Percy wanted it to be over. He had done his job for generations without ever questioning the orders. He had an exemplary record with the exception of losing control of Pablo. And that now was settled. But this time Jake had given him an order. The inflection and delivery produces the previously mentioned Pavlovian response. Jake must have been listening during the training or someone taught him the trick. A string of words, said just so, would incline the listener to comply. You can see it in action during emergency situations where the fire chief is calling out orders and directing personnel. No one questions, all obey. Percy was usually the one using the 'voice', controlling reuseables. Ironically, though, he was a reuseable and thus subject to the same response issues; Jake's order had all the necessary variables.

Percy crawled on, driven beyond what would be considered humanly possible. Shit happens. He clipped his bad knee on the corner of the survival chamber. Pain overwhelmed him but he did not cry out. Percy curled into a fetal position, cradling his knee with both hands. He had just maxed out the pain scale and beyond, but had no intention of stopping other than taking a moment to let the shock pass. Luckily he was able to brace himself to keep from being tossed around by the rocking vessel. The ship itself was beginning to act very strange, too. Somehow heavier and the deck was much closer to the water. A few moments passed while he took in the situation, then it hit him. BIG BROTHER IS GOING DOWN! He tried to crawl, only to find he had frozen to the deck. Percy was able to wriggle out of his jacket, freeing up his torso. The bitter wind stung, soothing bullet wounds. He untied his boots, loosened the waistband of his pants, and with no small amount of personal effort and pain was able to extricate himself. His kneecap dangled by a thread of flesh. Moving as quickly as he could, he pounded on the door while his feet froze to the floor.

Through the port the men could only see his face. It was a little worse for the wear but still stalwart and focused. Goldstein let out a yelp of joy before being pushed out of the way by another. The pecking order was changing.

Regina had watched the three men struggling on deck from the porthole at her end. Though she had actually seen very little, that Jake and Percy were working together to vanquish Pablo was obvious. She viewed in silence, not wanting to get people all worked up in such close quarters. The men who clustered in the doorway did nothing. The events of the day had castrated them, metaphorically.

Big Brother began listing to port. It did not right itself, as was the norm. The deck tilted another ten degrees. Everyone stumbled and fell to the port side at the mean tilt. Everyone but Regina that is. With the men out of the way, she didn't feel the need to be armed. She stuffed a spud wrench in her waistband just the same. Catching the eyes of a couple of her girls, she signaled them to watch out.

Another ten degrees and the deck was tilting at a 45 degree angle. Regina clung to seating, overhead storage, anything to make it to the door. Hanging on to the exit sign, she swung and kicked the release mechanism. The door swung inward to port violently, crushing the man that clung to the wall behind it. Percy pulled himself into the opening, ripping the soles from feet that had become frozen to the deck. His bulk tumbled into the chamber making a small space a lot smaller. Ignoring the pain, he stood and groped to the open door. The deck tilted more and this time did not stop tilting. Suddenly they were lying on the port side. Shoving panic stricken suits out of the way, he took an iron grip on the door and began to push. The door was built for strength and weighed 250 kilos. In the proper position a man could do it without exerting himself. The way it was now, he had to raise the door through 180 degrees of upward arc. He squatted and began to lift. Huge muscles grew bigger, bunching themselves for the lift of a lifetime. It started to come up. The deck kept tilting. Big Brother was going to roll. Percy was now paying the price for his injuries. What he would do to have Jake here now.

"HELP ME!" Percy yelled. He was beginning to lose the lift. "NOW!"

The men froze in panic. Regina was the first there, followed by all of her girls. Even the ones that were hurt did what they could. If the ship rolled before the hatch was closed it would be a cold and miserable death. They were losing it!

"NOW!" Percy yelled one last time. Each member of the team gave their all in that unforgiving minute, against pain, against panic, against the odds in a struggle for survival. Just as the ship rolled, the steel door banged shut to the seal. With hands as hammers Percy dogged the latches secure.

Now they waited. Upside down there was little they could do. The emergency lighting worked. "Turn the lights off, we should save the electricity," Percy suggested.

Regina was closest to the control panel but before she threw the breakers, she took a long look at Percy's body, focusing on the wounds. "Turn around," she said. He did, exposing the kneecap. "Oh my god. We will turn off all the lights but one. Girls, we need an operating room. Make do with what we have somehow. I'm going to see just how good the med kit is. Oh, Mary –" she was one of the girls, a petite thing for men into the young girl look. She had a good cut on the head but no med experience. Mary was, however, a first rate killer. A girl has to have a side job. She would make an excellent guard during the surgery. Regina tossed Mary a filet knife from a fishing kit. Whoever thought of putting a fishing kit in a survival chamber had to have his head up his ass. Regina was thankful, now, for that peculiar point of view.

There was a pause in the activity within the chamber. Water was splashing the portholes; moments later there was just water. Big Brother was sinking. The silence was intense.

"If any of those assholes get nosy, feel free to give them a reason not to be." Regina and Mary exchanged nods.

The med kit was packed. She couldn't do much but at least she had what she needed to do it with. She rinsed his feet and hands, slathered them with antibiotic ointment and wrapped them up. Regina bent low and whispered into his ear, "Would you like something for the pain?" He blinked yes and she gave him a triple dose. If the others knew it was available it would get ugly.

Regina had never finished medical school but she never forgot what she had learned and kept up study out of habit. In her business it was a handy skill, tending to her girls when clients got too rough. Doctors ask far too many questions. After removing the eighth bullet she quit counting. Percy's massive build had saved his life but made the extractions that much more difficult, having to probe deep into the thick muscles.

She had known Percy for years. Well, not actually known him personally, but he was always at major Megacorp corporate affairs.

So were Regina and her girls. You could say they knew each other by sight and would nod when they passed each other during the course of many evenings. An understanding by observance had created a quiet friendship. Each respected the other.

Percy may have been whipped on morphine but he was not under. When one of the bigger men pushed past Mary, (and would earn thirty stitches for the effort), Percy sat straight up and hit him with a right jab knocking him clear back to the men's end. The rest of the time in surgery was uneventful.

Jake cleared the cutters, putting some distance between himself and the ship before surfacing. Once he could breathe again he continued to swim away from the floundering tonnage. There was no doubt she would be heading to the bottom in short order and Jake didn't want to be anywhere near the suction that would be created when the sinking began. It usually happens pretty fast. He took a glance in the direction he was swimming. When he looked back, Big Brother was gone.

"Now this is a fucked up," Jake said to no one, treading water in the middle of the night on the open sea and trying to relax.

The black water below began to brighten and boil around him. Without a mask it is difficult to see well in water. What Jake could see amped him with a final surge of adrenalin. It was the sub. Johnny was hovering 20 feet below. Jake jackknifed and powerful strokes brought him down to the wet lock hatch that was conveniently open.

Crawling into the lock depleted his adrenalin along with the rest of his drive. It took considerable effort to close the outer hatch and lock it down. He dialed the wetlock to return to the ambient pressure within the sub and hit the green button when the lights went out. The superhuman effort and multiple injuries had taken their toll.

Once Jake was aboard, Johnny sent out an S.O.S., activated the E.L.T. (Emergency locating Transmitter), and launched a salvo of flares. He brought the sub down another fifty feet to get below the wave action and put the controls on autopilot.

Mirka, Hans and Johnny had been waiting 500 feet from the ship, watching the sonar and radar for the inevitable. Jake's plan of diving overboard to find the sub was nuts, but it worked. Hans was still shook. A clean, dry jumpsuit and cup of coffee was just what the doctor ordered; that and the comforting words of Mirka. The glimmer of young love sparkled in his eyes. He came to with the mouth of a beautiful woman on his. The act was more of an exasperating exertion to save his life than a passionate moment between lovers, but for the time being, Mirka would not break the young man's heart. Love is part of the healing process. When it may fail in matters of the body, it wins in reparation of the heart and mind. After what Hans had seen over the last few days, there was a lot of repair work to do.

Johnny sat back in the pilot's seat and put his feet up. He admired the compassion that Mirka manifested, a trait so rare, not only in their kind, but in the world at large, that he could not help but be moved by it. She was not play-acting or working the quid pro quo angle. No, it was something more beautiful than that. It was human kindness.

Jake had spoken highly of her and there was no doubt she had a brutal past. After all, she was a Megacorp op. Johnny had pulled up her file while killing time aboard Big Brother. The term 'brutal' was a gross understatement. To be a reuseable was hard and demeaning, no matter what your skill was. But to be used as a corporate whore was worse than anything he could imagine. Regina and her girls were trained professionals. They may have been working girls but it was a legit business. Their pay was excessive, as was the gratuity; the work dignified, sort of. If the suits wanted raunch, they would have to go work the streets to find it. Any crack whore or junkie would let themselves be abused and debased for a bag, then left in their own shit and blood. Of course, disease came along with such trysts and thus the need for Regina. She had contracts and rules of conduct. The cost depended on what was asked for, and they were clean.

At the time Mirka joined the club she had no contract and there were no rules of conduct. Johnny wondered how she did it. How did she not become a hardened bitch and the bane of those around her was beyond him.

Mirka had been listening to Johnny's mentalating. "Because I didn't want to be like that. It would have been too easy." She said this with a slight smile. "There were a few incidents that helped me decide which path to take."

"I am listening. Would you like another cup of coffee?" Johnny asked.

"Yes, please. Our friend, Kale, was the first to show me there was another way. Aside from killing some of the worst offenders, he rewrote my contract so that sort of thing would never happen to me again. He had an ace up his sleeve, though, and pulled it, before allowing me to sign."

Johnny handed her a cup of coffee and chinned to Hans, "Go on."

Mirka checked Hans' pulse and breathing. Nodding to Johnny with a smile, "He is resting comfortably. He must have thought we were out of our minds," She laughed lightly. "I had to agree to spend six months at an undisclosed location to live with and help a group of friends. It was damn near the best six months of my life. There was no religion or revival bullshit, just a way of life I had never seen before. It changed me."

"Kale knows some fine people. What was the other?"

"Jake."

Johnny cocked his head, looking at her slyly before cracking a smile. "Somehow that does not surprise me. He told me all about his time on Goliath."

"But from his point of view. The last few months aboard the rig were difficult for me, personally. I had been used for more than 75 years and was having a mid-life crisis," Mirka began.

"I am certain you put that as nicely as you could."

"To be sure. I had had enough and wanted out. The hard part about killing yourself is they just bring you back again. Your shame grows exponentially each time." Mirka sucked it up. "I had just been brought back for the sixth time when Jake arrived."

"A hard case, huh?"

"You might say that. Struggling for survival during those few days helped to give me a new understanding for what living is. Living is doing and Jake is a doer. Never have I seen a man completely disregard his own safety when the lives of others are at stake."

"That is Jake in a nutshell. He has always been that way, even before Megacorp took him," Johnny interjected.

"You knew him before?"

"I had been sent to keep an eye on him. To keep him from becoming unuseable until Percy became available." Johnny watched Mirka take in the news.

"And you're still friends?"

"Never closer." Johnny replied as sounds came from the wetlock. "Speaking of..."

Mirka woke Hans and got him into the co-pilot's seat to make room as Johnny spread a fresh blanket out, waiting for the green light. It lit moments later. Johnny spun the locking wheel and opened the hatch. Jake was balled up at the bottom of the lock, unconscious and bleeding.

"You were saying?" Johnny laughed to her, reaching into the lock and getting hold of Jake's harness. Without help he raised the limp body through the hatch and laid him gently on the blanket before closing the hatch.

The interior sub lighting had been kept low to conserve juice. Mirka brought them up and with the extra illumination came a gasp. Jake was beat to shit; his suit shredded and a half-inch groove cut into the bone along the side of his head inside the hairline. Unfortunately for Jake, the sub's previous owners had raided the med kit. A few aspirin and a sling was all that remained. Johnny produced a sharp knife, a couple single edged razorblades, the tweezers from a Swiss army knife, and the painkillers. The drugs would be saved for when Jake would become conscious. He also opened a nylon case like the one Percy always carried. In it were vials of the maintenance hit. At first Mirka looked surprised. She counted the days on her fingers and gave Johnny the chin.

Mirka leaned over, resting her head on Johnny's thigh. When he was done removing the air bubbles from the syringe, he did Mirka with all the care and love he had seen her give to Hans. It was definitely a new one for Johnny. Oh sure, he had done his girlfriends many times during the sex and drug days, but there was something strangely beautiful this time. The only thing that didn't jive was the irony.

Johnny did Jake with the same feeling. He filled a third point. "Would you mind?" he asked Mirka.

"It will be my pleasure. Just rest your head on my thigh like I did and relax. You're a good man, John."

Hans had been around reuseables for most of his working life. Unlike his mates, he had never formed an opinion of them one way or another. As long as they did their job he had no beef. Now though, he was creating an opinion. The last week had been an education unlike any he had ever had before. He'd seen a man turned traitor for the love of his son. He'd seen the greed in the men who took advantage of Skru's moment of weakness, using it to crush what remained of the little man. He'd seen men that he had been taught to distrust, despise and treat without respect, uphold what was right and good despite their orders. They had honor. He'd seen the leaders of the corporate world reduced to the basics and found them sadly lacking. They had no honor. Hans stared out the porthole in front of him, giving the people in the back their privacy. It was not their fault their deaths had been taken away. And the lessons would always be remembered.

Johnny set a course for Bergen. The sub was good for a month with an extra month in reserve. It would take two days to reach the coast. One hundred kilometers from the port, an armada of Naval and North Sea delegation ships was there to meet them and escort the little sub into the busy shipping channels and a berth.

The welcoming committee had assumed the sub's occupants were other than what climbed from the little conning tower. Top brass and big dogs sidestepped, drifting slowly back and away from the affair. Jake was the last out, arms folded around his broken ribs, his good hand protecting the bad one, and a big lumpy bandage around his head. He was ripped on a dose of medicine from Johnny that allowed him to stand.

A Naval officer dressed in black wool and brass buttons walked up to them, the corners of his mouth turned down as he scrutinized them. Captain Haaken pinned out the three reuseables, nodded to each, then directed his attention to Hans.

"I am Captain Haaken. I assume you are a crewmember of Big Brother."

"Yes sir, First Mate Hans..." he was cut off with a wave of Haaken's hand.

"Where is she?" Haaken said keeping a tight lid on his emotions.

"She is at the bottom of the sea, sir."

"How did this happen?"

"It's a long story, sir."

"Make it short."

"The captain and most of the crew were killed along with the Megacorp guards. She was scuttled."

"Are there any survivors? Members of the delegation and the Megacorp contingent?"

Jake was listening and so far Hans was playing it cool. He crossed his fingers.

"As she was sinking we could see movement within the survival chamber. That was all."

"So some have apparently survived."

"It would look that way, sir." Hans breathed a sigh of relief.

"What of the party that sank Big Brother?"

"He is dead." The moment of relief was replaced with instant anxiety.

"How do you know this?"

Hans lowered his head. "The diver killed him."

"I see." To all four of them Haaken said, "Then we must rescue the survivors. Please board the Reliant." Haaken pointed to the ship nearest them. "Remember..." the four froze in their tracks "...you are among friends. And one more thing: thank you."

An escort led the way down the pier to the gangway. He made polite conversation, explaining that special accommodations were being made for Mirka. Jake was slower, taking up the rear. He limped heavily with both legs. Mirka had done an excellent job extracting the slivers, never the less...

"Excuse me," Haaken said to Jake, "I didn't get your name."

Jake took a long slow breath in preparing to talk. Talking hurt like hell. "It's Jake."

"Welcome to the Reliant, Itsjake." Haaken mispronounced.

Jake was high and the faux pas hit his funny bone. He started to laugh which hurt worse than talking. The funny thing was it wasn't really funny at all. That's getting high for you. "Jake, just Jake."

Captain Haaken smiled, "Okay, Jake. Will you be able to dive?"

"You bet. Nothing I like better than diving in the open sea with broken ribs." Jake's sarcasm was quite evident and Haaken missed it.

"That is good, would you like a hand up the gangway?" Haaken didn't wait for a reply but picked Jake up and very carefully carried him up the stairs. Haaken was a big man; the effort had been nothing.

"Your room is that way. This crewman will take you there. I must go the bridge and prepare to depart. We leave in an hour. If there is anything you need just let me know."

Jake was humbled at the kindness and more by his very nature. "Do you have our maintenance hits?" Jake asked, embarrassed for no good reason.

Captain Haaken nodded. "And dive gear that I think you will like." He turned to leave.

"Oh Captain?" Jake said, remembering something important. Haaken paused and turned his head.

"Yes, Jake?"

"You're welcome."

***

The Reliant left Bergen on the evening tide, headed due west for the coordinates Johnny had given Captain Haaken. The Reliant was Big Brother's sister ship. Though the two looked similar, Big Brother was a support vessel while the Reliant was a salvage ship. A ten-meter recompression chamber had been put on the rear deck prior to departing. Welding crews were burning the midnight oil to retrofit the chamber so it would mate to the survival tank.

Jake put his feet up for a while but couldn't rest, so he made a pot of coffee and headed to where the action was. The rear deck was bustling with activity under the harsh glare of sodium lamps. The welders were not the only ones hard at work. There were riggers, the crane operator with his crew; food service and laundry personnel were all at it. And right in there with them was Captain Haaken giving orders and lending a hand. Gone was the formal black wool. He now wore a soiled insulated jumpsuit and looked like just another member of the crew.

Haaken saw Jake watching at the fringe and climbed down from the top of the chamber, where he had been tack welding a flange in place. He jumped from the ladder, weaving his way through the chaos and up a flight of stairs to stand next to Jake.

"Good morning, Captain. Cuppa?" Jake lifted a thermos.

"Good evening, Jake. Yes, please." Haaken accepted the cup, blew on the steam that rose from it and took a gulp. "It's a cold night. So much for global warming."

"Pretty funny, Cap. What do we have going on here?"

"We are going to try and get them in one shot. If we can mate to the other chamber they can just crawl on through. Disconnect, haul them up and we can all go home."

"What if we can't hook up?" Jake asked knowing the answer.

"You will have to swim them. Come on, the gear is in the chamber already. I guess you should check it out." Haaken led the way. Jake got nods and smiles from the working crew. He smiled in return but it sort of wigged him out. As a reuseable, he was used to the exact opposite behavior and was a little unsure of what it meant. He intended to ask Haaken about it once in the chamber.

Inside was lit brightly and organized with the exception of the dive gear, which was laid out for inspection. All of it was top of the line and brand new.

"It will take me an hour to set this stuff up," Jake said, admiring the shiny new toys.

"I was told it was all ready to go." There was a hint of irritation in Haaken's voice.

"It is, it is. This is all perfectly normal." Jake began trying to ease the creases in Haaken's brow. "A diver always sets up his own gear. It's standard protocol." Jake poured them both some more coffee and sat down to begin assembling some of the components. "You know, Captain Haaken, there is something I would like to ask you."

"Speak freely, Jake. This is not a Megacorp ship." Haaken replied, implying he did not exactly care for the corporation.

"Actually you just kind of answered my question. What's with the 'nice guy' treatment we've been getting? I am grateful but what's the catch? Even the crew..." Jake was silenced by the hand.

"Your cynicism is justified I would imagine. Unfortunately I do not have time now to explain. As you are grateful, so are we. The peoples of the North Seas, that is. Trust me. I am a friend." Haaken concluded his talk and downed the coffee.

Jake stood and shook Haaken's hand. "I'm not sure why but I believe you. By the way, what's with the big cruiser tailing us?" Jake pointed aft, out to sea where a huge shadow paced the Reliant.

"I am surprised you noticed. It is one of ours. Just in case. We will be on location in a few hours. Will you be ready?"

"Yes sir." Jake said with all due respect as Haaken left.

A few minutes later Johnny came into the chamber, banging his head on the low entry. He cursed in Italian before climbing the rest of the way in.

"Would someone explain to me why these goddamn things were designed so a man of decent height gets practically decapitated when he comes through?" The question was rhetorical. The red welt on his forehead was not. He folded himself onto a cot amidst the jumble Jake had created of the dive gear. "No rest for the weary, huh?" Johnny asked pouring coffee for them.

"I don't mind. You notice these are some fucking nice people?"

"Yeah. Kind of spooky in a way." Johnny sipped his brew. "The hose goes the other way," He directed.

"Oops. Thanks. Those were my feelings at first, too. But Captain Haaken is, like, *grateful.*"

"He should be. You know sometimes when you fuck up, Jake, things turn out aw'ight."

"Why thank you very fucking much, Johnny. I've always been fond of backhanded compliments. Just what do you mean?"

"Better than none at all. You mean you do not know?"

"Know what? Hand me that first stage will you?" Jake asked.

Johnny reached over and picked up the first stage then put it down and got another. "You mean this one?"

"Yeah, yeah. So?"

"Apparently Goldstein had not relayed the information of his little coup. He was saving the info for a triumphant return."

"But what about the party?" Jake asked, not taking his attention from putting the dive gear together.

"Just his cronies." Jake scratched his head, a little confounded. "You will figure it out." Johnny replied taking the regulator from Jake's hands and looking it over. "Reverse the quick disconnect and you should be all set. You sure you are ready for this? You seem kind of out of it."

"It's these goddamned broken ribs," Jake mumbled. He was never one to complain or let discomfort interfere with work. Johnny could tell Jake was way beyond discomfort. Misery was spelled in the beads of sweat on his forehead.

"The doctor is in," Johnny said with a sly smile. He pulled a pillbox and trickled a dozen little white pills into Jake's coffee.

"Thanks, man." Jake downed the coffee, swirling the dregs to get all the medicine.

"Oh, one more thing." Johnny reached into his case and withdrew a semi-automatic nine-millimeter, stuffing it into a pocket on Jake's dive harness. "Nevah know, brah."

The survivors in the chamber were unaware that rescue was not only on the way but was holding position directly above them. The hangover kept the suits incapacitated for the first eight hours or so of the confinement in the close quarters of the chamber. The moment of grace was needed to patch up Percy. His injuries would have killed a normal man, and would have killed him if Regina had balked and simply put dressings on the bleeders. She needed him as much as he needed her skills. Percy's knee was destroyed. Regina had left it for last. The damage was not life threatening, luckily, for there was nothing she could do. His broken patella was dangling by tendrils of flesh, which she clipped and put the kneecap in the little fridge.

Knowing most of the men at the other end of the chamber, Regina knew enough to be afraid. When they come around they would turn into a pack of mean bastards. Not that they weren't that already... however, remove the constraints of civilized society and watch the fuck out. Without Percy, the women would be easy prey.

"Are you sure they will be coming?" Regina asked Percy.

Percy could tell she was crashing. Post traumatic come-down. He had seen it often. Once the action stops, the mind – keyed to survival – slows down, becomes sluggish, and worry sets in. "We have Megacorp's top dogs sleeping it off over there. You can bet your ass they will be coming," Percy responded, a little stoned from the painkillers.

"But will they be coming for us?" Regina whispered not wanting to rattle the tenuous calm in the chamber.

"Of course they will." Percy knew the other women were listening. The chances were slim to none that any but the corporates would be rescued. It is just the way it was. Then again the corporate ladder to success was choked and the competition fierce. It was a toss up. Who the fuck cares about some suits and their hookers? No one, that's who.

Goldstein was the first to rouse and begin bitching. Water and aspirin had been left within easy reach of all the suits. Food on the other hand was being withheld. This last had been Percy's suggestion. You didn't want to energize fools, especially in close quarters. Goldstein's hands were swollen and purple. The skin had split where it could no longer stretch.

"Help me, goddamn it or none of you will get out of here!" he yelled.

Percy tossed him a roll of gauze. "Help yourself. Do you realize where you are?" Percy spat back.

Goldstein looked around in the dim lighting. The room was upside down, he thought. Slowly, through the residual alcohol content in his system coupled with dehydration, the realization of where he was and how he got there rose in his mind, like a drowned corpse that floats to the surface when the gasses of putrefaction make it buoyant.

"You can't talk to me like that!" Goldstein struggled to his feet, stumbling over suits to get to the radio. He grabbed Percy's collar, forgetting his hands and who he was manhandling. "Give me the radio! AAAAHHH!" he screamed as his broken digits rebelled at the grasp, to be followed with a right from Percy that flattened Goldstein's nose and sent him tumbling back into the pile of corporate vermin.

"Don't try that again, Ben. An S.O.S. has been sent. Now we wait."

"Are you threatening me?"

Jake sat on the threshold of the recompression chamber smoking a cigarette, planning how he was going to get the survivors from one chamber to the other, when Captain Haaken approached and sat down next to him.

"We'll be ready to go in about twenty minutes. You have any questions?"

Jake shook his head 'no'. "You have any?"

"Just one. Why are you doing this?" Haaken asked seriously.

"Because you asked me to. Besides, I have a friend down there, and a few others that don't need to die over this," Jake replied.

The Reliant's massive aft crane lifted the chamber from the deck. The boom extended over the stern lowering the chamber into the cold waters of the North Sea. Jake was inside and watched the last of the trapped bubbles trail up from the submerged unit. He pulled the nine-millimeter from the pocket, racked the slide back and dropped the magazine – ten rounds in the mag and one in the pipe. Jake had no intentions of using it, but as Johnny said, 'nevah know'. He put the gun back and put his feet up. The ride down would take a while. Time enough to meditate. Something inside told him this was not going to be an easy salvage.

The crane operator was good. The gentle bump that brought Jake around hinted at the man's skill. The comm crackled and a woman's voice came on.

"Good evening, Jake. My name is Katrina. I set you down ten meters from the stern of Big Brother. You have a go from Captain Haaken to, how do you Americans say, get it on."

Jake laughed. It just goes to show you how wrong you can be. "Roger that, Katrina. I'll be in the water in five minutes. Nice touch down by the way. Jake out."

Four minutes later Jake opened the hatch to the sea. The puddle of water on the other side was not inviting. So at five minutes Jake invited himself. The rush of the cold water snapped him into the here and now. There was the stern of Big Brother bathed in the glow of H.I.D. floodlights built into the chamber. She was upside down.

"Fuck me." Jake said solemnly.

"Come again. I didn't quite get that?" Katrina asked.

"Yeah, um. Can you turn up the heaters in the chamber from your end?"

"Can do. May I ask why?"

"Because its cold down here and I am going to have to swim them over."

"The temperature is coming up. Good luck."

"Yeah right. Thanks."

Jake swam over to the topsy-turvy deck and did a brief inspection before announcing his presence. He didn't have to. Every port in the chamber was filled with eager faces. He recognized Percy on the swim by and came up to the porthole nearest him. Jake wrote a message on a white dive slate and held it to the window long enough for Percy to read it. When he pulled it away Percy was nodding his head in the affirmative. Jake gave him the okay signal. Getting one in return, Jake moved to the external control panel and began dialing up the internal pressure in the survival chamber.

When Big Brother went down, the chamber was kept at sea level ambient pressure. In order to rescue them, the chamber had to be pressurized to the ambient pressure at a depth of 190 meters. The pressure had to be brought up slow to allow the occupants time to equalize their ears and sinuses. Jake erased the slate and wrote a new message and held it to Percy's port again. When he took it away it was the first time he ever saw surprise in Percy's eyes. Percy turned away to scribble a note and held it to the glass.

'The suits are losing it. Watch yourself. I can't swim.'

Jake gave him the okay signal again, waited till he got one in return. When the pressure equalized, Jake went to the hatch at the top of the rescue chamber, which was now at the bottom. He released the dogs and spun the locking wheel. The hatch dropped away on its hinge, opening a passage into the chamber. Jake climbed through the hatchway, pulling the nine. Two groups were huddled at either end of the chamber. Jake didn't remove his dive helmet. If the shit hit the fan he was going to drop back into the water and fuck'em all. Jake walked over to Percy and handed him the gun.

Speaking loudly so they could hear him through the helmet, "Women and wounded first! Who's in charge of the girls?" Regina stepped forward. "Well, get your girls ready. Percy will keep an eye on those assholes." Jake held up three fingers and three scared but tough enough women stepped forward. Jake pulled three dive rigs from the water. The rigs were small, easy to put on, and a no brainer to use. Stick the regulator in your mouth and breathe. With no exposure suits it was going to be cold. The girls understood that living and cold beats dead and cold. Without hesitation they followed Jake through the hatch. Having tied all three together prior to getting wet, Jake hauled them as quickly as he could to his unit and got them inside where it was a toasty ninety degrees. There was one more trip with three; then Percy, Regina, and the suits. So far – so good.

With six women in, Jake went back for the third time. Sticking his head through the little moon pool, he spied the situation in the chamber had changed. A pile of arms legs and bodies wrangled on the floor. That's to say the ceiling. Regina stood at the edge of the wrestle, bringing down a pipe wrench when she would get an opening. The screaming and wailing of people unaccustomed to fighting was high comedy but when the nine-millimeter rose from the pile, pointing in

Regina's direction, Jake had to act. The hand on the gun was too small to be Percy. At least Percy had understood that firing a gun in a submerged pressurize container is a calculated risk at best. The concussion alone would...

Jake pulled himself from the pool and dove into Regina as a finger squeezed on the trigger. The nine-millimeter hollow point caught him in the left shoulder, expanding as it passed through the soft tissue and breaking into a dozen pieces when it hit bone. The round spent its energy inside the joint, which is better than hitting the wall of the chamber.

The explosion momentarily increased the pressure within the chamber before escaping into the moon pool. In that moment every eardrum in the place ruptured. The gun clattered to the floor as hands went to heads in agony. It is a short-lived pain but if you are not used to it, it feels like your brain is coming out your ears. Too many years as a diver taught Jake how to deal with it quickly and that was to ignore it. Of course having your left shoulder rearranged was another way to cope. There was no time to assess the damage. He had to get the gun before someone else. He stepped quickly around the pile of bodies, picking the gun up off the floor. Percy's hand lay limp, sticking out from underneath all the suits. He grabbed the hand and pulled with all his might. If Jake had had the use of both his hands, he could have done it. Two small hands took hold of Jake's good arm and began to pull with him. Together they were able to drag Percy from the pile as the moaning suits relinquished their assault.

Percy had been beaten severely. The bandage over his knee was gone. It was obvious this was how they got control of the big man, by beating on his mangled knee. Jake was beyond pissed off. But once again, there was no time to deal with it. 'Fucking cowards', Jake said to himself, 'you had your chance.' Regina was not much worse for the wear. More frightened than anything else, helping Jake get the gear on Percy helped her to maintain. A roll of duct tape was used to secure the regulator in Percy's mouth. Together they rolled him to the pool and dumped him in. Not even the shock of near freezing water was able to revive Percy from his trauma. The steady pulse of bubbles from the regulator let Jake know he wasn't dead. Regina packed Jake's shoulder with gauze before putting her gear on. Jake cracked his helmet seal to speak clearly to her damaged ears. You can still hear with blown eardrums, just not very well.

"When you get in the water grab Percy and start walking to the lights. Don't stop no matter what! Now go!"

The shock of the cold water sent Regina back up through the pool. He didn't want to but with his foot he pushed her back into the water. She struggled for a moment, then accepted her fate, something a few more were going to have to do in the next few minutes. Jake knew he had little time. The women he had transported earlier were incapacitated by the time he got them to the chamber. Regina would be no different and he knew she wouldn't make it on her own. He tilted his helmet back exposing his face and turned to the group of suits.

"You stupid bunch of motherfucking whining assholes!" He raised the handgun and took aim at the first suit that lined up with the sights. Looking with deadly seriousness down the barrel at the three dots all in a row Jake said, "Fuck it! You figure it out." Jake dropped the clip from the handgun, letting it fall into the water. There was one round in the pipe. He racked the slide and ejected the bullet, letting it fall to the floor and tossed the gun into the group of men. Some scrambled for the gun, others stood there in awe at the realization of their fate.

"You can't leave us here!" Goldstein yelled from the pack.

"The fuck I can't," Jake said coldly, taking a side step and dropping into the pool. He locked his helmet down and flushed the cold water out. Jake looked up once to see the faces of the damned staring down at him. With his good hand he slammed the hatch closed and dogged it from the outside. They fought on the inside to keep him from spinning the locking wheel. They failed. Jake dropped away from the chamber and the muffled screams for help. Halfway to the rescue chamber Jake found Regina and Percy just the way he expected to find them; succumbed to hypothermia. By the time he swam them to the chamber and inside, he found himself too wasted from his wounds and cold to pull himself in. He hung on with his good arm until there was no more. Jake's grip relaxed as he went unconscious and began to sink into the blackness.

No one saw the men in the survival chamber again. Without a common enemy the group went at itself. Someone, it doesn't matter who now, got hold of the gun and found the round lying in a puddle of water on the floor. He stood once the gun was loaded. The floodlights from the Reliant's rescue chamber began to grow dim as it was hauled up from the seafloor. In the last glimmer the group lunged at the man with the gun. A flash lit the madness for a moment. With nowhere for the pressure to go, the concussion blew the portholes out of the chamber. The resulting influx of water crushed it like an egg, ending the careers of a dozen Megacorp suits.

***

Jake woke to the fluorescent lighting in the ship's hospital. Percy was in the bed next to him. His leg was in traction and face riddled with little black and blue marks from the futile punches he had received. There was, however, a hint of a smile on his lips that had nothing to do with the morphine drip. Jake stared at the upturned lips. He had never seen the man smile before and was taken by what it did to the face of his nemesis. Jake liked what he saw and was wondering where his drip was, when the door to the room opened. The long body of his tender, Johnny, came through with half a dozen babes in tow.

He gave Jake the chin along with his beguiling smile.

"Ciao Jake. You up for some company?"

It was as pleasant an afternoon as Jake could remember. The charming banter of women accustomed to being clever with men they did not know helped to dampen the blow when it came.

"Where's Regina?" Jake asked. The room went quiet.

"She did not make it, Jake."

What had happened in the North Sea had happened and it all happened quickly, too quickly for anyone to make sense of. Instead of an inquiry, the parties involved simply picked up the pieces and went on. The North Sea delegation was no longer the subject of an aggressive takeover by Megacorp. Instead both sides retreated to their positions before the events that led to the destruction of Goliath and subsequently, Big Brother. The new CEO and cabinet of Megacorp were not in alignment with Stimple and Goldstein on the takeover, viewing the results as a poor idea executed poorly. The embarrassing coup committed by an aging and unproductive board was round filed, written off, or whatever businesses do when these things happen.

The North Sea delegation took this opportunity to renew their strength as a union and refocus their sights towards surviving the next hundred years rather than fooling the likes of Megacorp.

The reuseables involved in the non-affair had been left in a grey area. There was no mention of them and it would seem they had ceased to exist. Yeah, right, ask them that. Mirka and Percy chose to stay on with the North Sea. The offer was fair to both sides. Jake and Johnny returned to Megacorp. It was their fate.

BLACK TIDE

PART THREE

***

The warm Kona wind heading north from the equator kept the chevrons aboard the Salvor whipping to starboard. It was night. The setting moon cast a silver trail across the dark water, lighting the bow that cut through the calm waters north of the Big Island of Hawaii on its way to Oahu. The Salvor was returning to its homeport in Pearl Harbor after drydocking in Los Angeles for new paint and engines overhaul. Well, maybe a little more. She was 90 years old and looked it, sitting atop wooden blocks when the water was pumped from the drydock. Patches of rust–like skin cancer bled fresh down the side of the ship. Better yet, small patches of healthy skin peeked through enormous scabs of spalling steel. This would be the second skin the Salvor had received in her life at sea. New hull plating, spool pieces, rudder, propeller, shaft bearings, seals, and sea valves.

Above the water line the work was just as extensive. The Salvor was being fitted for another ninety years. The shipyards didn't make them this big anymore. The facilities still existed to make them, but nobody knew how. Somewhere along the line key links in the industry had gone to meet their maker, leaving gaps that could not be readily filled. They died before their time from accidents in the industry or failure to cope with the changes brought upon them by the Reuseable Program.

One was Joe McMasters. Now that guy could build ships. You could say it was in the family. His grandfather had built the Salvor and the Nimitz. Joe built the Mammoth, the world's largest oil tanker and the Savior, a nuclear attack sub that would never surface once she planed beneath the waters of the Gulf of Mexico after being launched out of the McMasters' shipyard in New Orleans. Those were the ones he was famous for. He was also infamous for his stand against Megacorp and the Reuseable Program.

McMasters Maritime Inc. fought a long and ultimately losing battle opposing Megacorp absorption. But it wasn't for lack of trying. The problem was that everything was becoming Megacorp or a subsidiary of them. By refusing to do business with the giant corporation, McMasters cut his own throat. Literally. But that was after the takeover.

"Goddamn it, it just isn't right, that's all I'm saying!" Joe McMasters yelled at the Megacorp sales rep. "This is my business and we aren't going to use them!"

"Now Joe," replied Ted Mishap, "we are just making you an offer, and a profitable one at that. Once your men are rotated out, we will rotate them back in for you. No training, no learning curves, just back on the job at no cost to you. We have never made an offer to anyone like this before. So it shows you just how much we respect your business."

"You know my stand on this, Ted. You have been sucking up for years to get a chance like this. Let me make myself clear. McMasters will never employ reuseables. Nor will we allow our men to be 'rotated back in' as you say. A man lives his life, and then he dies. It's not much, but that's all anyone can really call their own, their death. And you take that away. It's just not fucking right."

"But..." began Ted.

"But nothing, Ted. When my time comes I'll look forward to it. Till then I got work to do."

"When your time comes, we'll be waiting." Ted Mishap began to gather up the portfolio he had laid out. He changed his mind and left it, closing his briefcase.

"Get out of here, Ted." McMasters said this quietly. Inside he was seething at the intimidation. It wasn't the first and certainly wouldn't be the last, but it was the first time the threat was made personal and was an augur of things to come.

Joe and McMasters Maritime didn't have to wait long for the shit to hit the fan. The offer from Ted Mishap was Megacorp's last. Because of the size and reputation of the shipbuilder, Megacorp had maintained the appearance of a non-aggressive merger. With the offer in a round file, there was no reason to keep up the charade any longer. Steel was life. Joe and his straight-up way of doing business kept the supply line of metals, stainless, bronze, copper, and black, flowing into the harbor in

New Orleans. Without the steel, McMasters Maritime would be sunk. As it was, she was sinking.

Instead of a direct assault, Megacorp went after the suppliers. Crushing a copper mine in Chile, an iron ore producer in Minnesota, and a Korean cargo shipper, was just the beginning. Taking out the small players would cripple McMasters. Megacorp had carried this scenario out countless times. They knew what they were doing. Only this time they wanted more than the company. Joe McMasters was the real prize. They wanted him: his knowledge and experience.

Jake climbed the ladder for the last time of the day. It was eleven-thirty P.M. and he had thirty minutes to grab a bite to eat and smoke before being put back in the water. Johnny met him at the top of the ladder, removing the dive helmet and relieving Jake of unnecessary tools and equipment.

"Stay here at the ladder while I hose you down. The C.O. does not want you dripping shit all over the deck." Johnny grabbed the hose and let Jake have it.

The outfall that serviced the greater metropolitan area of New Orleans had clogged, backing up toilets all around town. Raw sewage poured into the streets from broken mains that were not designed to be pressurized. Of course being a couple hundred years old didn't help either. 'Nobody ever thinks about these things until the shitter starts to overflow,' Jake thought, drying his hands and accepting a cigarette from Johnny.

"Find anything interesting," Johnny asked, handing Jake a cup of coffee.

"Tell me, Johnny, how the fuck do you flush a diaper?"

"The trick is not to ball it up..."

Jake rolled his eyes, exasperated.

"You asked," Johnny finished.

An outfall, in this case, a sewer outfall, is a large diameter pipe that runs from a facility on the land to deep in the sea. Everything, and I mean everything that gets flushed or goes down a drain winds up deep in the oceans via this pipe. No – your shit does not magically disappear when you flush. Well it does, sort of, as far as most people are concerned anyway, but it sure as shit doesn't vanish. It just gets relocated. In this case, it is at the bottom of the sea. Used properly a clogged outfall would never happen. However, once you start flushing everything into the magic disposer, shit happens. Let that toilet operate in reverse...

This project was typical of much of Jake's work. Ancient infrastructure operating at maximum capacity 24/7 is a bad combination. The aqueducts of the Roman Empire are a marvel to look at but they sure as hell don't operate any more. The system in current use under New Orleans was as worn out as any in the western hemisphere. It leaked like a sieve, you just couldn't smell it. Bad as it was, the leaks helped to relieve pressure during peak hours of usage. But now with the outfall clogged, everything changed.

Two cheeseburgers and four cigarettes later Jake stepped over the side of the workboat, making the fast drop to the pipeline. On the previous dive, he had suspended a fine mesh net over the outfall clean–out hatch. Lift bags suspended the 10,000 square foot net fifty feet above the seafloor to capture the debris when the hatch was opened. Built like a door, the clean–out hatch was hinged on one side and secured in the closed position by nuts and bolts on the other three. One hundred fifty, to be exact.

The city of New Orleans called in the Megacorp diver due to the nature of the emergency's toxic environment at the jobsite. It was a time-and-materials kind of deal that comes with emergency/hazardous pay that the corporation would clean up on. So instead of using automatic tools, Jake used a five-pound maul and slug wrench. Let sewage run in the street a few more days, who gives a shit when there is profit to be made? Megacorp also wanted New Orleans, and this little incident could give them the leverage they needed. Suffering and death are marvelous tools and Megacorp knew how to use them.

Hours of relentless hammering resulted in loosening all of the corroded fasteners, leaving the lever latch that would pop the lid when the order to open the hatch was given.

"Yeah topside, I'm ready to open when you are," Jake radioed while putting his tools away.

Johnny looked up from the comm unit to the commanding officer in charge of the emergency repair operation. "You get that?" Johnny asked.

"Have him double check the net connections. We don't want to lose control of that much shit," the C.O. said.

Johnny pressed the talk button. "Yo Jake, double check the netting then get back in touch, over."

"Roger that," Jake replied as he swam to the first of four connectors, each a series of shackles, cables, and binders. First was a visual inspection, followed by a hands-on. Twenty minutes later, "We look good to go. Sorry, man, couldn't help myself."

"Yeah we all agree it was a crappy pun." Johnny got the nod from the C.O., "Open her up!"

Jake slid a cheater over the latch handle and leaned into the effort. At first, nothing – it would not budge. Jake adjusted the cheater for maximum leverage. This time he put all he had into it. The corroded mechanism screeched as the handle moved away from the hatch, releasing the final catch that secured the lid. Once released, Jake backpedaled away from the pipeline as fast as he could. You just never knew what was going to happen, but you knew you didn't want to be anywhere near it when it did.

"Okay topside, the lid is free." Jake watched from the relative safety of a pile of rocks that was created when the pipeline was originally built. 'Wait for it,' he told himself. The visibility was poor but he could see that nothing was happening. The hatch remained closed. Normally, after a few moments, the internal pressure pops the unsecured lid rather spontaneously, followed by what could only be described as the effluence of society. The net was there to catch the floaters. Everything you could possibly imagine was within the mass, along with a lot of stuff you don't want to imagine, too. But nothing happened.

"Topside, we got nothing. The hatch is still closed," Jake reported.

"You sure you got all the nuts undone?"

"Double checked three times."

"Yeah okay, okay," Johnny said to the C.O. before responding to Jake. "Roger that Jake. The man says to pry it, over and out."

'You gotta be fucking kidding me ... and risk getting sucked up into a net full of shit?' is what Jake wanted to say. "Can do, heading back to the pipe," Jake said, accepting his duty. Under normal circumstances, a crane would be used to lift the frozen lid, but normal circumstances no longer existed for Jake and those of his ilk.

On the seafloor, next to the pipe, were all the tools Jake had brought down with him. Jake fished a prybar out. He would put the cheater on the end of the prybar to give some extra leverage. He approached the hatch cautiously, like a member of some bomb squad with a hot package. Sliding the prybar beneath one corner of the hatch, Jake smacked the end with a mall to drive it into the gap for a solid bite.

Jake had worked outfalls before and understood the dynamics involved. What the C.O. wanted him to do was insane. But he wasn't down there, Jake was, and Jake knew he had to work fast because all hell was just about to break loose. As he leaned on the prybar, he saw his life begin that slow parade that signaled things weren't going to work out too well.

Jake watched the corner with great interest as he put his back into the work. If the gap began to grow he could stop, get away and let the process continue of its own accord. You just needed to break the seal and the internal pressure would do the rest. He scrunched up his eyes, refocusing. Had it moved? Then in the blink of an eye the lid burst open. The rush of water pulled him into the rising mass of filth. He fought against the tide of trash but there was nowhere to go except into the net.

In the moments before the weight of the now buoyant shit crushed him into the netting he called to Johnny, "Don't let them just dump the net!"

"Why?"

"Because I'm in it!"

The C.O. stepped over to dive communications and turned off the comm box. "Drop an R.O.V. over the side and have them inspect the site and integrity of the net. Once we get the okay from the city that things are returning to normal, we'll have a tug tow the net out and dump it."

Johnny remained seated in an effort to keep his cool. "What about Jake?"

"Guess we lost him. That's what they're for." The C.O. watched Johnny boil under pressure. "You're good, real good. Just remember to keep it that way. It would be just as easy to lose you, too. Break down the dive station. You're done here."

Johnny did as he was told. It wouldn't serve him or Jake to be sitting in the brig. The Navy would contract out the tug work. Now if he could just get off this fucking boat!

As soon as the Navy shit bucket lowered the gangway Johnny was down it. The diving was done, his end of the contract completed and he was out of there. He didn't go far; McMasters Maritime was two piers away. They had been contracted to tow the net to deep water. After a security check, he was allowed onto the pier once the guards placed a call to the operations manager. In this case that would be Joe McMasters. It wasn't Johnny's papers that came into question. It was his nature, or lack of it, as the case may be.

Johnny walked along the pier to the office. Massive work tugs; hipped three deep, ran the length of the dock. Big equipment, bigger machines, silent now, would soon be grinding away somewhere in the Gulf or up the Atlantic coast. Behind his Ray-bans, he smiled at the industrial complex. Johnny knew all about the differences between McMasters

Maritime and Megacorp; in particular, Joe McMasters' personal view of reuseables. He was taking a huge risk to enter the property, especially with what he had in mind. He had nothing to offer but was willing to put it all on the table to save his friend's life.

Joe McMasters was at his desk when the call came in.

"Yeah, McMasters?"

"Sir, we have a Megacorp man at the gate."

"If it's Mishap tell him to go fuck himself. He is not allowed on the property!"

"It's not, sir. It's one of them."

"You mean..."

"Yes sir. His I.D. checks out. He says he wants to talk to you."

"Is he armed?"

The guard eyed Johnny from head to toe. "Doesn't appear to be. Want him searched?"

"Tell him it is personal," Johnny said loud enough for Joe to hear.

"Let him in. This I got to hear. Just him and no one else. You got that? What's his name?"

"Yes sir. He goes by Giovanni, I can't pronounce the last name."

"Thanks for the heads up. I'll meet him on the dock."

Joe hung up the phone and finished what he was doing before heading to the door. Joe wasn't the kind of guy who peeks out the window. He was more straight up and in your face than the conniving little fucks at Megacorp. A baseball bat sat next to the entry. He had used it many times over the course of the years to settle disputes. Joe thought about taking it with him. 'Not yet; besides some of the boys will be watching.' Hell, half the tugboat crews were watching already. Word travels fast in a shipyard. McMasters saw the gatherings of men on their boats, took a deep breath and opened the door.

The closer Johnny got to the office the more that sense of not belonging and imminent bodily harm grew. He saw the black gangs and deck hands gather for the show. Every one of them held a wrench or piece of pipe. They had their boss' back.

Joe McMasters stepped onto the pier. He was a big man that was in no way diminished by the size of the equipment that surrounded him. Backlit by the morning sun, he cast a shadow that engulfed Johnny. They both took a moment to look each other over and in the same moment, step toward each other stretching out an empty hand. Suddenly a half-dozen laser sights lit up Johnny's chest. He looked down at them, "Shit." Joe closed the gap between them with an uncommon swiftness for a big man. His arms went wide wrapping Johnny in protective hug. He saw the red dots, too. Who knows? The sudden movement, the tense moment, it didn't matter. One of the rifles that had been trained on Johnny fired.

The big man's embrace knocked Johnny back a step with the impact of the bullet. Johnny wrapped his long arms around McMasters, lifted him off the ground and made for the door that Joe had just exited. There were no more shots fired as Johnny closed the door behind them. Right now all that mattered was saving McMasters. A conference table covered in blueprints was large enough to serve as an operating table. Johnny laid Joe face down, thumbed his pocketknife open and slit the man's shirt. A single red dimple marked the spot just beneath his left shoulder blade. Johnny glanced about the office for one of those first aid boxes they always have mounted to a wall somewhere. Found, he ripped the box off the wall, and set it next to his bag on the table. The med kit was raided but still had plenty of gauze. His personal works had everything else he needed.

"How bad is it?" Joe asked through clenched teeth.

"Depends on whether it is a hollow point or not. What are your boys packing these days?" It was a rhetorical question.

There began a pounding on the office door that rattled the hinges. Johnny had just poured some painkiller into the wound when Joe rolled over and got to his feet.

"Best you stay here and out of sight. I'll deal with my people." Joe flexed his hand and worked his arm on the way to the door. Hefting the baseball bat he swung the door wide and stepped into the opening so no one could pass by him.

"Step back," he said just short of yelling. Those that hesitated understood the language of the bat better than words. "That man was invited onto our property. Since when do we shoot first and ask questions later?" It was another rhetorical query. "Now leave here and go back to work, all of you! If I need help, I'll ask for it! When I'm done here I want to talk with the man who pulled the trigger." Joe turned his back and slammed the door closed. In that flash of an instant you could hear the collective intake of breath as the men saw his back.

One step, two steps, on the third Johnny caught McMasters and brought him back to the table. Half an hour later, a bloody slug stained a blueprint that acted as a sheet over table while Johnny finished the last stitch. It was only when he was putting the works back together that he realized just how lucky both of them had been. If Joe McMasters had been a smaller man, things could have been so different. As it was, his build effectively stopped the nine-millimeter full-metal jacket without any real damage.

Joe sat up and went to his desk, "Hey man, have a seat." Joe waved at an empty chair with a bottle of bourbon he retrieved from a drawer.

"Thank you," he poured for both of them, "Now what is it I can do for you?" Joe was ever to the point.

"I need to be on the tug that is going to tow the net."

"Why? And don't make me play 20 questions with you."

"A friend of mine is trapped in the net. I want to get him out before you dump it."

"I heard about the diver. He like you?" Joe meant a reuseable.

"Yes."

"Then what's the point?"

"He is my friend."

"I imagine a friend is hard to come by in your shoes."

"Few and far between, Joe."

"What's in it for me and McMasters?"

"We will work for you when not otherwise engaged."

"McMasters doesn't use your kind. And we never will."

"Then I guess I got nothing."

"Give it to me straight boy, Mishap set you up to do this?"

"No."

"You dive?"

"No."

"Guess I'll be going with you."

McMasters handpicked a crew for the operation. Only volunteers were accepted, of which there were very few. There was only one exception; Scrandle, the man who pulled the trigger. He was relatively new to the employ at McMasters. Though Joe had never actually met Scrandle, he had an excellent reputation as a dive tender. Joe would be diving this one. He had to know whose side Scrandle was on.

Joe had checked with the other men that had their guns out. All, to a man, used high-velocity hollow-point bullets in their guns. The type of round that causes considerable damage, even if they don't hit the mark. Scrandle's were standard velocity full metal jackets. FMJs kill quite effectively but don't make a mess of everything. He was either an amateur or he had a plan. One thing for sure, you're not going to bring a man of Joe's size down with a nine, unless you hit him in the heart. Joe's lunge to save Johnny may have saved his own life. He just didn't know.

The tug arrived at the outfall during sunset. This enabled them to disconnect the net from the mooring and reconnect to the tug's tow wire while it was still light enough to see clearly and make the connection safely. After that they didn't want anyone to see anything. With darkness upon them Scrandle was told to set up the dive station while McMasters cleared the wheelhouse so that he could have a talk with Johnny. Joe stood easily at the helm while Johnny set to making coffee.

"You know we have coffee in the galley," Joe offered.

"Uchhh," replied Johnny.

The night was calm and moonless, the sea, an undulating sheet of glass. The only illumination came from a shielded floodlight at the dive station. Within the spot of light was a portable compressor connected to a neat coil of diving hose and old style fiberglass helmet. In its day, the Superlite 17 was the workhorse of the industry. Properly maintained they would last indefinitely. This one was and had. It was Joe's personal and hadn't been wet in years with the exception of the drool of divers that wanted to use it.

Joe adjusted course and set the autopilot. The wheelhouse had a good view of the rear deck. He watched Scrandle setting up while sipping on the fresh coffee.

"Mmmm. I see why you make your own. Who was the C.O. on the outfall?"

"Grimshaw," the dislike in Johnny's voice was apparent.

"No surprise there. Your friend wouldn't be the first he has disposed of."

"There is a difference between a reuseable and disposable," Johnny replied.

"Not much. What's it like being one of you?"

"If you do not mind being shit on all the time, it will do. Why do you ask?" His sarcasm ran like diarrhea.

"Got an offer a few days back. Figured you came to seal the deal."

"Megacorp does not work that way. They shoot you in the back."

"You referring to Scrandle," shot Joe.

"Could not say. He is not one of us though. That much I can tell you."

"I know. We screen everybody but there isn't a scanner made that will tell you what's going on behind their eyeballs."

A red light began flashing on the control panel. Joe idled the motors down and put the tug in neutral. "We're here."

Johnny sat back in the shadows watching Scrandle gear up McMasters. Small sea swells licked noisily at the hull until the compressor was started, scrambling the silence with a loud clatter of valves and combustion.

The deck crew reeled in the tow wire to bring the net closer to the tug but far enough away to let the wind carry the stench away. McMasters sat on the gunwale, back to the sea.

"Cleared to dive," Scrandle said into the comms.

"Roger. Keep an eye on the wind, Scrandle. It is going to shift in a few hours." With that McMasters rolled off the side of the tug into the black waters of the central gulf. His body disappeared into the turbidity. Only the glow of the lights taped to the dive helmet indicated his movement. That and the air line that passed through Scrandle's hands as he played it out.

"I'm at the net. Beginning a search pattern starting at the surface and work my way down with consecutive passes. With any luck I'll be able to see him, or part of him any way."

While in the wheelhouse, Johnny explained that Jake had been pulled into the debris just as the lid popped free. Action, reaction – that sort of thing and Joe understood. In theory Jake would have been pushed to the top of the net with the shit behind him, therefore visible, maybe. Joe swam next to the net. Visibility was only a few inches. When that diminished to nothing, he used his hands feeling across the surface for anything that felt right.

After two hours of futility, "Scrandle, is Giovanni near? Get him!"

"Yes Joe, 'sup'?"

"It's not looking too good. If your friend is buried..."

"Trust me Joe, Jake is a survivor. Anything out of the ordinary is probably him. Do what you think is best. Thank you, Joe."

McMasters could tell those last three words extracted a huge concession on the part of the man who said it. To a certain degree, Giovanni reminded Joe of himself – to the point, and gratitude comes hard. He had been ready to call it. Now...

Joe was meticulous with his faceplate pressed hard to the net trying to peer inside while his hands were shredded from debris that poked through the fabric. He finished the net from top to bottom at which point he was ready to end the search. Something in the back of his mind sent him on a reverse course, beginning the search again from bottom to top. The net was huge and it would have been easy to miss something.

At the apex of the bulge in the net Joe ran into a piece of pipe that had poked through. He grabbed hold and putting his feet against the net began to pull. With considerable effort he withdrew the pipe three feet before it stopped moving. Bringing himself next to the net again he fanned the water, looking closely. There! Just inside the net was a hand clutching the pipe. Excited now, Joe pulled a pair of cutters from his harness.

At that moment, a wave of nausea coursed through Joe. He tried to shake the feeling, becoming lightheaded.

"Scrandle," he called over comms. "Move the compressor intake!"

Joe's dinner surged up his throat. There was no way to stop it. Luckily you can puke in a Superlite. Joe battled against his dimming consciousness and the durable material the net was made from. Judging the cut big enough, for he could cut no more, Joe put the rest of his effort into pulling Jake from the netting. Everything began to go dim, even though his light was working fine. Then everything stopped. Joe hung motionlessly in the water, one hand grasping the harness Jake wore.

Johnny may have been sitting in the shadows but at no time did he stop paying attention. He felt the shift in the wind a few minutes before he heard the call from McMasters about the intake. Scrandle's response was no response. He ignored the comms but did glance in the direction of the compressor's exhaust and the diver's air intake. Johnny waited long enough to see if Scrandle was going to do the right thing. He didn't. The tall Italian stepped from the darkness making a beeline to the intake, grabbing it and moving it upwind of the exhaust.

"What the fuck is the matter with you, Scrandle? Did you not hear the call?"

Scrandle didn't respond, instead reached into his jacket and withdrew a nine-millimeter semi automatic and pointed it in Johnny's direction.

"It doesn't matter now, he has had enough monoxide to kill a horse."

Johnny knew right then Scrandle underestimated the man. Johnny's hearing was good. Above average you might say. Beneath the noise of the compressor he could hear the shallow breathing of McMasters, dying of carbon monoxide poisoning. Johnny went to the gunwale, picked up the diver's hose and began pulling it in.

"What are you doing?" yelled Scrandle, threatening with the gun.

Johnny paid no attention and continued to pull the hose in. When the two bodies were at the side of the tug, without hesitation, Johnny raised them from the water and laid them out on the deck. He was not pulled in different directions as to who to help first. He fell to breaking the seal on McMasters' helmet. Johnny had just pulled the hat off when the first bullet hit him in the back, face planting him on the deck. A second followed. In moments the rear deck was filling with anxious angry men.

"He was going to kill McMasters! I had to shoot him! AHHHHHHH!" Scrandle was flipping into survival mode.

The gun fell from his hands and Scrandle crumpled to the deck, his hands now wrapped around his crushed shin.

Joe let the pipe drop from his hands. "Help them!" He pointed to Jake and Johnny while pulling himself to his feet and shrugging off assistance. "NOW!"

The tug's doctor was able to take care of Johnny's wounds. Johnny took care of Jake.

At the dock, McMasters stood with Johnny and Jake at the bottom of the gangway.

"I must say this has been quite an experience. I didn't know men like you still existed. You have changed my opinion of reuseables. Though we at McMasters will never use you, it was a pleasure of sorts to meet you. Under different circumstances... "

"That's life for you. Joe. Thanks for the help. Couldn't have done it without you." Jake reached out his hand and the two shook firmly.

"It's Giovanni you want to thank. We would all be dead if it wasn't for his savoir-faire."

"Gio," Joe began turning to face him. "I believe we are even on all accounts. There are two things, though, I would like to ask of you."

Johnny tilted his head smiling indicating, 'you name it.'

"Should either of you need anything, call."

"Anything?" Jake asked in a perky manner.

"Within reason, Jake."

"And the other?" Johnny prompted.

"Don't let them do to me what they did to you.

"You understand what that means?" Giovanni said.

"Fully," responded McMasters with dead certainty.

"If you can't, have one of your staff call us. We'll get the job done. It's what we do," Jake replied.

"So I gather. Good luck." The three shook hands again and McMasters headed to his office. Jake and Johnny walked back the length of the pier to their reality. On the way Johnny said with a certain sardonic joie de vivre, "Jesus, Jake, you need a bath."

***

J ake and Johnny returned to the Megacorp facility where they were stationed. It was a great surprise to the admissions staff to see Jake. His file had been written off, closed, and finished; complete with a certificate of death.

"As you can see I'm still standing." Jake pressed his thumb onto an electronic reader. A green light flashed.

"So it would seem," replied the tech. It was unusual for a reuseable to show up after being wasted, but not shockingly so. They always returned, for the maintenance hit. None could withstand the depths of desperation and fear induced by missing a 'hit.' It was both hook and inspiration to keep the reuseables under control. And worked quite effectively.

Jake was flown to Los Angeles to hook up with the Salvor, which was just coming out of drydock. Johnny was sent to Megacorp headquarters. They had a bone to pick with him.

The Salvor stood huge in the drydock facility. It was always fascinating to see, in the dry, what you only knew of in the wet. Mouse had taken advantage of Jake's skills prior to docking. He wanted the work to go smoothly. The sharp tacks in the industry had become dull or worse – non-existent. There was nothing new being created.

But retrofit we could still do. We were good monkeys. We could imitate anything. Create anything new? Not. Not the big stuff anyway. The Ayn Rand business minset that ran most successful corporations was being siphoned off, crushed, fatigued, stressed and railroaded until they began to crumble under the weight of Megacorp.

Jake smoked a cigarette while sitting on the bow. He took advantage of Mouse's offer every night when the Salvor was at sea and he would tire of reading. Human companionship was not *de rigueur*. Over the years Jake got used to it. He didn't mind his own company, but it gets old. Some evenings Mouse would come and sit with him, share a smoke and some coffee before starting his day or ending one. They'd talk shop, maybe have a laugh at another's expense, but in general just listened to the waves and the silence between them.

"Hell of a job bumping that hull plating. Having them ready made... the new skin'll go a lot quicker."

"Helped some engineers do it years ago on a cruise ship. Just glad I remembered how they did it."

"There haven't been cruise ships in..." Mouse stopped himself from indirectly reminding Jake of what he was.

"Years, I know. Thanks, Mouse, but don't worry about it, man. I'd rather hear you talk freely than not at all, cause if you're going to start second guessing yourself that's what it will be. Not at all." The remainder of the early morning was quiet. Jake got up to leave; his time was up. "Any chance I can get some time off?" Jake asked.

"It'll be another two months until we are ready to go back to work. There is still plenty of retrofitting to be finished in the Honolulu shipyard. That is unless something comes up. You going to go for a ride?"

"Yeah."

"Where to?" Mouse asked Jake's back.

"I don't know and I don't care." Jake left for his room. The morning shift would be turning out any time now.

The flight to San Francisco and Muni rail ride to Oakland were both uneventful. Coming into the Bay Area was always accompanied with relief. It didn't matter what kind of freak you were, you were accepted. Plus, a line of people stranger than you went around the city. If your money was green you were treated like a person. Of course if you had no money you weren't treated at all, for you were invisible, just another consequence of civilized society. Jake felt for the street people as they whisked by the windows of the Muni car. Aside from the money thing, it was these people that he felt closest to. Like the oldster with the shopping cart scavenging in a dumpster for something to eat, Jake passed among men invisibly. He was something undesirable, a necessary evil, eking out a survival from the waste of a society that knew nothing other than what they were told, wanted more, and threw everything away.

Outside the Muni station the sun had yet to burn the morning fog away. Jake zipped up his leather jacket and put some motivation behind his footsteps. Kale's place was a dozen or so blocks away. The pace kept him warm. Oakland, the old part, that is to say, all of it, weathered the climates; atmospheric, political and financial. Its saving grace was an active port and the two remaining bridges that connected it to the north and south bay. The Golden Gate Bridge was history. Earthquakes and rust finally won a losing battle. Luckily for Oakland the collapse did not disrupt the navigable shipping lanes and the loss of the G.G. doubled the stream of traffic through the East Bay. This doubled the revenue generated by all the cars and trucks spitting dollars off the spinning tires.

The house was pushing a couple hundred years old. Kale had done just enough work on it over the years to keep it standing but never standing

out. He explained that it was just impossible to find a contractor worth
a shit. The ones that were around were perpetually busy with wealthier
clients. "Besides the house is just where I sleep."

It was only when you opened the garage door that you saw where all
the money went. Motorcycles. Jake's, the one Kale loaned him, sat in
the back covered with a tarp. The rest ran the gamut from vintage to
late models. Once in the house he made a pot of coffee, lit a cigarette
and found a note left for him.

'Jake, something came up. Didn't have a chance to prep your bike but
she should be ready. I'll catch up with you somewhere along the way.
Kale.' Attached was a computer generated map with a red line inscribing
the route.

The garage held everything he needed to perform a minor tune-up
on the old bike; oil change, plugs, adjust the valves, and check every nut
and bolt on the machine for tightness. It didn't take long. By midnight
the bike was loaded and ready to go. There was no reason to stay. Jake
poured a thermos of coffee, had a smoke and hit the road. Traffic would
be less at this time of night, and if he could get the hell out of California
before all the fruits and nuts got behind the wheels of their cars so much
the better.

The night was cool and clear. Big rigs dominated the highway. They
had the same idea as Jake, who, when he found a truck traveling at the
right speed, settled in behind it and cruised along. He was in no rush
and still had no idea where he was going, yet. Kale had indicated that
the route he marked was just a suggestion. Another suggestion was to
get gas at every opportunity. Jake would study the map later but had
made up his mind to follow the map as it was. Kale always had his
reasons for these things though they might not be apparent at the time.

Jake peeled off the interstate in Sacramento for gas and to find
Highway 50, which begins in the state capitol. The station attendant
was more than happy to give Jake directions off the property. After he
paid for his gas that is. By the time the first hints of blue caressed the
eastern horizon he was heading into the Sierras. It was a refreshing 40
degrees at an elevation of 6000 feet. Jake pulled over in Carson City for
gas, coffee, a cigarette and sunrise. With the map spread out, he got the
first real take on the trip. At one time Interstate 50 was a main artery
from east to west for vehicular traffic and parallels the original pony
express route. Of its history, Jake would learn more on the way, but at
first glance the road looked like two lanes to oblivion. He smiled. Kale
knew what he was doing. In the past there had never been any time for

riding unless it was to and from work. Jake knew there was a difference in going somewhere and going nowhere. Both are worthwhile destinations depending upon your time and circumstance. Going somewhere was what Jake had always known. Although, there are those that would argue otherwise, seeing Jake's life as going nowhere. Jake knew that one, too. But there is a difference between spinning your wheels and spinning your wheels. By choice he decided to take the route into oblivion, even though someone else had blazed it for him. But that's the way it always was for Jake. Someone else was always making the decisions. At least this time, they were made by a friend. The small wheels began to turn again. The big wheel never stops.

The micro-towns scattered across Nevada had been neglected by the net of cyber space and the clutches of Megacorp. Not untouched, just neglected. There were but a few giant flashing relay towers dotting the landscape and radar dishes that sprouted mainly from public buildings. Picking up gas in Aurora, he wondered at the lack of internet access. It was improbable that a large section of a state if not the country had chosen to ignore their computers. No, that was too much to hope for. The Megacorp mindfuck was that good. Lunch at Ma's diner educated him a little on this matter. Usually two or three vids would be operating in any given café. At Ma's, none. The food was good. Home cooked, home made and garden grown. You could tell.

Ma was strong. Big hands and well developed arms earned by hard work told her story. She was quiet but candid and Jake could tell she'd tell you to go fuck yourself without hesitation if you crossed her.

"We don't get too many riders out this way any more."

"No? It's just what I was looking for," Jake responded keeping his eyes to his plate. She hadn't pinned him out yet.

Ma looked him over closely. "If you like nothin', that's what we got."

"Can I ask you something, Ma?" Jake looked up at her removing his sunglasses.

"Sure sonny, I got nothing to hide." She was taking a good look at him now. "Ya know, you ought to get out of that leather and into the sun for a while. What do want to know?"

"How come you got no vid? No monitors even?" Jake considered his question normal.

Ma barked a laugh and slapped her thigh. "You come all the way out here and you want to watch TV? No wonder you're so pale."

"No, Ma, I don't want to watch. I just noticed you don't have any." Jake was apologetic.

"Can't afford it. Oh sure, they give you all the stuff for free. I got boxes full of it. Guess you just learn to live without it."

"Isn't this a Megacorp Co-op state?"

Ma laughed again but this time she wasn't amused. "Yes it is, but this far out there is no profit in it, so they pulled out and left us on our own."

"To let you die out?"

"You don't mince words, sonny. Yes. We work together as a community to survive." Ma was proud in a humble, beaten sort of way.

"I could tell, the food. How do you get gas?"

"I think that's enough questions for one day. Want some pie? Made fresh this morning."

"I'd be a fool to say no," Jake said smiling.

"No sonny, you'd be a fool to keep asking too many questions. Some folks might get the wrong idea. Here ya go. Fresh pear, first of the season."

Jake wiped the plate clean with his thumb. "Is there a bathroom I can use?"

"It's outside around back. You city boys get a kick out of it. Fill up your bike then come back for a cup a Joe and we can settle up."

Jake found the outhouse behind a stand of gnarled pine. After a healthy constitutional and filling the bike up with gas, Jake grabbed a screwdriver and returned to the outhouse to repair the door hinge and secure the seat in place. There was no paper, just a pile of bark. It took a few minutes of scouring the nearby woods to gather a few good handfuls of bark for the next person. When he returned to Ma's, a couple of good old boys occupied Jake's table. Jake ignored the bait and went up to the counter. Ma rolled her eyes to Jake. He smiled and lifted his chin in response.

"The bike took four and a half gallons." Jake pulled his wallet. This was one of the places where Megabucks or the Megacard were useless. You needed cash. He supposed maybe the boys were there just in case he couldn't pay. Regardless of that he liked Ma; he was just passing through while these other gentlemen lived here.

"That comes to eighty four dollars and fifty cents." Ma turned the receipt so Jake could do his own math.

A moment later Jake slid a 100 dollar bill from his wallet, handing it with the receipt back. "Keep it and thank you."

"Thank you and stop by on your way back through. We're always open."

"I will," Jake smiled reaching for his gear, which was under the feet of one of the men. "Excuse me," he said pulling on the suit.

"Otis!" Ma snapped only once. The feet were removed. Jake nodded to the boys and chinned Ma.

"They're just keeping an eye out for their old Ma."

"No harm done, ma'am." Jake breathed a sigh of relief. He was out of there without a disturbance. He was going to be polite if it killed him. Jake was just glad it didn't come to that.

Jake stepped out into the brilliant afternoon sun. He stuffed his full water bottles into a saddlebag and idled his way out of the dusty parking lot. He didn't want to kick up any more of the smut than he had to. The old lady had given him some advice that would probably serve him well in the future, all without the hefty price tag that usually goes along with these things, i.e. getting the shit kicked out of you in the process of gaining knowledge. Because so much of his education came with an inhospitable learning curve, Jake was always thankful for the few times it came easy.

As the blistering asphalt sped by beneath the tires of the old BMW, Jake let his mind wander back a few years to the debacle in the North Sea. 'Too many had died,' he thought. 'Oh sure, a few deserved what they got and even that was too good for them.' The thoughts came hard. His life had brought misery to many, so Jake was good at blocking the memories. When they did come, the coating of Vaseline over the lens of perception kept the details at bay.

Jake rolled on across the barren high desert, over the Rockies and into the high plains of the American west. The towns and people he met along the way were like Ma's in Nevada. They were simple and survived on less than nothing. Scattered like tumble weeds, the little towns were one step away from being blown across the flats themselves. One thing united them; the dun colored dust that seemed to settle on everything that hadn't moved in over a hundred years. Even the people, after living their lives on the windswept plains, resembled dust motes as they went about their business of living.

Ma's advice saved Jake's sorry ass more than a few times on the journey across, when even getting gas can be a life and death choice. Red necks and prejudice thrive in a hardscrabble environment and fresh meat is water for their thirsty roots. Jake had been there more than once and had no desire to wet the soil with any more of his blood. Long days in the saddle kept his contact to a minimum. He was here to ride, and it beat sitting around jawing with some local till you say the wrong thing and end up fleeing town, or worse, not getting out of town and living to regret it.

A few days into the ride, Jake became the rider, forgetting all else except the focus on the road ahead. It was one of the reasons he took to it. Riding is the closest thing to diving he ever found. Jake had been diving all his life. The splash of cold water when you entered snapped you into diver awareness. You became the diver. There was nothing else but you and what you had to do to survive the day. Any other mentality would get you killed. Death was always at your elbow and you knew it. But you never paid it any attention. To do so invites it in and 'how do you fucking do.'

The red line on the map headed north and Jake along with it. The late summer had harvest in full swing. Fountains of brown dust billowed off in the distance. The business of farming was open. The little towns took on a different look. The dust was rinsed off and windows sparkled. Satellite dishes sprouted like clusters of mushrooms atop every house and business. The people bustled, proper and clean. It didn't take long for him to realize he was somewhere now.

Four gallons of gas, a hot dog and a coke for under fifty bucks! Even Jake liked a good deal. The bill went on his Megacard. The price in stares of disgust and fear were applied to his soul. Part of him wanted to turn around and get the hell out and be no one again. Passing a mirror on his way out made him instantly regret type–casting the cashier. He was caked in dust from head to toe, unshaven, and his hair stood on end, basically looking like a wild man. He broke out laughing, which garnered him another round of frightful stares. Along with the return to somewhere came his old fears and paranoia as well. Jake assumed they were fearing his reuseable nature. The irony was too much to contain. So he laughed. He examined the bike on the way back to the pump. It looked like shit, too. On the way out of town Jake cruised into a truck stop. It was a big one with one of those power wash sudsing sprayers for cleaning the big rigs. Jake pulled into the empty stall and swiped his card. He blasted away at the brown bike, revealing the black paintjob underneath. Truckers gathered for the sight, having a good laugh at Jake's expense. Jake didn't mind but he wasn't through yet. The smiles would drip from their faces, kindness flush from the eyes and re-fill with fear and the Megacorp mindfuck.

Once the bike was done, he peeled off the leathers and let them have it. It was about now the smiles began to change to astonishment. He stripped to his skivvies, washed the jeans and tee, and then sprayed himself. His face and arms went from dull brown to dark wet brown till it ran in rivulets down his pale skin. Astonishment turns to abhorrence about now. Several of the truckers left only to return carrying those big sticks they use to check their tires. Jake concentrated on being quick and efficient, so as to get the hell out of Dodge before his moment of grace was used up. It was perhaps the extra minute he gave himself just letting the water run. Or maybe it was the time of day. That must have been it – the heat of the day. And there was Jake enjoying the cool water while others were in the hot sun. Whatever it was it came with a vicious blow to the back of the head that sent him to his knees. Another caught him in the kidneys.

The spraying of the water, the swings of the batons sent Jake on a post-traumatic flashback. He curled into a ball and took the hammering. How long it lasted he had no idea other than it was dark when he awoke. He felt about himself. Breathing told him he had several broken ribs. His skull felt like a dozen golf balls had embedded themselves. But it was the muscles of his back that took the brunt of the mob's anger. The truckers were drivers. They had never been trained to hit a man to inflict the most damage. Trained or not they made the message clear: 'Welcome home.'

A shadow crossed the shadow Jake was lying in. Someone dragged him off to the side and tended to the bleeders.

"You are awake. Come we must go." A shadowed hand reached into his line of sight. Jake took it.

"Mah dbi," Jake sputtered through a swollen jaw.

"Shhh man. Trust me, I am a friend."

Jake fell off the man's assisting shoulder into the crowded bed of a pick up. The heavy, wet motorcycle leathers were thrown in on top of him before the truck rumbled to life and disappeared from the lights of town. It was dawn by the time the truck got to where it was going. Jake had been sitting up in the bed for the last few hours watching the night go by and wondering what the hell happened. When the truck shut off he figured the answers would be coming soon enough.

"You're awake! That's a good sign," said the farmer from the truck.

"A good sign of what?" Jake replied, rubbing the knots on his head.

"That you ain't dead. The name's Tom Parker." Parker extended his hand.

Jake took it tenuously, making sure there wasn't a club in his other before fully committing to the shake. "I'd be a little concerned if I was you, too. Them boys sure took a liking to you. Lucky I come along when I did. They was having such a good time, you'd a looked like a road kill by the time they were done." Parker laughed.

It was the laugh that caught Jake by surprise in that early morning light. He had heard it somewhere before. Like the handshake, felt it before. As the sun crested the horizon and the day began in earnest, Jake was thankful for the seat on the bed of the truck when he realized where he was.

"This is Red Oak," he said, recognizing the stand of trees. Glancing about he saw the buildings and remnants of a life that had been. Jake's head fell into his hands. Tears formed in his eyes but did not fall. He sucked it up. "I was here a long time ago. Stuff, ya know," Jake snorfled.

"Yes. I remember. We moved shortly after your departure. I was a kid at the time and all I remember was something about being compromised."

"So what are you doing here now?" Jake looked at the older man's face, trying to see the young boy that once resided there. He pulled blanks.

"Returning the favor, I guess."

"Thanks, but can you fill me in?"

Parker began, "When I was young this biker guy shows up here with one of our teachers. He shot up the place saving us from some bad guys, then split. It's just that while he was here for a day or two, I can't remember, but he was nice to me. Made me feel like somebody by calling me a 'little fucker' and letting me turn a wrench. It's one of the reasons I'm back here. I'm restoring the place to be a school again. Anyway, you looked like him. You could be him for that matter. Seemed as good a time as any to pay back."

"As far as I'm concerned you chose a good time. Thanks Tom Parker. You doing this project alone?" Jake asked, not seeing anyone around.

"For now."

"What you need done?" Jake arched his back and smiled. This was his kind of world, a world where something needed to be done.

A few days of backbreaking labor did little to heal Jake's battered body. But it wasn't his body he was interested in healing. With the forecast for a dry late summer and fall, he tore off roofs and stacked them with shingles. A work crew was scheduled to arrive in a few days. The more that was prepped the more that could be done. Jake put his back into the effort, which made up for old Tom Parker's lack of agility on a slanted roof. Jake watched the old guy. Tom wanted to, he just couldn't any more. It was only after a particularly long and hot day that Jake saw why Tom struggled so. It wasn't old age. As the sun was setting Jake went around putting the tools away while Tom went to clean up. He threw a tarp over the equipment to protect it from the dew and headed to the well to rinse off the day. There was Tom Parker leaning heavily against the well's masonry. In his day Tom Parker had been a man. His shoulders had been broad with arms and back to match. Powerful legs kept him upright. It was then the clouds drifted from the sun. Long black and yellow welts crisscrossed his back, shoulder and buttocks. The front of his torso had a matching set. Jake quietly fell back into the shadow. The older man had taken quite a beating in saving Jake. Jake had wondered how he did it; now he knew. All men have their secrets. Jake let him keep his. He tipped over a wheelbarrow to announce his presence, waiting a few moments before coming into the open space around the well.

"Good day Tom. Why don't you put your feet up? I'll figure out something for dinner."

"Thank you, Jake. You check the chickens?"

"Nope."

"I'll get'em. The shower's yours." Tom ambled off into the brush in search of the nest.

Dinner was the same as breakfast. Pancakes and eggs. A tall stack and three eggs twice a day was hardly sufficient for the work they were doing. No matter how Jake tried to slow things, Tom struggled to keep up. They were tearing the shingles off the old milking barn when Tom's side of the roof went quiet. Jake continued working but the song of a single hammer is a lonely thing and it wasn't long before he set his down taking a look over the peak of the roof. Tom was on his knees, his body slouched forward, his forehead on the roof. Jake scrambled across the perlins and without stopping picked up Tom, leaping from the roof into the shade on the ground cast by it. His color wasn't good and skin was clammy and cool. An ice chest in the kitchen had enough melted water for Jake to pour over Tom in an effort to bring his temperature down. Tom's head lolled to the side, as the cool water soaked his clothes. His eyes opened, staring at nothing.

"Take me for a ride, Jake. I always wanted you to, but you had to leave so fast." Tom lapsed back into a coma.

Now Jake was in shock. He had not told Tom his name. They had survived the last few days with 'hey man', never using names at all. Something inside Jake told him there was more at stake here than heat stroke. It was becoming obvious that Tom had suffered internal injuries during the intervention. Tom was dying.

"Sure Tom, just rest here while I bring the bike around." Jake lowered Tom back to the ground, drizzling more water on him before leaving. He returned and left the bike idling while he soaked a sweatshirt in ice water and filled the helmet with cubes. Jake pulled the wet sweat over Tom's head then put the helmet on so the ice stayed inside, melting and cooling his head.

It must have been the cold. Tom became aware enough to wrap his arms around Jake's waist. "Just keep holding on," Jake yelled. Tom squeezed feebly in reply.

Hardly a breeze whispered across the cornfields. Their tassels stilled, pausing in their unending waving across the plains to witness the passing of one of their own. The rooster tail of dust kicked up by the wheels of the motorcycle hung in the air, describing the miles while circumnavigating the heart of the heartland. Jake rode without paying attention to where he was headed. Whichever way looked nicer was they way he went in an attempt to give old Tom the ride of a lifetime. Only the sun was paying attention in its march west. Dusk was upon them when Jake came to a four-way stop.

"Which way, Tom?" There was no reply. He reached down to his waist and put his hands on Tom's. At first he was relieved, they were cool. But they were also stiff. So were the arms. Jake closed his eyes, breathed deeply, squeezing gently on the lifeless hands.

A horn honked impatiently behind him. Jake was stunned into awareness. Where did it come from? He hadn't seen a car or truck all day. It honked again followed by the noise of a revved engine and cloud of swirling gritty dust, lifted by the passing auto that choked two of the three routes. Jake turned left into the clear and came to the realization he had no idea where he was. A mile later was the turnoff for the old school.

Jake stopped the bike and put the kickstand down. It took considerable effort to bend Tom's rigor mortised and tangled body from himself and the machine. The man had died some time before. Jake had not noticed when it happened. He was more thankful that the old man kept holding on at the time. There was a spot Tom would go after working to sit and look over the countryside in the last light of day. Jake took him up there now, leaning him against a tree so he could enjoy the view. As the last of the daylight crept away a wave of illumination caressed Tom Parker's face. In that moment Jake beheld for the first and last time the smile he had died with. He dug long into the moonless night, and in the hours before dawn laid Tom to rest.

Jake sat quietly until the sun broke the horizon. It was a habit he had seen among these 'friends.' There was no prayer or dogma when other people would do just that. No. Instead they would just sit quietly. It seemed appropriate and since Tom wasn't there to do it Jake did it for him.

Was the coffee boiling loud this morning or was it the quiet? Neither. Miles to the west a brown cloud was roiling up and headed in the direction of the school. There wasn't any time to wonder what it was because the advance guard was already pulling into the parking lot. It was Kale that stepped from the billowing fines that hid the bike's arrival.

"Good morning, Jake! That a fresh pot on the brew?"

"Certainly didn't expect to see you this morning," Jake replied. "Give it a minute."

"What did you expect, trouble?"

"Well... No cream, you'll have to take it black."

"Mmmmm," Kale vocalized. "Did you remember Tom? Where is he?"

Jake swirled his coffee wishing he could be pulled into the little vortex. He chinned to the hilltop. There was no one there. Just the tree.

Kale looked to the hill, to Jake and back to the hill. After relieving himself of his motorcycle jacket, he kept his coffee and walked up the mound. Kale was always good with math. He took his time of quiet before returning.

"It was a good place you put him."

"He liked it there."

"How'd it happen?" Kale asked pouring some more coffee.

"He interrupted some truckers who were practicing beating someone to death."

"You?"

"Yeah. They got him pretty good, too. Saved my life at cost of his own. He said it was payback for a good turn done to him long ago."

"Must have been something pretty nice," Kale said not bringing up the painfully obvious. "Tom heard you might be coming and wanted to be here. Ya know he had cancer?"

"He never mentioned it. Why?"

"No, he wouldn't have. Kind of takes after you that way. He was terminal. Couple of months tops. You get to take him for a ride?"

"Yeah we did. The last thing he ever did."

"Good because it was one of the only things he ever wanted to do. So how does it feel to see someone you knew as a child die of old age?"

"Kinda blunt, ya think, Kale?"

"A bit I guess."

Then Jake realized that Kale's kids must have died a while ago, too. "Gee, I'm sorry, Kale. You just don't think of things that way. They were good kids. They lived a better way."

"Thanks, Jake," He slapped Jake on the shoulder, "Let's see what you got done here." Kale got up, stretched his back taking a walk around the complex.

"I don't know, Jake. Looks like you might of worked old Tom to death," Kale said sardonically.

"Yah, real funny man. If I'd of known..." Jake began.

Kale turned on him, looking him hard in the face. "If you knew you would have treated him differently. Sparing him the dignity of manhood for the ignominy of the terminally ill. You would have treated him like a sick old man and forced him to watch from the sidelines. Ignorance can be bliss, Jake. In your case, it let Tom live for his last few days rather than die."

"Thanks Kale, I guess."

"It's a tough concept to grip. But it doesn't matter if you get it or not. What matters is you did the right thing."

"Yeah, uh, right. So what's the plan?" Jake asked changing the subject.

"The crew will be here in a few days. I say we put things in order and ride out of here tomorrow."

Jake looked at the unfinished work, shrugged his shoulders and looked over at his friend, "You're the boss."

Two motorcycles headed through the cornfields into the sunrise. Harvest was in full swing. A line of combines stretched from the road to the horizon. In staggered formation they reaped thousands of acres a day. The sky became dark with the cloud of dust kicked up by all the machines going at once. The corporate farms were huge. The largest, which they were passing through, was the Illiani/Iowa Gen Mo Co-op, a Megacorp subsidiary. Those combines would run twenty-four hours a day clearing the fields. Within a week the fields they were surrounded by would be tilled, sprayed, fertilized and replanted with a winter crop.

The co-op was relentless in its assault against the land, maximizing and squeezing every square foot of earth to death to fill its coffers.

As the miles went by Jake wondered about a lot of things. The death of Tom Parker rattled him more than he thought at the time. Jake had seen a man's life come full circle. The stuff in between was just that, stuff, dukkha. Kale spoke well of him. The days spent working with Tom had yielded the man's nature to Jake. It was easy to see that he had spent his life consciously, aware of what he was doing. Certain mannerisms, the way he would rub a nick on the feel of his hammer or dropped the lumber would hint at difficulties he was working on. Oh of course it may have just been the cancer, but it didn't matter. Tom was coming to closure on the issues in his life. No matter how good a life you lead you still have unfinished business. Jake envied Tom. Here, a man at the end of his life was wrapping things up. Making a bed or putting your tools away after a job are but poor metaphors for dukkha of a personal nature, but they hint at the way the man went at his business. Tom was dying consciously and Jake was part of it. The diver was honored, too, that he had been remembered and was part of the process.

Tom Parker achieved what Jake would always hold as his holy grail. Death. But not just dying, although that was a part of it. It was the dignity of a life well lived. In that dying breath, the hands open and the relief of a burden born righteously is seen briefly upon the countenance, before that too, passes. All that remains is death. The life that once was, now lives the dream of death.

Jake moved his ass around the seat of the motorcycle trying to find a fresh spot to sit on. His sore butt let him know he was still alive. If you have ridden all day you know what he was feeling. Pain is one of life's little reminders that you're still in the game. In Jake's case, it was the only reminder. It had become a constant companion years ago, but their relationship had just begun.

When houses began sprouting from the cornfields Kale signaled and pulled off the highway into a truck stop. They filled empty gas tanks and scrubbed bugs from the windshields and helmet shields. Grasshopper guts splattered everything.

"Where did all this shit come from?" Jake yelled as he peeled the bug carcasses from the screen over the oil cooler.

"Indiana's organic. We're done riding for the night. The bugs just get worse until the sun comes up."

They pushed the bikes across the parking lot to the motel. Kale pulled his Megacard at the reception desk. Jake tilted his head, "Megacorp? Organic?"

"Just another market, Jake. Since growing your own was outlawed, those that can afford it can still get organic, non-gmo ... well, organic and non-gmo as it gets, anyway. The farmhouses and homestead atmosphere is just for show. Underneath, it's all business. Just let one of those cute little farms come in under quota... " Kale explained.

"And the sodbuster gets fucked?"

"That's a nice way to put it. Good run today." They high-fived. "See you in the morning." Kale tossed Jake his key-card before disappearing into his room.

For once it was Kale that sat in the diner before sunrise absorbing coffee like a sponge. A laptop sat in front of him on the table. The face reflected on the screen was troubled. Jake had finished the pot in the room and was heading for more when he spotted Kale.

"Sup, Kale?" Jake motioned with his cup at the computer screen.

Kale grumbled, closing the tool to look over at Jake who was busy getting comfortable on the other side of the booth. "You check your phone lately?" Kale's face was business.

"No," Jake responded irresponsibly as he picked bugs from his motorcycle jacket.

"You should. McMasters' went down. You've been called out."

"Fuck me," Jake replied dolefully.

"That they will if you don't bring him up useable."

"Is he? I mean how does Megacorp know he isn't crushed or something?"

"They don't."

"That's a plus."

"Not for you, Jake. Doesn't matter what shape he is in. It's your ass. You got an hour to pack your stuff. A car is being sent to take you to the airport."

"What about... " Jake began.

"I'll get the bike to some friends. Just do what they tell you and walk away, Jake."

"I can't. I gave my word."

"I know."

The Salvor had been underway for several days by the time Jake arrived. He met the salvage vessel at Midway Island, where it stopped to refuel on its way to Wake Island. Wake was a leftover from WWII with a history as cruel and barbaric as any. In its day it was a pivotal outpost in the middle of the Pacific for communications, fuel, and a runway for landing bombers. Although its use as these had become outdated, the location still served as a runway for ailing planes and vessels in the area.

Due to the remote location, it also served as service station for the nuclear attack submarine Savior. McMasters had been flown in weeks before to rendezvous with the sub. She was one of a kind and only one man knew her well enough to do the work without having the sub surface, McMasters. In the military transport that brought McMasters was a mini-sub that he would use to survey the Savior. He would mate the two crafts and enter the big sub to finish with the inspection. Simple. What could possibly go wrong?

The Savior looked like a giant Cohiba with fins. There was no conning tower. Since she was never to surface there was no need. Without the tower she slipped through the water effortlessly. Due to the shape she had been dubbed 'the turd.' McMasters liked the cigar application better.

The exterior survey was uneventful. Since the Savior ran deep she was devoid of marine growth. Even then there should have been some growth but the molecular makeup of the paint inhibited even the toughest organisms. The painters' had called it 'liquid death.' That it worked was all that mattered to Joe. The diving planes and rudders, wings, all appeared normal. It was the propulsion system that was unique. Joe had slaved the idea from nature, creating a machine that operated like an octopus' jet. The bane of most sea craft was the propeller. In highly polluted waters entanglement was always an issue. The Savior had been designed to be tangle free.

The only unusual aspect of the survey was that it was done while the submarine was under way. During the course of her life she would never stop moving. When Joe arrived on Wake, he was given the coordinates of the Savior's route passing the island. He would pick up the sub while it was still a day out and stay with her until a day past the atoll, at which point he would ride the currents back within the confines of the mini-sub to Wake and go home. Although he had built the Savior to withstand the rigors of the undersea environment, it was the human factor that was ever being tested. All the crew had been volunteers, signing on for life. At over a thousand feet long, the Savior had room for most of the basic human requirements.

Normally when he boarded the big sub, McMasters would be

overwhelmed with conversation-starved personnel. News they had gotten via satellite. A new face, on the other hand, was something to be exploited. Joe had done this survey a dozen times already and so was prepared for the onslaught with a warehouse of stories and hearty handshake for every one of the men with whom he would come in contact.

The security check at the sub lock was cold and formal, leaving McMasters wondering who had died. After a brief meeting with the Captain, he was certain there was something amiss. It was all business. The Chief Engineer, normally a chatterbox, spoke like a repair manual. Joe remembered their conversations of past and most of them never dealt with the sub. Now it was nothing but. There was something, something in the man's eyes that was trying to tell him what the voice could not.

"Come on, Bill. What gives? You shipping out? Somebody die?"

"Nothing, Joe. We have orders."

Joe McMasters looked down hard on the engineer. "And just what would those orders be, Bill?"

"Keep our mouths shut."

"Well, you're doing a great job of it. I thought we were better than this, Bill."

"You are, Joe. They brought someone on board. They did things to us."

Joe saw the discomfort, if not misery, brought on by divulging that little bit of information. Those few words opened his eyes. Why had he not noticed before? The lack of natural sun he figured was taking its toll. But no, it was not the sun. A small scar on the side of Bill's neck explained the rest of the story to Joe. Not only had the Chief Engineer been bucked up to the ranks of reuseable but the entire crew as well.

Was this Megacorp's way of saying, 'See Joe, it ain't so bad?' The usual excuse for a delayed departure was excessive conversation. This time it was redundant systems checks. Oddly, Joe's personal anxiety was relieved upon discovering the state of the crew. That is, he worried more for their welfare than his own. He considered himself safe. The redundancies were simply military and he figured the sub would be foregoing any contact for some time to come. By the time he reentered the minisub, he was more acquainted with the Reuseable Program than ever before. The men worked hard, all assholes and elbows. Gone, though was the casual banter between men that was ever the bottomless money pit as far as business was concerned. He didn't like it one bit. Gone was the reason for living, and he wanted no part of it. Joe initiated the minisub's start up procedure, preparing to get underway.

Joe McMasters never smelled the gas that rendered him unconscious. Nor did he feel the needle that entered the big vein in his neck releasing the noxious infusion into his bloodstream. When possible, Megacorp would try and take key individuals while they still lived. It shortened the transitional curve usually involved in the creation of a reuseable. McMasters would not have to cope with death. It also helped retain the creative abilities. Automatons like Tommy, the crane operator, had their limitations. In most cases where the victim is taken alive, the change takes place in an unnaturally easy fashion. They simply wake with more drive and energy than they had ever had before and by the time they realized what has been done to them, well, it's too late. For those that were unable to accept their new reality there was still death.

History is filled with tales of the working class rising up to strike a blow at the powers that be. Is there anywhere the upper class bands together to deal with their oppressors? Not really. They are too busy watching their assets. It was with this mindset that McMasters was brought on board. Even though he was at odds with Megacorp, McMasters was a top dog in the industry and thusly was treated with deference, like one of their own. He was considered educated and understanding of the way things work, and most definitely unlike Jake and men of his ilk, i.e. working men who just might decide to take matters into their own hands. These Megacorp was afraid of and so beat, tortured and drugged them into submission. There was a difference.

McMasters was kept aboard the Savior until the med techs were certain the injection took. Joe was never allowed to regain consciousness during this time. At the end he was returned to the minisub, strapped into the captain's chair and set on a crash course with Wake Island.

Jake walked across the little bridge that connected Wake to Peale Island over the lagoon that separated them. There was nothing on Peale with the exception of the officer's lounge. Jake was more interested in the nothing part, which was at the north end of the islet, a few minutes walk from the bridge. Since boarding the Salvor Jake had felt hemmed in, constricted. Something was bugging him, he just didn't know what. It had something to do with what Kale had said about just doing the job and walking away. It was unlike Kale to look the other way, turn the other cheek maybe, but not to help his fellow man, even when that meant killing him? No, something was wrong and like most things Jake figured he would be finding out soon enough. The north beach did not stretch on for miles, but it was empty with the exception of a beachcomber at the east end. Jake settled into the warm sand, rolled a cigarette and poured some coffee from a thermos. As the sun burnt a path to the horizon, the skooch of a pair of rubber flipflops in the coral fines worked their way to where Jake was seated.

'Jesus, all you want is a little privacy...' Jake said to himself, looking up to see his tender. "What the fuck are you doing here?" Jake said without surprise.

"You are diving, yes?"

"Maybe so. When did you get in? There haven't been any jets."

"Came in with McMasters. You should check your phone more often," Johnny replied looking over his glasses at Jake.

"Am I missing something here? I mean just what the fuck is going on?"

"I was told you were given instructions as how to play your end. Just do what your told. Come on, it is time to go to work."

Jake sat on the gunwale that surrounds the fantail of the Salvor smoking a cigarette. He was dressed and ready to dive.

"Ten minutes, Jake. You need anything?" Johnny asked, prepping the dive station.

"A thermos of coffee. If McMasters is down there," Jake thumbed at the water, "and if he is alive, I'm sure he would like a cup."

"You are a weird person, Jake."

"Just putting myself in his shoes," Jake replied.

"You already are," Johnny said over his shoulder on the way to the galley.

Jake scratched his head at the comment, flipped his butt over the side and lit another. He was staring at the black water when Johnny and Mouse returned.

"Morning, Chief."

"Evening, Jake, you ready?"

"Yeah," Jake shrugged his shoulders. "What's the plan?"

"Ride the wire down, hook up to the sub and come home."

"That's it?"

"That's it. Just do your job and walk away, Jake."

"I get the feeling I'm not being given the whole picture."

"Nobody gets that, Jake. Don't take it so personal. It has nothing to do with you."

Jake reached for the thermos and clipped it to his harness.

"What's the coffee for?" Mouse asked

"Maybe I get thirsty. Don't take it personal, Mouse. It has nothing to do with you." Jake felt a stab of remorse for saying it back like that. He didn't mean it and Mouse didn't deserve it. "Sorry, Chief."

"I just don't want to lose you, Jake."

"You won't, I'm like a hemorrhoid that just won't go away."

"Come to think of it, you are a pain in the ass."

"Why thank you, Chief. I'm ready to dive. Let's get this shit over with."

Johnny raised the helmet to put on Jake. "You all right with this?" Johnny asked.

"Does it matter?"

The Salvor held position directly above the mini-sub. The largest crane, with its boom extended over the port side, lowered Jake into the deep clear black water. The sub was a thousand feet below and it would be ten minutes before he hit the bottom, giving Jake some time to think. McMasters sank his sub. So what. It probably wasn't the first time and, in Jake's mind, more of an expensive embarrassment than the vibes he was getting from Johnny, Kale and Mouse. He knew McMasters and liked the guy. He was probably a bastard to work for, but that was none of his concern and never would be. So what...

The wire came to a stop after hitting the rubble of coral on the bottom. Jake slid his foot out of the hook and scanned the area. Ten feet away sat the sub. If not for the red flashing light atop the little vessel and the dim glow of an LED bulb from the cockpit, it would have been just more sea junk – 20 million dollars worth of junk, that is.

"Yeah topside. We are on the bottom."

"How's she look?" came Mouse's voice over the comms.

"Buried in coral," Jake lied, buying himself some time. "Going to have a cuppa and I'll get right at it." Jake turned the comms and video display off to give himself some privacy at the risk of getting his ass chewed out for doing so. The sub was not buried.

Jake swam the sub. She was intact and rolled to starboard. He dimmed his headlights swimming over the top to look into the cockpit, so as not to blind McMasters. There he sat, deep in a meditation of sorts. This came as no surprise. Any time your air supply becomes compromised, you have to do something to stretch it. And although McMasters and divers in general are not the mediation type, they all know how to do it. Panic is not an option.

McMasters opened his eyes, nodded to Jake and gave a weak okay sign. Jake returned the hand signal, holding the thermos next to the window and signed that he was going to enter the wet lock. Joe's thumb pointed up. Fifteen minutes later...

"Morning, Joe," Jake said crawling into the cabin from the wetlock.

"Evening, Jake. I figured they would send you."

"Cup of coffee?" Jake watched a dark smile cross McMasters' face.

"Sure, Jake." McMasters leaned to one side, getting a hold of his cup and handing it to Jake. It was then Jake saw it.

"Turn your head to the side again, Joe?" It was about now that Jake began to put two and two together. 'Son of a bitch,' Jake said to himself.

"My sentiments exactly," Joe replied sipping from the hot coffee. "Johnny make this?" Joe was savoring the cup.

"Yeah but..."

"But nothing, Jake. What pisses me off is they didn't have to work for it."

"They're takers, Joe. The question is what are we going to do about it?"

"What do you mean we?"

"I mean you asked me to not let this happen to you."

"So I did. Too late now, ya think?"

Jake slipped his spud wrench out of his harness. "It's never too late, Joe."

"Yes it is, Jake. I've never been one to bitch about the hand I've been dealt. What's done is done. But what are we going to do about it? Well I'll tell you, 'cause I've had some time to sit here and think about it..."

It may have taken Jake ten minutes to hit the bottom, but the ride up took several hours. When the sub reached the surface Jake swam to the ladder and climbed out to a cigarette and cup of coffee.

"Thanks, Johnny."

"Thank you, Jake, for..."

"... doing my job and walking away."

"Something like that. Where is the thermos?"

"Shit."

When the little sub finally settled into the cradle on the rear deck, the locking wheel spun and the hatch popped open, followed by McMasters.

A cadre of black suits hustled him off the deck, but not before he got a nod to Jake as the diver was put into the recompression chamber.

The next morning the red light went green above the chamber door. As Jake climbed out a piece of paper was handed to him. 'Report to the rear deck, Chief Mouse is waiting.'

Jake made a detour to the galley for some coffee and Danish before making his way to the rear deck for his ration of shit.

"Afternoon, Chief," Jake said steeling himself for whatever was to come.

"Morning, Jake. What were you supposed to do yesterday?"

"I did what you asked, Mouse. What more do want from me?" Jake replied in such a way as to imply, 'that's all you're going to get.'

"We lost audio and video when you got to the sub. Care to explain?"

"Nope."

"What about this?" Mouse held the empty thermos out for Jake's inspection. "We found it inside the sub."

Jake shrugged his shoulders. "You want me to lie to you?"

"No, but you better come up with something better than that."

Jake was trying to come up with something clever to say when he was struck in the back with a cattle prod, dropping him to his knees and faceplanting on the deck. Mouse leapt forward to catch Jake. He was rewarded with a jolt from the electric stick. Black suits dragged Jake away for a little interrogation. Mouse woke on the rear deck, a large black burn spot on his forehead being tended by Johnny.

"They're going to hurt him, Johnny."

"Yeah I know. It will not be the first time."

"No but it may be the last. They have had it with Jake. If they find out what he did down there..."

The return trip to Honolulu aboard the Salvor was as hard a voyage as Joe had ever had make. For a week he sat with the suits while the techs tortured Jake in an effort to get him to divulge what had happened in the sub. Jake and Joe had discussed this possibility, with Jake taking the position of fall guy. Joe had never had the opportunity to get the 'training' Jake received when becoming a reuseable. Thusly, Joe, although tough as nails, had no idea how bad it would get. Jake did.

"I'm not going to ask you to take it for me. I'll fight my own battles."

"It's not up to you, Joe. In fact, I can't be certain you won't get your chance. All I know is you won't be able to endure. These guys got game, Joe. They know what they're doing." Jake peeled off the top of his wetsuit revealing innumerable scars. Giving Joe a good look he said, "These are just the ones you can see."

"Good god," Joe responded, aghast at the sight.

"No, Joe, he is not very good, but I appreciate the sentiment. If they can get you to crack, they'll work it till you split wide open."

"How can you be willing to do this for me?"

"I'm not. Its just there's nothing I can do about it. The moment I cut the comm feed I signed up for it. There is one thing."

"You name it."

"Stick to your plan. Don't make me go through this for nothing."

So Joe watched them do to Jake that which he knew he could not have 'endured.' More often than not Joe wanted to stop the proceedings by spilling the beans and letting Jake go. Every time the words would surge up his throat like vomit, Jake would catch his eye and hold it with a steely gaze until the pain forced his concentration from the contact. 'Don't make me go through this for nothing.'

McMasters Maritime died upon Joe's return. On the record they went back to work as if nothing had happened. It was the way Megacorp wanted it and Joe was happy to oblige, as long as it kept his cover intact. During the course of his life Joe McMasters had earned everything the hard way. From the strain of working with iron to dealing with the iron fist of Megacorp, he had thought himself one tough son of a bitch. But nothing, and I mean nothing, compared to what he had to tolerate, bear, thole during Jake's interrogation. He knew what pain was. It may have been Jake that bore the physical suffering but Megacorp was also searching for a weakness in McMasters. The harder they pushed Jake, the harder they tore at Joe's soul. Half way through the exercise in agony Joe knew that Jake had been right. He could not have taken it. As it was, it took every effort of will that he had to hold his tongue and keep his word.

'In another life we would have been friends,' Joe thought as one of the torturers dug rigid fingers into the spot just beneath Jake's solar plexus. It's a little move that stops you from breathing with unbearable pain and works quite effectively on just about everyone. When it didn't achieve the desired response, a set of jumper cords was attached to a battery. The other ends to each of Jake's testicles. Jake's body went rigid. Blood poured from lips that had been bitten through. When that didn't work, they put the jumpers, one to his tailbone one to the neck vertebrae. If they had stuck a light bulb in his mouth he would have lit up like a

Christmas tree. His jaw clenched to such a degree that teeth began to break. Jake spit the pieces on the floor when the electricity was stopped. He looked up at the inquisitors and through the broken mouth rasped, "Is that all you got?"

The phrase stunned McMasters into silence, for he had been ready to cave to Megacorp. But after seeing the bad guys give him all they had, then to hear him ask for more tempered Joe's emotions, hardening him in ways he never thought possible.

Never once during the proceeding had Jake cried out or begged for mercy. After being stripped and chained to a sturdy chair, Jake took what little time he had remaining to get to know his oppressors. They avoided looking directly at him while setting up the workstation. Jake was patient. Sooner or later he would catch one's eye and hold it. Jake wasn't psychic, yet could learn a lot about someone just by looking them in the eye. Of course a handshake works better but that was not an option at this point. In that moment he pushed the thought, 'You can hurt me but I will survive.' Whether they 'heard it' or not didn't matter to Jake. It was the affirmation that mattered, that he needed. So many times in life you say to others what you yourself need to hear.

When the business of torture began Jake went to that place he found so long ago during his 'training.' The place was work. Some job some where. He would relive every moment and detail. It was not an escape, for there is no escaping what they were doing to do to him, but a state of mind. He felt every electric jolt, bone break, skin burn, punch, kick, poke, and stab. So it wasn't a place like so much pleasant Zen, but a place you could survive, mentally. An ace up the sleeve of the damned. The body will heal, but damage to the mind does not. Not very well anyway. There was one other miniscule bit of knowledge that helped give him an edge. Megacorp needed him.

Hours before docking in Honolulu the session ended. The men made one hell of a mess with Jake, splattering the floors, walls, and ceilings. And it needed to be cleaned up. The best part, if one can consider a best part on a journey through hell and back, was when they unchained Jake. A gurney had been brought in to take him to the brig. No man could have walked away from the kind of vitiation that had been wrought. Jake remembered some thing Johnny had said years ago about being what they had created him to be, 'use the tool, it scares the shit out of them.'

Heavy hands took hold with iron grips to carry Jake from the chair to the gurney. His move was non-aggressive, for he had none left. It was more like, 'get your mother fucking hands off me,' kind of shrug. The men backed away, pulling weapons in preparation for what usually comes next. It didn't. Jake pushed himself up off the chair, broken fingers and shattered kneecaps resisted in agony, but succumbed to will. He raised his head and took in every face in the room. His eyes did not pause when they reached McMasters; Jake could tell he held tough and didn't want to give the Megacorp men another reason to continue this discussion.

Through shattered teeth and broken jaw Jake said, "Where do you want me to go?" There was no emotion. Jake was as dead serious as he had ever been. It was taking all he had just to stand there. Ambulation from here to there would merely be unbearable. 'Been here before. Here we go again,' he said to himself.

"Return to your room," one of the faceless suits remanded after regaining composure.

Jake nodded. You could hear the bones crackling with each step. When he got to the door no one moved to open it for him. 'You fucking bastards.' Both hands working together provided sufficient force to turn the knob and pull it open. He stepped over the raised threshold, a booby trap common in most ships, stumbling but catching himself on the jamb. Turning his head back he said to the group, "Have a nice day."

Johnny caught him as Jake collapsed into the shared room. He cooked up the usual dose of sedation along with a triple dose of the juice to speed the healing. Once Jake was out, Johnny went to work. He spent the next twelve hours putting Jake back together. There was nothing he could do about the teeth except pull them. Set fingers and foot bones, superglued the pieces of kneecap together, and went through two rolls of dental floss to stitch closed the bleeders.

Jake was given a week to heal and get new teeth. Then what, you may ask? Well, in a nutshell, Jake went back to work. Whether it was in water maintenance of ships, replacing rods in a nuke facility, or reinforcing the aging infrastructure of bridges, he was happy to be doing the work and not involved in some intrigue. Fucking with Megacorp would invariably leave him with reminders of why he shouldn't. The last business with McMasters left the kind of injuries that would remain purulent. It wasn't the teeth or bones that bothered him. It was rankle of personal damage incurred that exuded a pus of hatred that ragged him most.

Work was meditation and Jake got into it. Depending on the environment he would work around the clock, coming out of the water only when his batteries redlined, smoke three cigarettes, drink as much coffee as he could and get back in the water. The topside crews rotated out every eight hours. Some shifts he never met. Management didn't care. Why should they? Jake was a reuseable; this is what they were for.

As long as he was in the water Jake didn't have to deal with anyone. Water became an escape from the madness. The only problem was you had to come out sooner or later.

This was one of the few times in his life that he considered suicide as an option. On any given day, he had on hand numerous tools and equipment to do the job quickly and completely. The trick was to physically destroy the brain. A sharp drill held firmly to the temple only required the squeeze of a trigger. An underwater cutting torch would not only burn through your skull, but cook the grey matter suitable for eating, if you're into that sort of thing. Detonating cord and a blasting cap work pretty good, too. The list goes on but I think you get the idea.

So did Jake. In his mind he rehearsed each death he could think of, over and over. He was looking for the one to suit him best maybe, or the one that guaranteed. What it did do though was give him time. Time to get past the dukkha, as Johnny called it. Your personal shit. Getting through it did not come as an epiphany. You know, Wow! Life is worth living! Not. It took years of personal torment for Jake to find a place within himself that he could live with. In times previous when he had fallen into the depths of despair after some particularly murderous operation wherein his actions directly caused the deaths of many, some sick part of him would consider the sadism he sustained on the Salvor as penance for his 'sins.' The only problem with that is that the session ended. It should have lasted an eternity. If they had broken him perhaps things would be different, perhaps not. Either way Jake persecuted his very being.

Eventually he was himself again, sort of – just darker of nature and humor than times previous. It was not easy being the person he wanted to be, but it sure beat the alternative. Work had set him free again. He knew it wouldn't last.

Inevitably the projects would come to an end as far as Jake's work was concerned. With it came the interim waiting for the next one to begin. Usually this was short. Hop the next jet or chopper to another location, get briefed, set up the dive station and go back in the water. Then there were the longer waits. Jake chafed when involved with the general public at least as much as his presence excoriated them. These were the people that required his mistreatment so their lives might be lived 'uneventfully.' By that I mean boring, lacking true adventure. Everything remains nice and there is no challenge. All created, solved, and delivering satisfaction via high-speed internet service. Let that shit crash and there would be a world wide epidemic. Thus the need for Jake, Johnny, McMasters, and those of a similar dark nature, to make sure that wouldn't happen.

It was only when Jake considered the differences and similarities between reuseables and normal people that he was able to get a grip. The reality was there wasn't that much of a difference at all. Their diet was different, so what, everybody eats differently. Both had become tools for Megacorp. The bulk of the workforce was employed by Megacorp or one of its subsidiaries; all were used by the giant conglomerate. Every one had their minds ruined one way or the other. To a man, we had given up to instant gratification. Sure, Jake's abuse may have been beyond extreme but he considered the others, the real people. Surely somewhere within their opiation of streaming informationless virtual crap, they too must suffer the loss of true freedom, to think and do as you will, that surely pierced to the soul. The price was too high for it not to be painfully obvious. At least that was the way Jake felt about it.

In returning to an even keel, emotionally and mentally, Jake almost empathized with the society he serviced. Almost. He still had a sense of self and a will he could call his own. His days as an expeditor of getting the job done, a.k.a. being a murderous bastard, were far from over. He thought, 'perhaps I will be a little more discerning in the future... not!'

Joe McMasters buried himself in the business of business. The work had to be done and it allowed him to hide his nature, not only from the staff at McMasters' Maritime but from himself. Once a week he would drive to a Megacorp facility and get his maintenance hit. It was all very discreet. Joe played the good dog. It's what Megacorp wanted to see so he created the illusion. The reality was that Joe, like Jake, was buying time. The difference was Joe had no intention of sticking around any longer than was absolutely necessary.

With Joe's conversion to reuseable status, Megacorp eased back on limiting McMasters' access to vital metals and components, the lifeblood of the shipbuilder. They had him by the balls ... at least they thought they did ... and so let the man run his business. But Joe had no intention of running his business as usual. In fact, the plan was to run it into the ground. Not right away mind you, he didn't want to raise any red flags that would alert the mother company. But quietly, like scuttling a ship. Let the water in slowly, unnoticeably, and by the time anyone catches on, it will be too late.

Joe was working things on several levels. He was never one to put all his eggs in one basket. Plan 'A' and plan 'B' operated simultaneously. 'A' was to wipe out the company's cash, liquid assets and holdings. Quietly he opened accounts for each of his employees, regardless of their status. Each week a tidy sum was placed into the accounts. When McMasters Maritime's end came, Joe wanted his people to be taken care of. Only after his death would the staff be notified that they no longer had to work another day of their lives. The money came with a caveat: 'Take the money and run, disappear and hide yourselves.' Thus saving them from the fate to which he had ultimately succumbed.

Plan 'B' on the other hand had nothing to do with being a nice guy. Megacorp fucked him and as far as Joe was concerned he was going to fuck them right back. Hit them where it hurts, in the pocketbook. In the near future, two things were going to happen. One, the worlds largest oil tanker, the Mammoth was heading to New Orleans for drydocking. Number two; the Savior would be entering the Panama Canal.

For the Mammoth to drydock it had to enter the Mississippi, be turned around and pushed into its mooring. McMasters Maritime would be operating the tugboats responsible for the move.

"We're going to what?" exclaimed Jared, the head tugboat captain who spoke for all the operators.

"Like I said, Jared, we are going to get the Mammoth sideways in the river, then hold her there," replied Joe McMasters calmly.

"Do you have any idea what it's going to take to do that? The Mississippi has a seven-knot current. I don't even think its possible."

"I've done the math. If we use all the tugs we can hold her in place."

"But what the hell for?" Jared was never one to mince words.

"Do I have the word of all the men here that what I am going to say will never leave this room?" McMasters was dead serious.

Every head nodded in assent. Only Jared held out until all the men had made their decision. Reluctantly he gave Joe the chin and the go ahead.

"A few months back I did the survey on the Savior. This was my reward." Joe turned his head and peeled down the collar of his shirt. The room was aghast.

"What the fuck is going on here, Joe? You want all of us to do it, too?" Jared was pissed that he had not been given the skinny earlier.

Joe picked up on it. They had been friends for years. "I couldn't, Jared.

I'm sorry. I had to figure this out for myself. To answer your question – no, I do not want any of you to get this shit. Arrangements have been made for all of you regarding that."

"Okay," Jared began, "assuming we can hold the ship in place, what happens then?"

"We sink it," Joe deadpanned.

"We what?"

"You got a problem with your hearing, Jared? None of you will be involved in that part. Your careers, if that's what you're worried about, are covered. Now if you ram her into a bridge or levee, then maybe you got problems. Trust me, Jared. Have I ever let you down?"

"No, Joe, but why?" Jared expressed the sentiment of all the captains present.

"I have always had the deepest respect for business and was pretty honorable about it, too. Fair, just, responsible, all that shit. You could say I've had a change of heart."

The muttering around the conference room reflected that the men agreed.

"When they did this to me, without my consent mind you, I decided to quit being a nice guy. They fucked me and I am going to return the favor. If we sink the Mammoth across the river, in a particular location, we will effectively stop all shipping up and down the ole Miss, indefinitely."

"You know what that will do!"

"Yes I do."

"But what about the people that depend on it for survival and stuff?"

"The people will survive. No one will die during the operation. Will there be hardship? Of course. The point of the exercise is to cripple Megacorp. At least for a while."

"What about McMasters Maritime?"

"It will be over. Once the ship is on the bottom, dock your tugs, walk away and keep going."

"Easy for you to say, Joe! What about us, our families?"

"No it's not easy, Jared. Just the way it's going to be. Trust me. You all have been taken care of."

As mentioned, Joe's plan was twofold. Timing would be of the essence. The Savior was the only military vessel Joe had ever created; although a pacifist, he was young and the challenge of building such a thing was irresistible. It was a ship of death with a payload of nuclear warheads capable of destroying the planet half a dozen times over and survive to tell about it. Although who you would tell is somewhat of an obscure detail. With this in mind, Joe McMasters built into the computer system a failsafe. Should the Savior be taken over by the forces of 'evil', Megacorp decide to use it for business, or the crew go insane, all Joe would have to do was initiate a sequence of programs that would disarm, disable, and destroy the sub.

The Savior would enter the Panama Canal around the same time as the Mammoth was in Ole Miss. Joe may have been concerned about the men on the tugs, but the crew of the Savior were as dead as he was and would soon be as dead as he would finally be.

Jake would never forget the beating he received at the hands of Megacorp for the incident with McMasters. But he did do a good job of getting past it and moving on. That is, until his phone rang. Normally he left the damn thing alone, but since it was sitting right in front of him he thought maybe a new experience was in order.

"Hello?" Jake spoke hesitantly into the receiver like it would bite him or something.

"Jake," said the voice on the other end.

"Yeah?" He was more hesitant this time. The vibes coming 'over the wire' were heavy.

"Joe McMasters."

"Is it time?" Jake knew full well what the call meant. The question was rhetorical.

"March fifteenth."

"Beware the Ides of March, huh?" Jake wrylied.

"Something like that. Jake?"

"Yeah?"

"Thanks."

Jake shut the phone off by throwing it into the wall and shattering it to pieces. 'I'll never answer one of those goddamned things again!' He got up and went to Mouse's office. His knock was responded with a growl. 'Safe to enter,' Jake opened the door.

"What's up, Jake? I don't have much time for a chat." Mouse was all business.

"Need some time off."

"Sounds like you're going to take it whether I agree or not, right?'

"Yup."

"We're going to be in American Samoa on April first. Be there."

"Thanks, Chief. Can I use your phone?"

"Hey Kale. Where's the bike?"

The numerous flight connections, ending in Chicago, were uneventful, rendering Jake thankful, which was a good frame of mind for what came next. A middle-aged man, graying at the temples, dressed in plain but clean clothes held a sign, 'JAKE', at the luggage carousel. After hefting his gear Jake went over to him.

"You're looking for me."

"Oh good. I wasn't given any particulars. The car is in the lot. We can take a tram," he offered, seeing the size and guessing at the weight of Jake's bag.

"I'd rather walk if you don't mind. Too much sitting around. So, how do you know Kale?"

"I don't really. He's a friend of my dad's."

"What's your name and who's your dad?"

"The name's same as yours, Jake. I never met my dad."

"Sorry to hear that."

"Don't be. My mom said he was good man. It would have been nice to meet him though."

After navigating the maze of the underground parking, the old car headed out into Chicago. At least it was night, traffic less, therefore drivable. Jake didn't pay attention to where they were going. He didn't know the town and it didn't matter to him. The city blended into the urbs, into the burbs, and finally into the country.

"We have to make a stop before we get you to the storage. That okay with you?"

"As long as I'm outta here at dawn."

"That shouldn't be a problem."

Driver Jake pulled off the road into a parking lot that was half full. Jake was hoping it was a bar. It was not. Inside a group of people were mingling, all were quiet in speaking and mindful of their words. 'Oh great, an A.A. meeting. As long as they took care of the bike.' Jake thoughts were suddenly interrupted.

Driver Jake stood on a raised platform. "Everyone let us take our seats. We have a guest this evening. Friends, meet Jake. Jake, your friends." Nods and silent salutations came from all around the room. Jake could feel himself blush. When the greetings were finished Driver Jake said, "Let us begin."

Jake sat in the back and waited for things to 'begin.' He waited and waited and waited and waited. Finally an old farmer stood up.

"The corporate crop dusters hit my fields. My crop is ruined. How am I supposed to be thankful for that?"

"I have heard, Brother Justin, my farm too was hit," replied Driver Jake. "But only part. Whatever I have left I will share with you." The others in the group voiced a murmured consent. They would all help.

"I thank you, but it does little to appease my anger."

"Anger will not serve, it never does."

"No, but vengeance does."

"No, Justin. It will only bring us more trouble. We must turn the other cheek."

"My cheeks bleed already from turning so often."

"We argue this at every meeting. It is not what we are here for!" The voice came from an old short woman, so short Jake hadn't noticed her seated amongst the others. Even standing she was barely as tall as the seated. The voice however was distantly familiar, more American than it used to be. Jake's jaw hit the floor. The once black hair was now fully silver. The yellow skin was still taught and unblemished with the exception of a few distinctive crow's feet. The face, humble and proud. She turned and looked Jake straight in the eye, and smiled.

"It is easy to focus on the negative impact of our neighbors. It is not our way, never has been. Tonight let us be thankful for bringing an old friend home. It has been many years. Jake, welcome to this gathering of friends." Quan Yin worked her way out of the row of seats to meet Jake in the aisle. They hugged until a polite cough came from Driver Jake.

Through tears he said, "Quan, I always wondered what happened."

She waved her hand to their son. "Something good happened, Jake. We can talk afterwards. Let us finish first."

"Finish what?" Jake asked.

"We sit, Jake, with our thoughts. If something spurs us to speak, like Justin and I, we express it. There is no judgment, no guilt."

Another half hour passed. Some folks quoted the bible; others spoke of personal issues and challenges. Jake was moved by it. By their faith, lack of dogma, and especially the guilt thing. What moved him to speak he will never know, for if there had ever been time to clam up it would have been now. He stood.

"I've been listening to y'all speak tonight and it's been good to hear. I have a problem that has been a bit of a paradox to me. You see I gave my word to someone a long time ago. At the time I never thought I would be asked to make good on it. Well I have, and that's the problem."

"What is it, Jake?" Quan interjected, "Perhaps we can help."

"I'm sorry, Quan, but I don't see how that would be possible. I have been asked to kill a friend."

"Good god, Jake, will you never change?"

"It wasn't my idea ... well, yes it was. But considering the circumstances, I think you of all people would understand."

"What happened?"

"He was taken against his will by Megacorp and made into what I am."

After a period of thought Quan said, "Was this a personal agreement or a contract?"

"Personal."

"You have always had difficult choices to make, Jake. When the time comes, let your conscience be your guide."

"I was hoping for something a little more concrete."

You never heard a silence like the one in the meeting hall; a veritable black hole of quietude. The meeting was over. One by one the people dispersed until only the three remained.

Jake, Quan, and Driver Jake sat on the steps of the meetinghouse.

"Well. You sure killed that meeting, Jake," Quan said sarcastically.

"And you have acquired sarcasm. It just slipped out. Surrounded by all that goodness, I couldn't help myself."

"You're a reuseable, aren't you?" Driver Jake injected, a little out of context.

"Yes, I am," Jake said in a no-nonsense manner.

"Are you my father?"

Quan remained calm, letting Jake handle it.

"I wish I was. I'm 38. How old is Quan? Do the math. I like your name though."

"You really going to kill someone?"

"I hope not, but I don't see how it can be avoided and I'd rather not talk about it."

An uncomfortable silence followed. Jake's heart sank. He had just ruined everything.

"Can you take me to the bike? I really should be going."

"Sure, Jake. I thought you were going to spend the night?"

"I've wrecked enough for one evening. You want stories? Quan can give a few." Jake turned to Quan. "It's been too long. Thank you for everything."

"Thank you, Jake. It was good to see you, too. You have a long and difficult road ahead of you, Jake. Follow your heart. Listen to it when you can. I will never forget the adventure we had. May your rides in the future be less eventful." Quan hugged Jake long and hard, passing on the goodness within her to him.

Jake felt it and for a while was relieved of the burden his life had become. It was Quan's gift. The gift of love.

Driver Jake pulled the painting tarp off the bike. 'At least she's clean,' Jake thought. The last time he'd seen it, well, it had looked like shit.

"I tuned her up a week ago."

"A week ago I didn't even know I was coming. How did...?"

"Mom told me to. She has a knack for seeing things."

"All that time in meditation, I guess. Who taught you to turn a wrench?"

"Understanding tech came from Mom. Tom Parker saw I didn't mind getting my hands dirty, so you know, one thing led to another."

"Tom was a fine man. The world is less of a place without him," Jake mused.

"No doubt there. For me he was surrogate dad and big brother all in one."

"Speaking of jobs well done, how's the bike?"

"New trans seals, pistons, rings, clutch, rebuilt the carbs, and changed out the front forks. Those old Earles were never worth a shit. And now you have a disc. You can stop."

"Geez, I didn't expect this."

"Kale sent the parts and service manual to Mom. After that it was kind of fun. You sure ride hard."

"It's never my idea. Just sort of works out that way. You take it for a spin?"

Driver Jake looked at Diver Jake with a 'duh' expression that morphed into a shit-eating grin. "You'll really like those front forks."

After Jake loaded the bike, he squeezed into the old leathers and worked the joints to renew a little flex. With helmet on he reached out to the younger man. The hands mated naturally and strongly. Jake put a little more into it, only to find his son not only able to take it but kick it up an notch or two with a smile that said there was more if he wanted it.

Jake relaxed and released. "Thank you, Jake. I hope we meet again some day."

"We will, Mom told me so ... and we'll go for a ride." Deftly, like an artist removing the veil over a sculpture to reveal it to the audience, Driver Jake pulled another tarp. "It's a Vincent Black Shadow. Should have it running by the time you pass through again."

"Holy shit! I've never seen one before."

"And you never will again unless you come back and take it for a ride yourself."

"You can bank on it."

Jake's BMW fired on the first kick. He gave his son the chin. He had wanted to tell him he was his father. He really did, but there was too much baggage involved in the truth. Besides Tom and Quan had done a far better job than Jake ever could have. The world doesn't need another fucked-up kid because one of the parents happens to be an asshole. If Quan had wanted him to know, she would have told him. It was better this way. It just hurt more.

"One more thing," Driver Jake said, hustling to the workbench. He withdrew a sheet of paper and gave it to Jake. "Kale sent these directions along."

"Thanks, Jake. Take care of your Mom. What goes around comes around, ya know?"

"Yeah, she says that all the time, especially when she talks about you. Some of the friends say you're a murderer. Are you?"

"There are two sides to every story, Jake. You decide." Jake dropped the face shield, put the bike in first gear and rolled out the open garage door, away from goodness and into a nightmare. 'There's never enough time,' he said to himself, accelerating onto the entrance ramp for I-65, heading south.

Kale's map, like all the maps Jake had received over the years, kept him on a safe route to wherever he was headed. In this case it was New Orleans. But they could never navigate the twists and turns of his soul. These, Jake had to discover for himself. There was something, however, that overrode his torment. Quan's presence, her embrace, had filled him with a calm, the likes of which he hadn't felt in years.

Heading south into the spring rains kept the pace slower and more miserable than Jake would have liked. Regardless, Kale's map was as good as ever keeping Jake from entering redneck establishments and unfriendly districts. The shitty weather was enough without risking getting the shit kicked out of you at every opportunity. It also fit his mood. The lightness of Quan's love kept the harsh reality of the near future from overwhelming him.

Committing unspeakable crimes in the course of his work was a survival issue. When you're at the bottom of the sea only one thing really matters. And that is getting out of it alive. But this, this keeping his word was killing him. Did Jake kill? And do it on a regular basis? Yes. Was he an assassin like Pablo? No. If he was, McMasters' murder wouldn't be such a moral dilemma. There was only one thing that kept him heading south through the driving rain. He gave his word. In this life 'your word' is all you really have. It was Jake's golden rule. Keeping it was nearly impossible; sometimes, like now, unbearable as well. He supposed if Joe hadn't saved his life when trapped in the net, the issue wouldn't be an issue. But he did, and Jake owed him one. The irony, however, weighed like lead.

On March 14th Jake rolled through the gates of McMasters Maritime. Security had been notified. Jake was expected. He parked in the shade of Joe's office and stripped off the leather before knocking on the door.

"Come on in, Jake," McMasters yelled from inside.

"Have a good ride down?" Joe asked getting out of his chair to greet Jake.

"Shitty weather but it had its upsides. You?"

"Never better. It's one of the things that pisses me off about this. I feel like I'm twenty again."

"Try it every day for a hundred years. The thrill passes," Jake drolled.

"I'm sure it does. Drink?" Joe went to his desk and pulled out a bottle of bourbon.

Jake looked at his watch. "It's after noon somewhere."

Joe poured, handing Jake a glass, "Thank you, Jake. I have a feeling this is going to be harder for you than me."

"It's just that I like you, Joe. Besides you kept your word, too. You didn't cave."

"No, but you should have."

"Can't. I was taught long ago to never give them the satisfaction even if they tear your skin off."

Joe shuddered at the memory of the interrogation years ago. In brutalizing Jake, Megacorp had nearly cracked Joe. That was the point of the exercise. Like Jake, he had given his word. On this point they were of a single mind. Jake sat and put his feet up.

"You tie up all your loose ends?"

"I think so."

"Good, so what's it gonna be? You want me to cap you right now? Doesn't take much. Just mixmaster your brain. A .22 caliber works perfect. Bullet goes in and spins around inside your head, scrambling your eggs." Jake pulled a small caliber handgun from his breast pocket and set it on the table.

"Not just yet. Tomorrow we tow the Mammoth into the river for drydock. When we get her sideways to the current I'm going to sink her."

"You're what? You're fucking nuts that's what!" Jake replied astonished.

"That's not all. I built a failsafe into the Savior. Never did trust the Megacorp Navy. Well tomorrow, about the same time she will be passing through the Panama Canal, her nuke will overload and have a meltdown."

"Don't get me wrong, I appreciate all the work that will be generated for me, but man, you're going to kick Megacorp right in the nuts."

"With any luck," Joe raised his glass.

The morning was overcast, with humidity a comfortable 95%. Joe and Jake stood together on the bridge of the Mammoth as eight tugs pulled and pushed the giant ship against the current of the mighty Mississippi. They were alone on the tanker, no crew. The tugs churned a dark chocolate milkshake behind them as they muscled the Mammoth into her final position.

While this was happening, Joe McMasters had two laptops up and running in the wheelhouse. As he opened valves to let water into the Mammoth, he closed circulation valves on the Savior just as she entered the third lock of the Panama Canal. Within moments all of Joe's phones began ringing. There were six. He handed them to Jake.

"Could you throw these over the side for me?"

"My pleasure. I hate the damn things." Jake went to the open door, hurling the phones into the milkshake. "What made you choose this course of action, Joe?"

"Megacorp has been breaking our balls for years. We were big but could only absorb the punishment for so long. Creative bookkeeping has kept us in the black. Now that they cut our steel and copper, McMasters is as sunk as this tanker will be in a few minutes. Something in me just won't let me give it to them."

"I can dig that. I'm just wondering how I fit into this?"

"Hopefully you don't. You are plan B. I leaked word of what was happening this morning. No doubt Megacorp has snipers on the shoreline. So, as soon as I'm done here, we'll take a stroll out on the main deck to give them a clear shot."

"Not much of a plan, Joe."

"Maybe not, but if we can stick this ship in the mud they'll never get it out. They know it, and would rather kill me than kill a major profit supply line."

"You do understand the way these things work, don't ya?"

"Yes I do. Here we go!"

Eight tugs put the guns to it, straining the tow cables taught as guitar strings, holding the Mammoth at cross current.

"I spent the last few days unbuttoning the flanges to let the river water come in fast. Once the scoop injection valve opens..." Joe stopped as the Mammoth began to list. The holds meant for containing oils were filling. Joe and Jake stepped out onto the slanted deck. Jake lit a cigarette, watching the shore. Within a minute he spotted half a dozen reflections that were the scopes of the sniper rifles Joe had mentioned.

As the Mammoth leaned farther to port, it was obvious to anyone with or without knowledge of boats that something was going wrong. Just then a high velocity round slammed into the bulkhead at chest level right next to Jake.

"Jesus Christ! You sure they want you?"

"Easy, Jake. They are just sighting in, didn't want to risk hitting me."

Jake was suddenly on edge; the moment was near. From the west bank he spotted three puffs of smoke. Instinctively he grabbed Joe to pull him down. With his hands on Joe's shirt Jake dropped to his knees to get Joe out of the line of fire. He was too slow.

The first shot, as Joe mentioned, was practice. A shot to the heart was the ideal way to immobilize a reuseable. They'll drop dead. Throw in a new heart, zap'em and put them back to work. The method proved itself time and time again when a reuseable gets uppity.

Jake wasn't so much slow in reacting as underestimating the strength it took to pull a man of Joe's size down. It didn't help matters that Joe was resisting, standing staunchly, waiting to take it. In failing to get Joe out the way, Jake unknowingly kept his word. As Jake dropped, using his body weight to help bring him down, he was only able to lower Joe about a foot.

Three bullets arrived and would have punched a hole clean through Joe's chest. Instead they hit him in the head, exploding the skull and splattering Joe's brain across the deck of the Mammoth. For Jake it was dark poetry. There was no more shooting. Minutes later the Mammoth rested on the riverbed.

Jake surveyed the man-made disaster. Joe had done an excellent job of fucking things up. While waiting for a chase boat to come and get him, he saw something that stirred his sense of pride. One by one, each of the eight tugs began taking on water. Megacorp would get nothing.

Jake sat alone on the bow of the chase boat. The other operators and crew kept their distance. They had watched from the decks of their tugs as Jake failed to save the life of McMasters. Worse than a murderer, they considered him a coward. Jake bore his albatross righteously. 'Let them think what they want,' Jake thought, holding onto the bowline before lassoing a bollard and securing the line. He walked away from the men and their stink-eye. Jake already lugged enough Samsonite in the way of reputation. Another piece wouldn't matter. What the crews didn't know would save their lives. His agreement was with McMasters, not these men.

Jake rode off the pier just as news reporters and podcasters were descending on the scene like flies on shit. The Megacorp affiliates would put a terrorist spin on events with the poor corporation bearing the worst of it. If Joe had a face it would be smiling. The sinkings were a staggering blow to the status quo.

But all Jake wanted was out of town. Stuffed into his helmet was a map downloaded off the net. The only handwriting said, 'a friend.' That was good enough for Jake. He memorized the route through town before putting it in his pocket and rolling off the dock. Without the map Jake would never have gotten out of New Orleans. The sudden installment of a fifteen hundred foot levee was forcing water into the streets and highways. The floods usually come from the other direction. This time it was the volume of water that comes down the Mississippi diverting itself around the Mammoth, seeking and creating new pathways of least resistance on the way to the sea. In this was an ironic twist of fate.

It began with Hurricane Katrina years before. The ninth ward, Bourbon Street and the poorer areas were always the hardest hit when the storm surge would push the river back up stream. Each storm forced more of the poor out until there was some highly undervalued real estate available for a song. That tune would come in the form of strategically placed levees and seawalls. The remaining ailing and strapped residents were easily forced out. With the levees guaranteeing there would be no more flooding from the gulf, a new renaissance of upwardly mobile corporate types built new southern mansions, creating a ghetto of the rich instead of poor.

Jake hopped the bridge to the west side. It was called the Skyway and afforded a grim view of the disaster. Not only did he get a panorama of the river but the rear view mirror gave him snapshots of the flooding. This time it was the rich that were stranded on rooftops. You get the idea.

It would take four days of hard riding to reach Kale's house in Oakland. They passed in a blur as he only stopped long enough for gas. Jake couldn't risk missing Mouse. Why the man cut Jake slack he could never be sure. Because of it however, Jake was honor bound to keep his word.

***

Johnny was sitting on the empty pier where the Salvor was usually tied when Jake's taxi pulled up.

"Shit. I missed the boat," Jake said tossing his gear bags onto the dock.

Johnny flipped a butt into the water. "Got a chopper waiting. You know captains and their schedules.

"How long ago?"

"They should be just about hitting the open sea."

"Couldn't wait fifteen fucking minutes?"

"Like I said Jake..."

"Yeah, yeah, yeah."

"No one knew where you were. You don't answer your phone..."

"You knew."

"Yeah well, some shit went down in New Orleans and I figure you had something to do with it, so, to be honest, I did not want to get involved."

"Anybody else think I was there?"

"Not yet. I would lay real low, Jake and come up with a good simple story line you can keep with." Johnny laughed, "Shit, Jake. You should have seen the faces when news got out about the Mammoth. Your name was first on everyone's lips."

"But they got no proof."

"Unless you give it to them, no."

"Great, then I'm going back to work. What a bunch of bullshit. When's the chopper get here?"

Johnny looked at an imaginary watch, "Any time now." The sound of a twin Sikorsky split the air. Johnny smiled and Groucho Marxed his eyebrows.

Jake sat alone on the bow of the Salvor. It seemed like he was always sitting alone now. The sound of Mouse's footsteps precluded his arrival.

"Evening, Chief," Jake said without getting up.

"Morning, Jake. Glad you made it."

"Me too."

"You have a nice ride?"

"Yeah," Jake responded hesitantly.

"Where'd you go?"

"Is this an interrogation, Mouse?"

"No."

"Then the answer is nowhere. I just rode."

"I'd stick with that too, Jake. Sounds good to me. You know McMasters is dead."

"I heard it through the grapevine."

"I figured more like firsthand."

"You're not getting any more, Chief, so just quit digging. Trust me. I'm doing you a favor."

"So that makes us square?"

"No. Maybe some day I can make it up to you, but not today."

Mouse stood. He was fishing but knew there wasn't going to be any catching. "Thanks again for making it back, Jake."

"I'm as glad as you are."

"I'm sure you are, I'm sure you are. Just one thing. How'd he do it?"

"By staying one step ahead of the game. Take a hint."

"I will. The crew is starting to stir."

"Thanks, Mouse, I can take a hint, too."

Jake stayed on deck for one more smoke. He flipped the butt, waiting until it winked out in the waves before leaving the presence of men.

Jake could only suppose it was Joe McMasters' parting gift to Jake that he was never indicted in the Mammoth disaster. Jake knew that if he had been pinned out, it would have been the end. He gave Joe the chance to live the dream of death. Joe made sure he didn't have to pay for it. It's just the way things work among men with character. That was good enough for Jake, who, after docking in American Samoa, went back to work.

"See ya tonight, Johnny," Jake said into comms as he stepped over the side of the ship into the cold black water.

In his early years as a diver, Jake learned what pain was. Agony however was an acquaintance. Death was the companion. Fuck up just once and he was there to carry you home. That was incentive. You worked harder, smarter, better to stay one step ahead of the competition and half a step ahead of death. When they took away dying, all that was left was the pain and agony. The spectre no longer existed. At least for

Jake and those like him. For reuseables, the dissolution of death is akin to tearing half of their humanity from them. Our dying is interwoven with our living. Remove half the threads of a tapestry and what do you have? Nothing. Most reuseable's lived but half a life, the working half. The rest had been taken away. Empty. There was nothing there. They became zombies, automatons, functioning human machines and little more.

Jake had been heading in that direction since his induction into the society of the damned. Johnny, Kale, an unforgiving kismet, and his own conscience kept Jake alive. At least alive with the guilt of living. Ask any Jewish mother; it's more than enough. And Jake had a mother load. It's enough when there is nothing else left.

That the road of Jake's life is littered with dead would be an understatement. He may have been following his directive of the moment but never the less, it was Jake's finger that pulled the trigger. He never forgot it either. It was also clear that the future, along with whatever else it might hold, would be paved with the victims of his passing. That a few deserved what they got, did little to appease his guilt because there were far too many innocents who just happened to be in the wrong place at the wrong time. The irony of justice rode heavily upon his shoulders. The deceased never realized how lucky they were to be able to die. Of course they never really appreciated it either.

To live knowing that one day you will die is one of the greatest gifts self-consciousness ever gave us. It gives you your drive, a desire to accomplish something before you die, a reason to get out of bed. But, to have that taken away is a crime. Though there are those who would argue against that point, they argue from the point of view of the living and so, to be quite frank, have no idea what the fuck they are talking about. When the reason for living is taken away what else is there?

Work.

*****

Some eighty years have passed since becoming a slave of Megacorp. Time had become pointless long ago, along with any hope of the nightmare ending. What was mine I kept hidden deep with the recesses of my mind. My eyes may have reflected the Megacorp mindfuck, but behind them I still lived. Johnny had been my only friend through all of it, and Chief Mouse to only a slightly lesser degree. It was enough. Without them I would have died long ago and become a

'Tommy'. Needless to say, I was incredibly thankful and showed it every chance I got.

A crane barge, stacked with miles of pipe, was anchored off the coast of Oregon above one of the many faults that fractured the earth's crust in that region. Two workboats and half a dozen chase boats were all in position and standing by. It was summer, the ocean flat and time to go to work.

Dive station was set up on the rear deck of the 'Sea Matron'. The project had been slated for a summer installation, as calm waters were needed for the delicate operation. An earthquake had opened up one of the many fissures on the deep seabed. A molten river was exposed and the opportunity was not to go unexploited. My job was to guide a very special nozzle into the flow of lava at a specific location and secure it. From there on, it was the rough neck's job to attach the pipe sections together. In theory, the steam generated would run a turbine, generating electricity for the greater metropolitan area of Portland.

The procedure for tapping the fluid core of the planet was perfected in the relatively calm waters off the Big Island of Hawaii. Once the bugs were worked out, the system worked better than expected, supplying all the islands with as much juice as they needed with a minimal carbon footprint.

For the raging seas of the Pacific Northwest however, the system had to be ramped up, beefed up, and oversized to withstand the environment. While the designs were being forged in metal, the site was surveyed and entry location and angle pinpointed on the sea floor. Now they waited. Late spring brought the first activity of loading the vessels and moving them into position a few miles off shore. More waiting till one morning the ocean seemed like an endless lake. Flat.

The news came at three that morning. By four I was six cups into the day, working on a seventh and waiting for a chopper to fly me out. Johnny had left hours before to insure the dive station was ready to go. The low–level shuttle flight was like a thousand others I had taken. Pilots are ever taking advantage of a captive audience.

"The name's Browning, you can call me Joe."

"Jake, Joe. Big Day huh?" I inspected his neck as he craned his head searching for other aircraft. He was normal, explaining his attitude.

"Yeah, you the diver that's going to set the pipe?"

"That's me." There was no reason to burst this guy's bubble, so I rolled with it. It could always get ugly but doesn't have to start that way.

"You know all of Portland is behind you. We've been living on rationing for years."

"Glad I could help."

"Yeah - your picture's are going to be all over the place. They're even planning a celebration for you," rejoiced the pilot.

"I doubt that, but somebody will take the honors. Sure hope I don't fuck up!" Jake thought a joke was in order. His timing was off.

"What mister!" Blurted Joe as he set down on the rear deck of the Matron.

"Just yanking your chain, Joe."

Relief washed across the pilot's eyes. Jake smiled and chinned the pilot, giving him a geeky thumbs–up.

He lifted his gear bags, heading across the five hundred foot deck to the dive station. Halfway there, Jake set the bags down and rolled a cigarette, taking in the visual of the active barge before becoming part of it. Halfway through the scanning something caught his eye.

The set of a pair of shoulders, straight and squared off; the tangled mop of blond hair, the man's height, a hop in his step that had nothing to do with getting to where he was going. The hair went up on the back of his neck, as did the hair on the individual Jake had focused on. The blond head turned, followed by the body.

Jake was thrown mentally, back to the beginning, no real memories, just images - a waterfall, a girl crying, and this man. The man stared at him with the blank gaze of the Megacorp mindfuck.

'Poor fucker,' Jake thought. That is until recognition took place. It was Jonah, his eyes glazed over. Now Jake's heart plummeted. He was a Megacorp op.

He took a few steps closer to his old friend, never breaking contact with his eyes. It appeared Jonah had become a 'Tommy'; the skills remained intact while the personality died. The glazed eyes were as solid as any Jake had ever seen. His hand reached out to Jonah's.

"Never thought they would get to you Jonah, sorry, dude."

Jake was ready to break contact and head on his way - it can get ugly if you try and break through the mindfuck as he had learned with Tommy years ago - when Jonah's grip tightened. He returned the squeeze. It's a guy thing. Jake's eyes were looking right at Jonah, inches away from his face when the glaze over Jonah's eyes evaporated. A smile cracked on one side of his face that reached all the way across.

"And they never will, Jake. It's good to see you again and nice to know there is someone I can trust." Jonah gave Jake the chin and released his grip.

Jake replied in kind saying, "Anywhere, anytime."

The encounter lasted moments, almost as if it never happened, which Jake figured was the idea. Jonah's eyes glazed over and headed on his way. Jake took the hint and went to the dive station. His heart was heavy as his gear.

'Why couldn't we just sit there and talk for a few minutes?' Then he remembered. Shorty, Julie, a stupid ouothouse. Just as quickly he forgot or tried to anyway, Jonah and he didn't have the kind of memories that are best shared with a cold beer. No, these are the kind of recollections that haunt you every day of your life and in the end, will destroy you, if you don't keep a tight lid on them.

Crossing the deck Jake put a clamp on his emotions. Johnny was smoking a cigarette, looking out to sea with a thousand yard stare. Jake dropped the gear on the deck.

"Hey Johnny, what's our E.T.D?"

"Half hour," he replied turning around.

"Is there any more coffee in that thermos?"

After more than a lifetime in hell Jake realized this was just the beginning.

john g rees was a salvage diver in Honolulu for some years in the 80's and 90's, getting a lot of research for his novels the hard way – first hand. Working in Pearl Harbor on Navy vessels to Japanese fishing boats, he dived the watery field in his youth, only to see all the horror years later. He now enjoys just writing it down, albeit with a slant.

john g lives on a volcano on the Big Island of Hawaii and likes it there. He returns to the Mainland of the USA every few years for some weeks of hard motorcycle riding – enough to hold him for the next few years. Then back to the peace of the island. He spends his time writing and at home with his wife, cats and chickens, in the middle of nowhere in the middle of the ocean. He likes it that way.

Nothing like his novels...

You can check out his website at
www.blackwaterbooks.com

www.ingramcontent.com/pod-product-compliance
Lightning Source LLC
Chambersburg PA
CBHW050917250626
47155CB00001B/270